Volume Two

# SIERRA JENSEN COLLECTION

*Close Your Eyes*

*Without a Doubt*

*With This Ring*

# ROBIN JONES GUNN

Multnomah® Publishers *Sisters, Oregon*

THE SIERRA JENSEN COLLECTION, VOLUME 2
published by Multnomah Publishers, Inc.

© 2006 by Robin's Ink, LLC
International Standard Book Number: 1-59052-589-2

Cover Photo by Steve Gardner, www.shootpw.com

Compilation of:
*Close Your Eyes* © 1996 by Robin's Ink, LLC
*Without a Doubt* © 1997 by Robin's Ink, LLC
The C. S. Lewis quotation is taken from C. S. Lewis, *The World's Last Night and Other Essays*
(San Diego: Harcourt, Brace and Jovanovich, 1973).
*With This Ring*
© 1997 by Robin's Ink, LLC

Unless otherwise indicated, Scripture quotations are from:
*The Holy Bible,* New International Version (NIV)
© 1973, 1984 by International Bible Society,
used by permission of Zondervan Publishing House
*The Holy Bible,* New King James Version (NKJV)
© 1984 by Thomas Nelson, Inc.
*The Holy Bible,* King James Version (KJV)
*New American Standard Bible*® (NASB) © 1960, 1977, 1995
by the Lockman Foundation. Used by permission.

*Multnomah* is a trademark of Multnomah Publishers, Inc.,
and is registered in the U.S. Patent and Trademark Office.
The colophon is a trademark of Multnomah Publishers, Inc.

Printed in the United States of America

For information:
MULTNOMAH PUBLISHERS, INC. · 601 N. LARCH STREET · SISTERS, OR 97759

Library of Congress Cataloging-in-Publication Data
Gunn, Robin Jones, 1955-
The Sierra Jensen Collection Volume 2 / Robin Jones Gunn.
v. cm.
Previously published as separate works.
Contents: Close Your Eyes -- Without a Doubt -- With This Ring.
ISBN 1-59052-589-2 [1. Interpersonal relations—Fiction. 2. Conduct of life—Fiction. 3. Christian life—Fiction.] I. Title.
PZ7.G972Sie 2006
[Fic]—dc22

2006008136

06 07 08 09 10—10 9 8 7 6 5 4 3 2 1 0

# TEEN NOVELS BY ROBIN JONES GUNN

## THE SIERRA JENSEN SERIES

### Volume 1
Book 1: *Only You, Sierra*
Book 2: *In Your Dreams*
Book 3: *Don't You Wish*

### Volume 2
Book 4: *Close Your Eyes*
Book 5: *Without a Doubt*
Book 6: *With This Ring*

### Volume 3
Book 7: *Open Your Heart*
Book 8: *Time Will Tell*
Book 9: *Now Picture This*

### Volume 4
Book 10: *Hold On Tight*
Book 11: *Closer Than Ever*
Book 12: *Take My Hand*

# THE CHRISTY MILLER SERIES

Book Four

# CLOSE YOUR EYES

# one

"HOW COME THIS STUFF makes sense to you?" Randy Jenkins asked, tossing his wadded-up gum wrapper into the fireplace. A high school physics book lay propped like a tent on the floor in front of him, and a half dozen papers surrounded him.

Sierra pushed the painted enamel bracelet up her arm and cast her buddy an encouraging smile. "You almost have it," she said. "Give it one more try."

While Randy fussed over his homework, Sierra stretched out her legs and fondly gazed around the warm family room. The grand Victorian house, which had been in her family for more than fifty years, offered plenty of space.

Sierra tilted her head and tried to catch Randy's gaze with her gray-blue eyes. "You want to take a break and eat something?"

Before Randy could answer, Sierra's older sister, Tawni, burst into the room clutching the phone in her drooping hand. "Where's Mom?"

"She took the boys to get haircuts." Sierra noticed tears

glistening in Tawni's eyes. If Sierra guessed right, Tawni had been talking to her new boyfriend, Jeremy Mackenzie, as she usually did this time of day, every day. Conversations with Jeremy were prone to cause smiles and whispers, not tears.

"Are you okay?" Sierra asked cautiously. She and her sister had never been exceptionally close and such a question could embarrass Tawni, especially since Randy was there.

"Sure. Fine. I'm going to make cookies," Tawni announced and marched through the family room into the kitchen.

"Now I know she's upset," Sierra said in a low voice to Randy.

He was scratching a list of figures on a piece of notebook paper and didn't look up.

"Something happened between her and Jeremy. I bet he's not coming."

"What?" Randy said, looking up. His straight, dark blond hair, which was cut in what Sierra's Granna Mae called a "Dutch boy," fell into his eyes. "Were you talking to me?"

"Never mind," Sierra said. Gathering her long gauze skirt in her hand, she stood up and headed for the kitchen. "I'll be right back."

"Whatever," Randy muttered.

The counter was already covered with all the dry-goods canisters from the pantry, including one filled with pasta. Two eggs sat precariously close to the edge of the counter, and a large bottle of vanilla extract stood with its lid off, spreading its pleasant fragrance like a blessing over the baking event. Tawni was smearing butter on two cookie sheets as

Sierra entered. Her sister didn't look up but dumped the rest of the butter stick into a mixing bowl and furiously began to chop at it with a wooden spoon.

"Are you all right?" Sierra asked again.

"Of course I am! Just because Jeremy isn't coming to see me this weekend after all our planning doesn't mean my life should come to a standstill. I have lots to do. Lots and lots!"

"Why isn't he coming?"

"Money, school, finals. Take your pick."

Sierra lowered herself onto a kitchen stool and felt her heart sinking. During the weeks Tawni and Jeremy had been planning his visit from San Diego, Sierra had been busy secretly making her own wishes. Jeremy had a brother, Paul, whom Sierra happened to meet at the airport in London five months ago. Since then she had seen him around town twice and received two letters from him. Their brief conversations and correspondence had left Sierra with a treasure chest full of "what if's" buried deep inside her heart.

When she had found out Paul and Jeremy were brothers, it seemed inevitable her path would cross with Paul's. Then when Jeremy decided to come to Portland to see Tawni, Sierra had known her treasure chest was about to be opened. But now all those possibilities were crushed.

"So, is he going to come later? After school is out?"

"He's going to try." Tawni opened the cupboard door and began to move the spices around. "Where does Mom hide the chocolate chips?"

"In the pantry," Sierra said. "On the top shelf behind the paper towels."

Tawni went to the pantry and continued her search as Sierra tried to rearrange the dreams in her treasure chest.

"That's not so bad," she told Tawni (and herself). "Only a few more weeks. Besides, in June, Jeremy should be able to stay longer. This weekend would have been here and gone like that." Sierra snapped her fingers for emphasis. "Don't you think it will be much better if he comes for a whole week?"

"I guess. That is, of course, if he can pull together the money by then. His car needs new brakes, and his bank account is shot."

"Probably from paying his phone bill," Sierra muttered.

"What is that supposed to mean?" Tawni spun around with a roll of paper towels in her hand.

Sierra should have known better than to challenge Tawni when she was in such a mood—especially because, at eighteen, Tawni didn't put much value in Sierra's sixteen-year-old logic. But she spoke up anyway.

"You guys talk constantly on the phone. I'm sure it adds up. Neither of you has that much money. It doesn't make sense to me. Why don't you save some money by not calling each other all the time?"

"Sierra," Tawni said, shelving the paper towels, "you don't know the first thing about love!"

"You're right. I don't."

Surprised by Sierra's admission, Tawni didn't respond but continued her search for the chocolate chips.

"I guess love makes you do crazy thing," Sierra said. "Like spending all your money on a phone bill instead of a plane ticket."

Tawni pursed her lips together as if she were holding back a flood of words.

"It was only a suggestion," Sierra mumbled, holding up her arms in surrender.

*You're not the only one affected by this, Tawni,* she thought. *All my dreams of seeing Paul are dissolved now, too, you know.* Of course, Sierra would never admit that to her sister.

A stiff silence crowded the large kitchen as Tawni reached her arm into the dark recesses of the cupboard above the refrigerator. "Aha! Perfect!" She extracted a large, crumpled bag of M&M's.

"Those look like they've been there for a decade," Sierra said.

"So? The bag is still closed. Don't they put enough preservatives in these to keep them fresh into the next century?" Tawni pulled open the bag with a snap and poured the candy onto the counter. "Go ahead. Try one," she challenged.

"I'm not going to try one," Sierra said. "You try one."

It occurred to Sierra that she and her sister had somehow changed roles. All their lives, Sierra had been the daring, rambunctious one even though she was younger. When they were little, Tawni was the dainty, prissy one who insisted on using a straw to drink her milk lest she fall prey to the dreaded milk mustache.

Now Tawni was acting like Sierra by turning the kitchen into a war zone in her attempt to make cookies, and Sierra had turned into Miss Finicky. Funny how she would go against her true nature just to oppose her sister.

"Oh, this is crazy," Sierra spouted, grabbing a handful of M&M's. "Look, I'm eating them." She tossed them into her mouth just as Randy entered the kitchen.

"What's happening?" he asked.

"I'm making cookies," Tawni said. "And Sierra is acting like her stubborn self."

"I am not," Sierra said, her words coming out garbled through the M&M's.

It wasn't unusual for Randy to hear this kind of banter, which frequently flew between Sierra and Tawni. About three weeks ago, he had started to stop by Sierra's house regularly. At first it was on Friday nights, and any other night he wasn't working at his lawn-care business. He even came by one night and had dinner with Sierra's family when Sierra was at her friend Amy Degrassi's house. Sierra's parents encouraged "drop-by" friendships, so Randy had quickly become part of the family.

"I have only one question," Randy said, sitting next to Sierra and nudging the two eggs away from the edge of the counter. "When will they be ready?"

"Soon," Tawni said, measuring the sugar and double-checking to make sure it was exactly right.

"Let us know when you're ready for taste testers," Randy said, heading back to the family room. "I have to finish this homework tonight."

"Me too," Sierra said. She gave Tawni a pleasant look and added, "Just keep telling yourself it will only be a few more weeks before he comes."

Tawni looked surprised and tossed back an amiable, "Yeah, well, thanks for caring."

*Oh, I do!* Sierra thought. *More than you know, dear sis. More than you know!*

# two

"I THINK I CLOBBERED the last two problems. Only one more to go," Randy said. "I sure will be glad when school's out."

"Me, too," Sierra said, hiding a smile that was tied to her dreams of seeing Paul once school ended.

The phone rang, and a moment later Tawni called from the kitchen, "Sierra, it's Amy."

"I'll take it in the study," Sierra told Randy. "Call me if you get stuck."

She hopped up and hurried into the library, her favorite room in the rambling old house. Curling up in the chair by the French doors that led to the backyard, Sierra reached for the phone and punched the On button.

"Hi, Aimers!" Sierra heard the click as her sister hung up the kitchen extension.

"Is Randy over there?" Amy asked.

"Yes, he's in the family room finishing up the physics problems. Have you done yours yet?"

"Are you kidding? It's not due until Friday. And why do you always change the subject when I mention Randy?"

"I did not change the subject. However, I do have news for you."

"What?"

"Guess."

"I give up."

"You give up too easily, Amy."

"I know I do. Is that why you called? To harass me about being an underachiever?"

"I didn't call. You called me."

"Oh, that's right. Tell me your news quick, and then I'll tell you mine."

"Jeremy's not coming."

"And that means you won't get to see Paul, right?"

"Right."

"Bummer," Amy said.

"I know." Sierra let out a sigh. "I shouldn't be so obsessed with the thought of seeing this guy, but..."

"But you can't keep yourself from demonstrating a common characteristic of the obsessive-compulsive person. You won't be happy until you get what you want, and then when you get it, you won't be happy because the fantasy will be over."

"Oh please, Dr. Degrassi, stop with the psychoanalyzing. I am not an obsessive-compulsive person, and you know it."

"Okay, then you're lost in a fantasy."

"It's not that either."

"Then, what is it?" Amy challenged.

"I don't know. It's just that Paul is..."

"Unattainable?"

"Not necessarily."

"Can I tell you what I think?" Amy asked. Sierra could picture her dark-eyed friend sprawled on her patchwork bedspread, flipping her long, curly black hair as she prepared to dispense pearls of wisdom.

"From what you've told me about Paul, I'd say drop the dream right now and pay attention to Randy. You know he likes you. Paul is nothing more than a phantom, a mysterious stranger whose life momentarily intersected with yours. That's all. You both now spin in separate orbits, and it's not meant for you to share each other's paths at this time."

Sierra burst out laughing. "Where do you come up with this sci-fi psychiatry? I don't like it when you talk creepy like that."

"That's not creepy. That's poetic," Amy said.

"It sounds as if you're giving coordinates for the space shuttle, not talking about real people. Paul is a real person. He's not a phantom."

"All I'm saying, Sierra, is there's no point in wishing for something that's not going to happen when something great is waiting around the corner for you."

Sierra didn't answer.

"Okay, to be more accurate—when something great is waiting for you in the family room."

"Randy and I are buddies," Sierra said. "You know that. Why are you suddenly interested in directing my social life?"

"Because," Amy began, "I have a great idea. That's why I called. Why don't we fix dinner for a couple of the guys as an end-of-school party? My mom said we could do it over here. We could get a couple of lobsters from my uncle's restaurant and make it really fancy."

"Sounds fun," Sierra said. "When do you want to do it?"

"I don't know. Maybe next Friday."

"And who are you going to invite?" Sierra asked. "Drake?"

"Yes, that is, if he happens to acknowledge my existence this week. You'll invite Randy, of course."

Sierra didn't answer right away. She twisted her finger around her long blond curls and noticed that she needed to wash her hair. Too much de-frizzer this morning had made it feel sticky.

"Sierra," Amy repeated, "you will invite Randy, won't you?"

"Maybe."

"Oh, no! You're not off with that phantom in your head again, are you?"

"Maybe," Sierra answered, with a lilt in her voice. The really fun thing about Paul was that the more she had thought about him in the last few months, the more she had convinced herself she had a crush on him. No, more than that: She and Paul were brought together by God, and she just knew that something had to happen between them—hopefully, very soon.

"Okay, Sierra," Amy said, "try to let that brainy little head of yours grasp the full meaning of this poetic statement: 'A Randy in the hand is with worth two Pauls in the bush.'"

"If you say so, Amy." Sierra knew the best route to take was to give in. She could be agreeable on the outside, but nobody could unlock that treasure chest of dreams she had hidden inside her heart.

# three

"THESE AREN'T BAD," Sierra said, biting into one of Tawni's cookies the next day at lunch. "You want one? My sister made them yesterday."

Amy pushed aside her cafeteria tray with her cold fries and half-eaten hamburger sprawled across the plate, revealing its layers: bun, meat, bun. Amy was a finicky eater—when she ate.

Amy nibbled at the cookie Sierra handed her and was about to give an opinion when Drake appeared behind her and said, "It's not going to bite you back, Miss Amy!" He sandwiched himself between Amy and Sierra and made himself at home.

Drake's whole name was Anton Francisco Drake. Everyone knew that. And everyone simply called him "Drake"—even teachers. He wore his dark hair combed straight back and stuck out his jaw whenever he tried to emphatically make a point about something. At six foot two and as one of the school's star athletes, Drake had little difficulty making whatever point he wanted to. Right now, he was eyeing Sierra's cookies.

"You want one?" Sierra offered.

"Sure." Drake inhaled it in one bite. "You make them?"

"No, my sister did. She was in a strange mood yesterday afternoon and baked herself silly."

"You guys want to go to the Blazer's game this Friday? A bunch of us are. You can still get tickets if you want to go with us," Drake said.

"I'd love to," Amy said. "Basketball is one of my favorite sports."

Randy tapped Sierra's arm and said, "Are you going?"

"I don't think so. I'm trying to save up some money."

"You want to go, Randy?" Drake asked.

"Maybe. I'll let you know."

Drake picked at the uneaten fries on Amy's tray and said, "Let me know if you want a ride."

"I do," Amy said quickly.

It seemed to Sierra that, for the first time, Drake was catching on. He seemed to realize that Amy was interested in him. His expression lightened a bit as he grabbed a few more of her cold fries. "Better draw me a map," he said. "I don't think I've ever been to your house."

"No, you haven't," Amy answered sweetly. She glanced at Sierra and winked—her way of secretly signaling victory. "I'll draw a map for you today," Amy said to Drake. "What time do you want me to be ready?"

Drake gave his broad shoulders a casual shrug. "Around six-thirty, I guess."

"Sounds great," Amy said.

The bell rang, and the six people sitting at their table all rose and cleared their trays. The others went on ahead as Amy hung back, clasping Sierra's arm.

"Can you believe it?" she whispered to Sierra, her dark eyes aglow. "Drake finally asked me out!"

"Yeah, with a little help from you," Sierra teased.

"This is so perfect! We can start planning our nice dinner for the following Friday! I'm so excited!"

Amy didn't need to tell Sierra she was elated. It showed all over her face. She continued to ramble on with plans for their dinner as they headed for class.

*What a contrast this friend of mine can be!* Sierra thought. Sometimes Amy carried with her all the maturity and wisdom of the ages, wisdom that she gladly spewed, with or without an invitation to do so. The youngest of three girls, Amy had gathered many insights from her older sisters. Other times, like now, she was every bit the baby of the family, set on getting her way and sweetly finagling the situation to make sure that's what happened.

The two girls took their seats next to each other in class, and Amy leaned over to give Sierra her opinion. "Why don't you go to the game with Randy? The four of us could go out afterward. Come on, Sierra!"

Sierra shook her head, her wild curls chasing each other across he shoulders. "I already have a date with my civics book."

"You do not. You already finished that chapter. You told me so yourself."

"There's always the extra-credit questions, you know."

Amy rolled her eyes and shook her head. "You drive me crazy. You know that? You absolutely drive me crazy. Maybe Vicki and Mike will want to go with Drake and me."

"Probably," Sierra said.

"Okay, class," Mr. Rykert called over the rumbling of conversations. "Take out your assignments and pass them forward, please."

Sierra gave Amy her final thought on Friday night. "I hope you and Drake have the time of your lives!"

Amy flashed an appreciative smile. She looked like a little girl when she smiled like that—timid, yet with a crazy exuberance. Sierra liked that about her. It was part of their common ground.

Handing in her paper, Sierra tried to keep her eyes and her mind from wandering to the back of the classroom where Randy sat behind Vicki Navarone.

*Relationships are such illusive things. First Tawni and her lovesick groans over Jeremy. Now Amy and her overly eager attention toward Drake. And what's my problem? My brain is stuck on Paul. Am I only deluding myself that anything could ever happen there? And why is Amy so convinced that Randy likes me as more than a pal?*

She glanced back and noticed Randy and Vicki chatting away like old chums. *See? Randy's friends with a bunch of girls. I'm one of his many buddies, that's all.*

Randy and Vicki had gone out once, but nothing seemed to develop after that—additional evidence that he was pal material and nothing more.

"Okay, class. Let's open in prayer," Mr. Rykert said.

In Sierra's opinion, this had to be one of the advantages of going to a small Christian high school. Even though most teachers prayed only in their first-period classes, Mr. Rykert always led them in prayer in his class. Sierra loved to hear him talk to God. He prayed as if God were standing right there in the room with them.

Sierra silently formed her own prayer that her mind

wouldn't be so full of thoughts about guys. She prayed she would be able to finish the next few weeks of her junior year with the best grades she could get. Her older brother Wes had been pelting her lately with a barrage of information on college scholarships and awards. Sierra had the smarts to qualify for a lot of the programs, but this was the first semester she had thought seriously about college.

"Amen," Mr. Rykert concluded. Raising his voice, he announced, "This year for your final, I've prepared something a little different. You'll be writing a paper on a personal experience and presenting it to the class during the last week of school."

*Sounds easy,* Sierra thought. *I'll write about the outreach trip I took to England last January. Or maybe I'll write about what it's like to live with an aging grandmother and how my Granna Mae had surgery a few months ago.*

"And," Mr. Rykert continued, "I'm going to assign each of you a partner."

Amy and Sierra exchanged glances. Drake wasn't in this class, so it was likely Amy would want to pair up with Sierra. For a brief moment, Sierra thought it would be fun to partner with Randy.

"I will explain the assignment for your final and then tell you who your partner will be," Mr. Rykert said. "I have a list of agencies here in Portland that accept volunteer assistance. Each of you, as a team, will select one of the organizations on the list. No duplicates, please. You and your partner will contact your organization and go together to volunteer your assistance for a minimum of four hours. You will then prepare a report and give it in front of the class."

"Can we choose our own partners?" Amy asked.

"No, I will assign them. And no changes, please. What I'm passing out now is a list of organizations, a list of the partners, and a list of information you must include in your report. Any other questions?"

"When is this due?" Amy asked.

"You have two weeks to complete the four hours of service, and the written and oral reports are both due finals week. It's on the bottom of the page."

Sierra took the papers from the guy ahead of her and passed the stack to the girl behind her.

A girl in the front let out a mock groan and said, "Not Jonah! Please give me anybody but Jonah."

"Thanks a lot," Jonah said. "At least I have a car, and you don't. If you're real nice, I might even let you pay for the gas."

"Byron Davis," Amy whispered loud enough for only Sierra to hear. Her face lit up as she leaned closer. "Are all my dreams coming true today or what?"

Byron, the strong, silent, studious type, sat two seats up. He was a straight-A student, and being partnered with him almost certainly guaranteed Amy an A on this final. Byron was studying the list of organizations and apparently hadn't checked to see who his partner was. Or maybe he hadn't mustered the courage. Byron gave the impression, because he was shy, that he was afraid of girls.

Sierra wouldn't have minded a bit if Byron had been her assigned partner. They would earn an A for sure. And she wouldn't be caught in that awkward trap of always feeling like she was the smart one.

Before Sierra could force herself to turn the page, she heard Randy call out, "Hey, Sierra!"

She turned around to see Randy holding up his paper and smiling. "It's you and me—Jensen and Jenkins. We're going to ace this final, buddy!"

Sierra gave him a thumbs-up signal and turned back around. Amy caught her eye and gave her a knowing look. With a delicate lift of her dark eyebrow, Amy mouthed the name "Randy" and smiled coyly at Sierra.

# four

SIERRA IGNORED AMY and looked over the papers that had been passed out. The rest of the class time was spent reviewing the chapter in the textbook. When the bell rang, Sierra tossed her papers into her backpack and was about to leave when Mr. Rykert called her and Randy up to the front.

They stood together by his desk as Mr. Rykert waited until the rest of the class cleared out. "You probably noticed," he began, "that the partners were selected alphabetically. I considered changing it so that you," he nodded toward Sierra, "would be partnered with Tre."

She hoped the sudden twitch she felt didn't show on her face. Tre Nuygen had transferred into the class mid-semester and was either the shyest student in the whole world or didn't speak English well enough to fit in. Amy said he came from Cambodia and had arrived in the United States only a few months ago. Someone else said he had been kicked out of public high school, and Royal Christian Academy was the only school in Portland that would let him in.

Whatever the case, Tre was not a desirable partner, and Vicki had ended up being matched with him.

"I have a questions for you two," Mr. Rykert said. "Would you be willing to work as a foursome with Vicki and Tre?"

"Sure," Randy said with a casual shrug of his shoulders.

"Sure," Sierra said after a slight pause. "That would be fine."

"Mr. Rykert?" a voice called from the back of the classroom. Vicki stood by the open door. Worry ripples creased her forehead and gathered above her clear green eyes. Vicki had learned to use her good looks and popularity to her advantage.

"Come in, Vicki," Mr. Rykert said. "We were talking about you. I'd like you and Tre to partner with Sierra and Randy."

"Oh, thank you," she said, including Randy and Sierra in her gracious, sweeping glance. "I feel much better about that."

"And may I suggest the location?" Mr. Rykert said. "I'd like the four of you to go to the Highland House. They run several services for the homeless and low-income families. You'll be volunteering with the after-school Kids Klub. It's run by the Highland Outreach Ministries. Do you know where it's located?"

"It's not far from where I work," Sierra said. "I've seen it, but I didn't know what it was."

"The main goal of the Highland House is to get people back on their feet. They run a limited job-referral service and offer some career-training programs. The Kids Klub is for children whose parents are working. These kids would be on the streets otherwise, since many of them literally have no home. Others live in places that would be unsafe for them to go home alone."

"There are kids like that in our city?" Randy said.

"More than you would guess," Mr. Rykert replied.

"This ought to be an education," Sierra said.

"That's what I'm counting on. So," Mr. Rykert said, rubbing his hands together and giving the three of them a warm look of assurance, "you're all set. Randy, you tell Tre what's going on, okay?"

"Okay."

"Let me know if you have any questions."

"Thanks, Mr. Rykert," Vicki said. She turned to Randy and gave him a puppy-dog look loaded with appreciation. "I feel so much better about this."

Something began to simmer inside of Sierra. Why was she feeling this way? Hadn't she prayed about her feelings toward Randy less than an hour ago? Why was it that one hint of flirtation from Vicki made Sierra feel she needed to protect Randy? Or flirt back with him or something?

She hurried to her next class, asking God why things like this were beginning to bother her so much. It made her feel so immature. The teasing from Amy and the twinges of jealousy over Vicki were experiences Sierra wasn't used to. Why was God opening the floodgate of testing situations? Was He trying to see if she really meant what she prayed?

Slipping into her seat in her next class, Sierra thought about Vicki and tried to be fair. Sierra knew if she had been matched with Tre, she would have wanted Mr. Rykert to do exactly what he did.

*Besides,* she chided herself, *this isn't about relationships. This is about school. It's about getting an A on the final. That's all. That's the most important thing for me right now. And if this check on my emotions is some kind of final from You, God, I want to get an A on that, too.*

That evening, as Sierra was leaving her job at the bakery, she decided to take a little detour and drive past the Highland House to see what it was like. Sierra counted the blocks as she headed toward the Willamette River.

Eleven blocks down, she spotted the old manor, now changed by the brightly painted mural across the north wall. Tall cedars circled the front of the huge house, protecting it from the busy street. A dozen yelling kids ran after a soccer ball in the front yard, and on the wide porch two girls played jump rope. An oval sign at the front gate proclaimed, "The Highland House." Smaller letters underneath read, "A safe place for a fresh start."

Sierra pulled into an open parking spot alongside the house and noticed a third person on the porch, turning the jump rope. The director, perhaps. He leaned against one of the pillars, and Sierra could hear him counting in deep, resonant voice as the young girl jumped.

*I wonder what they'll want the four of us to do to help out here? I could turn the jump rope and count like that guy is. Or maybe they'll want us to help the kids with their homework. This will be a snap.*

Part of her wanted to hop out of her car, march in, and volunteer to help right then, especially because it appeared only one adult was present with the dozen or so kids. But it was Tuesday night, and she had a ton of homework. Her mom would most likely have dinner on the table, and her parents would be concerned if she didn't arrive home at her usual time after work.

Taking one last look at the cheerful house, Sierra whispered, "I'll be back!"

Then, by the side of the house, she noticed a long line of homeless people waiting to get into the Highland

Kitchen, where they served soup each night at six-thirty. A raggedly dressed old man with a bedroll slung over his shoulder shuffled past her, checking a can of soda resting on the low cement wall. The can apparently was empty. He stopped under the streetlight several yards from the soup kitchen line, and a look of hopelessness crossed his bearded face.

Sierra's heart went out to him. Before she thought about what she was doing, she grabbed the bag of leftover Mama Bear's cinnamon rolls from the seat next to her, got out of the car, and called to the stranger: "Do you like cinnamon rolls?"

Startled by her question, he eyed the bag curiously.

"Made fresh today," she explained, holding out her gift. "I thought you might like them."

Sierra had never offered food to a homeless person before. In the past, the homeless had seemed far removed from her world. Tonight, she felt differently for some reason. She felt responsible to do what she could. The sweet stillness of the late spring evening, along with the anticipation of helping out at the Highland House, bolstered her courage. She felt safe because the guy on the porch wasn't far away. If she needed to cry out for help, he was there.

She couldn't figure out why she felt so exhilarated about offering food to a homeless person. Perhaps it reminded her of when she was in Great Britain and the way she and her friends had boldly told strangers about a relationship with Christ. Maybe it was the delicate coolness of the evening breeze that reminded her of the description in Genesis of how God walked with Adam and Eve in the garden in the cool of the evening. Whatever it was, right now

God felt close...touchable...involved in the ways of humankind.

The scruffy-looking man slowly reached for the bag. "Thanks," he mumbled, turning his back so the others in line down the street wouldn't see what she had given him.

"You're welcome," Sierra said. "God bless you."

He didn't answer but dug his dirty hand into the bag.

She turned and headed back to her car. Glancing at the porch, she noticed the girls had stopped jumping rope. The guy was standing in the shadows, apparently watching her. She felt good and unsettled at the same time: good because she had done something that felt so right in reaching out to someone in need, unsettled because she had done so little to really help him. Where would he sleep? What would he eat for breakfast?

Driving home, she thought how she would be greeted by her wonderful family, a bountiful dinner, and a warm bed. None of those things were available to that man. A strength and determination began to grow inside Sierra.

*I want to do more. I want to learn to live boldly and bravely for You, Lord, to reach out and really make a difference in this world You made.*

Unfortunately, Sierra's parents had a different view of her experience.

# five

"I REALIZE YOU FELT SAFE," her father said, passing a bowl of peas at the dinner table, "but that's a rough area of town, Sierra. You don't know what could have happened."

"Yeah," her eight-year-old brother, Dillon, said. "He could have had a knife."

"Yeah," six-year-old Gavin chimed in, "or a machine gun."

"He didn't have a machine gun," Sierra said, scooping some brown rice onto her plate.

"You don't know," Dillon said. "It could have been in his bedroll."

"Yeah," Gavin said, "or up his pant leg. You shouldn't talk to strangers, Sierra. Isn't that right, Mom?"

Sharon Jensen gave Gavin the kind of tender smile a mother reserves for her youngest of six children. Turning to Sierra, her youngest daughter, she issued the same smile, adding a tightening of the space between her eyebrows, which was a sign of worry. "We would feel better if you didn't approach someone like that again unless another person is with you. We applaud your zeal, honey. We always have. Now season it with some common sense, and we'll all feel a lot better."

"I sent for them yesterday," Granna Mae suddenly chirped from her end of the table.

Sierra dearly loved her grandmother, as all of them did. Some days her mind was as clear as still water in a reflecting pool. Other times, like now, she would speak nonsense, and an invisible blanket of concern would fall on the family. Sometimes they would try to enter Granna Mae's world by responding to her random statements. Other times they would let them go.

Tonight no one seemed sure what to do. Their eyes checked the other family members' faces for subtle signals. Granna Mae looked coherent as could be. Sierra wondered, as she had so many times, how a person's mind could betray her and go AWOL like that.

Granna Mae looked at them, startled by the sudden silence.

"I hear what you're saying, Mom." Sierra picked up the dropped conversation. "But here we sit, with all this food and in this great big house. A lot of people out there need help. I don't want to pretend they're not there. And if I can help, I want to help."

"We're all for that," Dad said sternly. "All we ask is that you always have someone with you. Understand?"

Sierra nodded.

"Isn't that how Christ sent out the disciples? In twos?" Sierra's mom said. "It's the wise thing to do, Sierra."

Sierra nodded again. "You're right. I agree. I'll do that."

"How did I get the signals so messed up?" Sierra wrote in her journal later that night. "Here I think I'm doing something wonderful, giving food to that guy, and yet I upset my parents. How can something be so right and so wrong at the same time? Is it that I'm too impulsive?"

She was about to launch into a new topic, exploring the crazy avenues of how she felt about her dream of seeing Paul again and how immature she felt at the same time for feeding her crush. Just then Tawni entered their bedroom and slung her purse over the back of the desk chair.

"Hi," Sierra said. "How was your day?"

"Terrible." Tawni kicked off her shoes and wiggled out of her panty hose. "The results from this last month came in today, and guess who scored the absolute lowest in sales?"

"You?" Sierra ventured. "But I thought when you did that Valentine special, they said you were the top promoter or something." Sierra didn't know much about the ins and outs of Tawni's job at the fragrance counter at Nordstrom's, and she had never tried that hard to understand what Tawni meant when she rattled off news of her day.

"That was back in February," Tawni stated with an edge to her voice. One false move, and Sierra knew the edge of that verbal blade could slice right through her. Fortunately, a letter waiting for Tawni on her bed caught her eye, and she shut Sierra out.

Sierra pretended to refocus on her journal, but she was really watching her depressed sister as she slit the envelope with her long thumbnail and began to read the letter. Sierra had noticed the letter earlier but hadn't checked to see whom it was from. Jeremy probably—although he usually called instead of sending letters.

Over the top of her journal, Sierra could see Tawni's sullen expression lifting. She flipped to the second page of the letter, and a definite smile began to tug the corners of her lips, which now moved silently as she scanned the lines.

Sierra noticed how thin her sister's lips were. Tawni was beautiful, no question there. People would often turn and stare at her. Sierra had grown accustomed to that occurrence as they grew up, realizing all along that she would forever be the tomboy, destined to go unnoticed in the shadow of Tawni's beauty.

However, Sierra knew one thing: She had perfect lips. And now she realized for the first time that Tawni did not. Sierra had her mother's lips. Perfectly proportioned on top and bottom. And when she drew them back in a smile, her teeth fit in a neat row, and a dimple appeared. It comforted Sierra to discover that she had better lips than Tawni.

"I can't believe this!" Tawni half shouted, shaking the letter in the air and looking wildly at Sierra. "This is perfect." She jumped from her bed and burst through the doorway into the hall. "Mom? Dad?" she called out, running barefooted down the stairs.

"What?" Sierra said to the empty air surrounding Tawni's bed. A slight scent of gardenias had followed Tawni out of the room. Now Sierra had a decision to make. Should she go galloping downstairs to find out what her sister was so excited about? Or should she wait until Tawni returned?

An old conflict surfaced for Sierra. She and Tawni were sisters, and Sierra considered them to be friends as well. But they weren't super close, which was why Tawni ran to talk to Mom and Dad about her good news rather than stay in their room and let Sierra be the first to know.

Tawni had once blamed their lack of sisterly bonding on her being adopted and therefore not as intricately connected to Sierra as she would have been if they were blood relatives. Sierra claimed it was their personality differences.

She chewed thoughtfully on the end of her pen and kicked at a pile of clean socks at the foot of her bed. Glancing at her journal, she reread her last line: "Is it that I'm too impulsive?"

"Okay," she muttered, "then I won't be impulsive and run downstairs. I'll wait here, and when she comes back, I'll be sweet and interested and let her tell me her big news."

Snapping shut her journal, Sierra decided to put away her clothes. She matched up her socks and put them in the dresser drawer; then she hung up a mound of clean clothes draped over the chair. She even sorted out the papers in her backpack. Still Tawni didn't make an appearance. It was after ten, and Sierra was too tired to wait any longer. She got ready for bed and tried to select the best of all the options she had been contemplating about the letter's contents while cleaning her side of the room. Her conclusion was the letter was from Jeremy, and he was coming to visit after all. Tawni had run downstairs to tell Mom and Dad, and then, of course, she had immediately called Jeremy. That's where she was now, making plans with him on the phone.

As Sierra turned off the light and pulled the covers up to her chin, she began to sift through the possible things she could say when she saw Paul again. Because if Jeremy was coming, she would certainly see Paul.

# six

SIERRA OVERSLEPT the next morning and had to scramble to get ready. Tawni was still asleep when Sierra galloped down the stairs and bounded into the kitchen.

"What was up with Tawni and that letter last night?" she asked her mom, who was unloading the dishwasher.

Mom checked the clock and, handing Sierra a box of cranberry juice and a granola bar, said, "You'd better eat breakfast on the run. We'll talk about the letter when you come home."

These kinds of mysteries drove Sierra crazy. Charging out the front door with her backpack slung over one arm and the granola bar already stuffed into her mouth, she tried to punch the straw into her box drink.

*Okay, let's see. Jeremy is coming, but they didn't want to give me the details this morning because...*

No conclusion came to her mind except there simply wasn't enough time for a conversation. Slipping her free hand into her backpack, Sierra fumbled for her keys and started up the old VW Rabbit she shared with her mom.

During the eighteen-minute drive to school, Sierra went over all the assignments she needed to get cranking on. It was going to be a full week. She slipped into the first open parking spot she came to and hurried to her locker. Randy was waiting there for her.

"How you doing? You want to go to Lotsa Tacos for lunch?" he asked.

"Sure. Did you talk to Tre yet?"

Randy looked at her as if he didn't understand the question.

"About the service project at the Highland House."

Randy nodded and said, "No, but I called there last night and set everything up. We're going to have to go two times to finish our four hours."

"That's okay," Sierra said.

"Yes, that's what I thought. I'll tell Tre today."

"Guess what? I drove by there last night and—"

Before she could finish her sentence, the bell clanged loudly over their heads. Sierra winced at the sound and gave Randy a nod. "I'll tell you the rest at lunch."

He appeared at her locker right on time for lunch. The guy had an unmistakable charm about him. As he stood there with his crooked grin, he looked at Sierra as if she were the only girl in the world.

"What?" she said, brushing past him and spinning the combination on her locker.

"You ready?" he asked.

"Yes," she answered with an affirming slam of the locker door.

"By the way," he said, "do you mind driving?

"Oh, so that's it," Sierra said. "You asked me to lunch because you wanted a chauffeur."

"That wasn't the only reason."

"I suppose you want me to buy lunch for you as well."

"No," Randy said, taking her by the elbow and directing her out the front doors. "I got paid yesterday, so I have money for once."

"Good," Sierra said.

They crossed the parking lot to Sierra's car, and she climbed into the driver's seat. Reaching over to unlock the passenger door for Randy, she said, "I was only teasing you. The pay-your-own-way system seems to work best for us."

"That's 'cause we're a team!" Randy said, thumping the dashboard with fists. "Unstoppable."

Sierra smiled at his antics. "I'm happy to tell you that I put my whole paycheck in the bank last week. I'm saving every penny."

"What are you saving for?"

"You know, that's a good question." Sierra pulled out of the parking lot and headed for Lotsa Tacos, which was less than three blocks from the school. "I don't need anything. I think I'm doing this savings thing on instinct. We were always taught to save our money when we were little, but I don't know what I'm saving for."

Sierra pulled into the drive-through at Lotsa Tacos. The Rabbit hit the curb hard, and Randy said, "I know what you can spend all that money on. New shocks."

"I'd rather buy a new car," Sierra said. "Did you know Tawni bought her own car? I might need to do the same if this one decides to go belly up."

Four cars were in line ahead of them, and all of them were loaded with students from their school.

"So, what do you think they're going to have us do? At the Highland House, I mean," Sierra asked.

"I don't know. Paint, maybe. Isn't it an old building?"

Sierra pulled the car up to the speaker. "It doesn't look too bad from the outside. Do you know what you want?"

Randy leaned over and shouted out his order. Sierra added a soft taco and a milk and began to drive forward.

"A milk?" Randy questioned. "Nobody orders milk with a taco."

"I do," Sierra said, sorting through the change in the glove compartment. "Oops! I don't have enough money. Do you have an extra quarter?"

"Oh, so you're one of those, are you?" Randy teased. "You have all your money tied up in stocks and bonds and rely heavily on your innocent friends to bail you out when you need cash."

Sierra pulled up to the window. "It's only a quarter, Randy. You make it seem like a crime."

"The only crime here is that you're drinking milk with your taco."

"I happen to like milk."

"I do, too. With cereal, or cookies, or even a turkey sandwich. But not with tacos—never with tacos."

"Just a second," Sierra said to the cashier. Then turning to Randy, she asked, "Are you going to give me a quarter or not?"

"Put your money away. I have this covered."

"You don't have to pay for the whole thing, Randy. Just loan me a quarter."

"Excuse me," the cashier said. "Would you two lovebirds mind paying first and then move forward to continue your spat?"

"Lovebirds!?" Sierra and Randy said in unison. They looked at each other and burst out laughing. Sierra snatched the money from Randy's fist and paid the whole bill with it.

"Keep the change," she said and drove forward.

"Keep the change!?" Randy spouted. "You just gave him a dollar tip."

Before Sierra could explain her impulsive action, Randy hopped out of the car and dashed back to the payment window. She watched in her rearview mirror as Randy nodded his apologies to the woman in the car now in front of the window. He then pointed over his shoulder toward Sierra and spoke with the cashier, using lots of hand motions.

As the bag of tacos was handed to Sierra through her open window, Randy jumped back into the passenger's seat. He waved the dollar bill in his hand and said, "Got it! Ha!" He was smiling and didn't appear at all bothered by her rash actions.

Sierra handed him the bag of food and pulled into the street, heading back to school. "You know what, Randy? I think I'm dangerous."

"I could have told you that," Randy said.

She shook her head. "I don't know what my mind is doing lately. I'm being reckless and impulsive. That wasn't fair to give him your money. I'm sorry." She drove into the school parking lot and found a spot for the car.

"Whatever," Randy said. "That's you, Sierra. You're a

free spirit, and free-spirited people do crazy things sometimes. There's nothing wrong with that. Why are you being so hard on yourself? It didn't bother me."

"But it did bother you. Why else would you have gone back for the money?"

"Because I'm a tightwad." Randy opened the bag, pulling out her taco. He presented her with the carton of milk on his open palm as if he were serving it on a silver tray. "Your taco and milk, Miss Jensen."

"I feel as if I'm changing, Randy," Sierra said.

"People do," he said.

Sierra unwrapped her taco and asked, "Do you ever feel as if you're not sure who you are?"

"Sure. Everybody does sometimes."

"I never have before."

"Ever?" Randy said after he had swallowed his first bite of burrito.

"I don't think so."

Randy shook his head and stuffed another bite in his mouth. "Don't take yourself so seriously. You can act as impulsively around me as you want. I'll still be your friend. I might be out a couple of bucks now and then, but I'll still be your friend."

Sierra smiled and took a sip of milk.

"Are you sure you don't want to go to the game Friday night?" Randy said, changing the subject and wolfing down his last bite.

"Not particularly. Are you going?"

"I thought about it. It would be a lot more fun if you came with me—I mean, with us. A bunch of people are going. Come on, Sierra. I'll even pay if you don't want to deplete your Swiss account."

"You're too nice," she said, enjoying having a guy be so understanding of her mixed-up feelings and so eager to spend time with her. Basketball didn't particularly thrill her, especially because the tickets were so expensive. But it would be fun to go with Randy and see how things turned out between Amy and Drake.

"Well?" he prompted.

"Okay, I'll go. I have the money, so I'll even buy my own ticket."

"Cool."

Smiling, Sierra motioned to Randy that he had a shred of cheese caught at the corner of his mouth. Randy had to be the only guy at school who still said "Cool." "Cool" and "Whatever" were his favorite words. And he was so easy to be around. It occurred to Sierra that what Amy was mistaking for a crush was simply a great friendship between the two of them. Not every girl had a buddy who was so understanding. Amy certainly didn't. No wonder she couldn't see this as merely a friendship.

# seven

ON THURSDAY AFTERNOON, Sierra sat on the edge of her bed watching her sister wedge another pair of shoes into her suitcase and scurry to the dresser to pack her jewelry.

"I still can't believe you're going to Southern California," Sierra said.

Tawni had been floating ever since the mysterious letter arrived on Tuesday. In a few short days, it seemed as if Tawni's life had changed completely. Tomorrow morning, she and Mom and Dad were flying to Los Angeles for the weekend. Tawni's best friend from high school, Jennifer, had moved there with her parents. The letter was Jennifer's invitation for Tawni to come live with them.

"You didn't borrow my pearl earrings, did you?" Tawni asked, going through the neatly organized jewelry in her top drawer.

"Like I would," Sierra said, rolling onto her stomach. "What if Mom and Dad don't agree to let you move down there? What if you can't transfer to a Nordstrom's store in that area?"

"That's why we are going this weekend. To find out," Tawni said impatiently. "Now, where's my gold bracelet?"

"Didn't you already pack your jewelry last night?" Sierra asked.

Like a skittish rabbit, Tawni hurried back to the suitcase on her bed and checked the pouch in the back. "You're right. I must be losing my mind!"

"You are losing your mind," Sierra chimed in, "to suddenly decide to move to Los Angeles like this."

"It's not Los Angeles. Jennifer lives in Carlsbad. It's only half an hour north of San Diego. I already told you this. The airfare was cheaper into LAX, and Dad thought the drive down the coast would be fun."

"When will Mom and Dad meet Jeremy?" Sierra asked.

"Tomorrow night. We're having dinner with his parents. Did I tell you I called the agent this morning?"

"What agent?"

"The modeling agent your friend's aunt referred me to."

Sierra nearly tumbled off her bed. "Modeling agent! I thought you said you didn't want to model?"

"I've been thinking about it. If I actually do have a chance, I should at least try it, don't you think?" Tawni definitely had stars in her eyes now. "The money would be a whole lot better than what I'm making, and besides, it might be kind of fun."

"Fun? Haven't you read those interviews with models who starve themselves and work fourteen-hour days and say they feel as if people treat them like objects rather than human beings? How can you think that would be fun?"

"I'm not going to Paris, or even New York. It's a small agency, and I'd agree to model only clothing, not swimsuits.

Mom and Dad and I have already talked about it. They think I should follow my dream and see what happens."

Sierra repositioned herself cross-legged on her bed and folded her arms across her stomach. "Since when did this become your dream, Tawni? It's as if you've turned into a different person ever since Jennifer's letter."

Tawni stopped her frenzied sorting and packing for a moment and looked softly at Sierra. "Maybe I have. Maybe this is what I've been waiting for, a chance to be on my own, trying something new, enjoying the most fantastic relationship I've ever had with a guy. Living so far away from Jeremy has been torture. Would you expect me to turn this all down? For what? So I can stay here, where I have no friends, no future, no life?"

Sierra had known Tawni would leave home someday, just as their two older brothers had. She just hadn't expected it to be like this.

Neither of them spoke for a full five minutes. Tawni carefully folded and refolded a black blazer and then leaned on the top of her suitcase to close it. She stepped back, an expression of satisfaction crossing her beautiful face.

"Tawni?" Sierra said, getting up and shuffling the ten or so feet to where her sister stood. "I love you, and I'm going to miss you. I hope everything works out." Sierra offered a big hug, which Tawni received with surprise.

"Honestly, Sierra, we're only going for the weekend to check things out. I'm not moving yet."

Sierra wanted to push her sister on the floor, mess up her hair, and tickle her until she laughed. However, the technique hadn't worked when they were kids, and Sierra felt certain it wouldn't work now either.

"Well, just know that I'm happy all this seems to be working out for you."

"Thanks," Tawni said, picking up from her nightstand the "To Do" list she had written neatly on a flowered tablet. "Oh, right," Tawni muttered to herself. "Wrap thank-you gift for Jennifer's parents."

As Tawni set to work with her gift wrapping, Sierra retreated to the bathroom down the hall. Closing the door and locking it, she took a long look at herself in the mirror.

"What if I were beautiful like Tawni?" Sierra whispered to her reflection. "Would I want to run off to become a model? Or is it Jeremy she's really chasing?" Sierra grabbed a handful of her wild, curly blond hair and pulled it back from her face. She turned to the left and studied her profile.

Facing the mirror again, she smiled and watched her slight dimple appear. Her clear blue-gray eyes stared back, scanning each feature. Nose, chin, eyebrows, cheeks. All normal, she decided. A few too many freckles across her nose, perhaps. But then, there were always her lips—her perfect lips. She made a kissy face in the mirror and wondered if she were a little old to be doing this kind of self-image seeking. Didn't most girls do this when they were twelve?

At twelve, Sierra had been too busy riding horses and writing songs to stop and look in the mirror. At fourteen, she was still turning cartwheels in the yard with her younger brothers and raising rabbits for her 4-H project.

Now at sixteen, for the first time, Sierra realized she was almost grown up. Her family's move from a small town in the northern California Sierra Nevada mountains to the city of Portland had a lot to do with that. Her trip to England had also matured her. At least while she was there, she fit right in with the older students.

Sierra knew she was about to be left in the wake of her eighteen-year-old sister's departure. And all Sierra could think was that she wanted to go back and live her ideal childhood all over again. Who needed the pressure of striving to get straight A's? Or the loss of an older sister right when they were starting to almost get along? And who needed a phantom like Paul in her life, anyway?

Sierra let out a huge sigh. She didn't really feel like crying, but it would be nice to somehow expend these overwhelming emotions. Another long stare in the mirror brought a reflection of Paul to her mind. It must have been the eyes. Paul's eyes were the same color as hers. At least that's what the flight attendant had said when he looked at both of them sitting together on their flight to Portland.

With a tug at the drawer, Sierra pulled out her toothbrush, loaded it with toothpaste, and went to work scrubbing her teeth with all the vigor her emotions brought out.

*I'll never see Paul now that Tawni is going to San Diego. Jeremy has no reason to come here, so I have no reason to think I'll ever see Paul again. He's probably forgotten all about me.*

The foaming toothpaste began to drip from the side of her mouth. Sierra made a funny face like a raging monster before spitting it out.

*Amy's right. He is a dream I've made up. I do think about him too much.*

She rinsed her mouth and took a close look at her gleaming smile.

*And I'm probably too young for him anyway. Too impulsive and—what was it I told Randy the other day?—oh yeah, dangerous. I'm too dangerous for Paul.*

Sierra grimaced fiercely at her reflection in the mirror.

Unexpectedly, some of Paul's final words to her before they parted company in the airport baggage-claim area came back to her. "Don't ever change, Sierra."

Sierra stood before the bathroom mirror, gazing into her eyes, which had turned the shade of silent winter morning. In that instant, she remembered everything about Paul. The way he smelled like Christmas in Pineville, his searching blue-gray eyes, his leather jacket and Indiana Jones-style hat. The way he first approached her and spoke to her so openly.

Then, as Sierra had done a hundred times in the past few months, she closed her eyes and prayed for Paul.

# eight

THE NEXT NIGHT, Sierra sat home alone, except for Granna Mae, who was asleep upstairs. Settling in the swing on the front porch, Sierra picked at a box of raisins and listened to the plump doves cooing from the roof of the house across the street. Low clouds hung over the city, sending down a fine, warm mist.

Sierra felt so alone.

Randy, Amy, and Drake were on their way to the Blazers game at this very moment. Sierra had had to turn down the event because that afternoon Mom and Dad had left with Tawni. Someone needed to stay home and keep an eye on Granna Mae. Sierra was the only one available.

Earlier that afternoon, Sierra's brother, Cody, had picked up the boys to keep them for the weekend at their home in Washington State, an hour's drive away. Cody and his wife, Katrina, liked it when Gavin and Dillon came to their "ranch" and kept their son, Tyler, company. Three-year-old Tyler adored his young uncles.

Amy had called in a panic half an hour ago, asking

Sierra's advice on what to wear. As Amy began to describe the outfit she had on, she had hung up with a squeal before Sierra could make a suggestion. Drake had arrived early.

Sierra had tried to convince Granna Mae that a jaunt around the block would do her good. Granna Mae had broken her foot, and when the cast was removed not long ago, the doctor had encouraged her to exercise moderately. But tonight Granna Mae was weary and declined the offer, preferring the company of the television in her bedroom. Sierra had sat with her awhile watching a game show.

Within the first five minutes of the program, Granna Mae had nodded off. So Sierra had pulled a blanket over her and switched off the noisy television. The silence woke Granna Mae, and she irritably asked Sierra to "turn my program back on."

Sierra had obliged her beloved grandmother and then tiptoed downstairs and out onto the porch, where she now sat in her bunny slippers with her raisins and thoughts of Paul.

*Father God, are You tired of my praying about this guy? I don't know what it is. I just want Paul to stay on track with You. When I met him, it seemed he was falling away. Please keep him close to Your heart. I know it's his choice to obey You or to go his own way, but I pray that You'll keep Your hand on him always.*

It was unusually quiet, a strange occurrence around this old house. She thought back on how much things had changed. Her two older brothers had each left home, and now, if Tawni left, Sierra would be the oldest child there. Already she was experiencing the disadvantages of being the oldest, "responsible" child. She'd had to give up the basket- ball game to watch Granna Mae. In a small way, Sierra could understand why her sister was looking forward to being on her own, running her own schedule.

Sierra tapped the last raisin out of the box and scuffed in her bunny slippers back into the house, where she headed for her favorite room: the study. An entire wall was covered with built-in bookshelves that reached from the floor to the ceiling and were filled with old books Granna Mae had collected over the decades. Some of them were in her native tongue, Danish. Sierra flipped on the soft amber light by the overstuffed chair and glanced around the room. Dozens of books silently called out, inviting her to slip between their cozy covers and spend the evening with them.

In the back of her mind paraded the long list she had written in her notebook of all the studying she needed to do this weekend. Being a young woman of determination, Sierra shunned the beckoning books and turned on the computer at her father's desk. The familiar soft whirring sound of the "brain" coming to life put Sierra into a studious mood. The assignment before her called for a ten-page report. She mentally increased that to fifteen pages since she was conscientiously collecting every extra-credit point possible.

For almost an hour, she typed away furiously. Distant footsteps sounded on the wooden floor on the entryway. Sierra assumed Granna Mae had awakened and was coming downstairs for a snack. To Sierra's surprise, Wesley, her older brother, poked his head into the library.

"What are you doing here?" Sierra said.

Wes greeted her with a kiss on top of her head. "I didn't want you to be stuck here alone all weekend." Wes attended the University of Oregon in Corvallis, about a two-hour drive south of Portland. She would never admit to having a favorite among her four brothers, but in a lot of ways she was closer to Wesley than to the others.

"Where's Granna Mae?" he asked.

"Sleeping, I think. She was nodding off about an hour ago. I haven't checked on her since." Sierra clicked a few keys on the computer and closed down her project.

"You finished?" Wes asked.

"No, but a person can spend only so much time expounding on 'the benefits of the Industrial Revolution' on a Friday night before complete depression sets in."

"Why aren't you out with your friends tonight?" Wes seemed to have figured out the answer before he even finished his sentence. "Hey, I'm here now. I'll keep an eye on Granna Mae. Why don't you go do something? It's not that late."

"My friends are at a Blazers game."

"Wealthy bunch you're hanging out with these days."

"Not really. They buy the cheap seats. What about you? No interesting women to keep you company on a Friday night?"

Wesley stood with one shoulder leaning against a bookcase, running his fingers through his wavy brown hair. A slight smile graced his five o'clock-shadowed jawline. He looked just like their dad, or at least how their dad must have looked in his younger days before the crown of his head went bald.

"Not this week," Wes said casually. Sierra knew Wes had been interested in someone last Thanksgiving, only the woman hadn't seemed to return the interest. He hadn't talked about anyone since then.

"You want to do something?" Wes asked.

"Like what?"

"Rent a movie or go out for coffee."

"Sure. Do you think we should leave Granna Mae?"

"You're right," Wes said. "I forgot we're the only ones home with her. I think this is the quietest it's ever been around here."

"Strange, isn't it?" Sierra said. "It was worse the weekend I was alone with her when she had her surgery. This house is kind of creepy when it's empty."

"Have you checked the refrigerator yet?" Wes asked. "Is there any food?"

"I found some raisins," Sierra said, knowing that her brother hated them. Raisins, prunes, figs—any wrinkly fruit, he automatically boycotted.

Wes made a face. "Let's check on Granna Mae. She might be awake and feel like running out with us for a pizza."

"I doubt it, Wes," Sierra said with a laugh. "She's a grandma, not a college student."

"That's part of her problem," Wes said, leading the way upstairs. "Everyone treats her as if she can't do anything for herself. Granna Mae is one hearty woman. She climbed into the tree house out back with me when I was fourteen. Remember that? We had a picnic, just the two of us."

"Still, Wes," Sierra said, lowering her voice, "that was what—nine years ago? A lot has happened since then."

"People are only as old are they think they are," Wes said, tapping gently on Granna Mae's bedroom door before turning the knob to open it.

Granna Mae stood by the window in her flowered robe,

looking out into the night. The television was turned off. Mellow jazz music floated softly from her radio.

"I told you she would be up," Wes said to Sierra. Then raising her voice, he said, "How's my favorite lady?"

Granna Mae turned, startled to see them. Her eyes seemed preoccupied as they looked past Sierra and Wesley. Sierra involuntarily glanced over her shoulder to see if someone else stood behind her. Of course, no one was there. Granna Mae was experiencing one of her short-circuits of the brain.

"Yes?" she said cordially. She gave no indication that she had any idea who Sierra or Wesley was.

"I…" Wesley began. "Or rather, *we* thought we'd check on you."

It seemed to Sierra he wasn't prepared for this disengaged greeting from his dear grandma. Then she realized that he wasn't home often. Sierra didn't know how many times he had seen Granna Mae like this.

"Yes," Granna Mae said evenly. "I'm fine."

"Would you like us to bring you anything?" Sierra asked.

"It appears my luggage hasn't arrived yet," she said. "If it wouldn't be too much trouble, could you check on it for me?"

Wes looked to Sierra. She gave him an affirming nod, and she said, "Sure. We can do that. Anything else?"

"No thank you." She shuffled across the room to where her purse sat on an old embroidered footstool. "I'll give you a nickel now and another if you return with my bags within the hour."

Wes looked pale.

Sierra spoke up. "That's awfully kind of you, but there's no need. Really. It's all complimentary."

"Oh." A pleased expression brushed over Granna Mae's face. "Well, thank you."

Sierra and Wes exited, closing the door behind them and making their way down the stairs in silence.

"Should we take some suitcases up there?" Wes asked.

"I don't think so. If we do, she'll only ask what they're for. She doesn't seem to stay on track with her scattered ideas. We should stay home for sure, though."

"I agree," Wes said. "Boy, that's sure strange, seeing her like that."

"I know."

They entered the kitchen, and Wes tapped the light switch. The light turned on for a brief moment and then burned out.

"Whoa!" Wes said. "Where does Dad keep the light-bulbs? Out in his workshop?"

"In the basement, I think," Sierra said. She kept in step with Wes as they searched for a lightbulb and then returned to the kitchen and made quick work of replacing the burned-out one.

Out of habit, Sierra shook the old bulb and heard the slight rattling of the metal threads. Right before she tossed it into the trash, she thought of how frustrating it must be for Granna Mae to have a mind that didn't always make the connection, the way that burned-out bulb hadn't. For years and years, the switch automatically turns on and off at command. Then one day—poof! The switch turned on as always, but the connection isn't made. Sierra shuddered to think of the day Granna Mae would be gone.

The feeling somehow applied to Tawni as well. Her whole life, Sierra had shared a room with her sister. It was entirely possible that would soon change.

When Wes wasn't looking, Sierra took the burned-out lightbulb and tucked it in a drawer instead of pitching it into the trash. Later, when he wasn't around, she planned to take it up to her room.

# nine

SIERRA WORKED at Mama Bear's bakery from eight to five on Saturday. Amy came in during Sierra's lunch break, and they sat in the back room of the bakery eating broken bits of cinnamon rolls until they were sick of the gooey bakery goods. Amy talked nonstop about the game and Drake. Apparently, he had done everything right: opened the door for her, bought her a Coke, paid attention to her all night, and walked her to the door—the perfect gentleman. Amy was glowing.

"I told Drake about our plan to fix dinner for him and Randy, and he thought it was a great idea!"

"Did you say anything to Randy?" Sierra asked.

"Of course. He was sitting right there."

"Amy!"

"What?"

Sierra knew it was best to go along with the whole scheme and try not to change Amy's big plans. "Nothing," she said, reaching for a napkin and wiping her sticky fingers. "Go ahead. What's our plan?"

"Okay." Amy's dark eyes lit up. "Next Saturday, my house. We'll have lobster, baked potatoes, and...what else?"

"Salad of some sort?" Sierra suggested.

"Caesar," Amy decided. "And some kind of incredible dessert. Chocolate, of course."

"When are we going to make all this?" Sierra asked.

"We have to cook the lobsters fresh that night. I told you my uncle said he would give us four lobsters, didn't I? He doesn't usually serve them, but he can order them at discount, so he's going to give them to us."

"That's nice of him."

"Maybe he can get us some chocolate cheesecake," Amy suggested. "I asked Drake, and he said he liked cheesecake."

"I have a feeling Drake will like anything we serve him," Sierra said. Then, because Amy looked at her strangely, she added, "And Randy, too. Have you ever met a guy who didn't like to eat?"

"I have a cousin who hates pasta," Amy said. "In our family, that's like saying, 'I hate to breathe air.'"

Sierra glanced at the clock above the sink and said, "I have to get back to work. Let me know if you want me to bring anything. And it's next Saturday, right?"

"Right. I told them seven. That will give us a little time to get everything ready."

"Sounds fun!" Sierra adjusted her apron as Amy exited through the back door. "See you," she called out and then returned to the front counter where Jody was the only one helping a long line of customers.

"You should have called me," Sierra said. "I didn't realize it had gotten so busy."

"They all came at once," red-haired Jody answered.

"One little cloudburst, and everyone wants coffee." She turned the knob on the espresso machine, and Sierra stepped to the register to ring up the order.

Sierra glanced up to see two more customers enter—Randy and Drake. She smiled at them and kept ringing up orders as Jody expertly made one cappuccino after another. When Randy and Drake reached the front of the line, Sierra noticed that both had wet hair.

"Did you stop to take a shower on your way in?" she asked.

"It was the other way around. A shower took us," Drake said.

"He was helping me with some of my Saturday regulars, and we had to stop right in the middle of one of the lawns, it was coming down so hard. I made the executive decision it was time for lunch." Randy's crooked smile lit up his face. He had such a friendly way about him. Sierra realized she felt comfortable and at ease whenever Randy was around—sort of the way she felt the night before when Wes showed up to help her with Granna Mae.

"Randy tells me these are the best donuts in town," Drake said. He ran a hand over his dark hair, taming all the wayward strands into place.

"Actually, we serve only cinnamon rolls, no donuts. Mrs. Kraus is considering getting a frozen yogurt machine, though."

"Two cinnamon rolls, then," Drake said.

"With lots of frosting," Randy added. "You always have to remind Sierra about the extra frosting."

"Are these boys friends of yours?" Jody asked.

"This is Drake and Randy," Sierra said. "And, yes,

under pressure, I will admit that I know them both."

"Nice to meet you," Jody said. "Do you want something to drink with your rolls?"

"I'll have a mocha latte," Drake said.

Randy ordered two milks, and Sierra quickly said, "What you really need to go with those milks is a taco."

She was glad to see that Randy understood her teasing immediately and said, "No, no. Milk goes with cinnamon rolls, not tacos. This is what I've been trying to tell you."

"They have tacos here?" Drake asked.

"No," Sierra told him. "It's a little joke, that's all."

Drake glanced at Randy, who was still grinning, and then he looked back at Sierra. She realized that she had hinted at something she never thought she would. Private jokes are common between boyfriends and girlfriends, and Drake seemed to be reading their expressions to see how close the two of them actually were.

For some reason, that made Sierra feel uncomfortable. She scooped up their cinnamon rolls as the two of them pooled their cash.

"You see," she began to explain to Drake, "I like milk with tacos, and Randy thinks that's weird."

"I like milk with tacos," Drake said.

"See?" Sierra challenged Randy. Her silver bracelets clanged against the side of the cash register as she rang up their order.

"So, is this what we're having at Amy's next week?" Drake asked. "Tacos and milk?"

"No. Actually, she was just here. She'll be sorry she missed you. Didn't she tell you what we're having?" Sierra asked.

The guys shook their heads and reached for their rolls and drinks.

"Then I won't tell either," Sierra said. "It'll be a surprise."

Drake and Randy stepped to the side, making room for the next customer as they chomped into their rolls.

After Sierra had helped the last two people in line, Randy stepped back up to the register and said, "We think what you and Amy are doing is really cool."

"You haven't tried our cooking yet," Sierra warned. "You might want to reserve your opinion until after you've lived through the experience."

"I'm willing to risk it," Drake said, looking at her with an extra-warm smile that made her feel funny. He was such a contrast to Randy—taller, with striking dark features, broad shoulders, and that firm jaw, which he was now sticking out as he smiled.

*If Amy were here,* Sierra thought, *she would think Drake was flirting with me.*

But Sierra knew that Amy had little to worry about. Flirting back had never been at the top of Sierra's skills.

# ten

ON SUNDAY EVENING, a little after eight o'clock, Granna Mae and Sierra were sitting on the porch swing. That day Granna Mae had been lucid. Wes and Sierra had gone to church with her and to lunch afterward at her favorite restaurant. She had taken a nap in the afternoon while Sierra finished her paper and Wes took their St. Bernard, Brutus, for a run. Sierra had fixed grilled cheese sandwiches for supper, and Granna Mae had eaten hers with one dill pickle and a cup of strong black coffee, sipped from her favorite china cup.

All was normal. Sierra and Granna Mae had gone for a stroll around the block and now sat on the porch, chatting about birds. Cody and Katrina had dropped off Sierra's little brothers that afternoon, and Gavin and Dillon were on the front lawn wrestling with Wes and Brutus.

The peaceful May evening had just pulled down its shades, welcoming the night sounds and deep-shadowed hues, when Dad pulled up in the van. He honked and called out the window his trademark "We're homely-home-home."

The boys ran to greet Mom, Dad, and Tawni. In a few minutes, everyone was gathered on the front porch asking questions over Brutus's incessant barking.

"Well?" Wes said. "How did it go? What did you decide?"

"Are you going to be a famous model?" Dillon asked.

"Did your luggage arrive okay?" Sierra asked.

"Do tell us, Nee-Nee," Granna Mae said, using Tawni's childhood nickname, which Tawni couldn't stand.

Tawni looked at Mom and Dad. They both nodded their go-ahead. Facing the inquiring faces, Tawni announced excitedly, "I'm going! I'm moving to Carlsbad."

Even though this was the response they all had expected, a moment of silence hung over them as they each read the delight and eagerness written on Tawni's face.

"That's great!" Wes was the first one to find his voice.

"Wow!" Sierra blurted out. "You're really going."

Tawni nodded and flashed an appreciative smile at Mom and Dad. "I wish you could have all met Jeremy's parents. They are such wonderful people."

"Yes, they certainly are," Mom agreed.

"Jeremy wasn't too bad either," Dad teased. "Tolerable. Not like that other guy in Pineville. What was his name? Marvin?"

"Martin!" Sierra, Wes, Tawni, and Mom all answered in unison.

"Right," Dad said with a twinkle in his eye. "The Martian boy."

"I hope he wasn't like this around Jeremy," Sierra said.

"No, thank goodness," Tawni responded.

Granna Mae tapped Sierra on the leg and said, "Now who is Jeremy?"

Sierra leaned over and explained. "He's the guy Tawni met when she and I went down to Southern California for Easter vacation. He's friends with some of my friends from San Diego. Do you remember hearing about him? He's Paul's older brother."

A look of recognition came to Granna Mae's sweet, soft face. "Oh, yes. Paul. I do like that Paul. He brought me daffies, you know."

"Yes," Sierra said, "I remember. He visited you in the hospital."

"Yes, he did. I do like that Paul," Granna Mae repeated.

*So do I*, Sierra thought.

"We'd better carry the luggage inside," Dad said, turning to Wes, who was already following him to the van. "How was the weekend, son? We appreciate your coming up."

Sierra helped Granna Mae stand up as the women headed back into the house. Everything felt so right to Sierra at this moment. She had Granna Mae's silky hand in hers, her little brothers were running into the backyard with hulking Brutus barking and following at a gallop. Everyone in her family except Cody, Katrina, and Tyler was there within her view. She loved the scent in the air after the rain, the excited tone in Tawni's voice, the warm feeling that washed over her when Granna Mae said Paul's name.

Sierra wanted everything to freeze right there, even the moths on the screen door. This was her home, her family, her life. She didn't want it to change. Truth be told, she didn't want Tawni to leave.

How could she possibly feel this way? And since she did, how could she tell her sister?

An hour later, the two of them were alone in their room. Tawni bubbled over the details as she unpacked. Wearing her favorite pj's, Sierra was curled up in bed taking in every word.

Tawni seemed to have come alive since this adventure began. She was excited about everything. Already she had told Sierra about their meeting with the modeling agent on Saturday and how the agent has said he thought Tawni had a good chance of finding work right away. She also had explained to Sierra how ecstatic Jennifer was that Tawni would be coming to live with them. Now she was recounting that she would request a transfer to a Southern California Nordstrom's on Monday and move down as soon as she could. Everything seemed perfect.

Except for the pierced feeling in the center of Sierra's heart. She wanted to protest, "You can't leave. Not yet." She never had expected she would feel this way.

"I'm glad for you, Tawni. I really am. I just can't believe you're going," Sierra said, taking a deep breath. "Actually, I wish you weren't going. I'm going to miss you something fierce!"

In one fluid motion, Tawni swished across the room and flung her arms around Sierra's neck. She gave Sierra a light hug and graced her cheek with a kiss.

"Think of it this way: You'll have the whole room to yourself." Tawni's smile remained in place as she fluttered back to the nearly empty suitcase.

*How can she be so casual about this?* Sierra thought. *I'm opening myself up to her for one of the first times ever, and she's being sweet and kissing me. Why wasn't it like this before? Will it ever be like this for us again?*

# eleven

SIERRA HAD LITTLE TIME to contemplate her relationship with her sister during the next week. On Monday, in Mr. Rykert's class, they spent the period in their teams discussing their outreach projects. Randy had some notes on what they were supposed to do and started to suggest who should do what.

Vicki pulled a ponytail holder from her wrist and twisted her hair into it. "Will you guys excuse me a minute? I'll be right back." She went over to the corner where Amy and Byron were sitting and started talking to them. Amy and Vicki had been close friends when Sierra started attending this school in the middle of the year. Then Vicki began to date a senior, and Amy seemed ready for a new friend. That's when she and Sierra started to do things together.

"We're scheduled to go to the Highland House Tuesday and Friday," Randy said. "The director asked if we could tell a Bible story and maybe sing a song with the kids. Then we'll spend the rest of the time helping them with homework and playing with them."

Tre looked indifferent. Sierra couldn't tell if he was with them or not.

"You want to organize the story?" Randy asked, looking at Sierra.

"Sure. Sounds easy enough."

By the next afternoon, when the four of them stood inside the meeting room at the Highland House, Sierra discovered she had spoken too soon. Telling a story to this bunch of kids was not easy. Even sitting on the floor and listening was more than most of them could handle after being in school all day.

Sierra had worked until almost midnight cutting out, pasting, and coloring Bible characters that she had fastened to pencils so she could hold them up as puppets while she told the story of the prodigal son. She had enough puppets so that Randy, Vicki, and Tre could all help her hold them as she did the storytelling.

Tre didn't understand what she wanted him to do, so he retreated to a far corner of the large room to watch. Vicki didn't get into the spirit of the activity and spent all her time telling the children to hush.

But Randy jumped in enthusiastically, especially when it was his turn to hold up the pigs from the pigpen where the prodigal son had his change of heart. Randy had those pig puppets dancing and snorting and stealing the show. The kids laughed and started to imitate the pig noises.

"Randy," Sierra whispered, "the prodigal is supposed to realize he doesn't want to stay in there with the pigs!"

Randy kept the pigs dancing and leaned over to answer without taking his eyes off his captive audience. "Hey, at least they're listening. Come on, hit 'em with the moral of the story while we have their attention."

Sierra tried to conclude with the point that the young man returned home and his father was watching and waiting for him. Only, Vicki had the father puppet, and she held it out in front of her like a lit sparkler she was afraid would get sparks on her.

"And God is just like that," Sierra concluded, feeling frustrated with Vicki that she wasn't making the father-God figure a little more appealing. "He loves us and wants us to come to Him. He wants us to say we're sorry for all the wrong things we've done, and He wants us to turn our lives over to Him."

The puppets were then put to the side, and Sierra was the only one standing before the kids. She was losing their attention fast.

"If any of you would like to do that," she said, feeling herself stumbling over her words, "if you would like to pray and give your life over to God, then we'd like to talk to you afterward."

Several kids were meandering to the back of the room, anticipating the opening of the double doors so they could be released to play.

"Before you go," Sierra said, her voice rising and carrying a bit of a desperate edge to it, "I'd like to pray with you guys. Everyone please stop where you are and close your eyes."

She waited a moment, looking around the room. Only two little girls in the front closed their eyes, and one of them started to peek.

"Come on, you guys," Randy said loudly, stepping next to Sierra. "Stop where you are and close your eyes."

Now they were all looking at Randy, including the two girls who had previously had their eyes closed.

"Better go ahead and pray," Randy muttered to Sierra.

Sierra closed her eyes and bowed her head, knowing she was probably the only one in the room doing so. Her prayer was four short lines and her "Amen" came out faster than ever she imagined it would.

"Okay!" Randy called over the kids' rumbling. "You're dismissed." He didn't need to say it twice.

Tre, Vicki, and Randy followed the herd of noisy kids out the doors, leaving Sierra to pick up.

*Well, that was a bomb,* Sierra thought in disgust. *And look at this floor! How could these kids have made such a mess in so short a time?*

Smashed paper cups, left over from snack time, were everywhere. Some had been shredded into tiny bits and sprinkled across the floor like confetti. Muttering to herself, Sierra grabbed a trash can and began cleaning up the cups.

*They didn't hear a word I said. What a disaster!*

"Prodigals seem to be your specialty," a male voice behind her said.

"Hardly," Sierra said dryly, without looking up.

"Why? You think they don't ever change, Sierra?"

It was his voice, saying her name. Holding her breath, Sierra turned and looked into the face she had carried around in her memory for months. Paul's.

# twelve

SIERRA FELT THE BLOOD rushing to her cheeks and found her voice had taken a sudden vacation without telling her.

Paul stood only a few feet away, looking casual and unruffled. His thick, wavy brown hair fell across his broad forehead, giving him the look of a windblown adventurer. He was clean shaven, and a hint of sunburn flashed across his cheeks and his thin, straight nose. Or was it possible that Paul was blushing as well?

He held the prodigal puppet in his hand and twirled the pencil between his fingers, spinning it back and forth. He didn't speak but gazed at her through clear blue-gray eyes that smiled at her even though his lips remained still.

"Hi," Sierra managed to squeak out. She brushed her hair from her face and tried to take a deep breath. Her heart pounded wildly, and she felt her lips quiver as she tried to form a smile.

"Hi," Paul said calmly. "What happened to your boots?"

"You mean my dad's old cowboy boots?"

He nodded.

"The sole came off the right boot. I haven't taken them in to be fixed yet." *He remembers what I was wearing when we first met.*

"I never had a chance to thank you for the flowers you took to Granna Mae in the hospital. She really appreciated them."

"How's she doing?"

"Good. Great, really. She's doing fine." *Stop yourself, Sierra. You sound like a parrot!*

The room grew silent. Sierra and Paul held each other's gaze for a long, uninterrupted moment. For some reason, Sierra felt herself calming down and drawing closer to Paul even though she hadn't moved an inch.

"I want to tell..." Sierra began.

"There's something..." Paul said at the same instant.

They both released a nervous laugh, followed by a "You first," which also came out in unison.

"Go ahead," Paul said. This time he was smiling at her, not only with his eyes, but also with his lips.

"I, um...well..." Sierra couldn't get her thoughts and her words to cooperate. Part of her wanted to run into Paul's arms and say, "I've been praying my little heart out for you, and here you are at a Christian outreach mission. Does this mean my prayers have been answered? Are you done with walking away from the Lord?"

Another part of her was still in shock at suddenly seeing him. That part of her wanted to turn and run like the wind.

Suddenly, the double doors burst open, and two little girls with small braids all over their heads called out, "There you are, Paul. Come turn the jump rope for us."

Paul didn't answer them but kept staring at Sierra.

"Come on," they cried, running over and grabbing his arms.

Paul reached over and gently tapped Sierra on the forearm with the first two fingers on his right hand. "We need to talk sometime," he said in a low voice.

The persistent girls pulled at him, and he added, "By the way, Clint really appreciated the rolls."

"Clint?"

"Last week," Paul said as the girls urged him to come with them. "I saw you on the sidewalk out front. I saw you give Clint the bag, which he told me was filled with cinnamon rolls."

"That was you on the porch?" Sierra asked.

Paul nodded and allowed himself to be dragged from the room. As he passed Sierra, a fresh-from-the-forest scent touched her nose.

"Whose turn is it to jump first today?" he asked, wrapping an arm around each of the girls.

The doors closed behind them, and Sierra lowered herself to the floor with a plop. There she sat, stunned, trying to absorb what had just happened. She knew her friend Katie would call this a "God-thing," this coincidence that Paul just happened to be at the same place where she was assigned to do her service project. But why? What was he doing there? Obviously, the kids knew him, so he had been coming for a while. Did he work there for pay? Was he a volunteer? Why would he volunteer to help? This was the last activity she would have pictured him doing based on her first impression of him. But he seemed changed.

"Hey, Sierra!" a male voice called out, and the double doors swung open.

Sierra looked up expectantly.

It was Randy. "Are you coming out here? I could use some help at my homework table."

"I was just, um, cleaning up here a bit. I'll be right there." She wondered if her face still looked as red as it felt.

"Cool," Randy said, exiting with a single wave of his hand. Sierra quickly scooped up the final pieces of trash and stuffed the puppets into her backpack. When she picked up the prodigal, Sierra spun the pencil slowly between her fingers the way Paul had. What had he meant about her specialty being prodigals? Did he see himself as a prodigal who had come back?

When they had met, he had told her about his girlfriend, and Sierra lectured him on the folly of dating someone who wasn't a believer. Paul's reaction had been to pull back from Sierra, and that was that. Or was it? Had her months of prayers for him had an effect?

Her heart was still pounding fast when Sierra emerged from the meeting room and found her way into the former dining room of the old mansion. Several tables were set up around the room where the children could do their homework. Randy seemed to be the only person available to help the fifteen or so kids. Paul wasn't there. Maybe it had only been a dream. The lack of sleep last night, the stress of the rowdy kids...maybe she had only imagined that Paul had stood beside her, that he had looked at her and smiled, that he had reached over and touched her arm with his fingers. She touched the spot where Paul had tapped her arm, as if it might help her sort her dreams from reality.

"Over there," Randy said, pointing to a round table

where five kids sat with the same work sheet in front of them. "They're doing fractions. Can you help them?"

Still lost in her cloud, Sierra made her way to the table and sat down in a small chair. The little boy next to her smelled awful. The odor hit her like smelling salts, reviving her from the dream. She could hardly stand to be near him. The odor was so strong Sierra casually covered her nose with her hand. She remembered reading a book about a young schoolteacher in the Appalachians who had to carry a hanky laced with perfume because her students smelled so bad. Throughout the day, the teacher would hold it to her face, filtering out their terrible odor.

"Okay. You're done," Sierra said as soon as the boy finished. "You can go outside and play now."

He pushed back his chair, looking eager to leave. But instead of walking away from the table, he came over to Sierra and looked into her face. "Are you going to come back tomorrow?" he asked, his brown eyes pleading.

"Ah, no," Sierra said, trying to hold her breath and speak at the same time.

He looked disappointed, but he wasn't moving.

"I will be back on Friday," she added quickly.

His expression lit up. "I'm Monte," he said. "You remember me, okay?"

"Okay," she agreed. "I'll remember you." *Believe me, Monte, I'll remember you all right.*

"Will you do art with us on Friday?" one of the girls asked. "We don't have to do homework on Fridays, but we can do art if someone helps us."

"Sure," Sierra agreed. "I'll do art with you on Friday."

"Every Friday?" another girl asked.

"Well, at least this Friday," Sierra said. She now understood why the director had been so thrilled when their foursome showed up that afternoon. He said they were short-staffed. Sierra could see how desperately the kids wanted someone to pay attention to them.

The other children at her table finished, and they all wanted to go outside to play soccer with Sierra.

She let them lead her by the hands. When they went out front into the big yard, Sierra immediately spotted Paul. He wasn't playing jump rope. Tre had taken that position. The two little girls were turning the rope, and Tre was the one jumping. It was the first time Sierra had seen him smile or heard him laugh. Those little girls had accomplished what none of the teens at Sierra's school had been able to do. The girls made friends with Tre.

Paul stood in the center of the yard with a whistle around his neck and a soccer ball under his arm. He was calling out directions when Sierra was hauled into the mob by her new fan club.

"She's on our team!" they yelled.

Paul looked at her with what Sierra interpreted to be a mix of admiration and surprise.

"Okay, then," he called out, tossing the ball into the air. "It's every kid for himself. The goal is the oak tree."

He blew the whistle and immediately the twenty or so grade-school kids began to clamor for the ball.

"This way," the girls squealed, dashing after the ball.

Sierra jogged along with them, noticing that Randy had set himself up as the goalie. With a quick glance over her shoulder at Paul, Sierra knew once and for all that he wasn't a dream. He really was standing there, wearing that smile—

the one that started in his eyes and lit up his face. And he was staring right at her.

The soccer-playing little girls huddled close to Sierra as they charged toward the oak tree. It was a warm afternoon, and Sierra wished she had worn shorts instead of jeans. The lively gang of soccer players ran all over the yard, and Sierra trotted along with them until finally one of them hit the ball past Randy and made a goal by slamming it against the oak tree.

That kid then replaced Randy as the goalie, and the game continued. Only now Randy was jogging alongside Sierra, giving her advice as they went.

"Kick it out toward the front fence," Randy said. "I'll be waiting for it."

He started to run off as Sierra was saying, "But Randy, this is for the kids!"

Suddenly, the ball was before her, and without hesitation, she kicked it toward the front fence. Randy was ready as promised, and he slammed it into the tree before the goalie even had a chance to turn around.

"Yahoo!" Randy shouted, arms in the air. "Way to go!"

He ran over to Sierra and gave her a high five with both hands, leaning close to say in her ear, "I told you we make a great team!" Spontaneously, he wrapped his arms around her in a quick hug.

Sierra felt prickly from her neck up. Randy's gesture was the most affectionate thing he had ever done. She knew Paul had observed it. The blush crawled from her neck to her cheeks and then burst like a sunrise across her sweaty forehead.

"No fair!" the kids began to yell. "You two can't do that."

"You know what," Sierra said, wiping perspiration from her top lip as she saw Paul coming closer. "I think I'll step out this next round."

"Not now," Randy said. "With a little strategy, we can have this thing wired."

"Don't leave!" Sierra's little fan club cried, grabbing her arms.

"Come on," one of the older boys called out. "Throw the ball in, Paul. Let's play."

"Everyone ready?" Paul asked. He now stood less than six feet away, the group of eager players huddled around him. Sierra could smell Monte again, only she wasn't sure if her own armpits were contributing to the sudden air pollution as well.

"I'm out this round," Sierra said to the little girls beside her. "I need to check on something inside." She hurried away before anyone could see how red her face was.

She didn't look back, so she would never know what Paul's face looked like as he watched her go.

# thirteen

"THAT'S WHAT I'M SAYING," Sierra stated emphatically on the phone with Amy later that evening. She had repeated the whole scenario to Amy and concluded with, "The worst part is, nothing happened. Paul left before I did, and now I don't know if he'll be there Friday or not."

"So you're telling me that for one brief moment you two spoke, and now Paul is back to being a phantom."

"In a way, yes. But don't you think it's a God-thing?"

"Well," Amy said, "I hate to be the realist here, but nothing happened, Sierra. I mean, he was there, but all he did was look at you, say a few words, and disappear."

"I know, but when he looked at me, it was as if the rest of the room started to fade away into smeared watercolors."

"Oh, please!" Amy started to laugh. "You are so melodramatic, Sierra. Nobody really feels like that when she's around a guy."

"I'm not making this up, Amy. That's exactly how I felt."

"So where was Vicki the whole time?" Amy asked.

"She was playing jacks with a little girl on the back porch."

"She didn't see Paul, then?"

"I don't know. Why?"

"I was curious, that's all. If Vicki noticed Paul, I'm sure I'll hear about it."

There was a stretch of silence as Sierra tried to keep her imagination from spinning out of control. Vicki had a tendency to attract and hold the attention of most of the guys she set her sights on. Would Paul be the next one on her list?

"Why don't you come with us to the Highland House this Friday?" Sierra wasn't sure what this would prove, but it seemed like a good idea as she said it.

"I can't. That's when Byron and I are doing our service project. Oh, did I tell you that next weekend I'm going to start working at my uncle's restaurant?"

"Did another hostess quit?" Sierra was finding it difficult to be thrilled about Amy's news when her own news about Paul was still on the conversation table, even if Amy wasn't devouring it the way Sierra had. Amy wasn't even sampling it.

"Yes. He wanted me to start this Saturday, but I told him I already had a commitment. When do you get off on Saturday?"

"Probably four."

"Why don't you come straight to my house, and we'll start dinner for Randy and Drake. Did I tell you I got a chocolate cheesecake for us?"

Sierra had forgotten about the dinner. "Great."

"Oh, well, you sound excited. Don't you like cheesecake?"

"No. I mean yes. I like cheesecake."

"Okay. Good. I better get going," Amy said. "I'll see you at school tomorrow. Wait for me by my locker in the morning, okay?"

Sierra waited until the bell rang, but Amy never showed up at her locker the next morning. Slipping into class right before the tardy bell, Sierra pulled out her assignment to hand in. She had been up late again, trying to type her report in spite of the way her mind kept wandering to Paul. What had he thought of her? Why didn't he say anything more to her? Would she see him again?

So much had been going on at her house last night with all of Tawni's plans that Sierra hadn't tried to redirect the conversation to her and Paul. When Amy had downplayed the encounter, Sierra decided not to make a big deal about it with anyone else.

The funny thing was, she wanted to tell Randy. He was her buddy. She told him lots of things, including how she felt about Tawni leaving. And Randy was there at the Highland House. He had met Paul. Certainly, Randy of all people would agree with her that it was God-thing.

Somehow she couldn't bring herself to tell him. She was still trying to convince herself that his brief hug at the soccer game was only a brotherly expression of joy over their victory. Still, it had confused her. Funny thing—she hadn't even thought to tell Amy about the hug. Amy would have loved to hear all about it since it came from Randy. Sierra decided she wouldn't tell Randy about Paul and she wouldn't tell Amy about Randy's hug. It wasn't important.

Then, on their way to the cafeteria for lunch, Amy complicated things. She told Sierra she had been talking to

Vicki in the parking lot and that's why she hadn't made it to her locker that morning.

"I asked Vicki if she had met a guy named Paul, and she said she saw some guy out in the yard playing soccer with the kids, but she didn't know his name."

"You didn't tell her I knew him, did you?"

"Well…" Amy lowered her big brown eyes.

"You did. What did you tell her?"

"Oh, not much."

"You told her everything, didn't you?"

"Vicki and I have been friends a long time," Amy said, quickly defending herself. "She won't say anything to anyone. I told her not to."

"Amy, that really ticks me off!" Sierra turned to her friend and embarked on the first argument of the friendship.

"Sor-ry!" Amy retorted in an exaggerated tone.

"You knew I was telling you all those things about Paul in confidence," Sierra said, stopping in front of the cafeteria door and stepping to the side. "I feel betrayed. You didn't have my permission to share those things."

Students streamed past them. Sierra spoke only loud enough for Amy to hear her. Amy looked away as if she were a little kid who had just gotten in trouble.

Feeling her temper cool, Sierra said, "I wish you hadn't been so free with my personal life, Amy, that's all. Back at Easter when you found out I thought Randy had invited me to that formal dinner when really he had been asked by Vicki, you told me you were good at keeping secrets."

"I said that?"

The blood began to drain from Sierra's face. "You didn't say anything to Randy, did you?"

Amy's face gave away the answer. "I only told him because he was trying to figure out how you felt about him," Amy said.

"He could ask me that!" Sierra spouted. "Any time! Any day! He knows I'd tell him the truth." She caught her breath in the empty hallway and said, "Is that why you've been pushing for me to spend time with him? Because you told him I liked him, and now you're trying to verify your statement?"

"You make it sound so cold and cruel," Amy said.

"I think it was inconsiderate," Sierra shot back. "You were talking behind my back about my personal feelings and about information I had shared with you in confidence."

Sierra felt as if she were in junior high again, squabbling with her best friend. The image calmed her down. Maybe in a way she was still on a junior high level when it came to dating. She wasn't experienced like Vicki or eager like Amy. Instead, she was absorbed by this all-consuming crush on an older guy.

"You're right," Amy said, looking soberly at Sierra. "I said too much to Vicki and to Randy. I am sorry, really. I apologize."

Sierra let out a huge breath and said, "Apology accepted. Come on. Let's get some lunch." One thing Sierra did well was fight fair. She had learned early in her family to express herself openly and accurately. She also had learned the most powerful position in an argument was to be the first one to forgive and forget.

"You're not mad anymore?" Amy asked.

"I'll get over it. I told you I accept your apology, and I do. I won't hold it against you anymore."

"Wow," Amy said as they headed for their usual table.

"Wow?"

"That was the quickest I've ever been pardoned. In my family, you have to wash someone's car or make his favorite cake before he'll even begin to think about forgiving you."

Sierra smiled. It certainly wasn't that way in her family.

"Can we join you guys?" Sierra asked as they stopped at a table in front of Drake, Randy, and four other people. Vicki wasn't in the bunch, which made Sierra feel better, knowing that the topic of Paul was less likely to come up.

"You're really different, Sierra," Amy said.

"Thanks. I think."

"How is she different?" Drake asked, lifting a nacho chip to his mouth and catching the dripping cheese before it globbed all over the cafeteria tray.

"Is that all they have today?" Amy asked, avoiding Drake's question. "Nachos?"

"There are sub sandwiches, too." Randy said. "Did Sierra tell you what a great time we had at the Highland House yesterday?"

"As a matter of fact, she did. I heard a lot of interesting individuals were there." Amy's slightly raised eyebrows hinted that she knew more than she was saying.

Sierra held her breath, waiting to see if Amy would say anything more about Paul.

"I'm going to buy a sandwich," Amy said, letting her previous comment drop. "Anyone else want anything?"

Sierra shot her friend an appreciative glance for keeping her comments to a minimum.

"Hey, I had an idea, Sierra," Randy said. "When we go back on Friday, why don't we go for a pizza afterward?"

"Do you mean all of us? Tre and Vicki, too? And maybe some of the staff at the Highland House, if they're able to join us?"

"Oh." Randy sounded surprised. "Sure. That'd be fine with me."

Sierra turned to Tre, who sat quietly on the other side of Drake, and said, "Would you like to go out for pizza with us on Friday after we're finished at the Highland House?"

Tre caught her eye and nodded. She was pretty sure he knew what she had just asked. At any rate, she made the pizza event a safe situation. Regardless of what Amy may have said to Randy, now he couldn't read into their friendship any kind of message that Sierra was spending time with him because she wanted to be considered his girlfriend.

Digging her thumbnail into her orange, Sierra listened to the ruckus all around her in the small cafeteria and tried to figure out if she had truly calmed down after the confrontation with Amy.

*Is my heart with You, Lord?* Sierra thought as she slipped the first orange wedge past her lips and let the sweet juice burst in her mouth. *I don't want to get things out of whack here.*

But she had the feeling it was too late. Her life felt as if it were about to spin off into outer space.

# fourteen

SIERRA TOOK A LONG TIME to decide what to wear on Friday morning. She got up early to take her shower and to have ample opportunity to choose just the right outfit.

She was slipping into her third option when Tawni rolled over in bed and said, "What's with all the wardrobe changes?"

Since Sierra had time, she went over to Tawni's bed and gingerly sat on the edge. Talking like this with her sister was a new experience, and she approached it cautiously. She had so much stored inside her, things she hadn't said to Amy since the confrontation outside the cafeteria, things she couldn't tell Randy.

"I might see Paul today."

Tawni propped herself on her elbow and looked interested. "Oh?"

With this hint of encouragement, Sierra decided to tell Tawni everything. "Did Mom say anything to you about what happened at the Highland House last Tuesday?"

"No. You know Mom. She wouldn't say anything unless

you told her to tell me. With Mom, mum's the word!"
Tawni chuckled at her own little joke.

Sierra thought it was kind of irritating that Tawni was so
perky and happy lately, even first thing in the morning,
which used to be her worst time of day.

Sierra explained a little about Randy being on her ministry team. And then she plunged in and told Tawni about
Paul's coming into the room on Tuesday and saying what he
did about prodigals and then leaving at the end of the day
without talking to her again.

Tawni looked interested as the story continued.

"But now I might see him today, and I'm kind of nervous," Sierra confessed. "Actually, I'm terrified. I've never
gone through this before."

"First thing you do," Tawni said, now fully awake, "is
pray. Always pray."

Sierra almost laughed. "That's what I've been doing for
months. For months, I've been praying for Paul. Not that I
would see him again. I've been praying that he would get
really close to the Lord."

"You have?" Tawni's expression took a hint of awe. "I'd
say God is answering your prayers, because Paul is going to
Scotland this summer to work at a mission their grandfather
started."

"He is?" Sierra's heart sank. "When is he leaving?"

"I'm not sure. Pretty soon." Tawni snapped her fingers.
"You know what else I just figured out? The Highland
House is connected with the one their grandfather started
in Scotland. I remember that Jeremy asked me if I'd heard
of it because his uncle runs the one here in Portland. I
think Paul is staying at the Highland House since his school

already got out, and he didn't have the money to go home to San Diego and then fly to London."

Tawni's words, "fly to London," brought back all kinds of memories. Sierra wished she were going on another flight to London—the same flight as Paul.

"You know what we should do," Tawni said. "I'll ask Mom if we can invite Paul and his uncle to come for dinner one night before I leave for San Diego and Paul leaves for Scotland."

Sierra liked the idea immediately.

But before Sierra's imagination could spin a web of dreams, Tawni said, "Try to remember, Sierra, if it's meant to be, it's meant to be. If it's not, it's not."

For Tawni, that was a deep thought, and Sierra knew she was right. Even so, the many connections between Sierra's family and Paul's were intriguing as well as encouraging.

"Sierra," Mom called through the closed door, tapping it lightly with her fingers before opening it, "I need to keep the car today, so I'll drive you to school. Will you be ready in about ten minutes?"

"Yikes!" Sierra glanced at the clock on Tawni's dresser and sprang into action, pulling the rest of her outfit together. She settled on the basics: jeans, a white T-shirt with a cotton woven vest, and a braided leather and bead bracelet with matching bead earrings.

Sierra made it to school on time but found it nearly impossible to concentrate on any of her classes. So many feelings were colliding inside of her: eagerness to see Paul again, the possibility of his coming for dinner, and if she saw him today, the variety of things she could say to him. She had practiced several conversations in her head the night before while she was trying to fall asleep. One of the conversations involved being honest with Paul and not joking around or teasing the way she usually did when she talked to guys. She told Paul how much she had prayed for him over the months. In her half-awake, half-asleep state, she imagined Paul had taken her hand in his and held it tightly.

Sierra shook away the memory of her dream. She needed to catch the teacher's final homework instructions. It was time to put her thoughts of Paul into the invisible treasure chest in her heart and lock them up until at least the afternoon.

Randy met Sierra at her locker at lunch and told her that he and Tre were going to eat outside since the weather was so nice. Randy said he could use her help in preparing the story for the afternoon. Since Sierra had done all the work last time, Randy and Vicki were supposed to do the story this time.

Sierra joined Randy and Tre, feeling a little bit as if she were hiding from Amy. Her mind was so full of Paul that Sierra didn't trust herself not to say anything to Amy.

"Where's Vicki?" Sierra asked.

"She has other plans, I guess," Randy said, pulling out his guitar and tuning it up. He didn't seem bothered by the lack of assistance. "She said she would meet us there this afternoon."

As Randy strummed his guitar, he softly sang the three songs he planned to teach the kids. Tre seemed to watch Randy's every move on the guitar. "Do you want to try it?" Randy said, offering the guitar to him.

Randy's gesture touched Sierra. She pretty much

ignored Tre, but Randy treated him like a friend, even turning over his guitar to him. Sierra knew how highly Randy valued his guitar. He had brought it to Sierra's house one time and had played a song he wrote, but he didn't let Gavin or Dillon play it.

Tre shyly reached for the instrument and began to strum. To Sierra's and Randy's amazement, he started to sing old American pop tunes, accompanying himself on the guitar without flaw.

"When did you learn to play like that?" Randy asked. "You're very good!"

"My brother plays guitar," Tre said. "He taught me."

Sierra was certain it was the first time she had heard Tre speak a complete sentence. It made her wonder if perhaps he understood everything they had been saying all along, but he was actually too shy to enter the conversation.

It helped to see that side of Tre, because when she rode with him and Randy to the Highland House that afternoon, Sierra felt much more comfortable with Tre and more prepared to go at this project the second time as a team—even if Vicki hadn't been there to practice with them.

Randy pulled up in front of the gated yard and parked. A dozen noisy kids spotted them climbing out of Randy's truck and ran to the gate to welcome them. Sierra smiled and greeted the kids as they all spoke at once. Some wanted to play baseball. Others begged for a round of soccer. Two little girls came running up and reminded Sierra that she had promised to do art with them.

"First, we'll all go inside and have our meeting time," Sierra said. She looked over their heads, scanning the porch for any sight of Paul. "We have something really great planned for you today."

"I know what that is," one boy said to Randy. "You have a guitar."

"That's right," Randy said. "You want to come in and hear me play it?"

"Are you any good?" a kid asked.

"Not as good as Tre here."

All the kids turned their attention to Tre as they climbed the stairs to the front porch.

"Come on in, you guys." Sierra put her hand on the doorknob. "Wait until you see our surprise."

As she opened the door, Sierra stopped cold. Paul and Vicki stood there, only inches apart. Her face was tilted up toward his, and Paul was staring into her eyes, his right hand poised to stroke her cheek.

# fifteen

THE TROOPS EXPLODED into the room, but neither Paul nor Vicki moved. The kids started to call out snickering comments.

"He's going to kiss her!"

"Ooo! Puppy love!"

As Sierra and the others watched, Vicki blinked a few times, and Paul's finger gently dabbed underneath her right eye.

"There," he said, holding up his index finger in front of Vicki. "Got it."

"Thanks!" Vicki said. "This new lens won't stay in. It slides to the corner, and I can't get it."

Paul didn't seem to listen to her. He had turned to look at the group, and the first person his gaze rested on was Sierra.

"Hi," she said above the rumble of the kids. Her two sidekicks were each tugging on an arm, urging her into the meeting room, where the director was leading the rest of the children.

"Hi," Paul said back. He wore a light blue denim work shirt with the sleeves rolled up. A braided leather bracelet circled his left wrist, and a carpenter's tool belt was wrapped around his middle. From it hung a hammer and tape measure.

"Vicki," Randy said, stepping in front of Sierra, nearly whacking her with the end of his guitar case. "You want to help us with the songs?"

Vicki held out the wayward contact on her finger. Sierra noticed Vicki now had one aqua-blue eye while the other eye showed her true color, a subtle gray. "I'll be right in as soon as I fix my contact."

"I'm glad you're here," Randy called after her as she exited down the hallway. He turned to Sierra and said, "We'd better get in there."

Sierra's helpful parasites gladly fell in line behind Randy, leading Sierra away from Paul. Angie, the smaller one with long, stringy bangs, grabbed Sierra's right arm. Meruka, the more aggressive one with missing front teeth, locked on to Sierra's left arm. They pulled Sierra, arms first, into the meeting room. Just as the doors were about to close behind her, Sierra turned and looked back at Paul, who stood his ground in the entryway with his arms folded across his chest. He wore an amused expression.

"Will you be around?" she asked.

He nodded.

"Good," was all she could think to say as her arms received another hasty yank, and the meeting room gobbled her up.

Randy was telling the kids they needed to sit and listen. Most of them settled down. Sierra sat cross-legged on the floor between her adoring friends and did her best to hush the other kids as Randy extracted his guitar from the case and began to tune up. Sierra noticed Vicki slipping in the back door and standing in the corner with Tre.

*Where's Paul?* Sierra thought. *Is he going to come in, too?*

Randy plunged right into the first song, a common Sunday school number, familiar to most American kids. However, Sierra was the only one in the room who started to sing along on the chorus. Apparently, these kids had never heard this song before.

Randy sang a couple more songs, which he tried to teach to the kids. They seemed to pay more attention to Randy than they had to Sierra on Tuesday.

Instead of a Bible story, Randy told the kids how he had become a Christian. Briefly, he related his story, quoting several verses. He told them how he had grown up going to church and believing he would go to heaven when he died. Then one day when he was eight, the drawstring to his bathing trunks got caught in a pool filter, and Randy nearly drowned trying to get free. At that moment, he wanted to make sure he was going to heaven, so he asked Christ to forgive his sins and come into his life.

"Did an angel come rescue you?" one of the fascinated kids asked.

"No," Randy said, his crooked smile peeking out. "I wiggled out of my trunks and swam to the surface in my birthday suit."

The kids burst out laughing, and it was nearly impossible to get them to focus back on Randy's serious conclusion.

"You need to make sure you've turned your life over to God," he said, raising his voice. "God wants you to come to

Him. Remember the story of the prodigal son?"

Sierra wondered if any of them were listening at all. "Shhh! Pay attention now." *How can they understand?* she thought as she tried to quiet them down. Prodigal *is not a word they use every day. Why didn't I pick a different story? These kids aren't old enough to understand a prodigal losing everything and ending up in a pigpen.*

"Okay," Randy said in a last-ditch effort to corral the kids back in, "I'm going to pray now. Will all of you please close your eyes? That's right. Close out everything that's going on around you, and let's talk to God."

He prayed earnestly, and as if he had all the time in the world, not bothered by the rowdiness of the kids. Sierra prayed silently along with him, her head bowed, eyes closed.

"Before you leave," Randy said loudly as his prayer ended and kids scrambled for the doors, "we want you to know that God loves you. He wants you to come to Him and be adopted into His family as His very own kids.'

The doors burst open and out they flew.

"Time to do art," Meruka said, turning to Sierra with a grin that exposed the gap where her front teeth had been.

"You promised," Angie reminded her.

"Okay," Sierra said, rising to her feet and slipping an arm around each of them. "Let's first tell Randy what a great job he did. Great job, Randy!"

"Great job, Randy," the girls echoed.

He looked exhausted. "Do you think any of them were listening?"

"I was listening," Meruka said.

"Me, too," said Angie, swatting her long bangs out of her eyes.

"Good," Randy responded, smiling at them. He took

his guitar from his case. "Here," he said, holding it out to Tre. "Why don't you go out onto the porch and wow them?"

Tre's face lit up as he gratefully accepted Randy's offer.

"Come on," the impatient artists said. "Let's go!"

"Okay, okay. We're on our way." Sierra steered them toward the doors. As soon as they were in the hallway, she looked for Paul. "Girls?" she asked softly. "Do you know that nice guy who was in the hall here earlier?"

"You mean Paul?" Meruka asked.

"Yes. Have you seen him around?"

"Why? Are you in love with him?"

A tiny voice deep inside the treasure chest of Sierra's heart chirped out *Yes! Yes! A thousand times yes!* Sierra felt her cheeks turning flame red, and ignoring the incarcerated voice, she laughed lightly and said, "No, of course not."

# sixteen

SIERRA SPENT the next half hour directing her group of eager artists, which had grown to eleven kids. She thought of several ideas for easy art projects: bead stringing, clay figurines, puppets, masks, even colored macaroni necklaces. The ideas grew, and she wondered if the Highland House offered a summer program for these kids if they would want a volunteer art instructor. She also wondered if Paul would be gone the entire summer.

A sudden distinct odor wafted into the room. Sierra turned toward the door, and there stood Monte, a hopeful glimmer in his brown eyes. "Do you remember me?"

"Yes, I do. How are you, Monte?"

He looked pleased that she remembered his name. "Can I do a picture?"

"Sure. Why don't you join these guys?" Sierra directed him to a side table where two boys sat, trying to fold paper airplanes the way Sierra had shown them. "Do you want to make a paper airplane, Monte? Or do you want to color?"

The other two kids at the table started to argue over the

few pieces of paper allotted to them, saying there wasn't enough for Monte. Sierra could hear two of the girls at the other table saying, "Don't let him sit next to you. He kicks."

"I know. And he stinks, too."

"Get out of here, Monte!" one of the kids said.

Sierra found herself holding her breath again, wishing for all the world this small room had a fan she could turn on. The stench was overwhelming. Monte stood between the two tables, looking to Sierra for an answer.

"Ah, actually, Monte, did you want to go outside and play soccer with the other kids?"

He shook his head. "I want to make a frog."

"A frog," Sierra repeated. "Let's see. You want to make a frog." She quickly scanned the room. The door and both the windows were already open. It was as ventilated as it was going to get. "Why don't we move out to the porch?" she suggested. "It's such a gorgeous evening. We can take all our things with us. Everyone grab something and let's go."

The kids were reluctant to follow her instructions. Some of them abandoned their art projects altogether. By the time they had regrouped on the porch, only seven artists and Monte remained.

But for Sierra, the decision to move was a good one. The calm evening breeze skipped across the wide, open porch carrying the faint scent of honeysuckle mixed with bus fumes from the busy street beyond the yard. A long line was already forming at the kitchen next door. Sierra remembered hearing that they fed an average of 150 people a night. They also offered space to 85 people a night, with men sleeping in the annex and the women and children in the two upstairs floors of the Highland House.

It amazed Sierra how so many people seemed to appear out of nowhere to line up each night. Where did they come from? How did they end up there? Each of them had a story.

"Monte," she said, spreading out her armful of art supplies, "how old are you?"

"He's five," a girl answered. "I'm older than him."

"Where did you live before you came here?" Sierra asked.

"I don't know," he said, dropping down next to her and scrounging for a green crayon.

"Has the Highland House been able to find a job for your mom?"

"I don't know where my mom is," Monte said. "She left when I was a baby. My uncle takes care of me."

Sierra found she could neither hold her breath nor steel her heart against this kid any longer. "Come on, Monte. Let's see if we can make you a frog."

The cold reality of it all hit Sierra like a sledgehammer. These kids were real, and they didn't choose to be in this condition. Their problems weren't going to go away overnight. She realized the situation called for more than a quick four hours of trying to entertain some children to meet a class requirement. Sierra felt as if something inside her connected with the kids, and she was right where God wanted her to be, doing exactly what He had created her to do—make a frog with Monte.

"We need some round, buggy eyeballs," Sierra said,

reaching for the scissors. "And some long, good jumpy legs. Did you know that God made frogs?"

"I know that story about the prince," Angie said. "He got turned into a frog, and the princess had to kiss him to turn back into a prince."

"Right," Sierra said, smiling. "That's a good fairy tale, isn't it?"

"I would never kiss a frog," Meruka spouted, her tongue sticking out through her toothless gap. "Ewww!"

"Some people eat frogs," a little boy announced.

"I'd rather kiss one than eat one."

"Here, Monte." Sierra held out two bulging eyeballs she had made. "Are you ready for these?"

"Have you ever kissed a frog, Missy Era?"

"Missy Era?"

"That's your name, isn't it?"

"Oh. Miss Sierra," she decoded with a smile. "You can call me Sierra."

"Have you ever kissed a frog, Sierra?"

The truth was, at sixteen, she had never kissed any guy— frog or prince. "No, I've never kissed a frog."

The little girls giggled.

Suddenly, from the roof overhanging the porch, they heard a clamor of heavy footsteps. Sierra looked up and noticed for the first time the ladder leaning against the front of the house. Clunky boots appeared on the top rung and steadily made their way down the ladder. The circle of artists all watched as a pair of jeans appeared on the ladder above the boots. Next came a carpenter's belt topped with a blue denim work shirt.

Sierra swallowed hard. Paul had been above them the whole time. He must have heard her comments. Landing on the ground and hoisting the ladder under his arm, Paul slowly looked up, and Sierra caught his engaging grin.

He looked right at her and said only one word as he hauled away the ladder: "Ribbit."

# seventeen

AN AGELESS yet brand-new fairy tale danced inside Sierra's imagination. Was Paul trying to tell her he was a prince in disguise? She had already guessed that.

Only a week or so ago, she would have felt dangerous and impulsive—qualities that had bothered her about herself. Now she felt useful and determined. She was sure Paul had some interest in her—a curiosity if nothing else. It confirmed her daydream that an attraction existed between her and Paul, and it wasn't only her feelings.

Quietly humming to herself, Sierra helped each kid with his or her art project. Monte's frog turned out to be kind of distorted and silly looking. It didn't matter to him. He showed everyone, proudly boasting that Sierra helped him.

She collected the crayons and bits of paper from the porch as the children began to leave. Every now and then she looked up to see if Paul was around. She didn't want him to disappear this time.

The director came out onto the porch and shook

Sierra's hand, thanking her for coming. She pulled him aside from the three kids still coloring and asked if she could continue to volunteer.

"We'd love it," Mr. Mackenzie said. "You can see how much we need the help. My nephew speaks highly of you."

*Paul spoke highly of me?*

"I think very highly of Paul as well," Sierra said. "And Jeremy. My sister, Tawni, is dating Jeremy."

"Really!" Mr. Mackenzie had a gentle, engaging manner about him. "And is your sister here?"

"No. But we'd like to invite you and Paul to come some evening for dinner before he leaves for Scotland."

"He's told you, then."

"Actually, Tawni told me."

"We'll have to see about arranging a meeting in the next week since Paul is leaving a week from tomorrow. You knew that, didn't you?"

Sierra felt as if a load of bricks had been dumped on her stomach. "No. I didn't know he was leaving so soon." Sierra cleared her throat. "My mom said she'd call you. I'm sure we can arrange something before he leaves."

"Wonderful! It's a delight to know you, Sierra. You are welcome here anytime. Any amount of volunteering you would like to do would be greatly appreciated."

Sierra finished picking up the art mess. Most of the kids had gone. Her two faithful sidekicks, Meruka and Angie, eagerly helped her clean up. She could barely think straight with this new information about Paul marching across her brain.

"Are you going to come back tomorrow?" Meruka quizzed her.

"What? Oh. No, not tomorrow. I will come back another day. And maybe we can do some more art."

"Will you tell us some more stories with puppets?" asked Angie.

"Well, maybe. Would you like that?"

Angie looked at Sierra with innocent eyes and nodded her head.

"Hey, Sierra," Randy called from the yard, "you about ready to go?

"No!" she called out a little too urgently. She hadn't talked with Paul yet. "I need to put these things inside. I'll be a few minutes."

"We'll be waiting," Randy said.

Sierra scooped up the last scrap of paper and dashed into the house. Slipping the supplies back into the cupboard, she quickly tidied up the room and then took off to find Paul. She couldn't locate him anywhere.

*He said he would be around. And last Tuesday, what was it he had said when he touched my arm? Something about how we should talk.*

She took one last peek in the meeting room and gave up. If she would see Paul tonight—or ever again—it would have to be a God-thing. Gathering up her disappointment, Sierra walked to Randy's truck with long strides. She sat next to Tre, silently staring out the window all the way to the pizza place. The cloud of gloom hung over her while they ate.

Paul was leaving in a week. How could they have come so far in seeing each other and being around each other for hours, and yet still be so far away from each other?

Randy got Tre to open up and talk a little about his family and his interest in music. Sierra ate one slice of pizza and wondered if Mom had called Paul's uncle yet to set a time for them to come to dinner. When Randy dropped her off, she couldn't wait to run inside and ask Mom.

"Wait up," Randy said, following Sierra up the steps to her front door. She had forgotten how Randy usually hung out at their house on Fridays. It was only eight-thirty. Of course he would want to come in. That didn't mean she had to entertain him.

"Sounds like the boys are in the family room," Sierra said to Randy as they stepped inside. She planned to find her mom and make some dinner plans.

"Hey," Randy said as she made a beeline up the stairs, "I didn't come in to see your brothers."

Sierra stopped and looked down at Randy. His head was tilted, his eyes questioning. With a hesitant hand, he flipped his straight blond hair.

"I was hoping we could talk for a while," he said.

"Now?" Sierra realized how rude that must sound. Randy always had time to listen to her woes. How hard would it be for her to do the same for him? "I mean, can you wait just a minute?"

"Sure," Randy said, giving her a crooked grin. "I'll wait in the family room."

"Thanks," Sierra said and then took the rest of the stairs two at a time,

She found Mom in Granna Mae's room. They were playing a game of Scrabble.

"Mom," Sierra asked breathlessly, "you know our idea about inviting Mr. Mackenzie and Paul for dinner? Paul leaves for Scotland in a week. If we're going to invite them, we should do it tomorrow night because I have finals all next week."

"Take a breath, Lovey," Granna Mae said.

"I called him about an hour ago. We're all set for next Friday night," Mom responded.

Sierra lowered herself onto the edge of Granna Mae's bed. *Next Friday. A whole week, and I won't see him until the day before he leaves! I have to work out something else. Something more. I need a chance to tell Paul how I've prayed for him and find a way to let him know how I feel about him.*

"Help me out here, will you, Lovey? I have a *j,* and I can't figure out how to use it."

Sierra went over and stood behind Granna Mae, examining her letters and running the possible combinations through her head. They couldn't use the *j* this time, but Sierra managed to come up with "aft," and the *f* landed on a triple letter box. The game proceeded at an increased pace now that Sierra and Granna Mae were teamed up against Mom, the reigning champion of the house.

Forty minutes later, the scores were tallied. Mom won by seven.

"I suppose I should check on the boys," Mom said, stretching. "It's past their bedtime."

The image of her brothers watching TV brought back the memory of Randy. "Oh, no!" Sierra said, jumping up and running downstairs. She blasted into the family room and saw only her dad and her two brothers engrossed in the last five minutes of a video. "Where's Randy?"

"He left a little while ago," Dad said. "Is everything okay?"

"I hope so," Sierra said, charging out the front door and scanning the street for his truck. He was long gone.

Sierra tipped her face heavenward and whispered, "I'm

sorry." Here she had been so upset about Paul's disappearing and her not being able to talk with him, and then, without thinking, Sierra had disappeared on Randy when he said he wanted to talk with her.

The thought hit Sierra that perhaps her anticipation of talking with Paul was not mutual after all. Maybe Paul saw Sierra the way she saw Randy—a pleasant interruption. In the stillness of the dark, empty night, the tears came, bubbling up from someplace deep inside.

# eighteen

"MY LIFE IS FALLING APART," Amy said on the phone early the next morning.

Sierra was hurrying to dress for work, and she didn't feel a boatload of sympathy for Amy. Sierra's own emotions over not talking to Paul and ignoring Randy had kept her tossing and turning all night. She was not in a good mood.

"We can't have our dinner tonight because my sister has the flu and my mother thinks it's not polite to invite people to your house if someone is sick."

"Your mother's probably right," Sierra said, shuddering at the thought of getting the flu right now. "This is an awfully intense week ahead, Amy. Maybe we should wait until school is out."

"I guess we'll have to. I'll call Drake and tell him. I'm hoping he suggests we all go out to eat instead."

"That would be fine with me," Sierra said. She felt a little guilty about how clammed up she had been during the pizza outing the night before. First Sierra had made sure Tre was invited, and then she had ended up being lost in her own dreamworld the whole time. It would be good to see Randy tonight and get everything back on track. She couldn't do anything about Paul but wait until dinner next Friday. Or try to see him sometime this week at the Highland House. But that didn't seem like a great place to talk. At least she could apologize to Randy and feel better about that relationship.

All day at work, Sierra fought a headache. She attributed it to not enough sleep, stress over finals, anxiety over seeing Paul, and maybe that all she had eaten for breakfast was a mushy, spotted banana. Even the daily pan of "burnt offering" cinnamon rolls on the table in the back offered no solace. Jody offered her a packet of Energy Revive, a collection of vitamin B and ginseng tablets. Sierra believed vitamins were a good thing. But the way her stomach was feeling, it didn't seem likely she would be able to keep the pills down.

The instant the round tummy of the bear clock on the wall announced it was four o'clock, Sierra was out of there. What a relief to know she could go straight home since Amy's dinner party had been postponed. None of Sierra's friends had contacted her at work, so she didn't know if they were planning on doing something. If they were, she decided she would pass. All she wanted was a hot bath, some food, and a long nap.

Her heart sank when she turned down the street and saw Randy's truck parked in front of her house. A large mower stuck out of the back of the truck bed. Randy stood in the front yard in his lawn service clothes, wearing a blue baseball cap backward and talking to Sierra's dad. They both heard the noisy approach of her diesel-engine VW Rabbit and turned to watch her park. Both of them smiled and waved.

Sierra wished she could vaporize and not have to go through the humble apology to Randy. She knew he would understand about her deserting him last night. He always did. She just didn't like admitting she had forgotten about him.

"Hi," she called out, slamming the car door and forcing her brightest smile.

"What? No leftovers for the family this week?" Dad said, noticing she wasn't carrying the white bakery bag she usually brought with her each Saturday evening.

"Didn't I tell you? Mrs. Kraus decided to start donating all the extras to the Highland House."

"They need them more than we do," Dad said, patting his stomach. "Well, I have a project going out back. I'll see you around, Randy."

"'Bye," Randy said. Turning to Sierra, he cautiously asked, "Are you doing okay?" He looked adorable in the backward baseball cap with blond fringes of his floppy hair sticking out of the sides. He smelled like freshly cut grass, and his pants looked as if he had just lost a tackle football game.

"I'm okay. Randy, I apologize about last night."

He didn't halt her painful admission but let her continue.

"I don't know what to say. I meant to come down right after I talked to my mom. But then I started helping Granna Mae with her j in the Scrabble game, and I lost track of time."

Instead of his usual amiable laugh and crooked smile to

show he understood, Randy's face remained still. Sierra thought she saw a hint of hurt in his eyes.

"I knew it had to be something important," Randy said with a bite in his words. "Look, Sierra. If you don't want me to come around, just tell me. I thought we were getting pretty close. You know—buddies. Now I'm not sure what's going on. If I'm bugging you, I want you to tell me."

"You don't bug me, Randy. Not at all. Please don't ever think that. It's just that..." She didn't know how to tell him about her overwhelming feelings for Paul. He would probably understand. Randy was such a good listener, and he definitely kept confidences better than Amy. Still, it felt odd telling one guy that she liked another guy.

"What is it?" Randy said, adjusting his weight from one foot to the other.

"There's been a lot going on lately. I know I've been acting kind of strange. Please don't read anything into that about our friendship. I need you to hang in there with me for this next week or so."

Randy was quiet for a few moments, absorbing her words. "I can do that," he said.

"Good. Thanks." Sierra smiled her relief at him.

"I guess our dinner at Amy's was cancelled," he said. "I thought I'd see if you wanted to go do something."

A little night-light next to Sierra's heart suddenly lit in a soft glow. He was actually asking her to go out. It was so sweet of him. "I was planning to come home and crash," Sierra said. "I'm fried, and I still have to type up the written report for the Highland House. If you want to stay for dinner, I'm sure it would be fine with my parents."

Randy seemed to weigh the options. "I think I'll follow

your shining example," he said, the comforting, crooked grin creeping back into place. "I should go home and finish my report, too. Maybe we can do something next weekend—just the two of us—after the pressure of finals is off. How about Friday night?"

"Sure," Sierra said quickly. It felt good to have things cleared up with Randy. He turned to leave, and then she remembered. Friday was when Paul and his uncle were coming for dinner. "Ah, maybe not Friday. We have company coming. You and I could do something on Saturday, couldn't we?"

"Saturday," Randy repeated, as if trying to verbally stick a thumbtack in Sierra's words to get them to stay in one place. "I think there's a concert Saturday night."

"Great! That would be fun. See you Monday." She waved good-bye and made her way to the bathtub.

When Sierra did see Randy on Monday, it was right before they were to give their reports in front of the class.

"You go first," he said, then added teasingly, "We'll save the best for last."

Sierra stood before Mr. Rykert's class and gave her presentation, feeling at ease in front of the group. Public speaking didn't spook her the way it did a lot of her friends.

Coming to a conclusion, Sierra said, "For me, the best part about going to Highland House was discovering we can do lots of things to fulfill the commandment of Christ found in Luke 6:31." She looked down at her note cards and read, "Do to others as you would have them do to you."

Looking at her classmates, Sierra said, "Whether it's donating time or food or assistance of some kind, lots of needs are out there, and there's plenty we can do about them. I plan to volunteer at the Highland House. I'd like to close with a verse from Matthew 25:37–40.

"Then the righteous will answer him, 'Lord, when did we see you hungry and feed you, or thirsty and give you something to drink? When did we see you a stranger and invite you in, or needing clothes and clothe you? When did we see you sick or in prison and go to visit you?' The King will reply, 'I tell you the truth, whatever you did for one of the least of these brothers of mine, you did for me.'"

Sierra had begun her report telling about Monte and his paper frog. She concluded by saying, "Perhaps Monte would be considered one of the least of these. I learned that in serving Monte, I'm actually serving Christ."

Before she could take her seat, the class burst into applause. Randy stood up, clapping and whistling. Sierra turned and swatted her hand in his direction to get him to sit down and stop making such a ruckus. She had to admit, though, she did like the way Randy teased her.

"Wonderfully presented, Sierra," Mr. Rykert said, walking to the front of the class. "We'll hear now from Tre." He nodded at Tre, urging him to go up front.

Sierra's heart went out to Tre. He was perspiring and looked as if he would rather have his toenails lit on fire than have to stand in front of everyone.

"I went to the Highland House," he began, trembling and swallowing hard. "I helped with the children, and I played the guitar. I learned about the prodigal son."

He seemed to have difficulty saying "prodigal," and once again Sierra wished she hadn't picked that story. It was certainly too difficult for the children to understand.

"I know about the pigs," Tre continued. A ripple of

laughter moved through the classroom. "I don't want to have that life, so I made a choice at the Highland House to come back to the Father God, who is waiting for me."

It was completely still for a moment, as everyone tried to absorb what he had said.

Mr. Rykert stepped closer to Tre and said, "Are you saying you made a decision to turn your life over to God?"

Tre nodded. His expression seemed to relax as he said, "My friends showed me Jesus." Glancing first at Sierra and then at Randy, he added, "And I wanted to know Him, too."

Sierra looked over her shoulder at Randy. His mouth was open, and his eyes crinkled in surprise. Turning back to meet Tre's gaze, Sierra felt the tears rushing to her eyes, demanding to be released.

*Tre a Christian?! The prodigal story and those silly pigs made sense to him? I don't believe it. What a God-thing!*

Mr. Rykert appeared to be choked up. He stood beside Tre and placed his hand on the boy's shoulder. "I'd like to pray for you, son." And pray he did—rich, meaningful words of thanks to God.

The dismissal bell rang before Mr. Rykert finished praying. Everyone waited. Mr. Rykert said, "Amen." Instead of rushing out to class, most of the students went up front to say something to Tre. He seemed surprised and a bit confused by all the attention.

"That was close," Vicki said as she, Amy, and Sierra exited the room. "I was supposed to give my report after Tre. How do you follow that?"

"He didn't say all that just to get a good grade," Amy said.

"I know," Vicki said. "I was making a little joke. Relax."
She turned to Sierra and said, "Are you and Randy going to
the concert on Saturday?"

"Randy said something about it. I'd love to go even if he
doesn't want to. Do you want to go with us, Amy?"

"I'm supposed to start working at my uncle's on
Saturday. And what about our lobster dinner?" Amy said
with a pout. "Are we going to move that back a week?"

"How about moving it back two weeks?" Sierra suggested. "I'd really like to go to this concert."

"I have extra tickets if you want to buy one from me,"
Vicki said. "I'm going with Mike. You and Randy can
double with us if you want."

For the first time, it hit Sierra that other people
thought of her and Randy as a couple, not just buddies. She
wasn't sure how she felt about that.

# nineteen

MOM MADE MEAT LOAF for the Friday night dinner, and the house filled with the scent of it as it baked alongside a dozen fat potatoes. Salad, green beans, homemade soda bread, and an apple crisp with vanilla ice cream completed the menu. In Sierra's opinion, it was perfect.

At five-thirty, Sierra was still deciding what to wear. This was probably the biggest wardrobe decision she had ever had to make. And for the first time, Tawni seemed to understand what Sierra was going through.

"I think you should wear the skirt with the embroidered vest," Tawni said. "It's a nice, soft look, but not out of character for you."

"I don't know," Sierra said, eyeing five potential outfits laid out on her bed. "That's what I had on the day he saw me walking home in the rain with the armful of daffodils. I looked like a drowned rat," Sierra said.

"Is that why Jeremy says Paul called you the Daffodil Queen?"

Sierra nodded, remembering only too well the teasing

letter Paul had sent her after that frustrating experience. "Are you sure this gauze dress wouldn't be better?" She held up a long, cream-colored peasant dress. "With lots of beads?"

Tawni shook her head. "You look better with a little color by your face. That gauze dress looks like a nightgown. Trust me. Go with the vest and skirt. You can still wear all your little beads if you want."

Sierra gave in, knowing her sister was right. This was probably her favorite outfit of the batch.

Tawni wore a light blue skirt and jacket, which she had worn to work that morning. Today had been her last day. Her transfer went through to the San Diego Nordstrom's, and she would be moving within a week—two weeks at the most. The crazy thing was, for the first time in their lives, Tawni and Sierra were enjoying each other's company. Tawni had even invited Sierra to drive down to Southern California with her and then fly home. Sierra had put off deciding, saying she wanted to make it through finals week and this dinner with Paul.

Finally, Friday was here. No more papers or reports. Only one more final next week, and then she would be done. In a few minutes, Paul would be in her house, and she would be looking into his eyes. Somehow she would find a way to talk privately with him, and she would tell him how much she cared for him, how intensely she had prayed for him. And then...

Sierra didn't know what would happen then. Maybe they would write letters all summer. Maybe there would be a few overseas phone calls. When he returned in the fall, she would be seventeen and a senior. Paul wouldn't—couldn't—consider her too young then.

Slipping on her last bracelet and flopping a handful of curly hair over her shoulder, Sierra took one last look in the antique oval dresser mirror to make sure she hadn't messed up Tawni's expert makeup job. The mascara on her lashes was barely noticeable. She had let Tawni put makeup on her only once before. It was the first night Randy had come over. Even on that "first date," Sierra had been thinking of Paul and wishing he were the one coming to her front door instead of Randy. Tonight her wish was coming true.

Lightly taking the stairs down to the kitchen, Sierra smiled. She imagined she was glowing. Funny how much more understanding she now had for Tawni and her excitement over Jeremy. It only made the intrigue more inviting knowing that Jeremy and Paul were brothers. Sierra and Tawni now had so much more to share as sisters.

Just as she fluttered off the last stair, the doorbell rang. Sierra rushed to the door, then stopped and closed her eyes, drawing in a deep breath before opening the door to their evening guests.

"Randy!" she sputtered.

"Hey, you look nice," Randy said. Then, with a flash of recollection, he thumped his forehead with the palm of his hand and said, "Oh, yeah, you guys have company tonight."

Just then a car pulled up and parked across the street. Sierra bit her lower lip and tried to think fast.

"Is that them?" Randy said, peering at the guy who emerged from the car wearing jeans and a long-sleeved white shirt. His dark, wavy brown hair was combed off his broad forehead, and in his hand he held a small bouquet of daffodils. Sierra thought her heart was going to jump right out of her skin and go hopping down the front steps to greet him.

"Hey, isn't that Paul?" Randy said. "He's your company?" Randy's face took on that twinge of hurt.

"And his uncle," Sierra said quickly. "Mr. Mackenzie. Tawni's boyfriend is Paul's brother."

"Is that right? I didn't know that. Hey, Paul." Randy greeted him with a hearty handshake. "How's it going?" He looked behind him and said, "Isn't your uncle coming?"

"He sends his apologies," Paul said politely, looking at Sierra. "He was short on volunteers tonight to serve dinner at the Highland House. I hope it's okay that I still came."

"Of course!" Sierra said, eyeing the sweet bouquet.

"These are for Granna Mae," he said, holding them out.

"Oh, yes. Of course they are. Come on in." Sierra took the daffodils and held the door open for Paul. Randy followed him inside. Sierra swallowed hard, not sure what to do. This would not be the night of her dreams if Randy stayed for dinner, too. And of course he would be invited to stay since a place was already set for Mr. Mackenzie.

Sierra considered pulling Randy into the study and confiding her deepest dreams and hopes to him. Surely he would understand what a special night this was, and he would graciously leave. Randy would do that for her. She knew he would. If only she could figure out a way to tell him so it wouldn't hurt his feelings. He seemed to be wearing them on his sleeve lately.

"Short on volunteers," Randy said. "I'd be glad to help.

Do you think if I went down there, your uncle would be able to come for dinner?"

Sierra felt like giving Randy a big hug for being so sweet and sensitive to the situation. And she didn't have to say anything. What a great guy! *Now go, Randy. Go.*

"I'm sure he would appreciate the break," Paul said. "Thanks, Randy." Then, flashing a glance from Sierra to Randy as if trying to detect the relationship between the two of them, Paul added, "That would be great."

"Cool," Randy said. "I'll see you guys later." He looked at Sierra a little longer than necessary, and she wondered if Randy was doing the same thing as Paul, trying to pick up hidden signals.

"Thanks, Randy," Sierra said, smiling warmly, but not too warmly. All her best smiles had been saved for Paul. As soon as Randy turned away, Sierra took her best smile out and hung it from her perfect lips like a welcome sign meant only for Paul.

# twenty

PAUL MADE A BIG HIT with Sierra's family, especially Tawni, who kept saying, "You looked just like Jeremy when you said that."

"Uncle Mac," as Paul called his uncle, arrived right as they were sitting down in the large dining room. He couldn't stop praising Randy, who had come to his rescue. Uncle Mac sat next to Paul, who was seated directly across from Sierra. When her dad motioned for them to hold hands while he prayed, Sierra closed her eyes and wished for all the world she were sitting next to Paul instead of Gavin and Tawni. Then it would be Paul's stronger hand she was slipping hers into.

Several times during dinner, Sierra glanced up and thought she caught Paul looking at her. He always looked away, of course. Sierra couldn't wait until she had a chance to talk with him alone. She still didn't know how that would work out.

Granna Mae certainly didn't hide her affection for the young man. She loved the bouquet of "daffies" he brought her and had placed them in the center of the table.

Mom and Tawni were serving the apple crisp when Paul turned to Sierra's dad and quietly said, "I'd like to ask a favor. Actually, Jeremy asked me to do this as a favor for him."

"Sure," Dad said agreeably, without even knowing what it was.

"Would it be all right with you if I took Tawni and Sierra out for coffee after dinner?"

Sierra felt her heart immediately take an express elevator up to her throat. What a quaint "courting" approach. She loved it.

"It's fine with me if it's fine with them."

Paul looked at Sierra first. She somehow found the composure to suppress her ricocheting emotions and simply smile with a nod. Tawni kept serving, but a mischievous grin seemed to dance across her face.

The grin remained as the three of them drove off an hour later, heading for downtown Portland.

"Any place in particular?" Paul asked. "Jeremy said you had a place in mind."

Tawni directed Paul across the Burnside Bridge and into the West Portland hills to a tiny coffee shop. They parked on a hill and took a seat inside, at a small round table by the front window where happy red geraniums spilled from the wooden flower box. Only a few other customers gathered in the quiet shop. Sierra felt as if they had been transported to another country.

"You know what?" Tawni said. Sierra and Paul were seated, but Tawni was still standing. "A couple of shops are still open down the street, and I might not get back over here before I move. So why don't you two go ahead? I'll be back in a bit."

She disappeared out the door. Sierra was looking down at the place mat, her hands clutching each other under the table. "I think we've been set up," she said quietly.

Paul didn't answer, waiting for her to look up and catch his gaze. "It appears so," he said. "Would you like something to drink?"

"Do you suppose a place like this has herbal teas?" Sierra asked.

"We can find out." Paul lifted two fingers and motioned for the waiter.

In that moment, with Paul's profile to fill her view, the rich aroma of coffee filling the air, and the mustached waiter approaching them, Sierra believed this was a dream. A lovely jaunt to Paris for a cup of java on the Champs Èlysees. Only, in this dream, her eyes were open. She didn't want to close them for fear it would all vanish.

"Yes, one Black Forest," Paul said, "and do you have herbal tea?"

The waiter nodded and returned to the coffee bar.

"Did you want biscotti or anything?" Paul asked.

She was pretty sure he was referring to those long, hard cookies she had seen her parents dunk in their coffee. "No, I'm still full from dinner."

"Me, too. That was great. You have a wonderful family," Paul said. "Everything Jeremy said was true."

"Oh? And what did Jeremy tell you?"

"Well," Paul said, leaning back, "he said you're a pretty good surfer."

Sierra smiled.

"He also said you're a strong-hearted individual. But I could have told him that."

The waiter returned with a glass mug of coffee for Paul and a round, white teapot with a mug that fit on top. He presented Sierra with a basket of herbal tea bags for her to select from.

"Oh, and do you have any honey?" Sierra asked as the waiter turned to go.

"Jeremy also told me you're quite a prayer warrior."

Sierra felt this was the opportunity she had been waiting for. She dipped her bag of wild blackberry tea into the white pot and gathered her practiced phrases. Then she made them all line up and wait on the edge of her lips until the waiter placed the honey in front of her and left.

"What's that phrase? 'The warrior is a child'?" Paul sipped his coffee and looked at Sierra with an expression she recognized only too well. It was the same way Wesley looked at her. An invisible pat on the head. The endearing look big brothers bestow on kid sisters when they do something cute.

The world seemed to stop. It was as if her breath had suddenly been punched out of her lungs. *He thinks I'm a kid—a punk little kid. He's not thinking any of the romantic things I'm thinking about him.*

This changed everything. No way could she pour out her heart to this guy and tell him how hard and how long she had done battle for him. He wouldn't care that she had begged God to bring Paul to Himself when he was wandering off.

"My brother also tells me," Paul paused, a compassionate smile lingering on his lips, "that you have a crush on me."

Now Sierra could barely move. She felt her face heat up like a Roman candle about to explode. Her breath came back, rapid and sharp.

*A crush on you! Is that what you think this is? Me in some puppy-love phase of my young life and you the master, oh so mature and wise? Of all the nerve!*

Now she really didn't know what to say. Why did Tawni leave her? Had she set this up? Were Tawni and Jeremy trying to make fun of her?

Resisting the impulse to stand up and dump the table in Paul's lap, Sierra stared at her hands and made herself prepare her cup of tea. She went about the task slowly, giving herself time to calm down and respond to Paul in a way she could live with. This was the one time she refused to react impulsively, which would only prove his assumptions of her immaturity.

Paul waited quietly, his hands wrapped around his half-full glass mug.

"You know..." Sierra said, setting down her spoon and taking a sip of her hot tea. Paul seemed to be hanging on to her words, waiting for her response. As sweet and mature as could be, Sierra said, "I think God brings different relationships into our lives at different times to teach us different things." She wanted it to sound profound. It ended up sounding redundant.

After another sip, she continued, finally looking up, allowing him to see into her tearless eyes. "I wonder if perhaps God brought you and me together for one brief season so that I could learn how God really does answer prayer."

Paul seemed startled by her response. He had looked like this before at the airport in London. This obviously was not what he expected her to say.

"You're a lot closer to the Lord than you were when we first met," Sierra suggested.

"Yes," Paul said with a nod.

"And you're off to Scotland now for the summer to help at your grandfather's mission. That's a different direction than you were headed last January."

Again Paul had to agree. "I'm going for a year," he corrected her. "Not just for the summer. I'll be going to a university in Edinburgh."

Something pinched and twisted inside Sierra. Even though he had cut her down to size with his "puppy love" insinuations, the news still touched her somewhere deep inside. Going away for the summer was very different from going away for a year.

"I hope it goes well for you," Sierra said, dredging up one of the smiles she had been reserving for Paul only. "I'm just glad our paths crossed when they did." She was going to add something about them now traveling in different orbits, but it sounded too much like Amy's sci-fi psychology.

Leaning forward, Sierra was the one to lightly tap Paul's forearm this time. Looking through his eyes, right into his soul, she said in a whisper, "God has His mark on you, Paul Mackenzie. He's going to do something incredible in your life."

Paul didn't move. He continued to hold Sierra's gaze. "Thank you," he said, his voice low and husky. The earlier smirking look he wore seemed to have evaporated. "And thanks, too, for all your prayers. Don't stop."

Sierra paused before making her promise back to him. She took this seriously, whether he did or not. Was she willing to keep praying for him no matter where he lived, no matter whom he married, no matter what he did, no matter if she ever saw him again in her life? And would she be true to that promise knowing that the emotional connection she had felt with Paul was apparently one-sided?

"Okay," Sierra agreed, still holding his gaze. "I'll keep praying for you."

# twenty-one

SIERRA TOSSED AND TURNED in her bed. She had barely slept all night. She and Tawni had talked until after midnight, trying to figure out the evening. Tawni admitted she and Jeremy had rigged the meeting, but they had hoped it would allow Paul and Sierra a chance to open their hearts to each other and see what would happen.

As Sierra saw it, she was glad she hadn't opened her heart because Paul had made it clear he wasn't interested in her. Certainly not in the same way she had become so preoccupied with thoughts of him.

That realization had hurt something within Sierra, something she hadn't even known existed—a deep well of emotions from which she would have been only too willing to draw, if only Paul had asked. But he hadn't.

So, instead of those intense, womanly emotions having a chance to spring up, Sierra had capped them. She was fiercely embarrassed by having misread Paul's previous signals: his pithy letters, the way he seemed to have gazed into her eyes more than once, as if searching for his own reflection there, even his humorous "Ribbit" at the Highland House. None of these communications were intended to say anything especially personal.

Paul hadn't given her any more hints of his interest during their final hour together. He had finished his coffee; she had finished her tea. He paid the bill, and then they went outside into the spring drizzle. They stood close but silent in the glow of the antique streetlight under the café's blue-striped canopy.

Sierra noticed the geraniums and said absentmindedly, "Those are Martha Washingtons. The geraniums, I mean. They're my mom's favorite."

Paul had nodded pleasantly.

Sierra felt miserably ridiculous taking about stupid flowers. Here she had thought a whole world was open to her and Paul, when in actuality, there was nothing.

Tawni arrived and got in the car with them, jabbering about the great deal she had found on her favorite lipstick. They had driven home.

Paul walked them both to the door, and Tawni wrapped her arms around his neck in a hug.

"Have a great time in Scotland," she said. "I'm so glad I got to meet you before you left."

"I hope it's a wonderful year for you," Sierra agreed, managing one more smile for him. "Good-bye, Paul."

"Good-bye," Paul said. "God bless."

With a final look into Sierra's eyes under the porch light, Paul turned and took long-legged strides to his car. He started the engine and pulled away from the curb. That was it. He was gone. Out of her life forever.

As Sierra and Tawni hashed it all out in their beds with

the lights turned low, Sierra surmised a neat and convenient spiritual conclusion as to why their paths had crossed.
She told Tawni what she had said to Paul, that they were
brought together for a season and because of that, she had
learned how to pray consistently for someone. More than
that—to do spiritual battle for him. Sierra insisted, quite
unemotionally, that it was a lesson well worth learning.

Tawni apologized, saying she never would have imagined
things would go the way they did. In her mind, Tawni had
believed all kinds of potential existed for a long-distance
relationship between Sierra and Paul. It had worked for
Tawni and Jeremy; why shouldn't it work for Sierra and
Paul? It just hadn't.

The illuminated clock face read 5:27. Quietly rising,
Sierra tucked her feet into her bunny slippers and grabbed
her Bible and journal. She padded softly to the library
downstairs and began to pray for Paul, asking God to protect him as he was preparing to leave in a few hours for
Scotland.

Then, opening her Bible, Sierra noticed a bookmark
she had picked up at the Christian bookstore the last time
she had stopped by. It said: "He puts a little heaven in our
hearts so that we'll never settle for less."

"That's what it is," Sierra wrote in her journal. "I want
God's kingdom to come and His will to be done on earth as
it is in heaven. I desire God's best. At least I think I do—I
want to. So, in my heart, I hold all these treasures. They're
bits of heaven, and I won't settle for less. I don't know
exactly how this applies to Paul, but I want God's best for
him, and I hated seeing him settle for so much less."

She took a deep breath and continued writing. "That

season is over. The season for wondering if he felt anything for me the way I felt so deeply for him. He's gone. I release this whole relationship to You, Father. Please don't let me ever settle for anything less than Your best."

Now she was the one who felt like the prodigal. She had given in to runaway dreams with Paul, and they had taken her nowhere. She was back in her heavenly Father's arms now—a safe place to be. Isn't that what it said on the Highland House sign? She tried hard to remember and then wrote the words in her journal: "A safe place for a fresh start." Sierra read the phrase again and then added, "…in my heavenly Father's arms."

Sierra felt strangely calm and at peace all day at work. Randy stopped by and told her how much fun he had had serving dinner at the Highland House the night before. She thanked him again for filling in for Uncle Mac.

"No need to thank me. I had a great time. Let's go back there together sometime," Randy suggested. "I'd like to keep helping out."

"I would too," Sierra agreed.

"Do you want me to pick you up for the concert tonight?"

Once again Sierra had forgotten she had made social plans. She was really tired, but she had been looking forward to hearing this group. "Sure. Do you want to see if Vicki and Mike want to ride with us?"

"I already asked Mike. He said they're going out to eat first, so I told him we would meet them in front of the auditorium. A bunch of other people from school are going."

"Sounds like it will be great," Sierra said, feeling a little revived after her emotionally draining night. "I'll see you at my house later."

"Cool. I'll be there at six-thirty."

Sierra wasn't ready when he arrived. She had given in to a little snooze after coming home from work. Mom woke her, saying that Randy was downstairs eating dinner with them, and he said they were supposed to go to a concert.

Springing from her bed and rattling off the details to Mom as she quickly changed into a clean T-shirt, Sierra pulled herself together. Fifteen minutes later, she and Randy were on their way to the concert. The inside of his truck smelled of cut grass and mud. She was glad she had worn old jeans in case she picked up some grass stains from the seat.

The parking lot was jam-packed, and they had to park, as Randy said, "in Outer Mongolia."

"I told Mike we would meet them at the front door," Randy said as they hurried to the front of the arena.

They searched the thinning crowd for Mike and Vicki but didn't see them.

"I'll go inside," Randy said. "You want to wait here a few more minutes in case they're late?"

"How will I find you?" Sierra asked, sticking her hand in her back jeans pocket, making sure she still had her ticket.

"I'll be back," he said, taking off without further instructions.

Sierra felt a slight sense of loss as he hurried away. She noticed he was dressed nicer than usual. He had even brought her a tiny clump of wild violets, which she had hastily tossed on the kitchen counter as they were blasting out the door. She wondered if he was trying to compete with Paul's bouquet for Granna Mae, but Randy's explanation had been that he saw them while mowing a lawn and didn't have the heart to mow them down.

Watching, waiting, tapping her foot, Sierra began to feel nervous as the final few concertgoers hurried in the front door. Surely it had already started, and she was missing it. It wouldn't be that difficult to find Randy inside. Vicki and Mike had to be in there already.

She turned in her ticket and slid through the door. Muffled cheers rose from behind the closed auditorium doors.

*So, what do I do? Stand around out here or go inside?*

She opted for going in. The auditorium was packed.

People stood, applauding, and Sierra knew she had already missed the first song. Now she was irritated. True, it was her fault they were late, but why had Randy left her? She would never find him now. Slipping into an empty aisle seat next to a row of strangers, Sierra decided she could enjoy the concert and watch for Randy at the same time from this vantage point. If nothing else, she would have time "alone" to think, to finish processing her thoughts about Paul before locking them away forever.

A spotlight hit the center stage. The band started playing as the lead vocalist leaned into the microphone, filling the auditorium with her distinct voice. Sierra immediately knew she was going to like this group. Their music could soothe her soul and keep her company as she privately sorted out her life. This was exactly what she needed tonight.

# twenty-two

AS SIERRA LISTENED to the next upbeat song, she felt as if all the pieces were falling into place. The lyrics of peace and hope toned down her spiritual evaluations over Paul and soothed her emotions. She began to relax.

She watched for Randy but didn't see him. She knew he would understand why she had come inside. Randy was always understanding—understanding and patient. And he was kind and considerate of her as well. As a matter of fact, Randy was pretty terrific.

Thinking back on how he had handled the kids at the Highland House, Sierra found herself smiling. Randy was right. The two of them did make a great team. He willingly put up with her teasing—like that day at Lotsa Tacos when she grabbed his money.

Sierra realized he was the kind of guy she got along with best: someone who let her be herself, yet didn't let her dominate.

The song came to a velvety close as the soloist drew out the last note like a single breath. The auditorium exploded in applause.

Sierra looked around and had a curious thought. Was she the only girl who had ever misread a guy's signals the way she had misread Paul's? Of course not! She knew she wasn't. Being with so many other girls her age gave her a different sort of comfort than what she'd experienced trying to talk about Paul on a logical level with Tawni. Coming tonight had been a good choice, even if she had gotten separated from Randy. Settling into the moment, Sierra started enjoying the concert much more than she thought she would.

For the next hour Sierra swayed and smiled with the music. As the final song rolled over the crowd, the lyrics caught Sierra by the heart. Several lines were about holding on to the true friends in your life. The last few lines sliced into Sierra's heart.

> Think of all the dreamy times
> You wished upon a star
> Who was there by your side
> When the wishing star
> Fell from the sky?
>
> True friends are good friends
> And hard to find, it seems
> I found a true friend
> When I stopped looking
> In my dreams.

Sierra stepped into the aisle as the applause rose around her. Everything inside her told her to run out of there and find Randy. Maybe she was a little slow at this dating thing—

"a late bloomer," as Tawni once called her. Maybe she didn't know a good thing when it was right in front of her nose. Randy had been there for her all along, bringing her a rose before his big date with Vicki, volunteering to fill in for Uncle Mac, and even thinking of Sierra when he pulled up that endangered clump of wild violets.

Why hadn't she seen it before? Amy was right all along. Sierra had been too absorbed in her dream of Paul to pay attention to the true friendship she already had with Randy.

Dashing into the lobby, Sierra scanned the area, hoping Randy might be there looking for her. She didn't see him. Then, out of the corner of her eye, she noticed a lone figure standing outside the front of the auditorium, right where he had left her.

*That couldn't be Randy! Could it?*

Sierra pushed open the glass door and ran into the cool evening air. "Randy! Over here, Randy!"

He turned, and when he saw her, a look of relief spread across his face. Jogging toward each other, they met halfway, both spouting explanations at the same time.

Impulsively and wholeheartedly, Sierra threw her arms around Randy and hugged him. When she pulled away, Randy looked wonderfully surprised.

"You okay?" he asked, apparently trying to read her expression.

Sierra started to laugh, and with the laughter came unexpected tears cascading down her cheeks. She couldn't speak.

"Hey, what's wrong?" Randy didn't seem to know what to do with her. He stood awkwardly to the side, tilting his head and waiting for her to say something.

"Randy," she said, finally finding her voice, "I..." She brushed away her tears and felt all fresh and new inside. "I wanted to thank you for being my friend and for just being who you are. I think you're a wonderful person."

Randy looked at her as his crooked grin spread across his face. "Did you just figure that out?"

Sierra laughed again. She knew she didn't have to explain anything to him, nor would he ask her to. This is where she wanted to be. Right here, right now, with her buddy Randy.

"Do you want to go back inside?" he asked.

Sierra nodded and brushed away the last tears clinging to her eyelashes.

They turned to go, and Randy wrapped his big, rough hand around Sierra's and gave it a warm squeeze. She returned the squeeze, feeling a little bit of heaven in her heart.

Then, closing her eyes, Sierra made a wish that she would never settle for anything less than God's best for her.

Book Five

WITHOUT A
DOUBT

# one

SIERRA JENSEN TUGGED on her baseball cap's brim and wiggled her fingers to tighten her grip on the bat. Her long blond hair poked through the back of the cap in a wild, curly ponytail.

"Hey, batter, batter, batter, swing!"

Shooting a glance toward her friend Amy Degrassi, the heckler in the outfield, Sierra lowered her chin and eyed the pitcher.

"Come on, Dad," she called out. "Give me all you've got. I can hit anything you can send over this plate."

Sierra could tell her dad was enjoying this perfect, sunny Oregon Sunday. It was Father's Day, and he was surrounded by his family and a dozen neighbors and friends. Mount Tabor Park brimmed with families firing up barbecues, tossing Frisbees, and pushing toddlers on the swings. Only the Jensen group, with enough players to form two teams, occupied the baseball diamond.

"Come on, Lovey!" Sierra's Granna Mae called from her folding lawn chair planted behind the backstop. "Show me what you're made of!"

"I'll show you what I'm made of," Sierra muttered, adjusting her position. "I'm made of steel."

All eyes were on her. Mr. Jensen let loose with a slow-pitched, underhanded curve ball. Sierra swung and missed.

"Stee-rike one!" Randy Jenkins yelled, rising from his crouched catcher's position behind Sierra.

"You don't have to tell the whole world," Sierra snapped playfully at him.

Randy tossed the softball back to Sierra's dad and wiped his glistening brow. He wore his baseball cap backward and sported his familiar crooked grin.

"That's my job, missy. That's why they pay me the big bucks."

Sierra liked the way Randy could handle her teasing and dish it right back. Ever since they had attended a concert together a few weeks ago, Randy had come over or called her every day. She loved the attention.

His family had joined hers for this picnic celebration, and Randy's dad hollered from his spot on third base. "Let's go, Sierra! Bring me home, Slugger!"

With a glance at the player on third, Howard Jensen pitched the ball right over the plate. Again Sierra swung too late.

"Hey, I wasn't ready!" she squawked. "That shouldn't count."

"Stee-rike two!" Randy bellowed.

Sierra shot him a fierce look and choked up on the bat. With a slight sway, she watched her dad catch the ball, grind it into his mitt, and wind up.

"Hey, batter, batter, batter, swing!" Amy chanted from the outfield.

"Hit a homer, Lovey!" Granna Mae called.

"Right here. That's it," Randy muttered. "Send that baby right into my mitt, Mr. J."

Sierra ignored them all. She didn't blink as the ball came toward her. In perfect motion, she swung. The bat connected with the softball, and a beautiful SMACK sound filled her ears. Dropping the bat, she took off running for first base, not daring to look where the ball was flying. Tagging first base, she charged on to second with a quick glance at home plate, where Mr. Jenkins had arrived safely and was now cheering her on to victory. A quick tap at second, and her feet flew toward third base.

"Come on home, Sierra! You've got it! Come on!"Randy's dad yelled, waving his arms. Randy stood in front of him, one foot on home base, mitt in place, eyes fixed on the outfield.

Visions of glory danced in her head as Sierra gulped a quick breath and pushed herself off third base. She loved this adrenaline rush. If she made it home, their team would win, and she could thoroughly harass her eldest brother, Wesley, who had predicted that his team would win, especially since their dad was on the pitcher's mound.

Sierra pushed her leg muscles forward, her heart pounding. Only a few more feet. She felt her baseball cap coming off as she charged to her goal. Randy positioned himself like a brick wall beside home base. His arms reached up into the air.

She blasted toward him, screaming, "Move!"

With a final spurt, Sierra slid toward the base just as Randy jumped, reaching with his mitt. Her left leg skidded in the dirt, and her right foot caught Randy's, pulling him down with her in a tangled heap.

A cloud of dust surrounded them as Randy's dad yelled, "Safe! I saw it. She was safe!"

Coughing and shaking her now capless curls away from her face, Sierra tried to move. Randy regained his balance first and stood. He offered her a hand up. Sierra brushed herself off and coughed again, looking at her opponent. Dirt clung to his thick eyebrows like drops of rain on a screen.

"You're out," he said in a low, unemotional voice.

"What do you mean, I'm out?" Sierra shouted, "I'm safe, and you know it!"

Randy grinned and smugly held his catcher's mitt in front of her. He opened it slowly and dramatically, his eyes glued on Sierra's face as he prepared to show her the evidence. What Randy didn't see was the way the ball fell out just as he opened the mitt.

"Ha!" Sierra said, pointing. "I'm safe! You have to actually *catch* the ball before you can get someone out in this game, and it appears you have an empty mitt, buddy."

Randy looked at the mitt, looked at Sierra, and then gazed down at the ball in the dirt.

"I had it," he protested.

"Doesn't matter," Sierra said. "You have to keep it if it's going to count."

The other players had joined them at home base, each one barking out opinions.

"I'm safe. We won. Deal with it, Jenkins!" Sierra teased. As she started to stand up a slice of pain seared her left leg. Rivulets of blood coursed from a long scrape that began above her knee and ran all the way down her leg.

Amy, arriving from center field, noticed it, too. She had Sierra's runaway baseball cap in her hand and said, "That is so gross. How could you slide on your bare legs like that? You'd better clean that out, Sierra."

"We won!" Sierra answered Amy triumphantly. "I told you we would win."

"It was rigged," Sierra's brother Wesley said. He had the bat in one hand and a mitt in the other. Of all the Jensen kids, Wes most resembled their father, with his straight nose, wavy brown hair, and slim build. He especially looked like their dad around the eyes. When he smiled, he had the same pattern of laugh lines stretching like party streamers from the corners of his eyes. Only their father's were deeper and longer.

"Guess your star pitcher was no match for me," Sierra teased her brother.

"You were out, and you know it," Wes said, snatching Sierra's baseball cap from Amy's hand and plopping it backward on Sierra's head. Sierra's six-year-old brother Gavin had joined the mob. When he saw Sierra with her cap on like Randy's, he said, "Now you and Randy are twinners!"

To her surprise, Randy slipped his arm around her shoulder, pulled her close, and repeated. "That's us. Twinners."

Sierra heard a camera click and looked beyond Gavin and Wesley to see her brother Cody and his wife, Katrina, who had just arrived with their toddler son, Tyler.

"That'll be one for the scrapbook," Katrina said with a wink at Sierra.

The sharp pain in Sierra's leg had suddenly become

intense. Wiggling out of Randy's one-armed hug, she said, "I'll be back," and with a slight hobble, she headed toward the restroom.

She heard Amy behind her saying, "Do you want me to bring over a Coke for you, Wes? I was going to get one for myself anyway."

The thought had crossed Sierra's mind more than once that Amy might have a crush on Wesley. Now she was sure of it. Serving men food seemed to be Amy's way of reaching their hearts. It didn't seem to matter to Amy that nearly seven years stretched between her age and Wes's. Until a week and a half ago, all Amy could talk about was Drake, a guy from school. That was until Wes moved home for the summer from Corvallis, where he attended college. Now Amy was over all the time, and her dark Italian eyes followed Wes wherever he went.

Sierra didn't know how she felt about Amy flirting with her oldest brother. She couldn't blame Amy for being attracted to him. Besides his good looks, Wes was patient and kind, and he loved dogs, just as Amy did. Two nights ago, Wes had taken their bumbling St. Bernard, Brutus, for a walk, and Amy had volunteered to go with him. Sierra went along, feeling like a chaperone. Wes had been nice to Amy and talked to her about the things she was interested in. That's the way he was. Sierra doubted if Amy understood that.

Inside the chilly park restroom, Sierra picked at the wedged brown paper towels in the steel holder until she freed a corner. The first one she pulled came out in shreds. The next towel cooperated. She wet it and began to clean the stinging scrape on her leg.

She certainly understood Amy's attraction to an older guy. Sierra had been interested in an older guy named Paul, who had pretty much ruled her dream life for the last five months. Then Paul left for Scotland, and that was the end of that fantasy. Ever since Paul left, Randy had been, well...attentive. And she liked it.

The blood cleaned up quickly enough, revealing a small cut. It had stopped bleeding, but the cool water felt good as she held the paper towel to her leg.

So here she was. The summer stretched out before her, and her calendar was full of plans with her friends. The best part was, for the first time in her life, Sierra had a bedroom all to herself. Two days earlier, her only sister, Tawni, had taken off for Southern California, where she had big plans to break into modeling. Tawni had invited Sierra to make the two-day drive with her, but Sierra couldn't arrange the time off from work. She had already asked Mrs. Kraus at Mama Bear's Bakery for time off to go on a backpacking trip with her youth group at church. And then she had asked for a week off in August to travel to California for the wedding of her friends Doug and Tracy.

Tawni had understood. Their good-bye had been a tearful one, and Sierra wondered if she had made the right choice—backpacking with Randy and Amy over going with Tawni. Surprisingly enough, after sixteen years of living side by side as feuding sisters, she and Tawni were suddenly becoming friends.

*Friends*. Sierra liked that word. She had good friends, and she was looking forward to the fun they were going to have together this summer. Only one nagging question kept running around in the back of her mind. But she was ignoring it. For weeks she had been ignoring it.

After splashing some cool water on her face and neck, Sierra felt better. She turned her cap around, pulled her ponytail through the hole in the cap, and was ready to join the others. She stepped outside the dark, musty bathroom and into the bright afternoon sun.

Randy stood a few yards away, leaning against a tree. Obviously, he had been waiting for her. Randy smiled and walked toward her. The nagging question surfaced again: *Do I know what I'm doing?*

Again Sierra brushed the question away. Greeting Randy with a smile, she said, "No stitches required."

"That's good," Randy said. He looked almost shy as he stepped forward and held out his hand.

Not sure what else to do, Sierra slipped her slightly damp hand into his, and they walked together across the lush grass toward the picnic tables where the others were now gathered. A summer breeze laced its way through the ancient cedars towering above them. It seemed to Sierra as if the trees were whispering to each other, "Look! Look! They're holding hands. Isn't that cute? Oh, he likes her. And she must like him, too!"

Inside Sierra's heart, another voice filled her with doubt and anxiety, asking, *Sierra, do you know what you're doing?*

# two

JUST AS THEY APPROACHED the rest of the group at the picnic tables, Sierra conveniently let go of Randy's hand to adjust her ponytail, a task that required both hands. She hoped no one had noticed them holding hands. They would all tease her, and Wesley would be the worst. She had never had a boyfriend before—not that Randy was one, she reminded herself—but to start acting like that now, in front of her whole family, would qualify her for endless teasing later.

"There you are," Sierra's mom said, looking up with a serving spoon in her hand. "We're ready to eat. Howard? We're all here. Would you pray for us?"

"Sure. Why don't we all hold hands?"

Randy reached for Sierra's hand as the group formed a circle. She had to admit that it felt nice and warm and comforting. Randy had rough hands from working as a gardener. He had built up a nice little business mowing lawns for twelve regular customers. In Portland this time of year, lawns needed mowing at least once a week, so his business was thriving.

Sierra's brother Gavin took her other hand. As she lowered her head to pray, she noticed the pleased look on Amy's face across the circle. She was, of course, holding hands with Wes.

When Dad closed in a group-echoed "Amen," Gavin let go of Sierra's hand and headed for the front of the food line. But Randy kept hold of her hand and gave it a squeeze.

Now Sierra definitely felt embarrassed. If she let go Randy would think she was being rude. If she kept holding hands, someone would notice. She wondered why Randy wasn't embarrassed to have his parents see them holding hands like she was. With a halfhearted squeeze back, she let go and said, "Do you want me to get you something to drink?"

*Oh no! I'm starting to sound like Amy!* Sierra thought in horror.

"Sure," Randy said. "Coke, if any is left. I'll grab you some chicken."

"And lots of my mom's potato salad," Sierra added, heading for the ice chest. Reaching her hand into the cold ice, Sierra couldn't help but compare slipping her hand into Randy's strong grip and dipping her hand into the ice chest. She had never noticed before how sensitive hands could be. *All sorts of feelings at my fingertips,* Sierra thought ruefully.

"I like Randy," a voice beside her said softly. It was Sierra's sister-in-law, Katrina. She wore her thin hair straight around her face. Katrina had a gentle, couldn't-hurt-a-fly look. Sierra had always liked her but had never felt especially close to her. Perhaps it was because Sierra had been only twelve when Katrina married Cody. They had been high school sweethearts and married the week after they graduated. Sierra couldn't imagine herself being ready to marry *anyone* a year from now.

"Are you two going out?" Katrina asked.

"Going out?" Sierra echoed.

Katrina smiled and divulged her secret. "I saw you holding hands. I thought maybe you were going together."

"No, we're buddies," Sierra said calmly. "Just friends."

She dredged up a can of ginger ale and wondered why no Cokes were left. "Do you know if any Cokes are in that other ice chest?"

"I don't know," Katrina said. "Are you trying to change the subject?"

Suddenly, Amy stood in front of them. "She always changes the subject when the topic is Randy."

"I do not," Sierra said, plunging her hand back into the ice chest and fishing for a Coke.

Amy gave Katrina a knowing look by raising her dark eyebrows and pulling up the corners of her mouth.

"He's crazy about her, but she's not willing to admit how totally crazy she is about him."

"It's not like that, Amy, and you know it."

"The question is," Katrina said, looking Sierra straight in the eyes, "do you like him?"

Sierra looked away. Though she liked the attention from Randy, she didn't like Katrina's interest in her love life.

"Sure. Everybody likes Randy. He's a great guy. Oh, good. Here's a Coke. Gotta go."

She turned on her heels and delivered the icy soda to Randy. He was still waiting in line and hadn't dished up any food for them yet. As usual, he'd let everyone in the world get in line ahead of him.

"You need to be more aggressive in this family," Sierra told him. "Everybody else sure is. Start reaching, or you'll go hungry." She stretched her arm across the table and grabbed two paper plates. Within minutes the plates were loaded with food, and they were ready to chow down.

Sierra found two seats at the picnic table next to Granna Mae, who was sipping hot coffee from one of her favorite china cups. Granna Mae always drank from a china cup, and the family had gotten used to packing one of her cups and saucers whenever they picnicked.

Granna Mae returned the rose-painted cup to the matching saucer and said, "Hello, Paul. How are you today?"

Sierra bit the inside of her lip.

"I'm Randy. Paul's the one who went to Scotland."

Randy shot a sympathetic look at Sierra. He had been around her family enough to see Granna Mae when her mind slipped into a haze like this, and he knew it was best not to try to force the issue. "How's the chicken?"

"Well, dear, I haven't tried it yet. But I do like this fruit salad." Granna Mae speared a chunk of watermelon and held it up. With a quizzical look on her soft face, she asked him, "Rather sweet for this time of year, don't you think?"

"Very sweet," Randy agreed. "Great watermelon."

Wes stuck one of his long legs under the picnic table across from Sierra and plopped down his plate and said, "Have a little potato salad, why don't you?" His plate held three times the amount of potato salad she had on hers.

"Look who's talking!" she retorted.

"Hey, I've missed Mom's home cooking."

As Wes sat down, Amy slid into the place beside him.

"I thought my family was a bunch of big eaters," Amy said, making herself comfortable. "But now I think you Jensens could outeat a Degrassi any day. At least this one could." She turned toward Wes with a smile of admiration. Amy's long dark hair hung down her face, complimenting her molasses eyes. She was a striking young woman.

"And who's this?" Granna Mae asked.

"That's Amy," Sierra said, leaning close to her grandmother. "You remember my friend Amy. She was over a couple of nights ago for dinner."

"Oh, yes. The pork chops. I told Emma not to use onions when she cooked them." Granna Mae shook her head and took another bite of fruit salad. "She's always using onions. Onions, onions on everything. Even on pork chops. Can you imagine?"

"Actually," Amy said cautiously, "we had spaghetti the night I was over. And who's Emma?"

Sierra leaned back and shook her head, signaling to Amy there was no point in trying to enter Granna Mae's foggy world, nor would it help to try to coax Granna Mae back into theirs.

"So, Randy," Wes said, a half-devoured drumstick in his hand, "are you going on this backpacking trip Sierra's been talking about?"

"I plan to, if I can finish all my yards."

"I'm going," Amy said brightly. "Why don't you come with us, Wes?"

"I'm not in high school anymore."

"So? Come as a counselor. A trail guide. Assistant to the youth pastor. Why not have some fun this summer? After all, you don't have a job yet."

"Oh, thanks for the gentle reminder, 'Mom.'" Wes rolled his eyes.

"Come on, Sierra. Tell him it'll be fun."

"It'll be fun," Sierra said.

"Randy?" Amy asked, looking for more support.

"It'll be fun, Wes," Randy echoed.

"You two sound real convincing," Wes noted.

"Speaking of fun," Sierra said, "why don't you come with us tonight, Amy? We're serving dinner at the Highland House."

"Thanks, but we're having a big dinner for my dad tonight at home. And you changed the subject again, Sierra. Seems to be your specialty lately."

One of the things Sierra liked about Amy was her persistence—as long as Amy was on a personal mission for some worthy cause, that is. But when Sierra was the object of Amy's mission, she didn't like it one bit.

Amy didn't let up on Wes or on Sierra. On Monday afternoon, Amy came by the house on her way to work. Mrs. Jensen let her in and sent her upstairs to Sierra's room.

It was a big house, built in 1915 by Granna Mae's father, and Granna Mae had lived there ever since she was born. Sierra's family had moved here from northern California in January to keep an eye on Granna Mae. And Sierra and Tawni were given the large bedroom at the top of the stairs.

Amy tapped on the bedroom door and walked in. "Hi. I only have about twenty minutes before I have to be at my uncle's restaurant, but I was dying to find out how things went with Randy last night at the Highland House."

"What do you mean?"

"Sierra, come on! I saw you guys when you left the park—holding hands and looking so sweet and cute. He even opened the car door for you."

"So?"

"So, it looks like the beginning of a summer romance to me. What happened after the Highland House? Did he kiss you?"

"Of course not! Amy, how many times do I have to tell you? We're just friends." Sierra stuck a pair of rolled-up socks into her dresser drawer and returned to the pile of clothes on her bed. "Nothing happened last night. We left the picnic, went to the Highland House, helped serve dinner, and cleaned up."

"And nothing happened after that?"

"No. He drove me home, came inside, and watched TV for a while with my brothers. I came upstairs, wrote a letter to Christy, and went to bed."

"I don't believe you," Amy said, plopping down on Tawni's now vacant bed. "That isn't the way to catch a boyfriend."

"I'm not trying to catch a boyfriend."

"Obviously," Amy said dryly. She glanced around the room. "What's different here? Something is different."

"Tawni's gone, and so is all her frilly stuff."

"No, it's not just that. This room is looking, well...uncluttered. I've never seen your side of the room cleaned up before. And look at you! If I'm not mistaken, you're actually putting clothes away."

"Yes, I am." Sierra carried a bunch of clothes on hangers over to the closet and hung them in the empty space.

"What's come over you? You feeling okay?

"I decided to clean my room, that's all. It's a big room, and it looks better picked up."

"This is not like you."

"Maybe it is," Sierra said, sitting cross-legged on the bed next to Amy. "Maybe now that Tawni's gone, my true self will sprout in all kinds of ways. Like maybe deep down I'm really a tidy person. But I never explored that because my whole life I had a neat freak sister for a roommate, and she kept things spotless enough for both of us. Now maybe I'm finding out who I really am. Do you know what I'm saying?"

"You're weird."

"Oh, come on. You have older sisters. Didn't you change some when they moved out?"

"No."

"Not at all?"

Amy shook her head. "I was and always will be the baby of the family. Nothing changed when they left. Which reminds me, instead of fixing dinner at my house on Wednesday night, can we fix it over here?"

"Why?" Sierra was surprised that Amy was willing to make any adjustments to their dinner plan. For almost a month, Amy had been devising a scheme to get Drake to come to her house for dinner. Sierra had agreed to invite Randy so it could be a foursome. They had planned and scheduled and rescheduled. Finally, everything was set for Wednesday night. Why would Amy want to change locations?

"I thought it would be more fun over here," Amy said. "It's so quiet and boring at my house. My parents will lock themselves in the TV room upstairs, and I don't know, it just wouldn't be as lively as things always seem to be around here."

Sierra began to get the picture. "You mean Wes won't be around if we have it at your house."

Amy innocently blinked her thick lashes at Sierra. "Why did you say that? Why would I want Wes to be around when I'm on a date with Drake?"

"It was just a thought," Sierra said. "We wouldn't be able to make the dinner fancy here. My brothers would get into everything and join us at the table. If you want a quiet dinner for four like you've planned all along, we should have it at your house."

"Okay, okay. If you say so." Amy glanced at her watch and forced herself to get up. "I have to go. By the way, is Wes home?"

Sierra grinned at her not-so-subtle friend. "Nope. He's out job hunting."

"Well, tell him I hope he doesn't find a job until after the backpacking trip. Okay? Tell him I said that."

"I will, Amy. See you later."

Amy scurried out of the room, closing the door behind her. Sierra lay back on Tawni's bed and stared at the ceiling. Its uneven ivory stucco presented an interesting pattern. To Sierra, it looked like clumps of clouds floating in a winter sky, untouched by the earth below, unhindered by the heavens above.

That's how Sierra wanted to be. Light and free and unhindered. Why would she want a boyfriend? Or want things with Randy to be any different from what they were right now? Warm and nice and uncomplicated. Just friends. Sierra decided she wanted to float through this summer the way she had managed to breeze through almost everything else in life. Like a cloud. That's what she wanted to be—a cloud.

# three

"MOM, I'M LEAVING FOR WORK NOW," Sierra called out the back door the next morning. Her mother was bent over in the garden, stringing up green beans. She stood and motioned for Sierra to wait a minute. Stepping cautiously over the rows of strawberries, her mom jogged to the back door. Sharon Jensen was a slim, energetic woman who seemed to enjoy life and her six children to the fullest. She loved it when people told her she was too young to be a grandmother, which she had been for three years now, ever since the appearance of Sierra's nephew, Tyler.

Everyone told Sierra she looked like her mom except that her hair was blond and her mother's was light brown. They also said she had her mom's figure. Sierra had never liked her tomboy shape, though. Compared with her shapely sister, she felt unattractive. But every now and then, when she saw her mom like this, looking cute in her shorts and a sleeveless shirt that showed off her sunburned shoulders, Sierra hoped she would turn out just like her.

"Will you stop by the store on the way home for me?

There's a list and some money on the counter. You'll be home by six, won't you?"

"I should be. I get off at five."

"Good," her mom said, dabbing her sweaty nose with the back of her gloved hand. "Gavin has a friend coming for dinner. Do you know if Randy's coming?"

"Why would he?"

"Well, he's been stopping by at dinnertime a lot lately. I just wondered if he had said anything to you."

"No, I'm afraid I can't ever make predictions about Randy."

"He knows he's always welcome. There will be plenty if he shows up."

"Okay. Well, I'm off. See you at six."

Sierra grabbed the list and cash and headed for the '79 Volkswagen Rabbit parked out front. She slipped into the car and puttered down the street to her job at Mama Bear's. Parking in the lot behind the bakery, she walked in the back door at exactly 10:00.

The day flew by, as every day had since Mrs. Kraus installed a frozen yogurt machine. She had advertised in front of the shop with a giant yogurt cone perched atop the sign that read "Mama Bear's Cinnamon Rolls." As a result, the clientele had immediately grown to include neighborhood kids and the uniformed employees from the medical center a block away.

When Sierra started this job in late winter, she had been busy making specialty coffees all day. Now it was swirled yogurt cones. Mrs. Kraus had talked about adding a small hot pot for chocolate coating so they could offer dipped cones. Sierra and several other employees had begged her to reconsider. The yogurt was sticky and messy enough without adding quick-drying chocolate to the menu.

Sierra was preparing to leave that afternoon when Mrs. Kraus approached her with the schedule in hand. "Let me get this straight," she said, chewing on the end of her pencil. "You'll be working your regular hours this week, but you'll be gone next week. Right?"

Mrs. Kraus was a short, round, good-natured woman who had a thing about all her employees wearing matching aprons. She had changed the staff aprons twice since Sierra had started there. This week they were wearing hot pink ones with little ice cream cones and cherries sprinkled across the fabric.

Hanging up her apron, Sierra looked over her shoulder at Mrs. Kraus. "Yes, I'm going backpacking, remember? I can still work my regular hours next Saturday, though."

"Backpacking? How brave of you, dear! Where are you going?"

"Some place in Washington State. It's not far."

"Sleeping on cold dirt, eating dehydrated rations, and hiking until your legs ache…my, how wonderful it is to be young."

Sierra laughed. "We have tents. And it's not exactly strenuous. It'll be fun."

"If you say so, dear. Now, you leave on Monday." She was busy writing and erasing as she spoke. "Then can you work Friday of this week from noon to nine? I'm trying out the later hours on weekends during the summer, and I've been in a dither to get the time covered. Can you work this Friday?"

"I guess so. I usually help out serving dinner at the

Highland House on Fridays, but I think Uncle Mac will understand." Sierra ran her hands under the faucet, trying to wash off the stickiness.

Ever since she and Randy had volunteered at the Highland House as a service project for school, they had continued to go back and assist where needed. The Highland House ran an after-school program for kids and offered job-search aid to their parents. The center also fed and provided beds for dozens of homeless people each night. Sierra was preparing her own version of a vacation Bible school for the kids at the Highland House and planned to start the morning program in July.

Uncle Mac, the director, was thrilled to have Sierra working there. He had taken a special interest in her, not just because of her initiative in starting the Bible school program, but also because Tawni's new boyfriend, Jeremy, was Uncle Mac's nephew. As a matter of fact, the Paul who had moved to Scotland was Jeremy's brother. Sierra was sure it was all divine intervention.

"Okay. The schedule is all set," Mrs. Kraus said. "I'll see you Thursday morning."

"See you then," Sierra said, giving a wave and quickly stepping out the back door before they started to chat about something else. Mrs. Kraus was fun to talk to, but Sierra knew that if they got started, she would be there for another hour.

To her surprise, Drake was leaning on her car with his arms folded across his broad chest. His dark hair contained glints of amber in the afternoon sun. His square jaw was set firmly, and his eyes were on Sierra.

"To what do I owe the pleasure of this surprise, Mr.

Drake?" Sierra listened to herself, not sure where her brain had come up with such a coy remark. Maybe she had been watching too many black-and-white movies late at night.

Drake's full name was Anton Francisco Drake. He never apologized for his sophisticated name, but preferred that everyone simply call him "Drake," since it didn't seem one could glean a usable nickname from Anton or Francisco. And just like his name, Drake, the six-foot-two star athlete, was one of a kind.

"I'm killing time. I left my car at the shop across the street and thought I'd stop by to see you while I waited for them to fix the muffler."

"Oh, well, I just finished work, and I have to run to the store for my mom."

"Mind if I come along?"

Sierra was sure her face reflected surprise. "Fine."

She climbed into the car and leaned over to unlock the passenger door. Drake folded his tall frame into the small vehicle and immediately tried to scoot the seat back.

"You have enough room?" Sierra asked.

"Just enough."

"I think Amy's working tonight," Sierra said as she started the car. "Have you seen her much lately?" Sierra knew the answer but wanted to see how Drake would respond.

"Not much," Drake said, adjusting the seat some more. "She seems to be working or at your house whenever I call her."

"Oh, I see," Sierra said with a tease in her voice. "So you figured if you tracked me down, Amy wouldn't be far away."

"Actually," Drake said, "I wanted to see you."

Sierra felt her heart pounding as her car took the bump into the Safeway parking lot. Why would Drake say that? Could he tell that Amy wasn't interested in him anymore? Or was this Drake's method of moving from girl to girl and never letting anyone think he was going with a particular person?

Sierra didn't respond to Drake's comment but pulled into a parking spot and turned off the engine. "I have only a few things on the list. You want to come in with me?"

"Sure. This is much better than reading auto shop magazines."

"When will your car be ready?"

"Hopefully by six-thirty." Drake let her walk in front of him through the automatic doors and into the air-conditioned store. The blast of cool air felt good to Sierra and helped to clear the head.

*He's only killing time. Don't read anything into his comment. Drake is just being friendly,* she thought.

It felt strange walking up and down the aisles with Drake pushing the cart. Sierra made herself busy as she read the list, compared prices on pickle jars, and then checked the list again. She couldn't remember the last time she had felt so nervous.

"I think that's everything," she said, finally making eye contact with him. All through the store, she had felt his eyes on her.

Drake steered the cart into the ten-items-or-less lane and helped her unload the groceries.

"Make a guess," he said.

"A guess?"

"How much do you think this will add up to?"

"I don't know. Under twenty dollars I hope, because that's all I have."

"I think it will be eleven dollars and sixty-seven cents. Go ahead. You guess."

Sierra looked away from his good-natured smile and mentally priced the items rolling past her. "Nine dollars and seventeen cents," she said.

"I don't think so." Drake's eyes sparkled.

The total rang up as $14.92.

"Fourteen ninety-two?" they both echoed.

"What did I buy?" Sierra asked.

"Hey, fourteen ninety-two," Drake repeated. "Great year for sailing the ocean blue. Just ask Columbus."

He grinned. Sierra shook her head at his joke and handed over the twenty-dollar bill.

Drake carried the bag to the car for her. "I think it was the tomatoes," he said. "They're not really in season yet."

"And how do you know this, Mr. Tomato Expert?"

Drake shrugged and placed the groceries on the back-seat. "Our backyard is full of tomato plants, and they still have little green balls on them, not big fat red ones. That's how I know. Doesn't take a rocket scientist."

Sierra settled into the driver's seat and glanced at her reflection in the rearview mirror before Drake wedged himself in. Her cheeks carried the blush of pink she felt inside.

"You mind dropping me off at the auto shop on your way home?" Drake asked. "Or, actually, would you mind taking me there and waiting? They weren't sure they could fix it tonight."

Sierra waited as Drake entered the small shop and stood

at the counter, talking to the mechanic. A thousand swirling thoughts, like confetti in the wind, blew through Sierra's mind.

*Why is he being so nice? I never dreamed Drake would be interested in me. This is so flattering! I can't believe he stopped to see me.*

Drake jogged back to Sierra's car, looking like a football player entering the stadium and anticipating the crowd's roar of approval. Sierra rolled down her window. He leaned over, resting his muscled arms on her door.

"Well, it looks as if I'll have to come back tomorrow. They're not finished with it yet."

"Do you want me to give you a ride home?" Sierra asked.

Drake was so close to her that his face was only inches away. Before she realized what was happening, he reached over and, with a thick finger, brushed something off her cheek.

Sierra's hand instinctively reached for the same spot and began to wipe her cheek. "What was it?"

"A gnat or something."

"Probably a mosquito," Sierra said. "They're already coming after me. Mosquitoes love me."

"You know what they say. Mosquitoes only go for sweet blood."

"Oh, really?" Sierra said. "My mom says it's because I don't take enough vitamin B."

Drake sauntered over to the passenger side and got back in the car. Sierra felt herself blushing again.

*What is wrong with me? I'm rambling about mosquitoes and vitamins while Drake is sitting in my car!*

"So, where to?" Sierra forced herself to ask calmly as she started up the engine.

"That depends," Drake said. "Are you interested in going out to dinner?"

# four

SIERRA AND DRAKE walked side by side up the front steps of her home. She opened the door, and he carried in the bag of groceries.

"Anybody home?"

There was no answer. They went into the kitchen and heard voices coming from the backyard. Sounds always carried from the deck into the kitchen like a funnel.

Sierra motioned for Drake to place the grocery sack on the kitchen counter and peeked out the window over the sink. Mr. Jensen stood in front of the barbecue, swatting at the cloud of smoke with his spatula. Granna Mae reclined on a patio lounge chair under the shade of one of the huge oak trees that lined the backyard. Gavin and his friend were taunting Brutus with a stick, holding it up and trying to entice him to jump. Mrs. Jensen stood by the patio table with a glass of iced tea in her hand, talking with Wes. Sierra's eight-year-old brother Dillon was sitting at the table, ready to eat as usual. Sierra felt like an eavesdropper, spying on her family through the window.

"Come on," Sierra said, leading Drake outside. "They're all out back."

"There she is," Wes said, spotting Sierra as she stepped onto the deck.

"Hi, everybody! This is Drake, a friend of mine from school. Mom, do you mind if we have one more for dinner?"

"Of course not. How are you, Drake?"

"Fine, thanks. I appreciate your letting me crash your barbecue like this."

"No problem," Sierra's dad said from the grill. "We always have plenty. You're welcome anytime. The burgers will be ready in about three minutes."

"Oh!" Her mom turned to Sierra. "Did you pick up those items at the store? I need to cut up the tomatoes and get the condiments on the table." She disappeared inside the kitchen.

"Time to eat, Granna Mae," Sierra said, going over and giving her snoozing grandma a kiss on the cheek. "You hungry?"

"Oh, goodness me," she said, looking up at Sierra. "When did you get back?"

"Just a few minutes ago. Are you ready for some dinner?"

"Well, tell me about your trip. Did you have a nice time?" Granna Mae smoothed back her hair and shifted in the lounge chair.

"I had a very nice time," Sierra said, playing along and offering her a hand up from the chair. "Come meet my friend Drake."

They walked arm in arm to the table, where Granna

Mae stopped to take a good look at Drake. She smiled cordially and found her place at the table. Sierra felt relieved that Granna Mae didn't say anything more. Drake might not understand that Granna Mae's mind was fuzzy.

Drake and Sierra sat next to each other. All eyes seemed to be on Drake, waiting for him to speak. Sierra felt proud and confident. It wasn't every day she had someone important like Drake as her guest.

"Heads up!" her dad said. "Burgers coming through."

"They smell great," Drake said, rubbing his hands in anticipation.

"I better start you off with two," Mr. Jensen offered.

"If you're sure you have enough."

"We always have extra," Dillon piped up. "That's 'cause Randy eats with us a lot. Do you know Randy?"

"Sure do."

"Randy is Sierra's boyfriend."

"He is not!" Sierra spouted. "I mean, you know." She looked at Drake and then back at Dillon. "Randy's my friend, not my boyfriend."

"Then how come you hold hands with him?"

Sierra felt her face beginning to burn. She suspected her brother was old enough to know that his words would embarrass and upset her, and he seemed to enjoy his role as the pesky little brother.

Just then her mother stepped onto the deck with a tray of condiments. Her eyes were on Sierra, and in a flash Sierra knew why. Randy was right behind her. They had heard every word in the kitchen.

"You're just in time," her dad said, saving Sierra from the awkward moment. "You hungry, Randy?"

"He's always hungry," Gavin said.

"Join us," Mr. Jensen said.

"Hey, Drake," Randy said. "How's it going?"

He ambled over to the patio table, still wearing his grass-stained work clothes. Sitting next to Dillon, he acted like one of the family. He appeared unaffected by what Sierra had said while he was in the kitchen.

Sierra fidgeted, shifting her glance from Drake to Randy.

"How are you doin'?" Drake asked Randy.

"Good. I got two more offers today for lawns on Belmont Street. You sure you don't want to join me in the yard business this summer?"

"I'm locked in," Drake said. "I told my dad I'd work for him all summer."

Sierra watched the two of them share the bottle of ketchup and information about their summer jobs. Apparently, they didn't mind sharing their relationship with Sierra as well. So why was she flustered?

Dinner progressed at its normal pace around the Jensen table with lots of lively conversation, lots of food, and not a shred of evidence that anyone other than Sierra thought it strange that she had two dinner guests.

She eagerly volunteered to help clear dishes and serve the dessert. With full hands, she followed her mother into the house. From the kitchen window, she could hear Wes asking if anyone wanted to join him in a game of basketball after dessert.

"Is this normal?" Sierra asked her mom, turning away from the window.

"Is what normal?"

"Having two guys over for dinner."

"Feels normal to me. How does it feel to you?"

"Weird," Sierra said with a sigh, leaning against the counter. "I was so flattered when Drake stopped by to see me at work. I thought maybe he was, well, you know…interested in me or something."

"Did he give you that impression?"

"Yes. Sort of. I think. Oh, I don't know."

Mom pulled the ice cream from the freezer and began to scoop it into the line of bowls she had placed on the counter. "The strawberries are in the fridge, Sierra. Could you get them for me?"

"You know what I'm realizing?" Sierra said as she took out the large bowl of fresh strawberries. "I don't know much about guys. Tawni used to call me a late bloomer, and as much as I hate to admit it, I think she was right. This is all new to me. I mean, why would Drake come to see me at work when Amy is the one who's interested in him?"

"Easy," her mother replied. "Because you're not interested in him."

"So that makes me a challenge or something?"

"Something like that. Here, scoop the strawberries on top, will you?"

"But the thing is, I am interested in Drake. At least I think I could be if I knew he liked me."

"And what about Randy?"

"That's the weird part. I don't want Randy to go away just because Drake is here."

Mrs. Jensen glanced out the window and said, "Oh, I don't think Randy is going anywhere."

"But what about Amy, Mom? We're supposed to make

dinner for Drake and Randy at her house tomorrow night. Drake is her date and Randy is mine. Except now I feel like Amy would be mad if she knew Drake was over here tonight."

"Why?"

"Because she likes Drake."

"Does she?"

Sierra felt even more frustrated than before she had started talking with her mom. She was getting nowhere, and all her questions were only being answered with more questions.

"Aren't you going to tell me how a good little Christian daughter should handle this?" she pleaded.

"No."

"No?"

Her mother put down the ice cream scoop and gently cupped Sierra's chin in her hand. "I've been doing that for sixteen years, honey. It's time for you to show me what you've got. Show me what you're made of."

"Oh great!" Sierra said as Mrs. Jensen went back to scooping up the last two bowls. "You're leaving me to figure this out all by myself."

"You're never completely by yourself," her mom said. "You know that."

"Yes," Sierra said, topping off the last bowl with a generous mound of strawberries. "Aren't you going to quote me your favorite saying? 'Mothers couldn't be everywhere so that's why God sent the Holy Spirit.'"

"You *have* been listening." Her mom placed the bowls on a tray and headed for the back door. She turned to give Sierra an over-the-shoulder smile. It was a gleeful grin, like the smile her mother had given her last Christmas when Sierra opened up the present from her parents. It was a plane ticket to England for the missions trip she went on in January.

"Without a doubt, this is going to be your best summer yet, Sierra. I just know it."

Sierra watched her mother disappear and listened to the comforting slap of the screen door as it closed behind her. It seemed she and her mother had officially entered the next level in their relationship. An invisible door had closed on what was, and a whole new world had opened up on what would be.

# five

THE BASKETBALL GAME in Sierra's driveway lasted until nearly ten o'clock. Drake, Randy, and Wes hogged the ball, but Sierra and her dad both elbowed their way into the game and managed to score a few points. In many ways, it felt like any other summer night in Sierra's childhood. The sky stayed light until nine-thirty, crickets played their summer symphony in the cool green grass, happy shouts came from Gavin and Dillon amid eager barks from Brutus, and Wes and a bunch of his friends worked up a sweat and called out friendly insults. Only tonight, the guys in the driveway were Sierra's friends, not Wesley's.

Strange feelings surrounded Sierra all night. Her mom might have been confident that Sierra would figure out these relationships, but Sierra wasn't so sure. There were so many undefined pieces. Was Drake interested in her? Was Amy still interested in Drake? What would it be like tomorrow night at Amy's house if Drake was Amy's date, but he paid more attention to Sierra?

"I better get going," Randy finally said. "I have to start

work early tomorrow morning. What time are we meeting at Amy's?"

"Is that tomorrow night?" Drake held the basketball in the crook of his arm and wiped his chin with the front of his T-shirt.

Sierra sat on the grass by the driveway-basketball court. Her legs stretched out and crossed at the ankles. Leaning back on her hands, she tilted her head and asked, "Do you guys still want to have dinner?"

"Yes," they said in unison.

"Of course," Randy added. "Why? Are you and Amy having second thoughts about trying to feed us?"

"No, not at all." Sierra made a mental note that Randy and Drake acted as if nothing were unusual about both of them being here tonight. They both actually seemed eager to get together tomorrow. What could that mean?

"Okay," Sierra said, getting up and brushing off the seat of her jeans. "Six o'clock at Amy's. And remember, it's fancy." She noticed Wes standing to the side with a smirk on his face. "What's so funny?" she challenged him.

"Nothing. Sounds like you'll have a lot of fun." His grin got wider.

"Why don't you join us?" Drake said, tossing the ball to Wes. "I'm sure Amy wouldn't mind."

*Does Drake know about Amy's crush on Wes?* Sierra wondered.

"Thanks, but that's okay. Maybe another time."

"Okay," Drake responded; then he turned to Randy. "Hey, Randy, can you give me a ride home?"

"Sure. You ready to go?"

"Yep." Drake looked at Sierra and smiled. "Thanks for dinner, Sierra."

"Yeah," Randy said with a smile. "It was great."

They headed for Randy's truck. At the curb, they both stopped to wave good-bye.

"See you at Amy's," Randy called out.

The minute the truck pulled away from the curb and started down the street, Wes let out a hearty chuckle.

"What?" Sierra demanded. They were the only ones out front now, and it seemed that the night air had suddenly turned chilly. She hadn't noticed it while they were playing basketball.

"You are going to break some hearts, little sister!" Wes spun the basketball on his finger and caught it before it toppled to the ground.

She couldn't tell if he was teasing or complimenting her.

"How old are you going to be this November?"

"Seventeen," she said firmly. "You know that."

Wes's grin pushed up the crinkles in the corners of his eyes.

"Why is that so funny?" Sierra asked, annoyed.

"It's not. It's just that I guess I didn't see it coming. Little Sierra all grown up with a line of eligible bachelors at her front door. I remember when the phone started to ring off the hook for Tawni."

"Only she was thirteen, not sixteen, right?"

"Something like that." Wes sidled up to Sierra and put a sweaty, smelly arm around her shoulder, giving her a squeeze. "Now it's your turn, Golden Girl. Go easy on Randy, though, will you? I kind of like the guy."

"So? Who asked you?" Sierra said, ducking out of his hug.

"No need to ask. My expert opinions are always available free of charge. And it's my opinion that Randy is more your speed."

"Oh, yeah?" Sierra said, playfully tapping the ball out of his hand. "And exactly what speed is that?"

The ball bounced through Wes's fingertips and rolled down the driveway and into the street.

Wes crossed his arms, attempting to look threatening. "Go get the ball."

"I'm not your dog. You get the ball." Sierra stood on the driveway, hands on her hips, chin jutted out in defiance, waiting for her brother to tackle her, rough up her hair, throw grass in her face, or hoist her over his shoulder and cart her to the street, where he would make her pick up the ball.

Wes looked her over slowly, as if trying to decide which tactic would work best. Suddenly, a different expression washed over his face, a look of tenderness rather than teasing. Then he cleared his throat and said in a serious voice, "If you ever need someone to talk to about guys or whatever—especially now that Tawni's gone—I'll be around all summer. You know that you can talk to me, don't you?"

Those were the last words Sierra expected from her brother's lips. Had she somehow walked through an invisible door with Wesley the same way she had entered a new level in her relationship with her mom?

"Sure. Thanks," Sierra said, feeling as if that was the expected response.

Wes smiled and said, "I'll get the ball this time."

He hustled down to the street, and Sierra went inside, shaking her head. She climbed the stairs, trying to make sense of all that was happening in her life.

*Is there a sign on my forehead that says, "Treat me like an adult"? Or does everyone believe the door to my social life has swung open because Drake showed up tonight?*

Whatever it was, she didn't understand the change. And it certainly came as a surprise.

The next morning Sierra was in for another surprise when she came downstairs to breakfast. Her plan was to eat something and then call Amy to fill her in on the events of the night before.

She had carefully thought through her words in the shower. "Amy," she rehearsed, "I need to tell you that Drake came to my house last night for dinner. I want to know how you feel about that and whether you still want to make dinner for the guys tonight, because if you're not interested in Drake anymore, then..." Her words froze every time she got to the part about Drake. Certainly, a banana and a bowl of Golden Grahams would bring her thinking into focus, she decided.

But when Sierra stepped into the kitchen, she found Amy sitting at the kitchen counter, crying behind a barricade of cereal boxes. Wes stood at the kitchen sink, a glass of orange juice in his hand. They both turned to look at Sierra when she walked in.

"What's wrong?" Sierra asked quickly, looking first at Wes, then at Amy.

With a sniff and a deep breath, Amy said, "My parents decided to have a big yelling match this morning. My dad stomped out all mad, and my mom ran into her room and locked the door. I hate it when they do this."

Sierra sat down next to Amy and slipped her arm

around her shoulders. "I'm sure it'll work out. Doesn't it usually blow over in an hour or two?"

"Usually," Amy said with a sniff. "But I don't know what to do about our dinner tonight. I don't want to have all the guys over if they're going to fight again."

"You probably should stay clear," Wes said, getting his two-cents' worth into the conversation. "It might be better not to add any complications to the evening in case your parents need time to talk when your dad comes home from work. Why don't you guys reschedule your dinner?"

"We've already rescheduled four times!" Amy got up and went over to the side counter to grab a napkin from the basket. She wiped her eyes and blew her nose. "I guess we should cancel the whole thing and forget it. I'll tell my uncle we don't need the lobsters tonight after all."

"Lobsters?" Wes noted.

"We can have it here," Sierra heard herself saying.

"Are you sure your parents wouldn't mind?" Amy asked, her expression brightening.

Sierra knew Amy hadn't planned for her parents to quarrel. She wasn't trying to set things up so that Wes would be a part of their fancy dinner. But it sure was working out conveniently.

"I'm sure it'll be fine," Sierra said. "I'll call Drake and Randy to tell them. Do you still want it to be at six?"

"Sure. I can pick up the lobsters anytime this afternoon. We still have to shop for the salad and rolls and decide on some kind of vegetable. What do you like?"

"Zucchini," Wes jumped in. "The way Mom makes it."

"She didn't ask you," Sierra said, tossing her brother a "get lost" look.

"What are we going to have for dessert?" Amy asked.

The doorbell rang, and Wes left to answer it, giving Sierra the opportunity to try to have her heart-to-heart talk with Amy.

Sierra took a deep breath. "I need to ask you something. How are you feeling about Drake?"

Amy gave her a funny look.

"I mean do you still like him?"

"Of course I still like him. I've always liked Drake. Who wouldn't?"

This wasn't the answer Sierra expected.

"Why?" Amy asked.

"I thought you weren't that interested in him anymore."

Amy shook her head. "I'm totally interested in him! Drake isn't crazy about me, but I thought as he got to know me better, he would change his mind. That's why I wanted to do this dinner. Why do you ask?"

Sierra poured herself a bowl of cereal. "I need to tell you something."

She dipped her spoon into the bowl and tried to find a good opening line. Maybe Amy wouldn't care that Drake had spent last evening at Sierra's. *Yeah, right!* Sierra thought, shuddering. *What if this is the end of our friendship?*

"Amy, listen to what I say and don't get mad, okay?"

"Why would I get mad?"

Sierra knew she hadn't done anything wrong. Drake had sought her out, not the other way around. And there was nothing unusual about inviting a friend home for dinner. So why did she feel guilty?

Just then Wes walked back in with a UPS package in his hand. "Do you know if Mom is still around?"

"I don't know," Sierra said.

Gavin burst in the back door, laughing and running through the house. Dillon entered right behind him with a squirt gun in his hand.

"Hey, guys," Wes said in a booming voice, "take it outside."

"Okay, *Dad*." They chased each other around the middle table and out the back door.

"We can't talk in here," Sierra said, exasperated. "Let's go upstairs. You know, maybe we should postpone the dinner again. It'll be like this the whole time around here."

"No, it won't," Wes said. "I'll take everyone out for pizza. You guys can have the whole place to yourselves."

Amy's face clouded over. "You don't have to go anywhere, Wes."

The phone rang, and as Wes reached for it, he said, "Yes, I think I do."

"Come on, Aim. Let's go up to my room."

"Sierra," Wes called as they headed toward the hall, "phone. It's Drake."

# SIX

SIERRA FROZE.

"Let me talk to him. He probably guessed I'd be over here since I wasn't home." Amy reached to take the phone from Wes's hand and answered with, "Hi."

Wes stepped back and crossed his arms across his chest, amused by the scenario.

"Friday night?" Amy said. "I'd love to! I have to work till nine, so we'd have to go to the late show. What? No, this is Amy." She shot a glance at Sierra. "Who did you think you were talking to?"

Sierra pursed her lips together and looked down at her bare feet. Her heart was pounding like a drum.

"She's right here," Amy said and held out the phone to Sierra.

Tears began to well up in Amy's eyes as she grabbed her purse from the counter and spouted, "I can't believe you didn't tell me, Sierra! Forget the dinner." She brushed past Sierra and marched for the front door.

"Drake?" Sierra said into the receiver. "I'll have to call you back."

"I'm not at home," he said. "I'm at work. You want me to call you?"

"No. I mean yes."

Sierra heard Amy sobbing as she opened the front door.

Her emotions torn in two, Sierra said quickly into the phone, "I don't know, Drake. Whatever."

She hung up the phone and dashed to the front door. Amy was already down the sidewalk, unlocking the door of her Volvo.

"Amy, wait!"

Amy ignored her, got in, and slammed the door. Sierra bolted down the steps and ran to the curb as Amy started the car. She turned the key in the ignition, but nothing happened.

"Amy, we need to talk!" Sierra pounded her fist on the closed passenger window.

Amy ignored her and tried the key again. Nothing.

Sierra noticed the lock was up on the passenger door and quickly opened it before Amy could reach over to lock it. Plopping herself inside, Sierra slammed the door shut.

Amy forced the unresponsive ignition key again, and in a voice filled with anger, she said, "I have nothing to talk to you about!"

"Amy," Sierra said, trying to be calm, "don't do this. Talk to me. It's not what you think."

"Oh, really?" Amy turned her tear-streaked face toward Sierra. "Then what is it?"

"It's a misunderstanding, and we need to talk about it."

"No, we don't. Leave me alone!"

"I won't leave you alone," Sierra answered firmly. "I'm going to sit here until you talk to me. You can't walk out when you're mad. You'll never solve anything that way. Look at your parents." As soon as the words popped out of Sierra's mouth, she realized that was the worst thing she could have said.

*Oh, when am I ever going to learn to keep my mouth shut?*

Amy burst into tears and dropped her forehead onto the steering wheel. Sierra had never heard anyone sob so uncontrollably.

"I'm sorry," Sierra said, cautiously reaching over and placing a hand on Amy's shoulder. "All I'm saying is that you and I need to talk this out."

Amy cried and cried.

Sierra rolled down the window in the stuffy car and waited for Amy to calm down.

Finally, Amy lifted her head from the steering wheel and shouted, "Everyone is deserting me! Everyone I know has turned against me."

"I'm not against you," Sierra said in firm, even words.

"Oh please!" Amy glared at Sierra, her eyes puffy and her cheeks soaked with tears. "You steal my boyfriend and then you say you're not against me? You're a liar!"

"I am not a liar, Amy. And I didn't steal your boyfriend. I've been trying to tell you what happened."

"I don't want to hear it."

"Amy," Sierra said, struggling to keep calm, "don't act like this. Listen to me. Drake took his car in to be fixed yesterday, and then he came over to Mama Bear's right when I was getting off work. He said he was just killing time, so he went to the grocery store with me. Then I took him back to the garage, and they weren't done with his car yet, so I invited him to my house for dinner."

"Oh, that was convenient," Amy said, wiping her cheek with the back of her hand.

"Listen to me, Amy. Randy was there, too. My family was having a barbecue, and afterward we all played basketball. Randy gave Drake a ride home, and that was it."

Amy looked at her skeptically and sniffed loudly. "Randy was there, too?"

"Yes. Randy was there, too. He gave Drake a ride home. Nobody was stealing anybody's boyfriend."

"Why did he come to see you at work instead of me?"

"For one thing, the garage was right across the street. For another, he told me he had tried to call you the last few days, but you were never home."

"Yes, I was. He's lying."

"You can't go around accusing everyone of being a liar," Sierra stated firmly. "Look at yourself. You're falling apart over nothing."

"It isn't nothing," Amy said, brushing back her hair and reaching in her purse for a tissue. She blew her nose and blurted through tears, "My parents are going to get a divorce."

# seven

"DO YOU KNOW THAT FOR SURE?" Sierra asked. "I mean, have they actually said they're getting a divorce, or are you feeling that way because things were so bad between them this morning?"

"I'm positive," Amy said. "I heard them fighting once a few months ago, and they said they were going to wait until I graduated next year. Then they would sell the house and split everything."

Sierra didn't know that to say.

"The way things are going, I don't think they'll last until the end of the month."

"I'm sorry you're going through all this," Sierra said. "I'm glad you're telling me."

"I probably shouldn't be saying all this." Amy drew in a shaky breath. "I just don't know what to do."

"I don't think you can do anything. Except pray. Pray good and hard. This is something your parents have to work out."

They were silent for a few minutes. Sierra could hear

the morning birds singing their hearts out in the towering trees in the backyard. She remembered a saying she had once seen on a greeting card. "The blue bird does not sing because she has the answer. She sings because she has a song."

"Amy, let's put this morning behind us, okay? I don't have any answers for you. I just want to start fresh."

"You always do that," Amy said, looking Sierra in the eyes for the first time since Sierra had clambered into her car. "You spring back all the time. Don't you ever get depressed?"

"Sure. Sometimes. Everybody does."

Amy pulled her hair away from her face and reached for a ponytail holder hanging from her rearview mirror. With her hair back and her eyes wiped, she faced Sierra with a forced smile. "Okay. Fresh start. I can deal with Drake liking you."

"I never said he liked me."

"Well, Drake is interested enough to call and ask you to the movies Friday night, in case you hadn't figured that out yet. That makes it a bit awkward for us to fix dinner for the guys tonight and still assume that Drake is my date."

"Why should it be?"

"Sierra! Think about it."

"I never said I'd go to the movies with him. I never gave Drake any indication that I was interested in him."

"But you are, aren't you? I mean, if I hadn't picked up the phone, you would have said yes to the movies, wouldn't you?"

Sierra paused before answering, "I don't know."

"Come on, Sierra. You've always been honest with me.

Why can't you tell me the truth now? I can take it. Believe me! After all I've been through this morning, I can take anything."

Sierra let out a deep breath and lifted her thick hair off her clammy neck. How should she answer?

"I don't know how I feel, Amy. I just don't know." She shook her head and looked out the car window.

The front of the Jensen house looked like a picture from *Better Homes and Gardens* magazine. The wide wraparound porch was decorated with her mom's baskets of hanging ferns, and along the railing her flower boxes were alive with color. It all seemed so peaceful and inviting. A vivid contrast to the way Sierra felt inside.

"We can't fix dinner tonight," Amy said. "That's for sure."

"I still don't understand why not."

Amy gave her an incredulous look. "Do the math, girl! You would have two dates, and I would have none."

"Why can't we all just be a bunch of friends having dinner together and not divide up into couples?" Sierra suggested. "We're all friends, aren't we? Why do we have to match people up? I hate that."

"Why should you hate that? You're the one with all the male attention at the moment."

"So what do you want to do?" Sierra sighed.

"Nothing. I want to cancel the dinner. I want to go home." Amy paused. She reached for her sunglasses on the dashboard and slipped them on. "No, I don't want to go home. I don't know what I want right now. I just want to get out of here."

"Don't leave mad, Amy."

"I'm not mad." She turned the key in the ignition, and the car started immediately.

"Are you sure?"

"Yes, I'm sure. I'll talk to you later," Amy said.

"Well, call me or come by later or something. I have the whole day free now."

"I'll call you," Amy said. "But you call the guys, okay?"

"Okay," Sierra reluctantly agreed, opening the car door and getting out. "You will call me, right?"

"I told you I would." Amy pulled Sierra's door shut and charged away, making her tires squeal as she sped down the street.

*She's still mad, and she's not going to call me,* Sierra thought.

With her bare feet nestled in the cool grass, Sierra watched a puff of gray smoke rise from the old Volvo as it turned down the next street. Sierra felt hollow inside. There didn't seem to be any easy answers, no snap decisions that would make everything right and peaceful again.

*Why does life have to be so complicated? I should call Drake and tell him I can't go to the movies with him. Then Amy will have nothing to be mad about,* Sierra thought. *No, I can't do that. He never actually asked me. He thought he was asking me, but he really only talked to Amy.* Then Sierra had an idea. *What if Randy came with us? No, that's too strange.* She went back and forth. *No, it isn't. Randy's just a buddy. Or is he?*

The nagging little voice inside of Sierra was beginning to make her feel as if she were going crazy, causing her to doubt herself and everyone else.

A large white delivery van rumbled down the street and pulled up where Amy's car had been, interrupting Sierra's thoughts. The words on the side of the van read, "Bundle of Joy—Diaper Service." Sierra was sure the van was on the wrong block. None of their neighbors had a baby.

She turned to go inside when someone called from the van, "Hey, Sierra, wait up."

She whirled around and then nearly burst out laughing when she saw the delivery man jump from the front seat. Tall, handsome Drake stood before her wearing shorts and a white short-sleeved shirt with a "Bundle of Joy" monogram above the pocket.

# eight

"WHAT WAS GOING ON here when I called? Is Amy still here?" Drake pulled off his sunglasses and looked past Sierra to the front porch.

"She just left. You deliver diapers?"

Drake nodded. "It's my dad's company."

"I didn't know that."

Drake gave her a sly grin. "It's not the kind of thing I go around broadcasting, you know. Now tell me what was going on with Amy."

"We were trying to plan dinner for tonight, but now it's canceled."

"Why?"

"Amy felt uncomfortable about things."

"Why?"

"Well," Sierra said, "let me ask you a question. Are you interested in going out with her?"

"No."

"She's interested in going out with you."

"So?"

"So?!"

"Yeah, so? Does that mean I'm obligated to go out with her?"

"Drake!" Sierra put her hands on her hips and shook her head. "You don't get it, do you? You hurt her feelings this morning."

"I hurt her feelings? How?"

"Because when she picked up the phone, she thought you were asking her out. Don't you see? She started to say yes, and then you told her you wanted to talk with me. She likes you, and it hurt her to find out that you were asking someone else out."

"And it's my fault Amy picked up the phone and made me think I was talking to you?"

"She didn't mean to do that. You're acting like Amy and I planned this to confuse you."

Running his fingers through his dark hair, Drake looked frustrated. "Well, it worked. I'm confused, all right."

"Oh! And you think that's our fault?"

"I'm not saying anything is anyone's fault." Drake raised his voice.

Sierra folded her arms and bit her tongue before she said something she would really regret.

"Look, Sierra, I have to go. Do you want to come with me while I make deliveries so we can talk about this?"

"I don't have any shoes on."

"So go put some shoes on."

Sierra hesitated. She wasn't sure she wanted to run around town with Drake. Not because of the Bundle of Joy Truck, but because of her concern that Amy would get upset again, the way she had about Drake coming to Sierra's house for dinner. "I don't know," she said.

"Fine!" Drake said, exasperated. "I have to go. I'll talk to you later." He hustled to the driver's side of the van, hopped in, and took off.

"Men!" Sierra muttered.

She turned to go inside when another truck rumbled up to the front of her house. Sierra threw up her arms in surrender when she saw that Randy's white truck had pulled up to the curb.

"What is going on this morning?" she muttered.

Randy slid over and rolled down the passenger window. "Hi. How's it going?"

"Don't ask!?" Sierra spouted.

"Okay," Randy answered agreeably. "Let's start over again. I was on my way to my next yard job over on 52nd Street. I saw you standing out here, and I thought I'd bring you a friendly hello!" He flipped back his straight blond hair and offered her a big grin.

Sierra was not amused.

"Bad morning, huh?"

"Yes."

"Was that Drake's delivery truck?"

"Yes."

Randy cautiously ventured another question. "Is everything all set for dinner tonight?"

"No. We had to cancel the dinner."

"How come?"

"Don't ask. It's a mess."

"Is there anything I can do?" Randy asked.

"No."

Taking the hint that Sierra was not in a talkative mood, Randy smiled and said, "Well, I hope your day gets better."

"So do I."

"Oh, by the way," Randy said, "I invited Drake to go on the backpacking trip."

"You didn't! Oh, Randy!"

"What?"

Sierra grabbed her hair with both fists and, giving a pull, said, "Why do I feel as if I'm about to go totally wacko?"

Randy shrugged. "Did I do something wrong?"

"Just forget it. Now I have to call Amy and explain everything to her."

"Guess I'd better get going," Randy said sheepishly. "I'll talk to you later."

"You and everybody else," Sierra mumbled. She watched him drive away, following Amy and Drake's escape route. Then, taking the steps to the front porch two at a time, Sierra decided she needed to sit down and think things through. She retreated to the porch swing and stretched out on the soft cushions. Laying her arms across her forehead and shutting her eyes, Sierra began to sort things out.

Amy was a wreck. But maybe she was overly emotional because of her parents, and Drake wasn't really a part of the problem after all. Any other time it wouldn't have bothered Amy that Drake called Sierra. Actually, that wasn't true. It would have bothered Amy any time. She liked the guy. But it wasn't Sierra's fault.

Drake was the problem. Why was he being so nice to Sierra and giving her all this attention? She remembered the way she felt the day before when Drake's hand had brushed the bug from her cheek. She touched the same cheek slightly, reliving the sensation. She had never felt like that before, embarrassed and warm at the same time.

*I should have gone with him on his deliveries. Now he probably won't ask me out for Friday.* Sierra stopped herself. *What am I thinking? Even if he did, I wouldn't go out with him! I wouldn't do that to Amy. Or Randy. Randy? Why am I worried about Randy? He wouldn't care if I went out with Drake, would he?*

The nagging voice that had been plaguing Sierra whispered to her again, *Are you sure you know what you're doing?*

She sat up and tossed her wild curls from her shoulders, hoping to shake away both the annoying whisper and her mixed-up emotions. It was no use. The confusing feelings followed her as she got up and went inside. Heading straight for the kitchen, Sierra went searching for food. Actually, she wanted sugar. For the first time she understood why Tawni used to go on sugar safaris. Chocolate is the only known cure for emotional exhaustion.

The best she could come up with were some stale miniature marshmallows and a few spoonfuls of hot fudge. Sierra warmed a bowl of fudge in the microwave and then sat down with the marshmallows and a toothpick. Her "fondue" was ready.

"Sierra!" her mother said when she entered the kitchen a few moments later. "Is that your lunch?"

"Um-hmm," Sierra answered, a gooey morsel melting in her mouth.

"Wesley said you and Amy want to have dinner here tonight."

Sierra shook her head. "It's been canceled."

"Since when?"

"Since this morning when Amy was here."

"She was here earlier?" her mom asked. "I just talked to her on the phone ten minutes ago. I told her you were out with Drake."

Sierra dropped her marshmallow, toothpick and all, into the fudge. "You didn't."

Her mom nodded and tried one of the stale marshmallows. "When I got out of the shower, Gavin said you were out with Drake."

# nine

SIERRA REALIZED her little brother must have looked out the window and seen her at the curb talking to Drake. All Sierra needed now was for Amy to think that the minute she left, Sierra had gone out with Drake.

Sierra ran into the study and punched in Amy's number. "Amy, it's me. Don't hang up." Sierra sat down in her favorite chair in the study, staring at the ceiling in exasperation.

"I thought you were out with Drake," Amy said accusingly.

"I was out front talking to Drake. I wasn't 'out' with him. I was trying to explain to him that he hurt your feelings."

"You didn't say that, did you?" Amy's voice had an edge to it.

"Yes, I did. I wanted him to understand why it hurt you when you realized he was trying to ask me out."

"Sierra, will you just keep your nose out of my business?"

"What is wrong with you today? I'm on your side."

"No, you're not! Not when you go around telling Drake he hurt my feelings! That is so embarrassing. He obviously isn't interested in me. I'm not so dumb that I'm going to keep liking him."

Sierra stood up and began to pace with her hand on her forehead. "I don't get it. I was trying to stand up for you."

"I don't need you to stand up for me," Amy said coolly. "It's over."

"What's over?"

"My nonexistent relationship with Drake. He's all yours. Don't be shy. Go for it. Leave me out of your next conversation with him, and I guarantee he'll ask you out."

"How can you stop liking him so quickly?"

"A relationship takes two people," Amy said. "It was always one-sided with Drake and me. I just hoped it would change. It didn't."

"I don't know if I could go out with him, knowing that you liked him."

"Sure you could," Amy said. "In fact, I think you should."

Sierra let out a deep breath and slumped against the wall. "I don't get it. You really think I should go out with Drake?"

Amy sighed. "This whole dating thing is new to you, Sierra. Let me tell you, when a guy like Drake asks you out, you'd better say yes."

"Amy, your friendship means more to me than a date with Drake or any other guy."

"Sierra, hello! Wake up, girl! We're in high school.

You're supposed to go out with guys when they ask you, not turn them down because it might hurt some other girl's feelings. Nice gesture, but I'd never expect any friend to give up a potential romance for me."

"But I mean it," Sierra protested.

"I know. That's what makes you so sweet. That's why everyone, including Drake, likes you. And that's what makes it impossible for me to stay mad at you very long."

"So you're not mad anymore?"

Amy paused before saying calmly, "I'm fine with this. Really. I think you should go out with him. I'm sure he'll ask you again."

Sierra wished she could see Amy's face so she would know without a doubt that Amy was being honest.

That evening Sierra still felt uneasy about Amy's blessing and decided she would join Wes on a walk to Mount Tabor Park with Brutus. Maybe it was time to take Wes up on his offer to play big brother. He'd probably enjoy the opportunity to pour out his wisdom for her.

They put the leash on Brutus and were rounding the side of the house when Drake walked up the front steps.

"Hey, Drake," Wes called out. "Over here."

Sierra felt her heart pounding.

"How's it going?" Wes asked.

"Pretty good. You guys heading out for a walk?"

Wes glanced at Sierra and then said, "Sierra was looking for some company. You want to fill in for me, Drake?"

"Sure." Drake looked as if he had just stepped out of the shower with his thick, dark hair slicked back. The blue T-shirt and jeans were a contrast to the bright white Bundle of Joy uniform he had worn that morning.

Wes handed the leash to Sierra and said, "Make sure you have the big lug back by midnight."

"Which one?" Sierra muttered.

"I heard that," Drake said. "Which way are we going?" He reached over and roughed up Brutus's furry mane.

"Left, if you want to go to the park."

"Fine with me."

Brutus let out an impatient woof and took off. Sierra pulled on the leash. "The other way, Brutus. Go left."

"He actually knows his right from his left?" Drake asked.

"No, but we're working on it."

They walked a block and a half in awkward silence before Drake said, "Can I tell you my side about Amy?"

"Sure."

"I don't know what Amy has told you, but this is how I see it. A bunch of us went to the Blazers game. Maybe you remember—we were planning it during lunch one day at school. Amy sort of asked for a ride, and when I agreed, it was as if we were going out. I saw it as giving a friend a ride. I don't know what she considered it to be."

Amy had been so excited. Sierra recalled teasing her about how she had manipulated Drake into asking her out. Amy had also set up the dinner plans to encourage Drake's interest.

Apparently, Drake had never felt the same about Amy. Amy had been the instigator all along.

"I can understand your trying to defend Amy," Drake said. "But I'm not sure it was fair for you to make me out to be the bad guy."

"Maybe I jumped to conclusions," Sierra admitted.

"Jumped?" Drake echoed. "How about catapulted?"

Sierra laughed. "Okay, so I catapulted. All I know is that it hurt Amy's feelings when she answered the phone, and you were calling for me, not her."

"Whoa, wait a minute," Drake said. "I didn't know Amy was at your house this morning, and I sure didn't know she was the one on the phone. Are you telling me I don't have the right to ask a girl out if I know someone else is interested in me?"

Sierra saw his point. Still, Amy was her friend. Her good friend, which was something she didn't have an abundance of at the moment.

Drake continued. "What if I don't want to go out with her? Aren't I free to make my own decisions? Or do I have to sit at home, just so I won't potentially hurt her feelings?"

They came to a busy cross street, and Brutus lurched forward, galloping off the curb.

"Wait, there's a car coming!" Sierra yelled. She jerked on the leash and suddenly felt Drake's warm hand on top of hers.

"Here, I'll take him," Drake offered. He grabbed the leash and spoke firmly to Brutus. "Come on, boy. Hold up a minute."

If Sierra's heart had been racing before, it was sprinting now. She saw Drake in a new light. He was right. It wasn't fair for her to judge him only on Amy's view of what her relationship with Drake should be. Drake had a say in things, too.

"Look, I want to be straight with you, Sierra. I don't date a lot. I made a point last year to hang out with a lot of different people and not to go out with just one person."

Sierra knew that was true. Drake was friends with everyone and had even been called a flirt because he didn't go out with the same girl twice.

"I've been thinking about this a lot. Would you like to go out with me?"

"You mean to the movies on Friday?"

"Yes, but I mean more than that," Drake said. "I mean date. You know, be together this summer. I'd really like to spend time with you and get to know you better."

Sierra noticed that Drake's forehead was beginning to perspire. His voice sounded calm and confident, but she knew he must be feeling as nervous as she was.

*Well...he was right about Amy. And he is an incredible guy*, Sierra thought.

"Okay," she said.

*Boy, did that sound lame!* Sierra chided herself. *Couldn't you get a little more enthusiastic here? Drake just asked you out!*

Then, before Sierra could stop herself, she blurted out, "Why me?"

# ten

"WHY YOU?" Drake laughed.

"What I mean is, you can have any girl you want. Why in the world do you want to go out with me?"

Drake scratched the back of his neck. "I don't know. Do I have to have a reason? Isn't it enough that I like you and want to spend time with you?"

Sierra edged a little closer to Drake as they entered the park and turned up a tree-lined path. "I guess so. I'm flattered, that's all. I love this park, don't you? All the trees make it feel so secluded. Like a secret hiding place."

"It's nice," Drake agreed.

The trail wound upward, and they stopped talking and starting huffing with each rapid step. Drake's long stride proved to be a challenge for Sierra to keep up with. They didn't talk again until they reached the top of the hill where a spectacular view of the city hung low in the west, lacing the long row of scalloped clouds with a satin ribbon of peach.

"It's beautiful," Sierra murmured.

Drake casually slipped his arm around her shoulder,

holding Brutus's leash tightly with his right hand. "Beautiful," Drake repeated.

*This is so wonderful!* Sierra thought. *I love feeling his arm around me. I wonder if he's going to kiss me. Wait, what am I thinking? Why would he kiss me? We hardly know each other.*

It was the first time Sierra had been overwhelmed with such strong feelings about a guy. Everything was coming at her so fast. She both liked the emotional rush and felt threatened by it. It was liked the feeling she had on the Tilt-O-Wheel ride at the county fair when she was a kid. She loved the sensation of the gravity taking over, but felt anxious at the same time because she was no longer in control.

Something stronger than she was at work. With the rush of emotion came the fear of doing something she would later regret. On the Tilt-O-Wheel, she'd feared throwing up in public when she got off the ride. But with Drake, she didn't know exactly what it was she feared. Some kind of warning system was going off in her head, though.

"We'd better head back," Sierra heard herself say. "This guy's going to need a drink of water."

"I saw a fountain back there," Drake said. "Can he drink from there?"

"Sure."

They turned to go. Drake kept his arm around her shoulders. He seemed to think the gesture was completely normal. She hoped he couldn't feel her blood pumping at top speed through her shoulders, making her feel warmer than usual in her shorts and T-shirt on this mild summer's evening.

Drake led Brutus to the fountain and dropped his arm from Sierra's shoulders while he let the dog lap up the cool water. She immediately missed the warmth and security Drake's arm had given her.

When Brutus had had enough, he led Sierra and Drake to a bench beside a blooming rose garden, where he lay down.

"Looks like Brutus wants a rest before going home," Drake said. "Not a bad idea."

He sat down on the bench, and Sierra sat next to him. Not too close, not too far away.

The summer sky was still lit by the pastels that streamed across the evening clouds. It would be light for at least another half hour. The park was alive with people biking along the trails, playing on the swings, and finishing up their barbecue picnics. Sierra felt content.

"I'm glad we straightened things out," Sierra said. She felt like telling Drake that Amy had given Sierra her blessing to date him. But then she thought if she brought Amy's name up, she might say things the wrong way, and Amy would get mad at her all over again.

"Yeah, well, I knew you'd see the light," he teased. Drake had a way of jutting out his chin when he was after something he wanted. Sierra had noticed that before when he had begged cookies from her at school. Right now his chin was sticking out, firm and determined.

*This guy knows what he wants and goes after it. I still can't believe I'm the one he wants to be with! I love the way he's strong and so good-looking, and yet he's not too proud to drive a diaper delivery truck around town. This guy is perfect for me.*

"It's going to be a great summer," Drake murmured, slipping his arm around her shoulders again.

Sierra slid just a tiny bit closer. "That's what my mom

keeps promising me. But the way things were going this morning, I wasn't so sure I'd make it through the day, let alone the whole summer!"

"Oh, I think you'll make it," Drake said, smiling.

With energetic bursts, Sierra's mind flashed images of what the summer was going to be like. Drake hiking with her on the backpacking trip. Drake taking her out to dinner. Drake buying her popcorn at the movies. Drake sitting with his arm around her on the porch swing. Drake giving her her very first kiss.

# eleven

IT WAS NEARLY ONE O'CLOCK in the morning, and Sierra tossed and turned in her bed. She couldn't sleep. The whole evening with Drake had fueled her emotions. In the stillness of her room, she relit each feeling and let it burn itself out.

They had walked home from the park hand in hand. Her parents were sitting in the porch swing when they arrived. After putting Brutus in the backyard, Sierra and Drake had sat on the porch talking with her mom and dad. Then Drake scored extra points by asking Sierra's dad if it would be okay with him if Drake took Sierra to the movies Friday night.

Mr. Jensen said yes, and Mrs. Jensen wore a subtle, pleased smile. When Drake left, they all waved good-bye from the front porch.

No kiss. But then Sierra didn't want him to kiss her just like that the first night. The whole summer stretched before them.

She had gone to bed right after that and had stared at

the ceiling and kicked at the sheets for more than three hours now. Her mind refused to shift into a lower gear.

Part of her nervous energy was directed toward Amy. What would she say to Amy tomorrow? Would it really be okay with her if Sierra started going out with Drake? What would it be like for Amy and Drake both to be at the back-packers' meeting? Should she warn Amy ahead of time so it wouldn't be awkward for her to see Drake there?

And would Randy still feel comfortable coming around now that Drake was going to be a permanent part of her summer schedule? A smile curled Sierra's lips in the dark, silent bedroom as she thought of the contrast between Randy and Drake. Drake's hands weren't rough like Randy's, and they didn't smell like cut grass. Tawni would certainly be surprised when she found out she and Drake were a couple. Sierra glanced over at the vacant bed. If only Tawni were here now, then Sierra would have someone to wake up and listen to all of Sierra's plans for the summer.

Sierra never would have dreamed this day would have turned out the way it did. It had moved from Amy's crying in the kitchen that morning to Sierra's watching the sunset with Drake. Sierra smiled. This was a day to remember.

Feeling content with that thought, Sierra finally fell asleep.

The next morning, Sierra dressed extra carefully because she felt so special. She pulled back her hair in a loose ponytail and picked out her newest—and subsequently favorite—pair of dangly earrings. Her usual summer wardrobe of shorts and a T-shirt seemed blah today. She rooted through the back of her closet, searching for some-thing that would make her look as lighthearted as she felt.

The she saw it—the long gauze dress that Tawni called her "granny gown."

Sierra slipped it over her head and smiled at the thought that Tawni wasn't here to make any of her rude comments about the way Sierra dressed. She was a free spirit and had insisted to Tawni for years that her clothes expressed her art of living. Her sister would smirk and say, "They're an expression all right."

She placed a silver dove necklace on a long black ribbon around her neck, finishing off the outfit. Sierra looked in the oval mirror above her antique dresser and smiled approvingly. Drake's interest in her had given her much confidence. It felt good to be admired, to be wanted. Sierra couldn't remember the last time she had felt this way. It was terrific.

And no one could change her sunny outlook at work. She wore a permanent smile as she served cinnamon rolls and filled yogurt cones. And she was still grinning that evening as she helped her mother do the dishes before rushing off to the youth group meeting at church.

Since Sierra's family had moved to Portland, they had visited a number of churches. They attended one across the bridge in Washington for a while because Tawni was interested in their college group. But the church they ended up at was only a few miles from their house and also happened to be the church in which Randy grew up. His parents and Sierra's were in the same home Bible study group. Amy started going with Sierra since her family didn't have a church they attended regularly. Sierra wasn't sure of Drake's church background.

Sierra arrived early and glanced around the parking lot,

looking for Drake's car. It wasn't there yet. Neither was Amy's Volvo. Randy's truck was in one of the first parking spots; he usually came early. Sierra wondered if Drake had come with him. She entered the youth room and scanned the group, looking for Drake.

Randy spotted her and waved from the corner. For several weeks he had been trying to organize a band, and it looked as if they finally had everything in place.

Tre, a guy from school, stood in the center of the group, tuning up his guitar. Randy adjusted one of the speakers, and a few minutes later the room was filled with live music.

They sounded great, but Sierra was distracted. She nervously watched the door for Drake or Amy. As she waited, she practiced what she was going to say to Amy. But Amy never showed up.

Drake came in a few minutes late and stuck close to Sierra. She was proud to be with him, being keenly aware of the looks some of the other girls were giving her and the way they watched Drake.

"Do you want to sit down?" Drake asked Sierra after she had introduced him to all her friends.

They settled down near the front just as Shane, the youth leader, called everyone to find a seat. Of medium height and muscular, Shane had a commanding voice and boundless energy.

"Hey, you guys! We're glad you're here," Shane boomed to the crowd. "Let's get going."

For the first twenty minutes, they sang, accompanied by Randy's band. The room seemed much fuller than it had in weeks past. The band helped to boost attendance, Sierra was sure, and it added to the liveliness of the songs.

"Short-term pleasure, long-term pain," Shane said as everyone sat down after the last song. "That's our topic tonight. Short-term pleasure, long-term pain. I want you to form small groups and discuss what that means to you."

Sierra turned to Drake, and he said, "It means what it says. Some things you do are enjoyable for the moment, but they produce painful results."

"Like eating chocolate," said Jana, the girl on the other side of Drake, who had welcomed herself into their little group. "Chocolate makes me happy while I'm eating it, but it doesn't do my body any good in the long run." Jana wore her blond hair cut short above her ears. She had a wide smile and a button nose. She was thick around the middle and shorter than Sierra.

"Any examples?" Shane asked after a few minutes, looking around the room. "How about this group here?" He motioned toward Sierra.

"Chocolate," Jana called out.

"Okay, good answer. Chocolate can be a short-term pleasure that can produce long-term pain. Good. Next group?"

As Shane collected more answers, Sierra thought about Amy.

*I should have called her instead of waiting and assuming she would show up,* she chided herself. *I should have called her just to let her know Drake would be here—kind of with me. Well, hopefully she'll be at the meeting afterward, and I can try to explain things to her then.*

"Okay," Shane said, pulling everyone's attention back to the front, "let's look at a verse I believe will help all of us. If you have your Bible with you, I suggest you underline this one. And if you didn't bring your Bible, bring it next week, okay? Anyone who doesn't have a Bible, let me know, and we'll get you one."

A rustling noise filled the room as people reached for their Bibles. Sierra felt bad. She had forgotten hers, and that wasn't like her. But tonight she had been so preoccupied that she had run out the door without it. She would listen closely, though, and remember the verse Shane read. That way when she got home, she could mark it in her Bible.

Actually, quite a few days had passed since she had spent time reading her Bible or praying. It was easy to rationalize that lapse, because with the beginning of summer, her schedule had changed and her life had become hectic. Sierra knew she needed that regular time talking to God and listening to Him to stay on track. She silently promised herself and God that she would read extra chapters tonight.

"Got your Bibles ready? Here's the verse: Hebrews 12:11. It says, 'All discipline for the moment seems not to be joyful, but sorrowful; yet to those who have been trained by it, afterwards it yields the peaceful fruit of righteousness.'"

For the next ten minutes, Shane talked about what discipline meant and how Christians needed to be trained in discipline to have peace with themselves and with God.

Sierra tried hard to listen, but she kept wondering if Drake was going to reach for her hand or slip his arm around her while Shane talked. She wasn't sure whether she wanted Drake's attention. Unfortunately, all the anticipation and subsequent disappointment kept her from hearing Shane's message. Sierra did remember the

Scripture reference, though, and she planned to mark it in her Bible when she got home.

After Shane closed the meeting in prayer, Randy and the band played again. Then all the people going on the backpacking trip went into another room to meet. Amy didn't show up, which worried Sierra.

Shane handed out a list of everything they needed to bring, along with a permission slip that had to be filled out by their parents before they left Monday morning. Ten minutes into the meeting, Wesley walked into the room.

Shane looked up with obvious relief. "Good. Wes is here. You guys, this is our other trip leader, Wes Jensen. He's our wilderness expert. Any questions, you can ask him."

Sierra gave Wes a look that reflected her surprise. He winked in return and started asking if everyone had proper hiking boots.

Sierra smiled ruefully. With Wes as a leader, Drake as her new boyfriend, and the tension she was experiencing with Randy and Amy, this was going to be some trip!

# twelve

AS SOON AS SIERRA GOT HOME, she phoned Amy. But Amy's voice mail picked up the call. Sierra tried again the next morning and got the machine a second time. Finally, exasperated, she drove over to Amy's house, and Amy answered the door.

"I called," Sierra said. "Why didn't you answer?"

"I was in the shower." Amy sounded defensive.

She led Sierra to her bedroom. On the wall behind Amy's bed hung a gorgeous old quilt stitched together from patchwork squares by Amy's grandma. The bed wasn't made, and belongings were scattered around the room—a clump of dirty clothes on the floor by the closet, a pile of papers on the desk, a stack of magazines by the bed with a half-empty glass of milk on top.

Sierra sat in the chair by Amy's desk and began to chat as if there were no reason for things to be strained between them.

"You're still going backpacking, aren't you? I missed you at the meeting last night."

"I had to fill in for a girl at work who called in sick. I don't know if I'm going backpacking after all." Amy avoided Sierra's eyes.

"Why not? We've been planning this for a long time. You already asked for time off from work, didn't you? I brought you a permission slip. It needs to be filled out by your parents before we leave Monday."

"I heard Drake is going." Amy arched her eyebrows, waiting for Sierra's response.

"Yes, he is. I've been trying to find the best way to tell you what's happening."

"Did he ask you out?" Amy asked.

"Yes. Tonight."

"So you're going out with him! Are you excited about it?" Amy looked as if she were happy for Sierra.

"Yes."

"That's great, Sierra." Amy smiled and adjusted some books stacked on her nightstand.

"Do you really mean that? You're not upset about this?"

"No. I told you. This is high school. You're supposed to go out with guys when they ask you. Or at least the ones worth going out with."

"Thanks for understanding," Sierra said, relieved. "I didn't want things to be strained between us now that Drake is going backpacking, too. Oh, and did I tell you? Wes is also coming."

Amy looked up. "He is?"

"Yes. Shane asked him to come along as an assistant. You didn't have anything to do with that, did you?"

Amy shrugged her shoulders. "I just suggested it a couple of times. You know that."

Sierra lowered her voice. "How are things with your parents?"

"They seem fine. As if nothing happened. I'm waiting for them to blow up again, you know?"

Sierra didn't know. Her parents didn't have that kind of relationship, so she couldn't understand what it was like to have to tiptoe around your own home, trying not to irritate someone who was already upset.

"I really appreciate your understanding about Drake. He's a great guy. Thanks for being so nice about everything."

Amy looked down. "Don't thank me. You're the one who attracted him. He was never interested in me. Anyway, it seems pretty clear you two are getting along great."

"God will have someone special for you, Amy. Just wait and see." Sierra couldn't believe she was saying those words. Over the years, she had heard other people using that line, and she hated it. Why did it seem natural to say it now? What was happening to her?

"I have to do some things this morning before I go to work," Sierra said, changing the subject. "I'm working till nine tonight. New hours Mrs. Kraus is trying out. Come see me if you can."

"I'm working from five to nine," Amy said. "And all day tomorrow."

"Then I guess I'll see you at church on Sunday." Amy smiled as Sierra left and said, "Have a good time with Drake."

"I will. Thanks."

Sierra hopped into her car and drove downtown to the Outback Store to get her supplies for the backpacking trip. She wished she could feel settled about Amy, but a thread of tension still hung between them. Amy seemed to be holding something back. Or was she only imagining it?

Next door to the Outback Store was a pharmacy. Sierra decided she needed to buy some items there first, things she had never bought before. The biodegradable soap could wait. She wanted to buy some makeup.

That night, after a quick shower, Sierra slipped into her favorite jean shorts and white cotton shirt. With bracelets, necklace, and earrings in place, she started to work on trying to tame her hair.

*This is pointless*, Sierra thought after a while. No matter what she did, her hair cascaded in unruly curls from the crown of her head down to the middle of her back. For years, other girls had admired Sierra's locks and said they would trade hair with her any day. She would have been only too glad to accommodate them.

Sierra wasn't so concerned about her hair tonight. She was too excited about the small bag of cosmetics she had bought at the pharmacy. This was an adventure for Sierra. The only times she had worn makeup were the scattered occasions when Tawni had imposed her cosmetic skills on her.

Tonight, though, she was on her own. Twirling the mascara wand the way she remembered Tawni had done it, Sierra started from the outside lashes and worked her way toward the inside lashes. Leaning toward the bathroom mirror with her mouth open in an O, Sierra made each stroke with slow, deliberate care. Stepping back and blinking slightly, she felt pleased. Her eyes did look bigger, just as Tawni had said. She finished with a little brown eyeliner the way Tawni applied it—thin and even, then softened with a Q-tip. So far, so good.

For lipstick, Sierra had bought a gloss with a natural red shade. She liked it immediately, not only for the way it highlighted her lips, but also for the way it smelled like fresh strawberries.

*I wonder if Drake will notice.*

Sierra felt herself blush slightly as she pictured Drake kissing her tonight. She stuck the tube of strawberry lip gloss in her pocket and gave herself a final look.

*Ready or not, Drake, here I come!*

# thirteen

IT WAS A GOOD THING Drake showed up on time. If Sierra had tried to contain her butterflies any longer, they would have started to escape out her ears.

"You look great," he said when she greeted him at the front door.

After a few last-minute reminders from Sierra's parents, she and Drake were on their way.

Instead of Drake's old, beat-up car, an expensive-looking blue sedan sat at the curb.

"It's my mom's car," he explained as he opened the passenger door. Sierra slid onto the clean upholstery. "I told her I wanted tonight to be special, and she said I could use it."

"That was nice of her."

"She's a nice mom," Drake agreed, getting in and fastening his seat belt. "Sure beats the delivery van."

Sierra laughed. "I'm glad you didn't pick me up in that!"

Before Drake started the engine, he reached over and

took Sierra's hand in his. In the shelter of his large, cool hand, Sierra realized how clammy hers had become. Hopefully, he wouldn't notice.

"How're you doing?" Drake smiled at her.

"Great!" Sierra said. She was startled to hear her voice squeak out. She cleared her throat. "Well, maybe a little nervous. It was kind of a full day."

Drake gave her hand a squeeze, then let go and turned the key in the ignition.

Sierra tried to organize all of her thoughts, which were flying around in her head like popcorn kernels: her feelings about herself, her looks, her outfit, her posture.

Should she try to sit closer to him? Was that last squirt of "Vanilla Earth Scents" too much? Should she roll down the window? Would it be tacky to pull down the visor mirror and make sure her mascara hadn't smeared?

"My day was pretty full, too," Drake said. "Three new accounts in the Powell district and none of the delivery bags were loaded in the van. I had to go back twice because I thought they were all newborn, but one was the twelve-to-eighteen-month size."

Sierra started to laugh.

Drake glanced at her, and then realized how trivial his stress sounded to her. "Yes, siree," he said with a tease in his voice, "haulin' diapers around town is a mighty tough job."

"But somebody's gotta do it, right?" Sierra said.

"It's probably not quite as stressful as getting the swirl-e-que just right on top of those yogurt cones, is it?"

Sierra laughed again and started to relax. "You have no idea. And then there's the mixed factor. Some customers

want the chocolate and vanilla swirled and others want only
chocolate or only vanilla. I tell you, it's completely exhaust-
ing."

Drake smiled. He liked her, she could tell.

"I bought the tickets before coming to your house."
Drake said. "I wanted to make sure they weren't sold out."

They parked at the theater and walked inside, still teasing each other about their hard day's work. His six-foot-two
frame towered above her as they stood in line for popcorn.
She loved being so much shorter than Drake. It made her
feel dainty. Randy was only a few inches taller than Sierra,
and when she held hands with him, she felt more like his
twin.

Drake led her to a center aisle in the theater, and with
their tub of popcorn and two large soft drinks, they maneuvered past four other people. Settling in, Sierra felt her
crazy emotions calm down. They balanced the popcorn
between them and began to munch away. The movie
started. Sierra wondered if Drake was going to hold her
hand. It would be difficult since she kept using that hand to
scoop up the popcorn.

Sierra began to eat faster. The sooner the popcorn was
gone, the sooner their hands would be empty. Drake
seemed to be in no hurry and ate only a small handful every
five minutes or so. Feeling like a pig, Sierra settled back,
slowly munching the popcorn at the same pace as Drake,
and enjoyed the movie.

"How did you like it?" Drake asked as they left the theater.

"Lots of action!" Sierra said, looking up at his clean-
shaven face in the light of the lobby. "It was good. I can't

remember what other show I saw the actress in, but I liked her in this role a lot better."

"You hungry?"

Sierra folded her hands across her stomach. "Are you kidding? After all that popcorn?"

"Something to drink maybe?"

"I'm with you. Wherever you want to go is fine with me."

Drake slipped his arm around her shoulder, and Sierra wrapped her arm around his waist. No one could have described to her how good it felt. She suddenly understood lyrics to love songs, comments from girlfriends, underlying themes from romance movies. There was no feeling like this in the world.

Drake drove to the Brewed Awakenings coffee shop, and they sat at a table outside. He had hot chocolate; she sipped tea. They talked about their families, their plans for college, their favorite cartoon characters, and what the lyrics meant to a song that played in the background.

Sierra liked the way Drake looked directly at her when she spoke, as if drinking in her words. Never before in her life had she felt as special and sought after as she did tonight.

Drake drove her home, laughing over a joke she told him. He pulled up in front of the house and turned off the engine. Sierra felt her heart racing. She wanted to reach for the strawberry lip gloss in her pocket but decided that that would be too obvious. She undid her seat belt. Drake undid his. He shifted in his seat. She shifted in hers. Certainly he would notice in the glow from the streetlight how rosy her cheeks were turning.

"Sierra," he said tenderly, reaching for her hand.

She linked fingers with his, hoping her wildly pounding heart would calm down.

"Before you go, I want to ask you something."

*This is it!* Sierra thought excitedly. *Drake is such a gentleman that he's even going to ask me before he kisses me, the way he asked Dad if he could take me out.*

With a slight smile, Sierra invited his question. "Yes?"

"I don't do this with every girl I go out with," Drake said. His slicked-back hair had fallen forward on the right side, giving him a vulnerable, schoolboy look. "But you're different, and if you don't mind..."

He squeezed her hand a little tighter. Sierra held her breath.

"Yes?"

"Will you pray with me?"

# fourteen

SIERRA SLOWLY began to breathe again. A big lump refused to go down her throat.

"Sure." She closed her eyes, swallowed hard, and licked her strawberry-less lips.

His words were brief but seemed to be heartfelt, as Drake thanked God for their time together and asked for his direction for each of their futures. By the time he said, "Amen," Sierra had come down from her cloud.

"Thanks," she said. "I had a wonderful time."

"So did I," he replied. "Let me get your door."

Sierra remembered what Amy had said about Drake opening the door for her. She didn't remember Amy's mentioning anything about praying with him, though. They walked to the front door, and before Sierra could let her exhausted imagination come up with all the possible scenarios of what might happen next, Drake smiled at her and said, "Good night." Then he turned and hustled to the car as if he were on a tight curfew to get home.

Sierra felt drained. Happy and sad at the same time.

Delighted and frustrated. She opened the door and heard the TV in the family room.

"Sierra?" her mom called out. "Did you have a good time?"

"Yes, it was wonderful. I'm going to bed." She headed upstairs, still lost in a daze. It wasn't that she didn't want to pray with Drake. She thought that was great. It made her realize, though, how long it had been since she had had a good, long conversation with God. What had happened? What had crowded her time so much?

Ten minutes later, as Sierra climbed into bed, her mother tapped on her door. "How did everything go?"

"It was totally wonderful. He laughed at my jokes, opened my door, bought me popcorn, and prayed with me. I think I'm in love."

Mrs. Jensen laughed. "Are you serious?"

"Actually, I don't know what I feel. He held my hand and prayed with me. I liked that. A lot. It was just different from what I expected."

"What did you expect?" her mom asked, stretching out on Tawni's bed.

Sierra felt embarrassed telling her mom, but they had always been honest about everything. "Well, I guess I thought he might kiss me."

"And he didn't?"

"No."

"What would his kiss have meant to you?"

"Meant to me? I don't know. That he liked me. That he wanted to go out with me again. That he thought I was attractive."

Her mom propped herself up on her elbow and rested

her head in her hand. "You don't think he felt those things without kissing you?"

Sierra thought hard. "He made me feel all those things. I guess I just expected a kiss. I don't know. My emotions were running around in my head all night like escaped zoo animals."

Mrs. Jensen laughed. "Sounds normal to me. And Drake sounds better than normal. I'm glad he didn't kiss you."

"Why?"

"It's better for your first kiss, or any kiss for that matter, to be given only after you know what you're giving away."

Sierra was silent.

"Good night, honey. I'm glad you had such a good time." She got up to leave. "Oh, Amy stopped by tonight. She had some questions for Wes about her backpack. He helped her get set for the trip. Are you almost ready?"

"I think so. Mom? Have you noticed that Amy finds reasons to be around Wes? I'm sure she has a crush on him."

"Yes," was all her mother said as she stood by the open door.

"Don't you think it's ridiculous? Wes would never like her back the same way. She's only setting herself up to be hurt."

"Have you told her that?"

"Not yet."

"Then don't," her mom said and exited, closing the door behind her.

Sierra snapped off her light and shook her head in the darkened room. How could her own mother say that? Then she smiled. She couldn't wait to replay the entire night in her mind, reliving each feeling, as she had Wednesday night after their walk to Mount Tabor. Then she remembered she'd planned to mark that verse from Hebrews in her Bible. But she felt so tired. It was as if her emotions, which had been running wild all night, were finally tucked away in their cages, safe and sound.

As Sierra closed her mascara-brushed lashes, she fell asleep.

# fifteen

MONDAY MORNING SIERRA and Wes were the first to arrive at the church parking lot wearing their camping gear and sporting their full backpacks.

"Wes," Sierra said, deciding to take advantage of the few moments they had alone, "I've been meaning to talk with you about something. You said last week that if I had anything I wanted to talk about, I could come to you."

Wesley looked interested. "Guy problems?"

"No. I wanted to warn you about possible girl troubles."

"Excuse me?"

Randy's white truck pulled into the parking lot and roared past Sierra and Wes. The three backpacks in the truck bed slid forward as Randy came to a halt. They could hear laughter from inside the cab as he turned off the engine. Randy opened one door while Drake opened the other and got out. Amy rolled out behind Drake, laughing the hardest of them all.

A lump formed in Sierra's throat. "I'll talk to you later," she mumbled to Wes.

"If you're going to tell me what I think you are, don't bother. I'm not that naïve, Sierra Mae." Wes rolled his eyes.

"Hi!" Drake called out. A donut was wedged between his front teeth like a dog bone.

Amy had powdered sugar all over her hair and a blob of jelly on her nose. She was still laughing as she approached Wes and Sierra.

"Don't ever agree to ride with those two," she warned. "Especially if they're armed with food."

The lump in Sierra's throat swelled. Who put the jelly on her nose? Randy? Was he suddenly interested in Amy now that Sierra and Drake were together? Or was it Drake? Was Amy flirting with Drake and was he flirting back? A dark cloud of horrible thoughts crossed Sierra's mind.

*I think I want to go home,* she thought.

"Donut?" Randy held out the open box to Sierra.

"No thanks." She sat down on the grass next to her backpack. Drake came over and put his backpack down next to hers.

"Sure you don't want one?" Drake asked. "They're fresh as a winter snowfall." With that he demonstrated the powdered sugar sprinkling from his donut, which accounted for Amy's dandruff outbreak.

"Here, Sierra," Randy said. "Sniff this jelly donut and tell me what it smells like to you."

He had a gleam of mischief in his eye.

"Don't do it!" Amy warned. "If you smell it, he'll smash it into your face." She wiped the jelly off her nose with her finger and bent down to clean it on the grass.

Sierra tried hard to smile and enter into their banter. But it was their joke. The three of them were having fun together. Sierra hadn't been a part of it. Why did that bother her so much? All four of them had goofed around in the lunchroom during the school year, yet somehow this felt different. She and Drake should be the ones sharing personal jokes, shouldn't they? So why was he playing tricks on Amy?

Shane arrived with a car full of backpackers. Two other cars pulled into the parking lot at the same time. After nearly an hour of organizing, everyone talking at once, and finally a group prayer, they loaded up in the church van and took off.

Randy and Drake were the first to clamber into the van, and they headed to the back bench seat. Sierra made sure she was the next one in and planted herself beside Drake. It bothered her that he didn't seem to wait for her; nor did it seem that he planned to save a seat for her next to him. What was going on?

"Do you mind changing spots with me?" Drake asked before they took off. "There's a little more legroom on the end."

Sierra obliged and scooted over between Randy and Drake while he slid past her and stretched out his legs in the narrow aisle.

*Now this is really strange, sitting between Randy and Drake,* she thought. *A week ago I would have been sitting next to Randy, probably holding his hand or sleeping on his shoulder. Now I'm with Drake, so is he going to put his arm around me? How will that feel with Randy sitting right there? Oh, why is my head pounding?*

As the van moved north on the freeway, Sierra momentarily solved her problems by folding her arms across her middle and sliding down in the seat. With her eyes closed, she pretended to be asleep as she tried to figure everything out.

She could hear Amy's voice carrying from the front where she sat behind Wes, who was in the front passenger seat. She peppered him with questions about backpacking technique—questions like, "How tightly should I adjust the straps? Will it hurt my back? Should the pack ride on my hips or my waist?"

Unlike Sierra, Amy definitely had hips for her pack to ride on. She also had a tiny waist, which was emphasized today by her choice of hiking apparel. The shorts weren't exactly durable fabric, and when she reached up, her clean white T-shirt rose just enough to show her belly button. Definitely not a practical choice for the day.

Sierra had been backpacking many times before and she knew what worked best. That's why she wore rugged, six-pocket green army shorts and a dark green T-shirt covered with one of her dad's old flannel shirts. Now that was practical.

So why did she feel like such a slob? And why was Drake ignoring her and talking to Jana in the seat in front of them? Jana had a pocket-sized game of Connect Four, and she and Drake played it all the way to the hiking trail.

Every time Sierra peeked at Randy, he was looking out the window and appeared to be lost in thought. As the van sped toward Mount Adams, Sierra let her own thoughts unwind like a long roll of paper towels. And like a roll of printed paper towels, the same pattern kept repeating itself in Sierra's mind. Not long rows of blue geese with pink ribbons on their necks, but long, connecting thoughts on how she felt about Drake and what he felt about her. The pattern of Randy and where his friendship fit in all this also ran through her mind. And every time Amy giggled, Sierra wondered if she had made such a terrific choice in a best friend after all.

The more Sierra listened to Drake and Jana play their game, the more she felt left out. *I should do something to make Drake pay attention to me. No, it's better this way,* she decided. *It's like we're together, but we're still friends with everyone else. I should talk to Randy then. But what if he thinks I'm trying to flirt with him? Randy doesn't know that Drake and I are together now, does he? What if he tried to hold my hand? Would he do that? Why isn't Drake holding my hand?*

"Ha!" Drake's voice cut through her thoughts. "I did it. Right there. I connected four."

Sierra wished she could find a way to connect four of her unsettled thoughts—especially before this backpacking group hit the trail. She knew what it was like to enjoy the beauty of God's world in the backcountry and, at the same time, feel as if even God's creation has turned against you. Hiking was not a time for resolving unsettled relationships. It was a time for everyone to work together as a team. The last thing Sierra felt was that she was a part of a team.

# sixteen

"TURN HERE," Wes told Shane. "The map says to park in the area by the Pacific Crest Trail. That's down this road."

The van bumped over the dirt road, and everyone joked and made noise as if they were on a ride at Disneyland.

"Over there," Wes directed. "It's on the north side. Keep going."

"This road is ridiculous!" Shane said as they hit another big bump.

Sierra looked out Randy's window at the mountain looming before them. "Is that the one that erupted?"

Randy turned to her. "No. This is Mount Adams. Mount Saint Helens is the one that blew her stack. I've been there a bunch of times with my dad because he's worked on different geology teams, but I've never been here."

"I didn't know your dad was a geologist," Drake said, leaning close to Sierra and looking out Randy's window. "Are you the experienced nature boy when it comes to living in the wild?"

"Something like that," Randy said, his lopsided smile

appearing for the first time since the trip began.

"What about you, Sierra?" Drake asked. "Didn't you grow up near Lake Tahoe?"

Sierra nodded and leaned back, aware of how near he was to her and how equally close she was to Randy. They hit another bump, and her head banged against Drake's shoulder.

"Oops, sorry," she mumbled.

Drake slipped his arm around her shoulders as if he were a human seat belt. "Go ahead. What were you going to say?"

"I don't remember," Sierra said, realizing their relationship had now been revealed.

She glanced over at Randy. He turned his head and looked out the window.

"Did your family do a lot of camping and backpacking while you were growing up?" Drake asked her.

"Yes, but Wes is more of a pro than I am. So is Randy."

She hoped Randy would turn to them and come back into the conversation. He didn't.

"I'm sticking with you guys," Drake said, giving Sierra's arm a little squeeze. "You want to hear a confession? This is my first backpacking trip."

"I'm sure you'll like it," Sierra said.

"I've only been camping once. My dad's idea of roughing it is staying at a hotel that doesn't have cable," Drake joked.

Sierra laughed. Randy didn't.

The van came to an abrupt halt.

"This is the place," Shane said. "Now, I want everyone to help unpack the trailer."

They filed out, and their laughter tumbled out of the van with them. Sierra pitched in and hoisted packs out of the trailer. Many of the girls were giggling and standing around, admitting they weren't sure how to put on their packs and asking the guys to help them.

"Don't look at me," Drake said to Jana. "I'm the novice here. Ask Sierra. She's our nature woman."

"What do I do with this strap, Nature Woman?" Jana asked.

"That's for you to hang a water bottle or canteen on. Did you bring one?"

"No." Jana looked embarrassed.

"It was on the list," Sierra said.

"I know, but we didn't have one at home."

"I brought extra water bottles," Shane said, stepping into their conversation. "Who needs one?"

Five people responded, "I do."

Sierra caught her brother's glance, and she could tell he felt the same way she did about this trip. Shane hadn't said if he had done much backpacking, but he clearly was glad when Wes agreed to come along. Sierra was glad Wes was there, too. She had looked at the maps Wes was given the night before and was relieved to see it was an easy hike. Only twelve miles total and a gain of less then 2,000 feet in elevation.

The elevation at the trailhead was marked 4,750 feet. The morning air was still cool. Sierra hitched up her wool socks and stomped her heavy hiking boots on the heels.

"Is this an old Indian tradition?" Drake teased, imitating her heel stomping. "You look like a thoroughbred ready to race."

Her heart did some racing of its own as she looked up and read the kind expression in his eyes. "You ready?"

"I think so. I've been looking forward to this."

*I've been looking forward to this, too,* Sierra thought. *And I'm excited about spending time with Drake. But is he still glad we're together?*

Shane's voice interrupted her thoughts. "Okay, everybody, listen up. The hike this morning is nice and easy. We're only going about two miles. We'll stop at a place called Lava Spring. Stay on the trail. Stick together. I'll lead, and Wes will bring up the rear. If Wes passes you, you're in trouble."

"Roger-dodger, Ranger Rocky," one of the younger guys said.

Everyone laughed, and Shane called out, "Head 'em up, moo-oove 'em out!" Sierra waited for all the eager hikers to fall in line behind Shane. She knew it was a safe guess that Amy would be the last person before Wesley. Randy took off down the trail, and Drake waited for Sierra. The trail was too narrow to walk side by side, so Sierra went first with Drake behind her followed by Amy and Wes.

The trail's beginning provided an easy descent. As they hiked, the group's spirits were high and so were their voices, filling the valley and frightening any form of wildlife that might be within a mile of the trail. Sierra was frustrated. She had learned to hike silently, observing the beauty around her and listening for new sounds.

The only new sounds she heard on the trip, though, were Amy's questions for Wes.

"Is this strap supposed to rub on my shoulder like this? Do I have this buckled too tightly? Was I supposed to put the moleskin you gave me on my heels before we left, or do I put it on after I have blisters?"

Sierra wished she and Drake could walk behind Wes and take their time enjoying this gently valley. Before them spread acres of wild lupine, covering the wilderness like a royal-blue carpet. The way was dotted with pine trees, which framed a spectacular view of Mount Adams. The late-morning clouds lifted, and the great mountain jutted into the heavens in all its snowcapped glory. Sierra wished she had brought her camera to capture this sight, this feeling. A faint, familiar song began to rise within her heart. Having been born and raised in the mountains, Sierra couldn't help but feel as if she were coming home.

Glancing over her shoulder, Sierra caught the look on Wesley's face when the mountain came into clear view. He felt the same thing. She could tell.

Inside she laughed to herself. *We're like Peter and Heidi on our way to see the grandfather. All we need is a couple of goats and a girl in a wheelchair.*

The morning hikers all made it to Lava Spring without incident. When Sierra arrived, Shane and some of the other guys were peeling off their shirts and shoes, ready to go wading. "It's going to be cold," Randy warned them. "That water was snow this morning."

Shane was the first to plunge his foot in. He let out a whoop. "You weren't kidding!"

"You know," Wes said, speaking to Shane in a way that didn't put him on the spot, "I'm not so sure it's a good idea to pollute the water like that when it's so close to its natural source."

"Are you saying my feet are a source of pollution?" Shane teased. "Okay, you guys. Wes is right. We'd better not go in. I can tell you, it's freezing."

Sierra loosened her pack's arm straps and released the waistband. Before she could take it off, someone took hold of the side frame and helped her out. It was Drake.

"Thanks," Sierra said. "You want help with yours?"

"No, I got it. Thanks anyway. That was an awesome trail, wasn't it?"

Before Sierra could agree, they heard a squeal behind them. Amy had plopped down without taking off her pack, and she was now lying like an overturned beetle, with arms and legs flailing but getting nowhere.

"Somebody help me! Wesley! I'm stuck. You guys, this isn't funny!"

Sierra smiled. For the second time that morning she wished she had her camera.

# seventeen

THE HIKERS DECIDED TO EAT lunch at Lava Springs and
then head farther down the trail before setting up camp.
Sierra stretched out in the midday sun beside Drake and
savored her teriyaki beef jerky. She loved the sun on her
face, the salty taste of jerky, and the sound of Drake's deep
voice telling her about the time he had tried to catch a bird
when he was a kid.

Sierra noticed that Randy had taken off and was eating
by himself down by the stream. Amy was seated next to Wes
so he could examine her heels for blisters.

"That's all we get to eat?" Jana asked, sitting down next
to Drake. "Don't we have sandwiches or anything?"

"Nope," Sierra said. "The food they gave you to carry
this morning is all you get for the whole trip. Hopefully
we'll catch some fish tonight. The map shows a fairly wide
stream up ahead."

"I thought the trail mix stuff was just for snacks. I don't
even like nuts."

"You want some of my jerky?" Sierra offered.

"I don't mean to complain, but I don't really like jerky either. It's too chewy."

"You need to eat something," Wes said, walking over to their group. "And drink a lot of water. You can get dehydrated pretty quickly as this altitude."

"Isn't it beautiful?" Sierra asked Wes.

He took a long swig from his canteen and glanced around them. "This would be a great campsite for tonight. The trail ascends from here." He motioned over his shoulder. "Makes for chillier nights."

Sierra wondered if Wes was finding it hard to be a follower on this trip when in so many ways he might have been a more competent leader than Shane. If he felt that way, he didn't show it. And he was sure being nice to Amy as she followed him around.

The group hit the trail half an hour later, and Wes quietly took up the rear as Shane led them uphill and across a log bridge over a silty stream. The bugs were thick, so Sierra smeared her face, hands, and legs with repellent. She put on her baseball cap and pulled down the sleeves on her flannel shirt. Even though the mosquitoes flocked to her, the repellent worked well. Only one bite appeared on the back of her left hand.

Sierra watched Drake's red backpack sway as he hiked ahead of her this time. She set aside her happy mountain-girl feelings long enough to let some of her insecurities rise again. Over the last few days, she had been overwhelmed with emotions. Her feelings had taken over everything, and she was experiencing for the first time how strong they could be.

She didn't feel good about the way Randy and Amy were ignoring them. Did it have to be that way once a couple started going together?

She thought of how her feelings for Drake were different from what she had felt about Randy. *Randy was like my training wheels,* Sierra decided. *He helped to break me into this whole world of dating. He helped me keep my balance when I was just starting off. Now I can go on my own.*

Sierra liked her analogy. As the trail led into a peaceful forest of tall silver firs, Sierra pictured what it would be like tonight around the campfire, nestled in Drake's arms. Maybe they would go for a little walk and sit together on a rock, watching for shooting stars. He would kiss her, and it would be perfect—the most romantic first kiss a girl ever had.

"Wait till you see this!" Drake said. He was standing on a small rise in the forest trail a few yards ahead of her.

She caught up with him and gazed out at the sun-kissed meadow where thousands of brightly dressed wildflowers waved in the afternoon breeze, welcoming Sierra and Drake to their corner of the world.

"Wow," Sierra agreed. "It's beautiful. I love it!"

"I thought you would," Drake said, reaching over and taking her hand in his. It felt warm and strong. Drake held her hand tightly and said, "You're really at home here, aren't you?"

Sierra nodded, her eyes still drinking in the beauty stretched out before them. If she didn't have the bulky pack on, Sierra imagined Drake would wrap his arms around her and pull her close. Even though her face was covered with sticky bug repellent, Drake would look into her eyes and tell her she was enchanting, just like the meadow, and then...

"Are we taking a break? Tell me we're taking a break." Amy came up behind them with Wes and prepared to take off her pack.

"We're admiring the view," Drake said, casually letting go of Sierra's hand. "The others are way ahead of us."

"Can't we rest for a minute?"

"It's better if we keep going," Wes advised, adjusting the brim of his hat and surveying the meadow. "Wow. That's incredible."

"What's incredible?" Amy asked.

"Those flowers. The meadow. That view."

Amy took a glance and then looked down at her shoes. "Yeah, it's nice. My feet say it's time for a rest."

"Come on," Sierra said. She was glad Amy was at least sort of talking to them. "Let's keep going." She wondered if Wes had noticed that she and Drake had been holding hands. *Why should it matter anyway?* she thought.

The four of them hiked silently while Sierra returned to her thoughts. This was all new to her—guys, dating, dreams, hopes, and wishes. She hoped she could talk everything through with Amy once they set up their tent. Amy would understand her feelings since she'd had several boyfriends before. And Amy might have some good advice for Sierra on how to keep her friendship with Randy even though she was Drake's girlfriend.

The trail continued to ascend. When they finally met up with the rest of the group at Green Timber Camp, Sierra was tired.

But now the real work began. They had to clear the ground, set up their tents, start a fire, and catch some fish for dinner. Fortunately, the group was still in high spirits, for the most part, which helped the tent setup go quickly.

Sierra was surprised when Amy told her she had decided to share Jana's tent with her.

"Nothing personal," is all Amy said.

Sierra couldn't help but feel it was something personal. Even though Amy said everything was fine about Drake, she had turned aloof and barely made eye contact with Sierra.

As soon as Sierra had her tent up and sleeping bag rolled out, she grabbed her biodegradable soap and her cup and headed for the stream. So what if she didn't have Amy's or even Randy's friendship? She had Drake's, and that's what she really wanted.

Following the process her dad had taught her, Sierra filled her cup with the clear, cold water and walked away from the stream, where she used the soap to wash her hands, face, and neck. Then she rinsed with the cup of water and shook her hands to let them air dry. Pulling a clean bandana from her back pocket, she patted her face and neck. Sierra took a deep breath, feeling the cool mountain breeze sweep across her face.

"All fresh and friendly now?" a voice behind her asked.

"Drake! I didn't see you sneak up on me."

"I wasn't sneaking. You have some extra soap there?" He held up his mud-caked hands. "I feel like a slob."

Sierra held out her cup and the small bottle of liquid soap. She felt like telling Drake he didn't look like a slob to her. He fit the image of a mountain man, with his thick hair all windblown and a strip of sunburn across his nose. Teasing him, she said, "You look like the creature from the mud lagoon."

Drake made a zombie face and came lumbering toward her, his muddy palms poised to make contact with her clean face.

"Don't even try it," she said, laughing and standing her ground with her hands on her hips. Drake swooped toward her and grabbed her around the waist, hoisting her over his shoulder the way Wes used to do. Sierra couldn't believe how strong he was.

"Put me down, you big, scary monster," Sierra yelled, laughing and pounding Drake's back with her fists.

"Down?" Drake asked, heading for the water.

"No, don't!" Sierra squealed. Drake stopped right at the water's edge. "Oh, I forgot." He put her down, keeping his arms around her waist. "We don't want to pollute the water, do we?"

"That's right," Wes said from behind them.

They both turned, startled to see him standing there. *Did he see the whole thing?* Sierra wondered. She felt as if she had to explain that they were only playing around. But then, this was Wes, and they hadn't done anything wrong.

Drake dropped his arms from around Sierra's waist, and she walked away from the stream and sat in the dry grass. Wes quietly went about washing up. Drake lathered up with soap and was about to plunge his hands into the stream when Wes stopped him.

"Fill the cup with water and rinse away from the stream. You never want to dirty the water you might drink."

With an understanding nod, Drake followed Wesley's instructions and watched as he demonstrated. After rinsing off, Wes pulled a bandana from his back pocket, making good use of it as a towel before tying it around his clean neck.

"You know," Wes said, "the laws of nature tend to apply to other areas of life as well. That's certainly true here."

Drake looked at Sierra and then back at Wes. "I think I missed the point."

Wes scratched his chin. A sly grin edged up the corners of his mouth. "Most people do."

Drake gave Sierra a confused look.

"What are you babbling about, Wesley?" Sierra said, irritated. All she wanted Wes to do was leave so she and Drake could be alone.

"It's simple. Don't dirty the water. Even if you're not going to drink it later, someone else will." Wes turned to go, then added, "It's never right to spoil something pure."

# eighteen

"WHAT WAS THAT SUPPOSED TO MEAN?" Drake asked, sitting down next to Sierra in the tall, wild grass.

Her heart pounded, and her eyes followed her brother as he trekked back to camp, whistling as he went. She knew exactly what Wes meant. Their dad had used the same analogy once when they were backpacking and he was trying to explain to Cody why he and Katrina should remain pure with each other even though they planned to marry. Sierra was too young at the time to understand why Dad was telling Cody not to "muddy the water you're going to drink."

But she understood everything now. She was pure and innocent and had never been kissed, and in his big-brother way, Wes was warning Drake to not be the one to change any of that.

*What if I'm the one who wants to change that? What difference is one kiss going to make?* Sierra thought defiantly. *I want Drake to kiss me, and I don't care what Wes says.*

"Don't pay attention to him," Sierra told Drake.

"Is he with the Environmental Protection Agency or something?"

"Something like that," Sierra said, viewing herself as the environment and Wes as the protector. "So, how do you like backpacking?"

"Even better than I thought. You were right." Drake leaned back, laced his fingers behind his head and tilted his freshly washed face toward the sky. "It's so different out here. The sounds, the colors, even the way the sun seems so much closer. It's beautiful."

Then, turning toward Sierra, he reached over and touched one of the long curls hanging over her shoulder. "And so are you," Drake said softly. "But then, you knew that, didn't you?"

Sierra felt as if Drake's compliment had suddenly caused her insides to overflow with joy. No guy had ever said anything like that to her.

"No," she admitted shyly.

Drake smiled, twisting her curl between his thumb and forefinger. "Keep pretending you don't know how beautiful you are, Sierra. It's better that way." He let go of her hair, sat up, and stretched his arms over his head, trying to pull the kinks from his shoulders.

"Drake," Sierra asked, sitting up, "are you still glad we're going out?"

"Of course. Why?"

"I don't know. Do you think people treat us differently?"

"You mean like your brother?"

"Like everyone."

Drake shrugged. "Who cares if they do? Can you rub this shoulder? I have a knot right there," he said, pointing.

Sierra got on her knees behind Drake and started to

massage his shoulder. He was right. There was a big knot.

"Try turning your head to the side," Sierra said. She had had plenty of experience pounding out her brothers' sore muscles. Drake appreciated her expertise.

"How's that?" Sierra asked, after her hands began to cramp.

"Fantastic. You're much better at that than most girls," Drake said. "You want me to rub your shoulders?"

Sierra thought it would be wonderful to feel Drake's strong hands rubbing her shoulders. But when he said the words "most girls" she suddenly felt uncomfortable. It made her feel as if she was only one of many girlfriends. Not special and unique and only Sierra.

"That's okay," she said after a pause. "I'm doing all right."

"I guess we'd better go see if we can help catch some dinner."

He stood and offered Sierra a hand up. Pulling her to himself, Drake wrapped his arms around her in a close hug.

Her emotions plummeted. Instead of feeling warm and full of dreams about Drake giving her her first kiss, Sierra felt smothered. Caught. She slowly pulled away.

"You all right?" he asked.

"Yeah. I just feel kind of grungy. You know, all that hiking and the bug repellent and everything."

"You smell as sweet as a flower to me."

Sierra couldn't say the same thing about Drake. His face and hands may have been washed, but the rest of him had smelled a little gamy when her face had been against his chest. It wasn't how she expected it to feel at all.

Drake tilted her chin up toward him with his finger. His

smile showed his tenderness. "Hey, I'm not trying to rush you or anything," he said.

"I know. You're not."

She felt nervous and painfully inexperienced. Drake obviously wasn't.

"You want to go back?" Drake asked.

"We probably should."

They walked to camp hand in hand. When the others saw them arrive, Sierra couldn't help but blush, even though she knew she had done nothing to be embarrassed about.

Drake put together his fishing gear and took off with Wes. They both asked Sierra to come, but she told them to go ahead; she would catch up later. She wanted to be alone for a little bit.

Heading away from the campsite, Sierra found a boulder with a smooth surface and perched herself on it. The rock felt warm and soothing to her troubled soul. Gathering her knees up and hugging them tightly, she began to cry.

*What is wrong with me? I've been so happy the past few days, and now I'm falling apart!*

For nearly an hour, Sierra sat alone, crying, thinking, and offering up tattered bits of prayers. This was so unlike her. Usually she had everything figured out. Talking to God was as natural as breathing. Now she felt confused. Her mind swelled with doubts. Doubts about herself. About Drake. About her friendship with Amy and Randy and even about her relationship with God. Her only companion was that familiar voice in the back of her head saying, *Sierra, do you know what you're doing?*

Sierra gave in. For the first time, she admitted, "No, I don't know what I'm doing. Will You teach me, Father? Show me Your way. I need You."

She felt relieved when, a few minutes later, she heard Wesley's deep voice calling her, drawing her back to the campsite. The sun had ducked behind a grove of hemlocks, and the evening breeze turned noticeably more chilly as Sierra entered the camp. She retreated to her empty tent and put on a pair of fleece sweats over her shorts and pulled on her bulky jacket.

Three small, silver-scaled fish lay on the grill over the open fire.

"I still don't see how those three fish are going to feed all of us," Jana complained. "Unless this is a reenactment of that Bible story where Jesus multiplied the food."

"He won't have to," Amy said. "You can have my share."

She and Jana were sitting close to the fire, sharing an open sleeping bag across their shoulders.

"Didn't you two bring jackets?" Shane asked.

"Mine's too scratchy," Jana said. "And hers doesn't match."

They laughed and glanced at Sierra but didn't say anything to her.

Sierra had imagined herself sitting by Drake tonight, leaning against his broad chest. But Drake had seated himself next to Shane, and they were talking earnestly about the next portion of the trip. Sierra ended up standing to the side with Wes, moving each time the unpredictable smoke changed its course. She stood as she ate. Speaking little.

As the first stars made their stunning debut in the cloud-streaked sky, Shane announced that they were going to have a Bible study around the campfire. Sierra retrieved her Bible from her tent and sat down behind Drake. He turned around and invited her to scoot closer to the fire. She gladly obliged since closer to the fire meant closer to Drake. She could feel Amy and Wes watching her from across the fire ring. All the rumbling, unsettled feelings started up again in the pit of her stomach.

*I'm not doing anything wrong!* She silently argued with their stares.

Shane started to talk. "I thought we would discuss relationships tonight. Our relationship with God and with others. Let's open with prayer, okay?"

Sierra leaned a little closer to Drake as everyone bowed their heads. She hoped he would take her hand the way he had when they prayed together in the car the other night. But instead of reaching for her hand, or even acknowledging that her arm was only a breath from his, Drake shifted his position away from her. Rather than feeling Drake's sheltering arm around her shoulders, Sierra was aware of a chilly night breeze passing between them.

# nineteen

MOST OF WHAT SHANE had to say around the fire were things Sierra had heard before or thought before: Save yourself for your future mate. Hold out for a hero. Become the kind of guy worthy of a princess. Trust God to bring the right person into your life at the right time.

It was all future oriented, such as planning for marriage. What about right now? Why didn't anyone ever talk about the right way to start dating? Or how to understand changing emotions?

As if Shane had heard her thoughts, he pulled a slip of paper from his Bible and said, "This is a quote from C. S. Lewis. It helped me a lot when I was trying to decide God's will for me when my emotions were overruling my logic."

By the glow of his flashlight, he read, "Feelings come and go, and when they come, a good use can be made of them, but they cannot be our regular spiritual diet."

Sierra loved C. S. Lewis and had read many of his books. She thought he was a brilliant man. Even though the quote didn't sound familiar, she knew about feelings. She had been deluged with them the past week. Sierra could honestly say she'd never known her emotions could be so powerful. She wished she had someone to explain them to her.

Shane closed by challenging them to write out what they thought God wanted for them in a relationship. "Otherwise," he said, "when it comes to dating or anything else in life, it's like taking a dart and throwing it at that tree and then going over and drawing a circle around the dart and telling yourself you hit the mark."

Shane closed in prayer, and everyone retreated to their tents to warm up. But Sierra lingered by the fire, hoping Drake would stick around, too. He left with Randy and Wes, and all three said good night to Sierra, practically in unison. She sat alone for a few minutes, scanning the night sky for a familiar constellation. The clouds had increased, and only a few random stars shone through. It wasn't possible to guess which constellation they belonged to since they were out on their own. Sierra felt the same way—the lonely leftover.

She could hear Amy and Jana talking softly in Jana's tent a few yards away. Some of the guys burst out laughing in their tent. Sierra retreated to her lonely abode and crawled into her sleeping bag. A dozen thoughts and feelings circled her head, buzzing like a toy airplane on a shoestring.

*Why did Drake pull away from me at the fire? Was it because I pulled away from him down at the creek? Or did Shane's talk make him think we needed to set better goals for our relationship? Maybe he was trying to be sensitive because I said I thought people were treating us differently.*

As the rest of the camp settled down, Sierra's thoughts kept spinning. *Wes must have said something to him when they were fish-*

*ing.* Sierra camped on that thought a long time and concluded, *That's probably what happened. I'd better have a talk with that
overly well-meaning brother of mine.*

Fumbling for her flashlight and sticking her stocking
feet into her cold boots, Sierra quietly slipped out of her
tent and tiptoed to the guy's area. She remembered Drake
and Randy setting up a tent close to the trail. Her flashlight
revealed only one pair of boots outside a small tent. That
had to be Wesley's.

"Wes," She whispered, crouching down and slowly
unzipping the opening. "I have to talk to you." She slipped
inside and cautiously reached for his foot at the end of his
sleeping bag, giving it a playful yank and saying, "It's me—
Sierra. Are you awake?"

"Harumpf," he mumbled.

"Wake up, will you? I need to talk to you."

"What's wrong?" the sleepy voice asked.

She had her flashlight pointed toward the front of the
tent because she knew how much Wes hated people to shine
flashlights in his face. In the muted light, she saw him prop
himself up. He looked as if he had a stocking cap on his head.

"You said something to Drake, didn't you?" she whispered, hoping none of the people in the nearby tents were
still awake and could hear her.

"Huh?"

"Well, just listen to me, okay? Don't cut in and try to
give me advice. Just hear me out, because I've been giving
this a lot of thought."

Sierra adjusted her scrunched-up, cross-legged position at the foot of his sleeping bag, and with a deep breath,
she plunged in.

"I think I've been running on emotions lately, you know? Everything I've done or said has been based on how I felt. It's like I'm being swept away by my emotions, and I don't even know what I truly feel anymore."

She ran her hands through her unruly hair and said, "For instance, when Randy and I started to hold hands, I liked it. I loved the attention."

"Sierra," he whispered.

"Let me finish, okay?" She had intended to yell at her brother for whatever it was he said to Drake. Now here she was, pouring her heart out to him. "What I'm realizing is that I loved the attention more than I loved Randy. Not that I loved Randy, or that I thought I loved him and now I don't, but I mean...well, you know what I mean. The attention was more important than who it was coming from. Well, when Drake came over that night, he put his arm around me, and that felt even better than with Randy, you know? My feelings kept growing, and then all I could think of was whether Drake was going to kiss me."

"Sierra," he whispered again.

"Don't worry, Mr. Don't-Pollute-the-Water. He didn't kiss me. But I really, really wanted him to. And then, after you left the stream, I don't know why, but everything changed. I suddenly didn't want him to kiss me."

Sierra caught a quick breath and said, "He told me I was beautiful today. Do you know what that does to a woman when a guy tells her she's beautiful? I felt like I could follow him to the ends of the earth just because he paid attention to me and made me feel wonderful. Then everything flip-flopped inside of me, and I realized I didn't want to be one of his many girlfriends. Do you know what I mean? My feelings totally changed. It's like Shane's quote from Lewis. I've had a steady diet of all my feelings and nothing else. I haven't been reading my Bible, and when I try to pray, my mind wanders. I'm full of all these feelings, but you know what, Wes? I feel so empty."

He reached his hand out of the sleeping bag and gently touched her arm. "Sierra," he whispered more urgently.

"I'm such a jumble of feelings, Wes. Last week Mom told me to show her what I'm made of, and I think I'm discovering that I'm full of mush. All feelings and no substance at all."

"That's not true," he said, sitting up. Something was funny about his voice. "Listen, I've been trying to tell you—"

Sierra reached for her flashlight and shone it in the face of the man who had been hearing her confession. Her heart stopped. Before Sierra could shriek, Randy leaned over and covered her mouth with his hand.

# twenty

"SHH," RANDY URGED, his hand still over her mouth. "Don't say anything. I'm going to take my hand away, but you have to promise me you won't say a word."

Sierra nodded. Her heart was pounding in her throat. *How could he have let me say all those things? I told him everything! This is so humiliating!*

"Now it's your turn to listen to me," Randy whispered. "Don't say anything. Just listen."

He sat in front of her, the flashlight now tilted toward the back of the tent.

"I think you're right about your emotions being in control, Sierra. But don't beat yourself up just because you're a sensitive, emotional person."

"Randy," she whispered.

"Shh. Let me finish. We're all learning. I have to admit I was getting pretty emotionally involved when we started to hold hands. I'm glad I got to hear what you just said because now I know it meant something different to you. I was starting to think we were more than friends. I didn't know you liked Drake so much."

"Randy," she tried again.

"I'm not done. What I want to say is, don't start using guys to build your self-esteem. It's not fair to us. I think you've already decided it's Drake you want. Fine. Just know you can't have it both ways. If you go with him, I'm out of the picture."

"Randy, you're my buddy."

"Not the way I have been. Not if you have a boyfriend. I wouldn't do that to you or Drake."

"Do what?"

"You really don't get it, do you?" Randy said.

Sierra started to feel angry. Hadn't she just poured out her soul, expressing how confused and mush-headed she felt? Why did he have to throw it back at her? Fresh tears welled up, and her lower lip began to quiver. Refusing to let Randy see her cry, Sierra took the easiest way out—she camouflaged her hurt with anger.

"Just forget everything, Randy. Forget we had this talk. You're the one who doesn't understand."

He reached over and took her arm in an effort to calm her down. "Sierra," he said.

She jerked away from him and scrambled to get through the closed tent entrance. As she gave the zipper a yank, she caught her hair in it and let out a muffled yelp.

"Wait," Randy said. He leaned forward, fumbling to help with the zipper, not knowing her hair was caught.

"Don't!" Sierra snapped. She leaned too far against the side of the tent, and the whole side began to sag. "Randy!" She called out, just as the tent caved in on them.

The flashlight was buried in the fall, and so in utter darkness and confusion, Randy and Sierra clamored over each other trying to set things right. "My hair," Sierra cried. "Let go of my hair."

"I haven't got your hair! Get off my leg. I can't move."

"My hair's caught in the zipper. Ouch! There, I got it loose. Randy? Where did the main pole go?"

"I can't see a thing. You're blocking the light."

"I am not. You're sitting on it."

From outside, Wes's voice boomed above their squabbling. "What's going on in there?"

"Get me out of here!" Sierra pleaded.

Other voices joined Wes's. "Is that Sierra in there with Randy?"

"I thought the girls were supposed to stay out of the guys' tents."

"What's she doing with Randy? I thought she was going with Drake."

"Somebody shine a light over here," Shane said.

Within three seconds, the area around the tent lit up with half a dozen spectators' flashlights. Sierra found the zipper and opened the tent the rest of the way so she could crawl out. A dozen curious faces loomed above the searching flashlights.

"Sierra," Wes said, sounding exactly like their dad when he was mad, "what were you doing? You know the rules."

"I thought it was your tent," Sierra said, wiping back a runaway tear.

"I tried to tell her," Randy called from inside the collapsed tent.

"Why did you want to get in my tent? To steal my socks?"

"No," Sierra said, glancing at the audience and then

back at Wes. "I wanted to talk to you. I thought it was your tent, and I didn't think the rule applied if I was talking to my brother."

"In the middle of the night?" Shane asked.

"It was important."

"I can vouch for that," Randy called out. "It was important."

"Randy, don't say anything," Sierra pleaded. "You guys, can we forget this ever happened? It's freezing out here."

"Okay," Shane conceded. "Everyone back to bed. Their own beds."

As the group dispersed, Sierra could only imagine what they were all thinking. Especially Randy. And Drake.

She turned, and Drake stood before her.

"Are you okay?" he asked quietly.

Sierra couldn't see his expression in the dark, but she couldn't miss his broad chest wrapped in a down jacket.

"Where were you?" For some reason she felt mad at Drake. This whole mess was his fault.

"I switched tents. There was more legroom in with Wes." He turned his flashlight toward her feet. "Come on, I'll walk you home." He accompanied her the twenty or so feet back to the girls' side and to her "front door."

"Is everything all right?" he whispered.

"I don't know."

She scooted into her tent before Drake could ask any more questions. Right now she didn't want to talk to anyone, except maybe God.

# twenty-one

AFTER A RESTLESS NIGHT, Sierra woke with cold feet and a cold nose. She had placed the hood of her sleeping bag over her head sometime during the night and pulled the drawstring so only her nose stuck out. Fiddling to undo the thing, she noticed she could see her breath.

Reluctantly, Sierra wiggled out of her warm sleeping bag and unzipped the door of her tent. Smoothing back her mane of matted curls, she poked her head out, ready to greet the new day. The new day greeted her right back with tickles of snowflakes on her upturned face. A light, powdered-sugar dusting of snow covered the campsite. All the tents bore a fine layer of snow on their seam lines, and the tree boughs looked flocked and ready for a Christmas tree lot. The campsite had turned into a fairy world.

Wes was the only one out of his tent. He wore his bandana around his head like a pirate and was trying to start a fire.

Sierra had slept in all her warm clothes and jacket so the only items to put on were her baseball cap and her boots, which were extremely cold. Shuffling through the silent wonderland, she joined Wes and gave him her best smile.

"Hi," she said.

"Hi."

"Am I in trouble?"

"When are you not in trouble?" Wes teased.

Sierra fed kindling into his smoldering attempt at a fire.

"What did you want to talk to me about last night?"

Sierra looked over her shoulder to make sure no one else was up. "Guys and feelings and being all mixed up."

"You're just discovering what a basket case you are?"

Sierra playfully punched her brother in the arm.

"Do it again," he said. "That felt warm."

"I'm serious. Will you help me figure all this out?"

Wes gave her a crinkle-eyed smile. "Of course." He put his arm around her, gave her a squeeze, and kissed her on top of her baseball cap. "This is a big step for you, isn't it? Asking for help, I mean. You're usually so independent."

Sierra nodded and snuggled closer to him for warmth.

"Last night while I was trying to sleep, I realized I was being too independent because I was separating God from a whole area of my life. I wasn't getting off to a very good start at dating."

"It's never too late to start over. His mercies are new every morning, you know."

Sierra looked up through the trees at the stuffed cotton sky and tried to catch a snowflake on her tongue.

"I hope my friends feel that way, too."

Behind them, they heard a tent unzip.

"Hey, it snowed!" Shane exclaimed. "Wake up, every-body. We have to get off this mountain."

They broke camp immediately, packed up, and began the steady descent back the way they had come. The wind sliced their face, which made the going difficult and the group silent. It was quite a contrast to their hike the day before. The trip was supposed to last another day, with their making camp three miles up the trail at the 6,000-foot elevation. That wasn't a good idea now.

Sierra and Wes seemed to be the only two who were comfortable with the snow and perhaps the only hikers prepared for the cold. Sierra encouraged the others to keep eating as they hiked and to drink even if they didn't feel thirsty. Wes briefed them on the early signs of hypothermia and made sure everyone started out with dry clothes.

The strenuous journey back provided Sierra with a lot of time to think. In some ways, this hike symbolized her adventure into dating. She realized she had entered into the experience with a light heart, enjoying every bit of it as she went along. Retracing her steps in the wind and snow made her think of three potentially stormy conversations she needed to have and how difficult they were going to be.

Her first conversation was with Amy, and Sierra launched into it when they stopped halfway for some rest and food. They were only 1,000 feet below where they had camped, yet here there was no trace of snow, and in the shelter of the forest, the wind bullied the trees but pretty much left the hikers alone.

Sierra pulled Amy off to the side, away from the others. They sat together on their backpacks, and Sierra offered Amy half of her granola bar.

"I owe you an apology," Sierra began.

"What for?"

"For the way everything started out with Drake. I knew you were interested in him, but I didn't know how much. I don't think I was listening well enough. I think I would have handled things differently if I had understood your feelings better. I'm sorry, Amy."

"It's okay," she said. "No big deal."

"Yes, it is a big deal. You told me it was fine with you if I went out with Drake, but as soon as I did, things changed between you and me. I value your friendship, Amy. I don't ever want a guy to come between us."

"Thanks, Sierra." Amy's cheeks were red from wind-burn, and her lips looked chapped. "I have to be honest with you and say that although I was really interested in Drake a few months ago, my interest started to drop off when I saw he didn't feel the same about me. Then, when he started to pay attention to you, I felt jealous. I thought if I couldn't have him, why should you?"

Sierra rubbed the tops of her thighs to warm them. "I understand."

"It wasn't right for me to think that. I had a hard time with it when he asked you out. Now I feel okay about it. And you're right, our relationship did get kind of weird. I shouldn't have acted like everything was fine. I just didn't know what to do. Sorry I ditched you and went in Jana's tent."

"That's okay."

"Last week was a bad week for me, with my parents fighting and everything. I don't know what's going on with them, but they seemed fine when I left Monday. Things were back to normal."

"Are things back to normal with us?" Sierra asked.

"Only if we can start to walk again," Amy said. "I'm freezing."

They helped each other up and joined the group with their arms linked.

*One down, two to go.*

The rest of the journey, Sierra prayed. Her thoughts were coming together more clearly than they had in a while. She had a lot to pray about.

"What a beautiful sight!" Shane said as they entered the parking lot and saw their van and trailer, the only vehicle there. "Does anyone remember where I put the keys?"

Shane quickly deflected their looks of disbelief. "I'm only kidding, you guys. Lighten up!"

Lighten up they did. The packs were eagerly stowed in the trailer, and the tired, dirty bunch packed into the van. This time Sierra ended up sitting between Amy and Jana, and the three of them slept on each others' shoulders all the way home.

When they arrived at the church parking lot, they saw evidence that it had rained earlier, but now the summer evening lit up soft halos around the cherry trees lining the parking lot. Everything looked just as they had left it.

"How come I feel like a different person," Amy asked, "and nothing changed here?"

"I was just thinking the same thing," Sierra said. "A little hardship is good for a person. We need to get our world rattled every now and then." Reaching for her backpack, she added, "I think it shows us what we're made of."

"Well, I can't believe this whole backpacking thing is your idea of a good time," Amy said. "I can't wait to have a hot shower and microwave something. I definitely would not have made a good pioneer woman!"

Wes handed Amy her backpack from the trailer. Sierra thought she saw a hint of a smile on his face. The right woman for Wes would be one who knew how to start a fire with one match and looked good in a bandana.

The other weary hikers said good-bye and drove off. Randy, Drake, and Wes helped Shane unhitch the trailer and haul it around to the church's side yard. Then Shane took off, and Wes, Sierra, Randy, Amy, and Drake were the only ones left.

"You guys want to come over?" Wes asked, looking at Sierra out of the corner of his eye. She wished he hadn't invited them. Everything felt settled with Amy, but Sierra was still processing her thoughts and wanted to have a chance to talk with Drake and Randy separately.

"I don't know," Randy said, glancing at Drake and Amy. "I'd be glad to drop you two off at the Jensens', if you want."

"All I want is a hot shower. Would you mind taking me home?" Amy asked.

"Sure," Randy said.

"I'll come over," Drake said, giving Sierra one of his warm looks.

"You want a ride?" Randy asked Drake, not looking at Sierra.

"No, I'll go with Wes and Sierra," he answered.

"Hop in," Wes said.

Sierra watched Randy drive out of the parking lot, and she felt awful. Randy was doing exactly what he said he would. He had stopped being her friend.

# twenty-two

EVERYONE AT THE JENSENS' was surprised to see Sierra, Wes, and Drake home early. Mom offered towels all around and sent them to the four corners of the house for each to take a shower before they were allowed to sit down and eat.

Drake borrowed some of Wes' clothes, and Sierra put on a pair of jeans and a baggy sweatshirt. It felt so different dressing this time than it had when she had gotten ready for her first date with Drake. Now she wasn't concerned about impressing him. Had roughing it on the backpacking trip done that, or were her emotions finally calming down?

After they ate, Sierra and Drake ended up on the front porch swing. This was one of the special summer moments she had dreamed of. Now that she was actually sitting next to Drake, though, it felt different from what she had expected. Probably because she knew what she needed to say.

"Drake," Sierra plunged right in, "do you have a goal for dating like Shane was talking about?"

"Yes. My goal is to spend time with you and get to know you better. Why?"

"Because I don't have any goals yet. I feel like that example Shane gave of throwing the dart at the tree and then drawing a circle around it and saying I hit the mark. I'm just not ready to go out with you yet."

"Too late. We already went out," Drake said, stretching his arm along the back of the swing and attempting to nudge Sierra closer to him.

"I mean 'go out.' You know, be together like this. Spending time with just each other." She felt his warm hand resting on her shoulder.

"What's wrong with this?" Drake asked in a low voice.

Sierra wanted to melt into his arms and say, "Nothing. This is perfect, and so are you. Forget this nagging little voice." But she couldn't. Instead she pursed her lips together and did the hardest thing she had done in a long time. She slowly pulled herself away from Drake and his warm closeness.

Leaning against the cold armrest of the porch swing she faced him and said, "I have to figure this out for myself. I need to set my own goals and draw the circle first, before I start to throw the darts. Do you know what I mean?"

Drake gave her a look that was a blend of mild shock and teasing. "Are you breaking up with me after less than a week?"

"I don't know. Is that what I'm doing? All I know is that I can't let myself get close to you like this and act as if we're going together when I haven't even figured out what that means."

She thought about her mom's comment that it was good Sierra hadn't been kissed yet because she needed to understand what she was giving away. It was beginning to make sense.

"So, what are you saying?" Drake looked surprised.

"I'm saying I want to spend time with you and get to know you this summer, but not at the exclusion of our other friends. I need to think through my goals in dating. It's not you. You haven't done anything wrong. Everything you've done has been wonderful."

Sierra looked up, hoping to catch the tears that were beginning to gather in the corners of her eyelids. "It's me," she said. "I'm too immature, I guess."

"There's nothing immature about you, Sierra."

"Well, something about me isn't ready yet. I have to get myself balanced. Do you know what I'm trying to say?"

Drake pulled his arm off the back of the swing and folded his arms across his chest. "You're saying you just want to be friends."

"More than friends," Sierra said quickly. "Buddies. Good friends, but not boyfriend and girlfriend. I want us all to be able to do things together and not to be exclusive. You know?"

"I guess." He didn't look mad. A little hurt maybe. From what Sierra had gathered, she was the first girl Drake had asked to go with him and he was probably startled that Sierra wanted to go in reverse after such a short time together.

"It's like the backpacking trip," Sierra explained. "I've camped a lot, but this was your first time. Now you know what to do differently next time—what to take with you and what to leave behind. I'm the one who's new at dating, and you're the experienced one. You're much more comfortable with it than I am."

"This feels like the backpacking trip," Drake said, "because we're turning around and going back too soon."

"Sort of," Sierra agreed. "Is that frustrating to you?"

"Only when I get stuck out in the cold," Drake said, nodding toward Sierra's distance from him across the seat. She knew he wanted to feel her warmth and closeness the way she felt drawn to him.

"I need to figure out this whole physical affection thing for myself before I start dating, too. I mean, do you think holding hands means the same thing to you as it does to me?"

"Probably not," Drake said.

"And have you kissed a lot of girls?" Sierra continued in her up-front manner.

"Not a lot."

"What did it mean to you?"

"I don't know. It was just a kiss." Drake laughed, a tinge of nervousness showing.

"I think it needs to mean something more than that to me before I kiss a guy. It should be the beginning of a commitment."

"You think too much, Sierra."

"Maybe. But that's got to be better than going totally on my feelings like I have been lately. I need to find a balance."

"Does all this mean you don't want me calling or coming by?" Drake asked.

"No, of course not! You're always welcome. And I still want to do stuff together. But in a group instead of just the two of us."

"So you want to go back to where we were before we took the walk with Brutus in the park."

"Exactly," Sierra said. "Is that okay with you?"

Drake thought a minute, then pushing out his chin, he said, "Yes, I can live with that."

"Good," Sierra said with a smile. She felt about fifty pounds lighter. Instead of wondering whether Drake was going to kiss her before he left, she was thinking about calling Tawni and telling her everything that had happened and asking if she had ever written out her dating goals.

When Drake did leave, Sierra felt as if everything between them was settled. Somehow they had managed to put their relationship in reverse, and Drake could live with it.

The last person she needed to settle things with was Randy. She considered calling him right then, but it was late, and she was exhausted. She decided to wait until the next morning.

When Sierra called, Randy's mom said he'd already left to mow the yard on 52nd Street. Pulling on a pair of shorts, tennis shoes, and a T-shirt, Sierra bounded down the stairs.

"Tell Mom I'll be back in half an hour," she yelled to Wes in the kitchen.

# twenty-three

SIERRA HOPPED INTO THE CAR and headed for 52nd Street. She drove by Mama Bear's Bakery, then on impulse decided to stop and run in as a customer. Mrs. Kraus was surprised to see her.

"Yes, we all survived the trip," Sierra said. "I need to buy two rolls, one with extra frosting, and three milks."

"Glad to see that a little time in the wilderness has made you appreciate the finer things in life," Mrs. Kraus said, handing Sierra the white pastry bag.

Sierra stopped counting out her change and said, "You know what, Mrs. Kraus? A little time in the wilderness has made me appreciate a lot of things."

She flew out the door and puttered in her old car over to 52nd Street. Randy had on the earbuds to his iPod and didn't hear her when she drove up.

"Randy!" Sierra yelled over the roar of the lawn mower. "Hey, Randy!"

In that moment, Sierra realized how awful her senior year would be if Randy weren't her buddy. She couldn't stand to think that he might ignore her as he appeared to be right now.

Boldly approaching the path of the lawn mower, Sierra held out the bakery bag. "Refreshments!" she hollered.

Randy cut the motor on the mower and looked at her. He seemed cautious. Guarded. Not sure if he was happy to see her.

"Can you take a break?" Sierra asked.

"I guess."

Sierra ran to the back of her car and pulled out an old blanket her mom kept in the trunk for emergencies. They spread it in the shade of an elm and sat down.

"What's up?" Randy asked.

Handing him his usual two milks, Sierra suddenly felt like Amy, bringing food to a guy because she wanted his attention. Maybe there was something to this technique.

"I want to go back in time," Sierra said. "Back to when we were buddies."

"What about Drake?" Randy asked.

"I told him last night I just wanted to be buddies with him, too. I want all of us to go back to being good friends."

Randy took a bite of the roll and waited for Sierra to continue.

"I've realized I need to figure out quite a few things before I start to date. This is my summer to set goals and get my thoughts together before my emotions have a chance to take over." She motioned to Randy that he had a bit of white frosting on the side of his mouth. "So, what do you think? Can we go backward?"

"No," Randy said. Then he took another bite without explaining.

Sierra took a little bite of her cinnamon roll and waited.

"We can't go backward, Sierra. Only forward."

"But I want to erase a bunch of stuff. Like the other night in your tent. I want you to forget everything I said."

"Why?"

"Because I told you everything I was feeling."

"Sierra, you probably haven't figured this out yet, but you can trust me with your feelings. Don't be afraid of them. They're part of you. I know they're going to change. Everybody's feelings change. Don't be ashamed of that."

Randy took another bite before finishing his comforting speech. "I'm glad you spilled your guts in the tent. I understand you better now. And I meant what I said. If you want to go out with another guy, I don't want to be in the way. I'll step back. I need to figure out a lot in my life, too."

"I'm not ready for a boyfriend," Sierra said. She took a bite of her roll. "Just buddies. I need a lot of buddies."

A crooked grin pulled up the corners of Randy's mouth. "Then we're buddies," he agreed.

Sierra took a long gulp of milk and savored her last bite of cinnamon roll. Over their heads, four chattering birds departed across the wide, blue sky. A squirrel ran along the telephone line before hopping to the elm and taking shelter under the thick, green leaves. Two kids across the street shrieked as they chased each other barefoot through the front yard.

Sierra leaned back on her hands and breathed in the scent of cut grass. She noticed that the little voice in the back of her head was silent. No longer was she wondering if she was doing the right thing. Everything was beginning to feel right because it was right. In balance.

Even Randy was right. They couldn't go back, only ahead. And since each step she took with her friends seemed to be bringing them closer to the Lord and to each other, Sierra had no doubt this would be her best summer ever.

Book Six

WITH THIS
RING

# one

WITH ONE LAST GLANCE in her bedroom mirror, Sierra Jensen slipped a silver bracelet on her arm and called out, "Mom, tell him I'll be there in a second."

Sierra wondered if she should change into jeans. The short dress she now wore was a little too fancy for her. But this July night in Portland was hot, and the thought of jeans sounded uncomfortable. A dress was the way to go. But maybe not this dark, straight dress. What about a long gauze skirt?

Sierra began to rifle through the volcano of clothes that had erupted in the middle of her bed.

*Where is that blue skirt?* she wondered. *I saw it a few minutes ago when I was looking for my other shoe. Oh, yeah, under the bed.*

For a few weeks after Sierra's older sister had moved out, Sierra had kept her room neat. Then, as summer progressed and she became busier, the clutter seemed to expand to fill any empty space it could find within her bedroom. More than once Sierra had set out to clean the messy room, but the weeks of junk buildup had turned it from a one-hour cleanup to an all-day-with-a-shovel event. So she kept putting it off.

Bending down, Sierra lifted the dust ruffle. A half-eaten graham cracker greeted her, along with two cotton balls, a pair of socks, a magazine, a ponytail holder that had turned into a dust-ball magnet, and her A+ essay on Marie Antoinette. No blue skirt.

"Sierra!" Mrs. Jensen's voice came from above Sierra. "What are you doing?"

Pulling herself out from her unladylike position under the bed, Sierra faced her mom. Sierra's wild, wavy blond hair had flopped across her face. "I didn't hear you come in," she said.

Sierra's Granna Mae stood behind her mom. Both of them were smiling. Sharon Jensen, a trim woman in her forties, looked more like an older sister than the mother of six children.

"It's not polite to keep a man waiting," Granna Mae said. "Are you ready to go, Lovey?"

"I guess," Sierra said, straightening her dress and smoothing back her hair. "I was thinking of changing into a long skirt."

"You look fine," her mother said. "He's taking you to a nice restaurant, you know. You wouldn't want to dress too casually."

"I know. But I feel so silly about this," Sierra confessed. "I don't know why he asked me to go out to dinner with him."

"You don't have any idea?" her mom asked.

"No, but I suppose you do."

"Maybe," her mom said with a smile in her eyes.

"Okay, I'm ready. I just wish you guys weren't all making such a big deal out of this."

"You've become quite the young lady," Granna Mae said. "You'll certainly turn his head tonight."

Sierra impulsively gave her grandma a peck on the cheek as Sierra swished past her and headed down the stairs of their large Victorian home.

"I think you two are enjoying this milestone in my dating life more than I am."

She felt her cheeks beginning to blush when she noticed her date standing in the hallway by the front door.

He had on a sports jacket and dress slacks. The faint scent of his evergreen aftershave rose to meet her. He turned to watch her coming down the stairs, and Sierra could see he held a clear plastic box tied with a purple ribbon.

*I can't believe he bought me a corsage! This is getting way too corny. What if I tell him I've changed my mind and don't want to go after all?*

"You look beautiful." His deep voice was soothing. Sierra looked up into his familiar, clean-shaven face, framed by short brown hair with a receding hairline. The corners of his eyes crinkled up the way they always did when he was trying not to cry.

"Dad," Sierra said softly, "I know this is supposed to be some kind of special father-daughter event, but I really feel lame dressing up and going out to dinner. If you want to tell me something, can't we just go in the study or out to your workshop?"

"This is for you," her dad said, unaffected by her attempt to squelch their plans. "I had them make it into a wrist corsage because I didn't know if you would want to wear it on your dress."

Sierra looked down at the small corsage of delicate pink baby rosebuds. She recognized the name of the flower shop on the gold sticker. ZuZu's Petals. It was just down the street from Mama Bear's Bakery, where Sierra worked. She had applied for a job once at ZuZu's Petals and found that the owner knew Granna Mae. Now they probably knew her father. Did he tell them why he was buying the corsage?

"Maybe I should leave this here in the refrigerator," Sierra said cautiously as she took the box from him. "They're so pretty. I'd hate to squash them."

Her dad looked disappointed. Then he said, "Well, it's up to you. They're yours."

A tiny card peeped out from the top of the box. Sierra flipped it open with her thumb and read her dad's message. "You will always be my daughter, and I will always love you. Dad."

Sierra bit her lower lip and tasted the lip gloss she had put on fifteen minutes earlier. How could she reject the flowers? Even though she didn't understand what this father-daughter bonding night was about, Sierra knew she couldn't leave his corsage in the refrigerator.

"It's really beautiful," she said with a catch in her throat. "Thanks, Dad. I'll take it with us."

"Good. You all ready then?"

Mrs. Jensen, who had been hanging back at the top of the stairs, called down, "Wait a minute, you two! I need to take a picture."

Sierra forced a smile as her mom scurried down the stairs.

*This is going to be a long night!* she thought. *I hope we don't see anyone I know.*

"Okay," Mrs. Jensen said, squeezing one eye shut and holding the camera steady. "Put your arms around each other. That's good. Come on, Sierra, smile. Okay, hold that!"

The camera clicked, and immediately Sierra's mom said, "Wait! I want to get a close-up now."

Tucking her short blond hair behind her ears, Sharon Jensen coerced them into posing again.

"'Bye now," she said after the camera clicked once more. "Have a great time, and remember, Howard, my daughter needs to be back by her curfew."

"Yes, ma'am," he said, opening the door for Sierra.

They headed for her brother Wesley's new sports car. It was actually an old sports car, a 1969 Triumph, that Wes had bought almost a month ago. He and Mr. Jensen had spent hours fixing it up, and now, according to them, the little baby "hummed." Sierra was glad her brother was working tonight and hadn't been there to tease her.

"I thought you might find this a little more appealing than the family van," her dad said as he started up the engine. "Ah! Purrs like a kitten." He pulled out of the driveway and headed down their quiet street.

This part of Portland was known for its rows of restored Victorian homes. Sierra's great-grandfather had built the one they lived in, and many of the original owners or their families still resided along this tree-lined street.

"So, where are we going?" Sierra asked.

"I thought I'd keep it a surprise," her dad said.

He headed toward the Burnside Bridge that would take them over the Willamette River and into downtown Portland.

Sierra glanced at the corsage box in her lap and noticed how short her skirt was. She tried to tug it down a bit. Funny, it hadn't seemed short when she bought it or when she put it on this evening. But now, sitting next to her dad, Sierra wished she had changed into the long gauze skirt.

"How are things going at the Highland House?" her dad asked.

"Great. Did I tell you about the macaroni necklaces?"

"No. I noticed the kitchen was full of bowls of dyed macaroni last week. What did you do with them?"

"I had no idea the kids at the homeless shelter would get so into making necklaces. I took all the macaroni and let them string their own bracelets and necklaces, and they went crazy! Some of them did a really good job. I told the older girls I'd bring beads for them next week."

"Your mom and I are proud of the way you've been helping out there this summer and keeping up with your job at Mama Bear's. You've been busy."

"It's been a good summer," Sierra said, slowly removing the corsage from the box in her lap. The pink rosebuds trembled as she lifted them to her nose. There was only a slight fragrance. The mist clinging to the roses and feathery fern leaves dotted the end of her nose with moisture.

"And the summer isn't over yet," Sierra said, dabbing her nose with the back of her hand. "I'm really looking forward to going to California next week."

*Maybe I can carry the flowers into the restaurant without anyone seeing them and keep them beside my plate,* she thought. *It would sure make Dad happy.*

The car came to a stop, and Sierra looked up. *Oh no!* she inwardly groaned.

"Here we are," her dad said.

*Not here! Please, Dad! Of all the restaurants in Portland, why did you have to pick this one?*

# two

"I'VE HEARD YOU AND WES talk about this place so much that I thought it would be fun if we checked it out," Mr. Jensen said as he opened the door for Sierra.

She forced a smile and carefully held on to the corsage. She tried to get out of the sardine-can sports car without her short skirt hiking up and her hair falling in her face. She found it to be a difficult task.

"May I offer you a hand?" her father said gallantly.

"No, I'm fine," Sierra said. She pushed herself up and out, trying to appear graceful. Fortunately, no one was in the parking lot, watching her.

Offering her his arm, Mr. Jensen prepared to escort her into the Italian restaurant that was owned by the uncle of Sierra's friend Amy. Amy worked there as a hostess, and she had arranged for a lot of their friends to get jobs there. Wes was a waiter; he was working tonight. Sierra felt certain her dad was so into this that he probably had arranged for Wes to wait on them. Her buddy Randy was a busboy, and so was Tre, another guy from school who played in a band with Randy.

Sierra barely touched her dad's arm as they walked into the restaurant together. What would people think if they saw this sixteen-year-old girl, all dressed up—with a corsage, no less—being ushered into a nice restaurant by a middle-aged man with a receding hairline, who was grinning from ear to ear? This was so embarrassing.

Her dad opened the door for her, which gave her an opportunity to let go of his arm and walk slightly away from him. A dozen people were seated on antique benches, waiting for open tables.

The first person Sierra noticed when they entered was Amy. She had on the lace vest she had bought two days ago when she and Sierra were out vintage-store shopping. It looked cute over her navy dress. Her long black hair was pulled back with one tendril cascading down the right side of her face. Amy had a glimmer in her dark eyes that indicated to Sierra that she knew about this father-daughter date and had been expecting them.

"Good evening," Amy said formally. She made a mark on the seating chart in front of her. "Reservation for Jensen, party of two. Right this way, please."

Sierra fell in line behind her friend and whispered, "Okay, Amy, cut the act. This is humiliating enough without your playing along."

"Who's playing along?" Amy whispered over her shoulder as they wound past the round tables in the packed restaurant. "This is what I do every night."

Sierra wanted to playfully pinch her friend, but before she could, Amy turned, and with wide eyes, she whispered to Sierra, "There he is. Over there by table seventeen. That's Nathan. Is he a dream or what?"

"Table seventeen? Where's that? I don't see any dream."

"Over there," Amy said under her breath. "By the window. He asked me tonight if I have to work next Tuesday."

"Oh," Sierra said.

Amy had been raving about this guy for the last two weeks, ever since he had started to work there. That was about the same time Amy had given up trying to snag Sierra's brother. Wes was nice to Amy, and she had hoped all summer for something more. But when nothing happened and Nathan came to work at the restaurant, Amy quickly readjusted her goal.

Sierra glanced at Amy's new dream boy again. Nathan looked as if he were about twenty. He had bleached blond hair that was combed straight back and dark eyebrows over deep-set eyes. His severe looks didn't appeal to Sierra. She knew he had really made an impression on Amy, though.

Amy stopped at a booth in the back corner of the restaurant and motioned for Sierra to slide in.

"Don't you get it?" Amy whispered. "Tuesday is Nathan's night off. I think he's going to ask me out!"

She handed Sierra a menu and then handed one to Sierra's dad.

Clearing her throat and switching back to her hostess voice, Amy said, "Wesley will be your server tonight. He'll be here in a moment to tell you about our specials. Enjoy your dinner."

Amy gave Sierra a little raised-eyebrow gesture, and as Sierra watched, Amy walked the long way back to the front of the restaurant just so she would have to walk past table seventeen, where Nathan was writing down an order. He turned his head slightly as she passed, and Sierra knew

Amy's guess was probably right. She had attracted his attention, and he would undoubtedly ask her out.

The whole scenario didn't feel right to Sierra. Maybe the unsettled feeling came from watching Amy's dating life unfold while Sierra sat with her "daddy," trying to find a way to hide her rosebud corsage. She placed it next to her fork, then unfolded the cloth napkin and laid it in her lap. Sierra realized she owed it to her dad to be appreciative of all this attention. He had obviously gone to a lot of effort.

"Hi," Wes said, stepping up to the table. He was a younger version of their dad in many ways, including his lean build and clear brown eyes that crinkled in the corners when he laughed. The biggest difference between the two was that Wes had a full head of wavy brown hair.

Pulling out his notepad, Wes asked, "Would you like to hear about our specials?"

Mr. Jensen closed his menu and said, "Why don't you give us your expert recommendation?"

Sierra felt relieved that Wes hadn't done anything to tease her. In a way, it felt as if they were a bunch of little kids playing grown-ups.

"The manicotti is superb tonight. That's what I had on my break. You might want an antipasto salad and an order of Tony's Romano bread, too. The bread is our house specialty and is made with bits of tomato and melted cheese on top."

"Sounds good to me," Mr. Jensen said. "What would you like, Sierra?"

"That sounds good to me, too. Just a small salad, though. And I'd like some mineral water."

"I'll have water and coffee," her dad said.

Wes's pencil scratched across the notepad. He picked up the menus and gave his dad and sister a nod as if they were any other customers on any other night. "Very good. I'll get those drinks right out for you."

As Wes walked away, Randy, who was busing the table next to theirs, stepped over. He held a tubful of dishes and had a white apron tied around his waist. She hadn't seen him in the white-shirt-and-black-bow-tie uniform before. The waiter outfit looked normal on Wes, but Randy, with his crooked smile and chin-length, straight blond hair parted down the middle, looked as if he were dressed for a costume party.

"Hey, Sierra! Hey, Mr. J.! Did you hear about Drake's accident?" Randy said.

"No. What happened? Is he okay?"

"Yeah. He was driving the delivery truck and hit a phone pole. Blew out the front tire. It was over in Laurelhurst, and I was there doing lawns. I heard this huge crash and ran down the block to see what it was, and there was Drake. The engine was smoking. He was pretty ticked. He said he swerved to miss a cat."

Sierra knew how her dad felt about cats and hoped he wouldn't throw out a comment about how it would have been better to rid the world of that cat than to crash because of it.

Fortunately, Mr. Jensen only said, "What kind of delivery truck?"

"Bundle of Joy," Randy said, readjusting his posture so that the dishes rattled slightly.

"It's his dad's business," Sierra explained.

"Bundle of Joy diapers?" her dad asked.

Sierra nodded. She knew what he was thinking. Anyone who met tall, dark, and athletic Drake would never picture him driving a diaper delivery truck.

One of the other waiters came up behind Randy and said, "Table seven, and can you hurry?"

"Gotta go," Randy said. He turned, and then with a quick look over his shoulder, he added, "You look real nice, Sierra."

"Thanks," she murmured, feeling a tinge of pink rising up from her neck.

"You have great friends," her dad said after Randy disappeared.

"I know I do." Sierra thought how nice it was that Randy had been so comfortable around her. She and Randy had seen each other nearly every day this summer. At the beginning of the summer, they had acted as if they were dating. Then, after an adventurous backpacking trip, they had settled back into their "just buddies" relationship, and everything had felt normal since then.

Sierra had considered dating Drake for a while, too. They did go out to the movies once, just the two of them. But when everything had started to unravel in her other friendships, Sierra decided she wasn't ready to exclusively date one guy. Her other friendships were too important to her. Drake had said he understood, but he didn't pursue her too much after that. As interested as he said he was on their first date, he cooled off when things didn't continue on the course he had set.

Wes brought the drinks and a warm plate of Tony's Romano bread. Sierra began feeling a little more comfortable and settled into this evening with her dad. The scent of garlic immediately piqued her appetite.

"Are your plans all set for next week? When do you leave?" Mr. Jensen asked.

"I fly down to Orange County on Wednesday afternoon. Tawni is going to pick me up."

"And who is it that's getting married?"

"Doug and Tracy."

"Oh, right. He was the group leader on your outreach trip to England last January."

Sierra nodded. "And he's friends with Jeremy." She wasn't sure if her dad remembered the connection between Doug and Tawni's boyfriend. "Jeremy and Tawni are going to the wedding, too."

"Right. I think I remember hearing that. Sounds like a fun week for you." Her dad sipped his coffee.

"I'm ready for it," Sierra said. "Did you know I worked forty-two hours last week at Mama Bear's? Everyone decided to go on vacation at the same time. Mrs. Kraus was great about letting me have the time off. She has a new person coming to train while I'm gone since I'll have to go back to my twelve hours a week when school starts."

"Here you are," Wes said, placing the salads before them in bright blue and white Italian pottery bowls. "Would either of you care for grated cheese on your salad?"

"No thanks."

"Not for me."

"Enjoy!" Wes said, walking away with the cheese grater in his hand.

"Would you like to pray with me?" Mr. Jensen asked Sierra. He always prayed when they ate out, so it seemed natural to Sierra. She bowed her head and closed her eyes while her dad thanked God for the food and for his beautiful daughter.

When he said, "Amen," Sierra looked up and said, "Thanks, Dad."

He gave her a little wink, and they started on their salads.

Sierra had hardly swallowed her first bite when her dad said, "I guess you're wondering why I asked you out like this."

For some reason, Sierra's heart began to pound again. She lowered her fork and waited to hear what her dad had to say.

# three

"YOU KNOW," Mr. Jensen began, clearing his throat twice, "ever since you told your mom and me a couple months ago that you were going to write out your goals and standards for dating, we've been talking about what we could do to encourage you."

Sierra slowly took a bite of her salad and waited for him to continue.

"That's what I wanted to do tonight," her dad said, clearing his throat again. It seemed to Sierra that he was a little nervous about all this, too. "I wanted to find a way to show you how special you are. Not only to your mother and me, but to God."

Sierra nodded. "Thanks, Dad, I appreciate that. But you don't have to do all this to make me feel special."

Mr. Jensen munched his salad. He seemed to be thinking. Either that or trying not to look nervous. This was all a little awkward. She knew her parents loved her, and she knew God loved her. But the ceremony of dressing up and going out to dinner seemed like overkill.

"I'd like to know what you ended up writing out," her father said. "Your goals and standards, I mean. What's on your list?"

"I'm not sure I remember. I mean, I remember, but not the exact words. I wrote two different lists. One is sort of like my criteria for the kind of guy I'd go out with, and the other list, I guess you could say, is my creed."

"Your creed. Sounds interesting. I'd like to hear about both of them."

"Well," Sierra said, putting down her fork and pushing her nearly finished salad to the end of the table, "I only had three points on the boyfriend list."

"Yes?"

"The first one was that he has to be a Christian. And not just a believer but a really strong, growing Christian. A God-lover."

"A God-lover?"

Sierra nodded. "That's what Doug and Jeremy and their friends call themselves."

"I like that."

"So do I," Sierra said. "The next requirement, or whatever, is that he has plans to serve God with his life. I think what I wrote down is that he's committed to God and is planning to serve God in his future career."

"Are you saying you only want to date future pastors or missionaries?"

"No, that's not what I mean," Sierra said. "You don't have to be a pastor to put God at the center of your work. Like with Doug. He's an assistant to a financial planner. He'll probably be a businessman all his life because that's

where his strengths are. But Christy told me that he and
Tracy are budgeting to live on half his income so they can
give the other half to missionaries."

"Really?" her dad said, raising his eyebrows.

"I don't know if they'll be able to do it or not," Sierra
said. "But I like that Doug puts God at the center of his
career, and even though he's getting married, his goals
don't change."

"Quite noble," her dad said.

Wesley arrived at the table with plates of steaming manicotti and placed them before Sierra and her dad. "Some
grated Romano for either of you?"

"No thanks," Sierra said.

"Sure, I'll take a spin," her dad said.

Wes twisted the handle of the fancy cheese grater and the
thin white flakes floated down.

"That's good," Mr. Jensen said.

"I'll be back with more coffee," Wes said. He looked at
Sierra and then at her right hand. With a glance at Mr.
Jensen, he turned and left.

"Go on," Sierra's dad urged. "Any guy you date must be
a God-lover who is planning to honor God with is career.
What else?"

Sierra felt a little embarrassed telling her dad this one.
She sunk her fork into the soft pasta and said, "Well, I guess
the way I wrote it down was that I have to be attracted to him
and vice versa. And that we're both committed to saving
ourselves physically for our future mate."

"Sounds as if you have some pretty serious and stiff
guidelines."

Sierra was surprised. She took another bite of the delicious dinner and then asked, "Do you think my goals are too high or something?"

"Oh, no! They're terrific. I can tell you've really thought it through. What about the other list? Your creed. I take it you mean a creed as in a summary of what you believe."

Sierra nodded.

"Where did you come up with that idea?"

"You're going to laugh."

"Try me."

"I saw this poster in a music store at the mall when I was there with Randy a couple of months ago. It was called 'The Rocker's Creed,' and it had a list of ten points for people who believe in hard rock. It was supposed to be funny. Like, 'If it's too loud, you're too old.'"

Her dad smiled.

"Well, my creed is what I believe about staying pure." Sierra took another bite and chewed slowly. She had felt so spiritual a few months a go when she wrote all this out. Now she felt silly and embarrassed talking about it with her dad. She knew she shouldn't feel that way, but she did.

"What does your creed say?"

"It just says that my body is a gift and that God gets to decide who to give the gift to, not me. And the best presents are the ones that are all wrapped up, not the ones that have been opened and rewrapped and now the paper is torn or the bow is squished or the tape no longer sticks. Do you know what I mean?"

Her dad was smiling softly, and his eyes were starting to get all crinkly in the corners. He nodded, urging her to continue.

"That's it, basically. I believe God's best plan is for me to be like a wrapped present. Then, when I get married, I can completely give myself to my husband for the first time, and he'll know that I'm a special gift just for him."

*There. That wasn't so embarrassing. Why do I feel so self-conscious about all this?* Sierra wondered.

A tear glistened in the corner of her dad's eye, and he tilted his head down, moving his manicotti around on his plate. Then, lifting his face, he said, "That's beautiful, honey. I could never have said it better. That's exactly what you are: a very special and wonderful gift. I'm proud of you."

Amy stepped up to their table and leaned toward Sierra, breaking the moment.

"Sierra, guess what?" Amy said breathlessly, her dark eyes dancing. "He asked me out! For Tuesday, just like I thought. We have to go shopping this weekend, Sierra! I have to get something new to wear."

"Okay," Sierra agreed. It was hard to switch into Amy's dreamworld when she and her dad were in the middle of this delicate conversation.

"Aren't you excited for me?" Amy said.

"Yes, of course I am. That's great." Sierra wished she could really feel happy for her friend—Nathan didn't impress Sierra as exactly the catch of the day. But maybe she was jumping to conclusions.

"I'm so excited!" Amy said, giving Sierra's arm a squeeze before hurrying back to the hostess station.

"Girl talk?" her dad asked.

"Yes. Sorry."

"No problem. I'm about ready for dessert. How about you?"

"Sure."

When Wes stopped by their table a few minutes later, they ordered the tiramisu based on his recommendation. Sierra also ordered herb tea and watched Nathan out of the corner of her eye.

"May I take those plates for you?" Randy reached for Sierra's plate and empty bread plate. "Oh, you guys had Tony's bread. Good stuff, isn't it?"

"It was," Sierra agreed. "So was the manicotti."

"It looks good tonight," Randy said. "I get my break in ten minutes, and I think that's what I'm going to have. I'll see you later."

With the table cleared, Sierra's dad brushed away a few crumbs and then pulled a piece of paper from inside his coat pocket. "I wrote down a few things," he said, "but I don't know if I need to say many of them since you've taken such a strong position on protecting your purity. I went to a men's group a couple of weeks ago; I don't know if you remember. Anyway, the challenge to us dads was to help direct our kids toward purity."

Sierra remembered how excited her dad had been after that all-day meeting at church. Randy had said his dad had been, too. Now the dinner and this heart-to-heart conversation made sense. This was his assignment, or at least his challenge, from the men's meeting: to talk to his children about abstinence. Sierra hoped he wasn't going to list all the reasons for remaining sexually inactive the way her science teacher had last spring. She wasn't in the mood for a list of STDs right before dessert.

"The first thing on my list here," her dad began, "is that I want you to know we trust you and your judgment when it comes to relationships. But if at any time you have questions or doubts of any kind, I want you to come to your mother or to me. Okay? You can trust me, as your father, with anything, no matter how embarrassing you might think it is."

"Okay," Sierra agreed.

"I mean that, now. You can always talk to your mother and me."

"I know."

"The next thing I want to say is that God's way is always the best way. It's the only way, really. And God's Word clearly says He created sex for one man and one woman to share only inside the commitment of marriage."

Sierra started to feel embarrassed again and wished her dad didn't have such a loud voice. She hoped the people next to them couldn't hear what he was saying.

"I have a verse here I wanted to read to you," her dad said, unfolding the piece of paper in his hands.

Sierra noticed all the tidy little letters lined up in outline form, which was his typical way of writing. He even outlined grocery lists. His letters were all in capitals and always straight, even if there were no lines to follow. She could tell he had spent some time on this.

"I Corinthians 6:19 says, 'Or do you not know that your body is the temple of the Holy Spirit who is in you, whom you have from God, and you are not your own?'" Mr. Jensen looked up from his notes and said, "Actually, that's just what you were saying. Your body is a gift, and it's up to God to decide who gets that gift."

Wesley approached them with a teapot in one hand and a scrumptious-looking chocolate-layered dessert in the other. "Tiramisu for two, cherry almond tea, and I'll be right back with some more coffee." He disappeared as quickly as he had come.

"Let me read you verse 20," her dad said. "'For you were bought at a price; therefore glorify God in your body and in your spirit, which are God's.'"

Sierra dunked the tea bag into the white pot and decided she didn't want her tea too strong.

"I know you believe this already," her father said.

"I do," Sierra replied.

"I'm proud of the way you've given yourself guidelines and written out your creed. I know from experience that being a virgin when you get married is the only way to go."

Sierra had heard her mom say before that she and her dad were virgins when they married. It sounded a little different coming from her father, though. Comforting. It gave her a sense of hope that maybe somewhere in the world, quality guys were saving themselves for their future wives.

# four

SIERRA SANK HER FORK into the tempting dessert and let the first bite melt in her mouth.

"Oh, this is good," she said.

Mr. Jensen folded his page of notes and tucked the paper back into his pocket. As Sierra was digging in for a second bite, she noticed her dad was pulling a small black gift box from his inside pocket.

"This is for you," he said, placing the jewelry box in front of her. "Mom and I wanted you to have this. It's our way of supporting and affirming your choice to remain pure and to save yourself for your future husband."

Sierra quickly swallowed the bite in her mouth and looked up with surprise. "What is it?"

"Open it and see."

She lifted the hinged lid on the velvet-lined box. There, wedged in the padded slot, was a simple gold ring.

*Gold!? I only wear silver. Why did they get me a gold ring?*

"Look on the inside," her dad urged. His face was red with anticipation. Sierra didn't dare mention that she never wore anything gold.

Inside the thin band was engraved "1 Cor. 6:19–20."

"Those are the verses you read to me," Sierra said.

Mr. Jensen nodded enthusiastically. "It'll be a reminder to you always that you belong to God and that, as you said, your body is a gift that should stay wrapped up until your wedding night."

"Thanks." Sierra didn't know what else to say.

"Try it on."

She wasn't sure on which hand such a ring should be worn. She decided to slip it onto the ring finger on her right hand. It somehow felt as if that was where it ought to be.

"It's nice," she said, giving her dad the smile he was waiting for. "Thank you."

"I'm glad you like it." He plunged his fork into the dessert before him.

Sierra glanced at the ring and then took another bite of dessert. It seemed strange to wear jewelry she hadn't selected for herself. And the gold was really going to take some time to get used to.

Wes returned with the check and looked at Sierra's hand again. He smiled at Mr. Jensen and said to Sierra, "Do you like it? I helped him pick it out."

"Yes. It's nice."

"Dad said you only liked silver, but I convinced him that the gold is what would set this ring apart. This way it doesn't look like costume jewelry. Makes it unique."

As Wes was speaking, Sierra noticed for the first time that he wore a similar gold band on his right hand. "When did you get that?" she asked, nodding at his ring.

"Last week when Dad got your ring. He bought one for Tawni, too."

"You and Dad went out on a 'date,' and I didn't hear about it?" Sierra teased.

"No. He gave me my ring in the car on the way back from the jeweler. Only you and Tawni get the special treatment." Wes picked up the small tray with the check and Mr. Jensen's credit card. "I'll be right back."

Sierra turned to her dad and asked, "When are you going to give Tawni her ring?"

"I'm not sure," he said, drawing a deep breath. "I thought about having you take it to her next week when you go visit. It wouldn't be as special as this, of course, but I don't know when she'll be back up. Either that or I might just have to make a special trip down there."

"She would probably appreciate that," Sierra said. She didn't feel confident she would be able to deliver such a ring to her sister and that it would have the meaning it was supposed to.

Mr. Jensen signed the credit card voucher, and as he took his copy, Sierra noticed he left an extremely generous tip for Wes. He got up to go. Sierra scooped up her corsage and held it more confidently as they walked through the restaurant.

As they were about to exit, Randy came up and said, "Are you going to the Highland House tomorrow?"

"No, not until Monday. I work all day tomorrow."

"Me, too," Randy said. His job busing tables was only two nights a week, but he also had a lawn-care business that kept him busy five and sometimes six days a week. "I'll see you later," he said before hustling off to clear more tables.

Amy pulled Sierra to the side before they left the restaurant. A throng of people were in the waiting area. "Call me tomorrow morning before you go to work, okay? I was thinking I wouldn't have to buy anything new if I could borrow your blue gauze skirt. It would go with that crushed velvet top I just bought."

"You can borrow it," Sierra said. "Only you'll have to come over and help me dig for it. My room is a mess."

"I know what you mean. I haven't been home long enough to clean mine."

"That's the excuse I keep using, too," Sierra said. "I'll call you."

Sierra's dad held the door open for her, and they strolled to the parking lot. She didn't feel nearly as embarrassed as she had going in. She wished she had worn the corsage, just to make her dad happy.

"You know, I hope you don't lose any of your spunk," her dad said.

"Lose any of my spunk?"

"I'm just saying you have your own style. Your own charm and vivacity. I just hope you always keep that when it comes to your relationships with guys."

He opened the car door and Sierra got in, carefully pulling on her short skirt to keep it down.

"Are you afraid I won't?" Sierra asked once her dad was in the car. "I mean, that I won't keep being myself around guys?"

"No, I believe you will always be yourself no matter whom you're around. That's one of your strong suits. I guess what I'm trying to say is that you have some pretty high standards, and I support all of your goals 100 percent."

"But…" Sierra nudged him on.

"Just don't forget you're a teenager. You're supposed to have fun during this time. You can keep all your virtue intact and still enjoy yourself. That's all I'm trying to say. Don't get too serious, thinking that any guy you go out with is on trial as future husband material. Relax and enjoy the chance to make a lot of friends. God will bring the right man into your life at the right time."

Sierra took her dad's words to heart and wrote them out, as best as she could remember them, in her journal that night. Her dad was right. She needed to have fun, too, and not always feel as if she were scoping out every guy to see how spiritual he was.

Closing her journal and snapping off the light, Sierra snuggled under the cool sheets. She felt her new ring with her thumb and twisted it around her ring finger. It felt smooth and light.

Outside her open window, a frog had joined the chorus of nightly cricket chirpers. The warm summer breeze ruffled her sheer bedroom curtains, making them look like dancing spirits in the glow of the streetlight below.

Her thoughts floated to Paul. For many months she had prayed for him. At the end of the school year, her brief dreams of a romance with him were dashed when he had the nerve to ask if she had a crush on him.

What Sierra felt for Paul Mackenzie did not fall into the "crush" category. It was something so deep that she didn't even know what to call it. Maybe it was the intense spiritual connection she felt from all the times she had prayed for him. Or maybe it was nothing but an illusion she had allowed herself to entertain for too long. Sierra knew she was capable of talking herself into anything—even into believing there was still something between her and Paul.

But she had no pinch of evidence that he was interested in her. In many ways, Sierra was better off forgetting all about him. It made much more sense to pour her emotional energy into her friendship with Randy. That was a relationship with genuine openness and honesty. A friendship of daylight and solid evidence, not one of fleeting wishes and dreams in the night.

The hardest thing for Sierra was that she didn't feel she could talk about these things with Amy or anyone else. The only friend who would understand was Christy. She would see Christy next week, and hopefully the two of them could have a real heart-to-heart. Christy seemed to understand about holding someone in your heart, not only because she was older than Sierra, but also because Christy had found the true love of her life—Todd. They were waiting for God's direction in their relationship. Christy was the person Sierra admired and wanted to imitate.

She fell asleep praying for Paul and for his time in Scotland, that going to school and visiting his grandmother would be full of rich spiritual growth. The thousands of miles between them couldn't stop her thoughts from reaching out to Paul. And she knew nothing could stop her prayers for him.

# five

AMY CAME BY SUNDAY EVENING, still excited about her date with Nathan and still determined to borrow Sierra's blue skirt. The two of them hunted through Sierra's bedroom for half an hour. Actually, Sierra hunted while Amy sat in the overstuffed chair and chattered endlessly about Nathan.

"I found out at work last night that Nathan loves peanut butter cookies. So I thought I would make some for him as a surprise on Tuesday night. Did I tell you he moved here from Seattle? He says it's hotter here in the summer than in Seattle. Hey, is that it? Right there under the jeans. That's your blue skirt."

"You're right," Sierra said. "This is so ridiculous. I should have been hanging up this stuff while I was looking. Here you go. It's a wrinkled mess, but you can borrow it. If you decide to wash it, make sure you do it by hand in cold water, then wring it out and let it hang dry."

"It doesn't look dirty to me. Isn't it supposed to be wrinkled? I think it's perfect." Amy admired the skirt, then turned to Sierra. "So, are you getting excited about your vacation?"

"I don't know if it's really a vacation. I guess it sort of is. But I'm definitely looking forward to it." Sierra opened her closet door and pulled out a few hangers for her clothes.

"I'd better go," Amy said. "It's after nine o'clock already, and Nathan might call." She stood and turned her ear to the open window, listening. "Is that a frog?"

"Yes. He showed up a few nights ago. I guess he's trying to compete with all those crickets. Their concert last night kept me awake."

"They are pretty loud. They must like the flower garden. So many places to hide."

"That must be it," Sierra agreed. "Be sure to call and tell me how everything goes with Nathan. My plane leaves at 10:00 on Wednesday morning. So call me when you get home if it's before eleven or else before nine in the morning."

"I will. Thanks for the skirt. See you later."

Amy left in a whirlwind, and Sierra surveyed the rearranged mess in her room.

She flopped onto her bed and listened to the night creatures. Tucking her chin, she lowered her voice to the basement of her range and tried to imitate the croaking frog.

*I'll clean my room tomorrow*, she decided.

However, Sierra's good intentions didn't work out. Monday night after she finished volunteering at the Highland House, she ended up going with Randy to his band practice. For almost two hours, she sat in a stuffy, closed garage, listening to the four guys work and rework the same song. She couldn't believe she had agreed to come.

When she and Randy finally left, they stopped for something to eat, and by the time she got home, all she wanted to do was crash. Not even the cricket chorus kept her from floating off into dreamland.

Tuesday was just as hectic. She worked at Mama Bear's Bakery in the morning, went to the Highland House from two to five and then back to Mama Bear's for two more hours.

Finally, at eight-thirty on Tuesday night, Sierra scrambled to throw a bunch of clothes into a travel bag and wrap her gift for Doug and Tracy.

Knowing how much Tracy liked tea, Sierra had found a unique Polish potter teapot at the Portland Saturday Market a few weeks earlier. She had discovered teacups at another stand that went nicely with the pot, and now she was having a terrible time trying to wrap it all in tissue and find a box big enough for the gift.

By eight-thirty the next morning, Sierra had all her things together and was lugging her bag downstairs when Amy called. Mom came into the entryway where Sierra had dumped her bag and handed her the phone.

"Hi," Sierra said. "I was just leaving. I'm glad you caught me. So? Tell me everything really fast. Where did you go? What did you do? Did you have a good time?"

"I can say it all in a few words. I'm in love." Amy sighed on the phone.

Sierra laughed. "Come on. Be serious."

"I'm completely serious. Nathan is perfect for me. First he took me to dinner. It wasn't fancy. Just a '50s hamburger place off Belmont. Really cute. Then we went for a long walk in the park. He held my hand, and it was so romantic!"

"Sounds wonderful," Sierra said.

"Oh, there's more wonderful. We went on the swings at the park, and he pushed me for like half an hour. Then we went on the merry-go-round and down the slide together. I laughed so hard. Oh, and your skirt tore just a teeny, tiny bit. You can hardly see it. I'll fix it."

"How did that happen?" Sierra tried not to sound upset.

"It got caught on the slide. It's not really noticeable. Don't be mad."

"I'm not mad. I was just asking."

"Do you want to hear the rest or not?"

Sierra's mom stepped into the entryway and looked over at Sierra where she was sitting on the bottom step. Mom tapped on her watch and gave Sierra a "let's go" look.

"Yes. Talk fast."

"We drove around went up to this place where you can see the lights all the way down to the river. It's really beautiful. So peaceful. And then…Are you sure you want me to tell you?"

"Of course."

"Well, first he kissed me, then I kissed him, and then we kissed some more and…"

"Amy!" Sierra squawked into the phone. "Are you serious? Why did you do that?"

"Relax, Sierra! Man! You scared me. All we did was kiss. There's nothing wrong with that. It was really romantic. He had music on and—" Amy stopped and suddenly changed her tone of voice. "I can't believe you just snapped at me like that. I know this was our first date, but there was

absolutely nothing wrong with what we did. I don't appreciate your trying to make it seem like I did something wrong."

"Amy, I didn't mean to sound so harsh. But you guys
just met. I think you should take it slower, that's all."

Amy didn't say anything. Sierra could hear her breathing on the other end of the line.

"Look, Amy, I'll call you when I come back Sunday
night. Maybe we can get together and talk next Monday.
Okay?"

"I don't think there's anything to talk about. I try to tell
you about the most romantic night of my life, and you
judge me. Why can't you just be happy for me? I didn't
expect this kind of reaction from you, Sierra."

Mrs. Jensen picked up Sierra's bag and said in a firm
voice, "Sierra, we need to go right now if you're going to
make your flight."

Sierra nodded at her mom. "I have to go, Amy. I'll see
you in a couple of days. Don't do anything..." Sierra wasn't
sure how to end that sentence.

"What? Don't do anything you wouldn't do?" Amy
added sarcastically. "I'm not a nun, Sierra. But I'm not a
sleaze, either. So don't try to make me feel like one."

"I wasn't," Sierra said. "I'll call you when I get home.
'Bye." She pushed the "off" button and stood to take the
bag from her mom.

"Everything okay?" her mom asked.

"I guess so. I don't know. Amy met this guy at work, and
now suddenly she's in love." They walked down the front
porch steps to the van. "Amy's so impulsive. I worry about
her sometimes."

"I understand." Mrs. Jensen got into the van and stuck

the keys into the ignition. "Do you have your ticket?"

"Yes, in my backpack," Sierra said, pulling her ever-faithful companion off her shoulder and unzipping the front pouch. "Right here." She flipped it open and read the printed information. "It leaves at 10:12. We should make it with no problem."

"And you have the gift?"

"In my bag. That's why it's so heavy. I hope it doesn't get thrashed."

Sierra sat back as Mrs. Jensen headed for the freeway that would take them to the Portland airport. Something about the words Sierra just said echoed in the back of her mind. The image of her beautiful wedding gift mangled with the bow squished and the corner torn wouldn't go away. She thought of how embarrassed she would be to hand such a gift to her friends.

Then she thought of Amy. *That's why I reacted so strongly when Amy said she and Nathan had sat in his car and made out,* Sierra realized. Only a few days earlier, Sierra had told her dad she saw herself as a present that she wanted to give to her future husband, and she wanted the wrapping to be perfect.

Maybe what Amy did with Nathan wasn't wrong according to Amy's standards or values. But how could her "wrapping" help but get messed up? Sierra wished she'd had more time to talk with her friend. She and Amy had never discussed their standards before. Maybe Amy didn't have a creed like Sierra did. But would she even be willing to hear Sierra's opinions?

At the departures lane of the airport, Sierra gave her mom a hug good-bye and checked her luggage. Since she had packed in such a hurry, she had taken more clothes than she needed. The thought comforted her, knowing that all the layers of clothing would serve as protective padding for the wedding present.

With her ticket in hand and backpack over her shoulder, Sierra hurried to the gate and arrived just as the passengers began boarding her flight. She got right on, and stuffed her backpack under the seat in front of her, and looked out the window.

Sierra decided the first thing she would do when she came back was call Amy. The only problem was that Amy might not want to hear what Sierra had to say.

# SIX

STANDING WITH THE REST of the travelers, Sierra waited for the mob to move down the center aisle of the plane and head out the door into the airport. She knew Tawni would be waiting for her. Tawni was meticulous about many things. Being on time to pick up people was one of them.

Sure enough, as Sierra entered the baggage-claim area of the airport, the first person she laid eyes on was her stunning sister. Only, Sierra was startled to see that Tawni had colored her hair. Instead of her natural blond, Tawni's hair was a rich mahogany. The brownish-red color made her look even more sophisticated and grown-up.

During Tawni's months in California, she had landed a job modeling for a small local company. In every way, she looked like a model standing there waiting for Sierra.

"Were you at the back of the plane?" Tawni said, giving Sierra a less than exuberant hug.

"No, the middle."

"Oh. It seemed to take so long for you to get here."

"Can't you say, 'Hi, Sierra! I'm so glad to see you'? Why

do you have to criticize me for taking too long to get off the plane?"

"I wasn't criticizing you. Of course I'm glad to see you."

They waited silently, side by side, for the baggage carousel to start moving. Finally, Sierra said, "I'm sorry, Tawni. I had some stuff on my mind, I guess. Your hair looks nice. How's everything going?"

"Terrific. I have another offer for a catalog shoot, so that's good. They pay pretty well. At least better than the jobs I've been getting this past month modeling in restaurants."

"Modeling in restaurants?"

"I work for a boutique that's next to a nice restaurant in Carlsbad. Every day for the lunch rush, I walk around the restaurant in different outfits from the boutique. I tell people about what I'm wearing and give out cards from the boutique. The money is okay. It's not many hours, though."

"I've never heard of that kind of modeling."

"It's popular here. The shoot for the Castle Clothes Catalog will be in La Jolla, which isn't too far from where I live. It's four or five days of work. That should add up to some decent money."

"How's Jeremy?"

"Wonderful," Tawni said, a contented smile curling her lips.

"Did Christy call you? I don't know where I'm staying."

"At Marti's. Christy didn't tell you?"

"You mean at Christy's aunt and uncle's house? Am I the only one staying there?" Sierra asked anxiously. She had been to the luxurious beach house before, and although it was a fantastic place, Sierra wasn't too fond of Christy's Aunt Marti. Tawni was, though, because Marti was the one who had encouraged Tawni to start a modeling career.

"Don't worry. Christy and Katie are staying there too."

"There's my bag. I'll get it."

Sierra carefully lifted her bag from the carousel and followed Tawni out to the parking lot.

"Are you hungry?" Tawni asked. "Do you want to stop for lunch before I take you over to Bob and Marti's? I took off the afternoon, and they're not expecting you at a specific time anyway."

Sierra noted this friendly gesture on Tawni's part. It wasn't often that Tawni volunteered to spend time socially with Sierra, so Sierra knew she had better take advantage of the offer.

"Sure. Where do you want to go? It'll be my treat. I've been working like crazy all summer, and I have way too much money."

Tawni raised her delicate eyebrows as she unlocked the car door. "Well, then I will let you pay. It'll only be a matter of time, though, before you buy a car or move out. Then see how quickly money evaporates."

They drove down to the beach and found a quiet little café a few blocks from the ocean. It was a garden restaurant, and entrance was through a white picket gate. Honeysuckle vines laced their long fingers in and out of the garden's latticework and sprinkled their sweet fragrance over Tawni and Sierra as they entered.

"I saw this place a couple of weeks ago and thought it looked fun. I tried to talk Jeremy into taking me here, but he wasn't too thrilled. I guess it's more of a sisters kind of place."

Tawni's words warmed Sierra. *We really must be growing up*, she thought. Going to lunch together at a garden cottage restaurant was something women, not girls, did with their sisters.

The hostess ushered them to a round patio table under a pale yellow canvas umbrella and handed them menus printed on long sheets of paper with bright daisy borders. Everything was made fresh that day, according to the menu. The specialty of the house was, of course, garden salads.

For the next two hours, Sierra and Tawni talked and laughed and fully enjoyed each other's company—Sierra loved hearing all about Tawni's relationship with Jeremy. Deep down, she knew it wasn't only because Jeremy was Paul's brother. Hearing about Jeremy was, in a tiny way, like hearing about Paul.

When the bill came, Sierra was shocked to see that it totaled nearly forty dollars. She had brought twice that with her, so it wasn't a problem paying. It was just hard to believe that two salads, an appetizer sampler tray, and two raspberry iced teas could add up to that much. She decided this must be the price of passing into womanhood. Times like this with her sister were worth it.

When they got back into Tawni's car, Tawni said, "I noticed your new ring. I was waiting for you to tell me who gave it to you."

"Oh," Sierra said, fingering the gold band with her thumb. "Well, actually..." She didn't know if she should tell the whole story about dinner with her dad and the ring he also had for Tawni, or if she should brush it off as nothing important.

"Did it come from a secret admirer?" Tawni asked with a tease in her voice. "Randy maybe?"

"No, it's definitely not from Randy. It's actually from Dad."

"From Dad?"

Sierra nodded.

Tawni pulled her sedan out onto Pacific Coast Highway, her eyes wide with surprise. "Dad gave you a gold ring?"

"It was Wesley's idea to get gold. Dad was going to buy me silver, but I think Wes wanted gold because he got one, too. It's a purity ring. There's a verse engraved inside, and it's a reminder that I've promised God I'll stay pure until marriage."

Tawni didn't say anything.

"Dad bought one for you, too," Sierra said. "I don't know if I was supposed to say anything. He asked if I wanted to bring it with me, and I said I thought he should give it to you. He's going to figure out when he can come down. You could call him and tell him I told you, and he could just send it to you."

"That's okay. It doesn't matter."

Sierra got nervous when her sister said things like that. Tawni was the only one of the six Jensen kids who was adopted. Every now and then it seemed she saw herself as the outsider. Sierra knew it was possible that Tawni would feel that way now about the ring. She wished she would have realized how important it would be to bring the ring with her so she could give it to Tawni.

"A purity ring is a nice symbol for someone your age. I'm glad Dad got it for you."

"I'm sorry, Tawni. I should have brought yours."

"It doesn't matter. Really."

A thick silence enveloped them for a moment.

"I suppose I should tell you the plans, or at least the plans I know about, for the weekend," Tawni said, smoothly changing the subject. "There's a shower scheduled tonight for Tracy at her parents' house, and the guys are having a party for Doug at his parents' house. Tomorrow I have to work, and then I'll be back up Friday afternoon right after work for the wedding, which is here in Newport Beach."

"I just realized," Sierra said, "I don't have a gift for the shower."

"You could split the cost with me on my gift if you want. It could be from both of us."

"That's a great idea. How much do you want for my half?"

"Just twenty-two dollars."

*Twenty-two dollars! I'm going through money like water!* Sierra thought.

They pulled into Bob and Marti's driveway. An old VW bus was parked in front of the house, looking out of place in the upscale neighborhood.

"What is that doing here, I wonder?" Sierra thought aloud.

"Didn't you ever see ol' Gus? That's Todd's bus. The last I heard, he was thinking of burying it for good. He must have found another burst of life in the guy."

Tawni set the parking brake and popped open the trunk for Sierra.

When Sierra pulled out her bag and closed the trunk, Tawni was already at the front door, ringing the doorbell. Marti, a petite, well-groomed brunette, answered and greeted Tawni by kissing the air on each side of her cheeks.

When Marti saw Sierra, she graciously extended her manicured hand and said, "So nice to see you again."

Sierra lumbered her way through the front door, trying hard not to bang her luggage on anything. They had barely closed the door behind them when Christy's Uncle Bob came bursting in from the family room and gave each of the girls a hearty hug.

"Welcome, welcome," he said. "Here, let me take that for you."

Sierra found it hard not to stare at him. When she had first met Uncle Bob over Easter vacation, he had impressed her as an energetic, healthy man. Shorter and stockier than her father, Bob was tan, with thick, dark hair and a friendly twinkle in his eye. He was a good-looking man, not movie star material but definitely attractive. But that Easter break, he had been in a terrible accident when a gas barbeque exploded.

Now Sierra could see the extent of his burns. From his ear, now deformed, down the entire left side of his neck, Bob's skin was red, shriveled, and scarred. Even though Sierra had been there when the accident happened, she had no idea how bad it was.

The trauma had deeply affected Bob. At the end of that week, he announced that he had given his life to Christ. The accident had made him realize how short life was and how he needed to make peace with God. Sierra had left Newport Beach at Easter thinking the accident had had a happy ending.

Now, seeing what Bob had to live with day in and day out for the rest of his life, Sierra wasn't sure the ending was so great. Bob was headed for heaven, but for the rest of his life on earth he would be scarred.

Sierra's thoughts flipped back to Amy. What if she kept going further and further with Nathan? Sierra shivered. *Although something good can come from an "accident,"* Sierra realized, *somebody always ends up scarred for life.*

# seven

"COME ON IN," Bob said to the new arrivals. "Todd and Christy are out on the patio. Would you like something to drink? How about lunch? Are you hungry?"

"No thanks. We stopped on the way." Tawni checked her watch. "I should get going. I'm supposed to pick up the cake for the shower tonight, and I'm not sure how long it's going to take me to get it and drive to Tracy's."

"Go ahead," Bob said on his way upstairs with Sierra's bag. "Come back whenever you want. We have plans for dinner here, you know. The invitation is open to anyone who wants to come."

"Thanks," Tawni said. She turned to Marti. "If Jeremy calls, would you please let him know where I am? I'll probably be back here at about five-thirty. He's coming up with some of the guys from San Diego, but I don't know how late they will arrive."

"I'll tell him," Marti said. "Would you like to take my cell phone with you? That way you can check in if you need to."

"That's okay," Tawni said.

"No, really. I insist." Marti reached for her purse, which sat on a marble-top table by the staircase, and handed Tawni the phone. "Here. You have our number with you, don't you? Call and check in."

"Okay. Thanks. I'll see you later, Sierra." Tawni swished out the door with the phone in her hand, leaving Marti and Sierra alone in the entryway.

Sierra smiled.

Marti smiled back.

It might have been her imagination, but Sierra didn't think Marti liked her much. Sierra felt a little guilty because she didn't particularly care for Marti either.

Marti lifted her chin and said sweetly, "Well, I suppose we should try to find Todd and Christy."

She led Sierra through the elegant living room toward the back patio.

"Oh, Christy," Marti called out before they reached the patio door. "Your friend is here, Christina."

They stepped out onto the patio that faced the glorious beach and deep-blue ocean. Christy and Todd were sitting across from each other under the umbrella of the patio table. They were holding hands and looking intensely at each other.

Sierra felt certain she and Marti had just interrupted a private moment. She wished they hadn't burst onto the patio.

Todd sprang to his feet and gave Sierra a welcoming hug. Christy was right behind him with another big hug. The two friends pulled apart and looked at each other with joyful smiles and excited hellos.

Sierra could tell that, despite the smile, tears were brimming on Christy's eyelids. She was holding them back with willpower, but Sierra was sure Christy would have let them roll down her cheeks if Sierra and Marti hadn't interrupted them. Sierra knew she wouldn't be at peace until she had a chance to ask Christy privately if everything was okay.

"How was your trip down here?" Todd asked. His warm smile and steady gaze comforted Sierra. Either Todd wasn't as upset as Christy, or he was much better at concealing his feelings.

"Fine. It was a smooth trip. Tawni and I stopped for lunch at a really fun place, which was nice," Sierra replied.

Bob joined them on the patio. Sierra casually gave Christy another look. She seemed to be swallowing her tears quickly.

"Your bag is up in the guest room," Bob said. "Now, is there anything else? Did you want to call home and let them know you arrived safely? Or don't you jet-set kids do that kind of thing anymore?"

"I can call later," Sierra said. "Actually, I'll need to call a friend, too."

"You're welcome to make the calls now," Bob said.

Sierra wondered if Amy would be home. "Then I guess I'll go ahead and try to call, if that's okay."

"Sure. Help yourself. Nearest phone is in the kitchen."

"Yes. I remember," Sierra said, heading back inside. The kitchen phone was the one Christy and Sierra had run to when they called 911 the day of Bob's accident. It felt strange to retrace those steps now, months later.

Sierra dialed her home number and got their voice mail. She left a quick message letting her parents know she had arrived safely and that everything was fine. She knew her parents would appreciate her checking in.

Then she called Amy. Her voice mail picked up Sierra's call, and since she didn't know what kind of message to leave or who might listen to it, she simply said, "Amy, it's Sierra. I'll try to call you later. 'Bye."

*What a wimp! You could have left some kind of coded message like, "Don't forget what I said this morning." Right. Like that's going to change anything. She thinks she's in love with this guy. They're probably together right now.*

"Father God," Sierra prayed in barely a whisper, "I don't know how to pray for Amy. Would You please protect her? Don't let anything bad happen between her and Nathan, please. I really want her to be strong in You and stay pure."

Sierra mouthed an "Amen" to close her prayer and headed back to join the others. But nothing inside her felt comforted. How could she be peaceful when her closest friend at home was in over her head with some guy, and when her dear friend Christy was nearly in tears?

*Relationships! Why do I think I'll be able to figure out my own with a simple list and a creed? I can't even cope when my friends are involved in intense relationships.*

Sierra stopped in the middle of the living room and realized her thinking was wrong. She wasn't in charge of her friends' lives or their relationships. All she needed to concentrate on was her most important relationship, the one with the Lord.

A not-so-favorite feeling stirred in Sierra's stomach. Whenever she had these little glimmers of insight, it usually meant God was about to teach her something. And that meant she was going to be stretched. She didn't like this part of growing up.

Sierra slipped quietly out onto the patio. Bob was standing by the low brick wall, talking to a neighbor. The older, nearly bald man had been walking his little terrier on a retractable leash. Marti sat with Todd and Christy at the table under the shady umbrella; she was talking animatedly and had the couple's attention.

Not quite sure where she fit in, Sierra walked over to the wall and held out her hand to the small dog. It yipped loudly, and its owner pulled on the leash.

"Sorry," Sierra said sheepishly.

"Nothing to be sorry about," the man said. "You hush, Mittsey."

Christy came up next to Sierra and said, "Do you feel like going for a walk?"

"Sure."

"We'll be back in about an hour," Christy said to her uncle.

"Okeydokey."

Sierra noticed as they stepped over the brick wall that Marti was still talking at full speed to Todd, but his eyes followed Christy as they left.

"Do you mind walking in the sand?" Christy asked.

"I love it. I'm glad you suggested this."

"And I'm glad you're here," Christy said. She pulled a ponytail holder from her wrist and gathered her nutmeg brown hair into a high ponytail. Christy was taller than Sierra and moved through the sand with what Sierra considered a casual gracefulness.

Christy wasn't elegant like Tawni. And she wasn't particularly beautiful. But what made Christy striking was her open face and clear-eyed honesty. She had distinctive blue-green eyes, which were once again filling with tears.

"So much has happened in the last few days," Christy said as she directed Sierra toward the shore, where they could walk more easily in the firmly packed sand. "I feel as if my head is so full of information that it's going to crash like a computer hard drive."

"What's going on?" Sierra slipped off her sandals and let her toes mesh into the hot sand.

Dozens of beachgoers were scattered along the shoreline. Little kids played in the water, laughing and squealing. The carefree scene around them was a stark contrast to the downcast mood that hung over Christy.

She let out a long, deep breath. "I just found out I've been accepted at the school I wanted to attend. They turned me down last spring, so I went on with other plans. Now they have an opening, and I have two weeks to decide if I'm going."

The curling hand of an ocean wave unfurled at the their feet, shocking Sierra's toes with its cold fingers.

"And you're having a hard time deciding if you still want to go?"

Christy nodded.

They walked quietly for a few minutes, letting the playful Pacific grab their ankles and then run away. Sierra glanced at Christy and saw the first tear break over the rim of her lower lid and slide down her cheek.

"The school is in Switzerland," Christy said softly.

# eight

SIERRA WALKED ALONGSIDE CHRISTY in silence. Sierra knew such a decision would be hard for Christy. What would happen to Todd and Christy's relationship if she were far away? Would it be jeopardized by the distance between them? Then there was the adventure factor. The two friends had talked about this on the phone. They had decided that the trip to England, when they had met the previous January, had been more to Sierra's liking than to Christy's. Even though Christy said she liked the trip and wouldn't change any of the things God did, by nature she was more of a homebody.

"I can see how this would be a hard decision for you," Sierra said.

"It shouldn't be, I suppose," Christy said, sounding irritated with herself. "I mean, who wouldn't want to go to Switzerland? It's a unique program that gives me college units along with work-experience credits, so it would be almost like two years of study in one."

"You would be gone for a year?"

"Yes," Christy said, her voice growing dim. "It's a minimum commitment of six months, but they really want you to stay a year. The work experience is at an orphanage, and it's too hard on the children if the workers leave every few months."

As they walked on, Christy explained more about the program. She knew it would prepare her for what she wanted to do—to work with small children in a ministry setting. "But it means I'll be leaving Todd and my family for all that time, and I don't know if I want to do that."

"What do your parents think?" Sierra asked.

"They think it's a wonderful opportunity and that it's up to me to decide. I've been offered a scholarship. My parents could never afford to put me through a program like this. They said they'll support whatever I choose to do. They're praying I'll make the right decision."

"And Todd?" Sierra ventured.

Another tear skittered down Christy's cheek. "He's praying I'll make the right decision, too."

Sierra tried to imagine what it would feel like to make such a gigantic decision. She knew if it were her choice, she would fly off to Switzerland in a second. But if a guy like Todd were in her life, she knew it would be much more complicated. Her next question was simplistic, but she had to ask it.

"Could Todd go to Switzerland, too?"

"Not really. He's taken his college courses in too many pieces. He's been to three universities and then worked on a correspondence course while he was in Spain. He needs almost a full year of courses before he can get his B.A. There's nothing in Switzerland that we know of that would provide that for him." Christy stopped walking and let out a sigh. "Do you mind if we sit for a while?"

"Not at all."

They trudged through the sand to an open spot away from the summer crowds and sat down.

"Man, this sand is hot!" Sierra said.

"Try scooping off the top layer," Christy said, demonstrating. "That's what Todd does. Either that or he turns his flip-flops upside down and sits on the bottoms of them."

Sierra tried to scoop the hot sand away and settled back down. "Much better," she said. "But I felt like a cat digging in its litter box."

Christy laughed. It seemed to break the tension.

"So, tell me what's been happening with you," Christy said. "I've been giving you all my problems, and I haven't even asked how you're doing."

"There's not much to tell," Sierra said with a wink. "I'm not being offered scholarships to schools in Switzerland."

"Yet," Christy said with a smile. "Your chance will come soon enough."

"And you will have gone through it all and have made all the right decisions," Sierra teased. "So when it's my turn, you can tell me what to do."

Christy laughed again. "Don't count on it! If there's one thing I've learned, it's that God is a very creative author, and He writes a different story for every person. No two lives or stories are alike."

"Next thing you're going to tell me is there's not another Todd floating around in this world just waiting to meet someone like me."

A tender smile curled Christy's lips. Then she pursed

them together in a tight, contemplative expression. "You know," she said slowly, "everyone thinks Todd is the perfect guy."

"And you don't?"

"He's not perfect," Christy said. "He's an only child, and his parents are divorced. So sometimes it's hard for him to connect and be open with people."

"But he's close to you, isn't he? And your family?"

"Yes. I guess what I'm trying to say is that this decision about Switzerland is really hard for me, and I don't think he completely understands because he's done so much moving around. He would have no problem picking up and leaving for a year. He's done that before. To me it's an overwhelming decision."

"May I ask you something kind of personal?" Sierra asked.

"Sure."

"Are you afraid your relationship will fall apart if you go away to school?"

"I don't know. I think it would last. We've been through a lot already. But then, a year is a really long time. People change."

"Did you change when Todd went to Spain?"

"Yes, I suppose I did."

"But you were still right for each other when you met up again."

"Yes."

"This might be naïve," Sierra said, shifting her position in the sand, "but what's one more test of your relationship after all you've been through? I mean, true love waits, right?"

Christy swallowed hard and nodded. "Yes, true love waits," she repeated. "But don't ever let anyone tell you it's an easy thing to do."

Sierra looked over at Christy, smiled, and said with confidence, "I think you should go to Switzerland, and you and Todd should write letters to each other every week. It would be the ultimate endless romance. Then one day when you're sitting in your rocking chairs and all your teeth have fallen out, you can show those letters to your great-grand-children, and they'll have them bronzed or something."

Christy burst out laughing. "You really have a way of putting things into a different perspective, Sierra."

Sierra laughed with her. "Think about it," she said more seriously. "You have the rest of your life to be with Todd if he really is the right guy for you, which none of the rest of us seems to doubt. But you might not always have the chance to go to Switzerland."

"I know, you're right," Christy said.

"Not that it makes it any easier to take off for a whole year, and not that I have any idea how hard it would be or how much you would miss Todd. But think of it, Christy— Switzerland!"

Sierra did her best to imitate a carefree yodel, which made Christy laugh.

"There's only one flaw in your romantic scheme," Christy said.

"What's that?"

"In all the years I've known Todd, I've never gotten a single letter from him."

"Then I'd say it's about time he started writing!" Sierra said. She felt a little pain in her heart after she spoke. Paul had written to her months ago, and her response had been flippant. What did she know about starting up a romantic correspondence? Who was she to give advice to Christy and Todd?

"You know what?" Sierra said. "You shouldn't listen to me. I think you should pray, and I'll pray, too, and whatever God directs you to do, that's what you should do."

Christy nodded. "This is my story, I guess, isn't it? I have no clue what will happen in the next chapter of my life. All I know is that I want God to be free to write with His pen. Do you feel like praying with me now?"

"Of course. Sure."

Under the deep blue August sky, Sierra and Christy bowed their heads together and asked the Lord, the Author and Finisher of their faith, to write the next chapter of both their lives with His grace and majesty.

Then, done praying and ready to face the others, they sauntered through the sand back to Bob and Marti's house.

"I'm so glad you came," Christy said. "I feel lighter somehow. I still don't know what I'm going to do, but I feel a lot better about everything. I know everything will work out. It always does."

Sierra thought of Amy. *Will everything turn out okay for her? Or does it only turn out okay for those who diligently see God in every area of their lives?* Sierra knew Amy wasn't doing that, though. How could she be seeking God if it was so easy for her to physically express herself with a guy she barely knew?

Amy was settling for less than God's best. That's what Sierra would tell her. And Amy would see Sierra's point, and once she did, she was sure to change her opinion about Nathan.

# nine

SIERRA TRIED TO CALL AMY again after Sierra and Christy arrived back at the house. This time Sierra left a message on Amy's voice mail. "Hi, Aim. I've been thinking about our talk this morning, and I'm still positive I'm right. I just wanted to encourage you to never settle for anything less than God's best. You know what I mean. I'll talk to you when I get home. See you."

She hung up with a sense of accomplishment. *Now I can concentrate on my friends here.*

Just then the doorbell rang. From the sounds that echoed from the direction of the open door, Sierra knew Katie had arrived. Katie Weldon, an exuberant redhead with a quick wit, was already teasing Uncle Bob.

"Be careful with that bag, mister. My only nice clothes in the world are in there, and they're already ironed. Better keep that in mind or there won't be a tip for you."

Sierra stepped into the entryway, and Katie's mischievous green eyes flashed in her direction.

"Sierra!" she screamed. "When did you get here?" She rushed to tackle Sierra in a hug.

"A few hours ago," Sierra answered, her face crushed against Katie's shoulder.

The only one who gave wilder hugs than Katie was Doug. Sierra had a feeling she was going to get her fill of hugs from all her buddies this week.

"All right! Let the fun begin!" Katie said, looking over her shoulder at Todd, Christy, and Marti. "Who else is here?"

"This is it," Todd said. "The other guys are over at Doug's. You know about the shower tonight for Tracy, don't you?"

"Yep. Got my present in my bag. Hey," she called up the stairs, "be extra careful with that bag, mister. Valuable gifts are inside."

Bob appeared at the top of the stairs and played along with the bellboy role. "Would you like me to hang your garments for you, miss?"

"No thanks. You can tell me how to order room service, though. I'm starved."

"Aren't you always?" Marti said under her breath.

Sierra guessed she was the only one who heard it. She wondered how long Marti had been carrying on this love-hate relationship with Christy's friends. Katie was certainly not one of Marti's favorites, like Tawni was. In a way, Sierra felt glad for her sister. In their large family, Tawni had never been anyone's pet. Sierra always felt Granna Mae paid more attention to her than to Tawni. Maybe this made a good balance. Finally Tawni had someone to dote on her.

"The lasagna should be out of the oven in five minutes," Bob said, checking his watch as he came downstairs. "Anyone want to help me throw together a salad?"

They all agreed to help and made their way into the kitchen while Katie chattered nonstop. Sierra was given the task of setting the table. Todd went to work with Christy tossing the salad in a big wooden bowl, but Bob kept finding new items in the refrigerator to add to the mix. Marti slipped out. Katie talked about her new job at a coffee bar inside an upscale bookstore.

"If you guys want, I can whip up some killer cappuccinos for dessert. You still have that espresso machine around here, don't you?"

"It's in the cupboard above the oven," Bob said. He pulled cans of soda from the pantry and filled glasses with ice. "Cappuccinos sure sound good to me. I'd better get this garlic bread in the oven. Could you help me, Sierra?"

Sierra took the long loaf of sourdough garlic bread from Bob and wrapped it loosely in foil. As she opened the oven door to slide in the bread, the whole kitchen filled with the mouthwatering aroma of lasagna. The tomato sauce along the edges of the huge pan bubbled over the sides.

"Man, that smells good," Todd said. He popped open a can of soda and leaned in to have a look at their dinner. "Did you make that, Bob?"

"Sure did."

"You'll have to teach Todd your secret recipe for tomato sauce, Uncle Bob," Christy said. "He made some spaghetti last week at his dad's and it was, well..." Christy gave Todd a tender look and didn't finish her sentence.

"It was out of a can," Todd said, unaffected by Christy's gentle criticism. "The only kind I know how to make."

"It's all in the spices," Bob said.

The doorbell rang again. A minute later, Tawni and

Jeremy entered the kitchen. Broad-shouldered, dark-haired Jeremy had a wide grin on his face and his arm around Tawni's shoulder. They looked good together, even though Sierra was having a hard time adjusting to Tawni's mahogany-colored hair.

"Smells like we came to the right place," Jeremy said. "Hi, Sierra. How're you doing?" He came over and gave her a sideways hug. "Tawni said you had a good trip down. It's nice to see you."

"It's nice to see you, too."

Jeremy greeted the rest of them. Bob pulled out two more plates and added them to the stack at the end of the buffet serving line he had set up on the counter.

"Any of the other guys coming?" Bob asked.

"I think they're all eating at Doug's," Jeremy said. "Tawni said you had enough for one more person."

"There's always enough," Bob said. "And you're always welcome. Where's my wife? We're about ready to eat. Todd, why don't you pull out the lasagna and let it cool a few minutes? I'll go find Marti."

Todd obliged and placed the heavy pan on top of the stove. Sierra retrieved the warmed bread, and Christy turned off the oven. They lined up, ready to dig in.

"She'll be here in a minute. She's on the phone," Bob said, stepping back into the kitchen. "Shall we pray?"

Todd reached for Christy's hand and bowed his head. Jeremy took Tawni's hand.

"Why don't we all hold hands?" Bob asked. "I like it when we do that."

He reached for Sierra's left hand and Christy took her

right. Then Bob prayed the most unique prayer Sierra had ever heard.

"Will You just look at us here, God? You did all this. You brought us all together again, and I'm grateful to You for it. We have some food here, which, of course, You provided out of Your bountiful goodness to us. We appreciate that, too. Now we want to ask for something. Will You let Your kingdom come and Your will be done on earth as it's all planned out in heaven? That would be great. I'm asking this in the name of Christ Jesus."

Sierra kept her eyes closed, waiting for an "Amen." There wasn't one. Everyone leg go of hands and began to talk at once. A sweet closeness enfolded the group.

Sierra felt close to Randy, Amy, and her other friends from school, but it wasn't the same as this. Sierra's relationships here somehow felt clearer and less complicated.

"It's so gooey!" Katie said as Todd tried to serve her a slab of the steaming lasagna.

"The only kind of lasagna worth eating is gooey lasagna," Jeremy said. "Better get your plate in here, Sierra, before Todd. I've seen that guy eat more than any human being should."

"Except Doug," Katie corrected him. "Nobody eats as much as Doug."

"Yeah, good ol' Doug," Todd said, giving Jeremy a mischievous look. "I wonder how the ol' bachelor is doing about now?"

"He's fine now," Jeremy said. "Try asking that question again around midnight."

The two guys exchanged knowing glances and chuckled.

Sierra had no idea why Doug should be any different at midnight that he was right now. The wedding wasn't until Friday, two days away.

"Wonderful news!" Marti said, bursting into the kitchen and waving some papers above her head. "They're still valid. I made the reservations for Sunday. It's all set!"

Everyone looked at Marti, then at each other, and finally at Bob for an explanation. Bob shook his head. He was as much in the dark about Marti's exciting news as they were.

"What's all set?" Christy asked.

"Switzerland!" Marti announced. "We're going to Switzerland!"

"Who's going to Switzerland?" Christy asked cautiously.

"Why, you, Todd, and me, of course."

Todd looked the most surprised of all. "What? When are we going?"

"Sunday. Weren't you listening?"

"This Sunday?" Todd and Christy said in unison.

"Yes, this Sunday! I'm cashing in our last three vouchers, and the travel agent is making the hotel reservations right now. Don't look so shocked. We'll only be gone for a week."

Todd looked at Christy and then back at Marti. "There's one minor problem," he said.

"What's that?" Marti asked.

Todd stuck the spatula back into the lasagna and, without looking up, said calmly, "I can't go."

# ten

"DON'T BE ABSURD," Marti said. "Of course you can go! I've planned this whole trip so Christy can see the school and the orphanage. The least you can do, Todd Spencer, is show some support for Christy and come along so you can help her make this important decision."

Todd looked at Marti. It seemed to Sierra that his chin stuck out in a gesture of resolution. "Christy is capable of making decisions without my telling her what to do. God is the One who will help her make this choice, not me. I can't take the time off from work. I've already used up my last time off for Doug's wedding."

Marti looked stumped. "This is not what I expected you to say, Todd."

"I'll go!" Katie volunteered.

"Fine." Marti slapped the three airline vouchers on the counter and dramatically held up her hands in surrender. "They're all yours, Christina. Three seats on Sunday morning's flight to Switzerland. Do with them as you will. You probably don't even want me to go. That's fine. It's my gift

to you." Marti's voice toned down a notch and some of the
edge softened. "I know this has been a difficult decision for
you. I remembered we had these free flight credits, so I
thought it might help if you could see what the school was
like. Then you would know if you wanted to go or not."

Christy put down her plate and stepped over to her
aunt. Giving Marti a warm hug, Christy added a quick kiss
on the cheek. Sierra had to admire Christy. It seemed more
appropriate to shake the woman rather than hug her. Why
hadn't Marti asked anyone before plunging forward with
her grand plan? And what about Bob? Why didn't she plan
for him to go on the trip?

"I really appreciate it, Aunt Marti," Christy said. "I
know you meant well. But I don't need to go. It's okay. You
can use these for another trip for you and Uncle Bob."

"No, I can't." Marti sniffed and looked at Todd. "I've
already transferred them to the Sunday flight. I won't
change my plans. You have no reason you can't go next
week, Christina. So there are the three tickets. One for you
and two for whomever you wish to invite. You don't have to
include me in the trip if you don't want."

"You know what?" Christy said. "I'd like to have some
time to think about all this. Would it be okay if I let you
know a little later?"

Marti slowly picked up the vouchers. "I suppose. Let me
know what you decide. The sooner the better."

"Okay. Thanks, Aunt Marti. I really appreciate it."

The crowd quietly carried their plates over to the
kitchen table. Once they were seated, the noise level began
to increase. Sierra sat next to Tawni and noticed Marti had
left the kitchen, still wearing a hurt expression. In Sierra's

opinion, Christy deserved a medal for the way she handled the awkward situation. Sierra was certain she wouldn't have been so gracious.

They talked and ate for almost an hour. First they consumed the lasagna, garlic bread, and salad. Then they indulged in Katie's expertly prepared coffee beverages. The evening continued at a leisurely pace until Tawni noticed the time and suggested they leave for Tracy's shower.

Bob went to see if Marti was ready to go. Katie ran upstairs for her gift. Christy stepped into the family room to talk privately with Todd, and Tawni slipped out to use the restroom. Jeremy and Sierra were left alone to clear the table.

"How has your summer been?" Jeremy asked.

"It's gone fast," Sierra said.

"I hear from my uncle that you've been doing amazing things with the kids at the Highland House. They sure are glad you've helped out."

"I really enjoy it," Sierra said. "The kids seem to appreciate everything I do with them. Two weeks ago, a couple of the younger girls asked when I was going to tell them some more Bible stories. That was definitely a change from when I first went there."

"Paul told me your first few Bible story attempts didn't go over so well."

The minute Sierra heard Jeremy mention Paul's name, her heart began to beat wildly. She had wanted to ask about Paul earlier but hadn't. She was surprised, though, at the way her heart pounded at the mere mention of his name.

"I guess so. I mean, he's right, they didn't." Sierra paused and swallowed hard as she lowered a stack of dishes into the sink. "H-how is your brother?"

*Since when did I start stuttering? And why did I say "your brother"? Is it so hard for me to use Paul's name? What's wrong with me?*

"My brother is doing extremely well, thanks. He'll be glad to hear you're doing well."

Sierra could feel Jeremy's gaze on her. Was he trying to see if she was blushing? She kept her head down so he couldn't see her face. She remembered how Jeremy and Tawni had rigged up a meeting between Paul and Sierra a few months ago, before he left for Scotland. That night, Paul had made it clear that he wasn't interested in Sierra. Why was Jeremy looking for anything more from her? So he could tease her? *I won't give him the satisfaction*, Sierra decided.

Lifting her head and shaking back her wild blond curls, Sierra faced Jeremy and said, "And how about you? Have you had a good summer?"

Jeremy hesitated slightly before heading back to the table to clear off the rest of the dishes. "It's been great having Tawni down here. Did she tell you about the sailboat my friend bought? We've been out on it a couple of times. Tawni and I both really love sailing."

"Sounds fun," Sierra said.

Bob entered the kitchen and said, "Thanks, Sierra. I can take it from here. You'd better join the other women. I think they're all ready to go."

"Thanks for a great dinner." Sierra smiled at Bob and imagined that her smile showered him with encouragement. Encouragement was probably something this man didn't receive a lot of from his wife.

"Have a wonderful time," Bob called after her as Sierra hurried to join the others.

"Do you have the present?" Sierra asked Tawni.

"Yes, it's in the car. Let's have everyone go in my car since parking might be a problem."

"I don't think we'll all fit," Marti said. She had changed into a pair of wide-legged pants with a long, kaleidoscope-colored silk jacket. It appeared she had bounced back from the rift with Christy and was ready to be in control of something new. "Let's all go in my car. It's bigger."

No one argued. Tawni grabbed the gift from her car and joined them. She slid across the leather backseat of Marti's new Lexus and balanced the large gift box on her lap.

"What did we get her?" Sierra asked.

Tawni gave a feathery laugh. "Oh, you'll see."

Sierra wasn't in the mood to play one of her sister's guessing games, so she let it go. They drove the few short blocks to Tracy's house. Marti slowly edged her car into the driveway and set the parking brake.

Inside Tracy's parents' house, half a dozen women had already gathered. Light instrumental music played in the background. Sierra realized she was underdressed when she noticed the dining room table. On top of the lace table-cloth sat a silver tea service and china teacups. In the middle of the table, candles, flowers, silverware, and china cake plates surrounded the cake Tawni had brought earlier. It was white with light blue rippled frosting along the sides and was trimmed with real flowers.

Next to the table stood Tracy's mom wearing a flowing summer dress. Sierra glanced down at her shorts and T-shirt. Even Katie had put a jean jacket on over her cotton shirt, and although she had pushed up the sleeves, the look was dressy. Sierra felt like a tomboy who had dropped out of her tree house into the neighbor's yard and landed in the middle of a proper tea party.

Slipping away from all the visiting women, Sierra found the bathroom down the hallway. She took one look in the mirror and groaned.

"You have to grow up sometime, girl," she scolded herself. "Next time you're invited to a bridal shower, you could at least try brushing your hair before you go."

Using her fingers to untangle some of the wind-whipped snarls, Sierra tried to smooth her hair. She washed her face and brushed her teeth with her finger. Then, shaking out her T-shirt in an effort to scare away some of the wrinkles, Sierra looked at her reflection.

"Why can't you be like the others?" she muttered to herself. She didn't like this uncomfortable feeling.

*What is my style? My image?* she thought. *At the dinner with Dad last week, I was uncomfortable being dressed up. Now I'm out of place because I feel underdressed. Where's the middle ground? Who am I trying to be?*

As she joined the party, which had now swelled to nearly twenty-five women, Sierra told herself she was just being Sierra, and that was fine. She didn't need to change inside, nor did she need to change her outfit.

But then she saw Tracy, the star of the event. Tracy's heart-shaped face absolutely glowed. She wore a cotton sundress and a gold cross on a necklace; her hair was cut shorter than Sierra had ever seen it. She looked older than Sierra remembered from their time together in England. Was it her hair? Or the knowledge that, in two days, she was going to become a married woman? Sierra felt her own confidence shatter. She would have been better off staying in her tree house.

"There you are!" Tracy said as she came over to greet Sierra. "I'm so glad you came. I really appreciate it. Would you like some tea? I know the weather is kind of hot for tea, but I wanted to use my new silver teapot. Did you see it? It was my grandmother's. She gave it to us as a wedding gift. Come over and meet my grandmother."

Sierra knew that Tracy was the kind of friend who looked at the inside. The shorts and T-shirt didn't faze her a bit. That knowledge helped Sierra to hush the condemning inner voices that called her "unrefined" and "immature."

While meeting Tracy's relatives, neighbors, and women from her church, Sierra found out this was Tracy's third shower. Many of the women here were ones who hadn't been able to make it to either of the other two showers. She accepted a cup of tea from Tracy's grandmother, who poured it with her wobbly hand. Thanking her, Sierra found a place to sit down.

She carefully balanced the delicate china cup on the saucer and looked around the room. Everyone was so excited for Tracy.

*And they should be*, Sierra thought, sipping her tea. *Tracy held out for a hero and look who God gave her.*

The tea immediately warmed Sierra inside. Or was it the cozy, peaceful sensation that came from watching Tracy, her family, and her friends celebrate? The thought helped to redirect Sierra's feelings of insecurity.

*This is how I want it to be when I get married. Granna Mae pouring the tea, all my friends laughing and hugging me. And I want to look just like Tracy. She's so beautiful!*

Sierra glanced down at the fine china teacup and noticed that the gold band on her finger caught the glow of the candlelight from the end table next to her. It was a strong contrast to the silver bracelets on her arm. That was exactly how she felt in this room—like the silver among the gold.

# eleven

THE GIFT-OPENING PORTION of the shower was in full swing when Tracy lifted a small card from its envelope and announced, "This gift is from Tawni and Sierra." She carefully pulled off the thick white ribbon and handed it to Christy, who was sitting next to her busily making a bouquet from a paper plate and the ribbons taken from Tracy's gifts.

"Almost broke that one," Katie teased. She had announced earlier that every ribbon the bride broke represented a baby she would have. Katie predicted that Tracy would break nine ribbons.

"I did not." Tracy slipped her long thumbnail under the wrapping paper and smiled at her mom.

Sierra mouthed the words, "What is it?" to her sister across the room. Tawni only smiled and nodded toward Tracy, indicating Sierra should watch and see. The gift box bore the name of the boutique Tawni modeled for in Carlsbad. Sierra guessed her sister had received a discount on whatever it was. *And it had better be good for the twenty-two dollars I contributed*, she thought.

Tracy opened the gift box, laid back the tissue, and expressed surprise and delight. Her cheeks began to turn pink.

"This is beautiful!" she exclaimed, lifting the sheer white fabric carefully from the box for everyone to see.

A chorus of oohs and aahs reverberated around the room. Tracy held up a floor-length white gossamer gown. A string of white ribbons and tiny pearls lined the front.

Tracy lifted the robe all the way out and handed it to her cousin, who sat on the other side of her, listing all the gifts as Tracy opened them. Then she drew from the box a short, sheer nightgown with thin straps.

"This is so pretty!" Tracy said. She held the elegant yet very revealing nightgown in front of her. Every woman in the room had something to say.

Sierra pursed her lips together and glanced around at the delighted guests. Tawni looked pleased that Tracy liked her selection, smiling as if she wouldn't mind having such an outfit for her honeymoon. Christy was feeling the fine white fabric and smiling at Tracy. Tracy's mom admired the nightgown and whispered to Tracy's grandmother that it was a special gift.

"Doesn't leave much to the imagination," Katie quipped.

The women chuckled softly.

Tracy glowed. She shot her mom an excited grin and then carefully folded the gown and robe and tucked them back in the box.

"Thanks so much!" Tracy said, catching Tawni's eye and

then looking over at Sierra. "I love it, and I think Doug will, too."

All the women chuckled again. One said, "Oh, you can be sure of that!"

Sierra felt like crying. She was surprised at her reaction. At first, she was embarrassed and a little annoyed at her sister for buying such a revealing outfit and for not telling her ahead of time what it was. Now she felt like crying. It was an emotional experience to watch her friend become excited about her honeymoon and shamelessly show how much she was looking forward to giving her body to her husband for the first time.

Swallowing quickly, Sierra held back the glistening tears that had risen to her eyes. She decided this was a powerful celebration for all the women partly because of Doug and Tracy's purity. They hadn't even kissed yet. Doug had vowed he wouldn't kiss a girl until they were standing at the altar on their wedding day, and he had kept that vow. In two days, he would stand before God and many witnesses and promise himself for life to this special woman. Then he would seal that promise with their very first kiss.

The tears welled up in Sierra's eyes again. She had never kissed a guy, and at this moment, she was intensely glad about that. She didn't know if she wanted to wait until her wedding day for her first kiss, but she knew that when she did kiss a guy, it would mean a lot. A lot more than a first-date experiment, as it seemed to have been for Amy and Nathan.

Tracy held up a bottle of bath oil and lotion from the

box on her lap. "Thanks, Heather," she said. "You remembered." She sniffed the top of the bottle. "I love this fragrance."

"There's another box there, too. It has the same wrapping. It's for Doug, but you can open it," Heather said.

Tracy tugged at the ribbon, and it snapped in her hand.

"Aha!" Katie's short red hair swished as she announced, "That's one! And on Doug's present, too. Must mean your first child will be a boy."

Tracy handed Christy the broken ribbon and gave a cute little shrug. She opened the box and started to laugh. "Oh, he'll love this."

"I thought we shouldn't leave Doug out of all the bathtime fun," Heather said.

Tracy lifted out a big bottle of Mr. Sudsy bubble bath.

"That's perfect!" Katie said. "Now you have to name your first child Mr. Sudsy."

Everyone laughed, and Tracy passed the box around the circle.

Forty-five minutes later, Tracy finished opening the gifts. All of them were personal items for her. She received four other nighties, including a long black one from Aunt Marti. The only duplicate gifts were lotion, but Tracy insisted she would use them both.

The gifts made the rounds of the women sitting in the big circle. Soft music played in the background, and candles gave off a faint scent of lilies.

"Before we cut the cake," said Tracy's mom, standing and trying to get everyone's attention, "I'd like to say a few things."

Sierra noticed Tracy's mom had a note card in her hand, which was trembling slightly. It reminded Sierra of her dad at the restaurant. Why was it so hard for parents to speak to their children about the things deepest in their hearts?

"When Tracy was born, she weighed only four pounds and two ounces. We had to leave her in the hospital for almost three weeks because her lungs weren't fully developed. I remember sitting by her in the hospital one night, wishing I could take her out of that incubator and hold her in my arms."

The room had grown still as each woman listened. Looks of tender compassion brushed across their faces.

"I remember the day the doctor told me I could take you home," Tracy's mom said, looking over at her daughter. "I thought, 'This is it! This is what I've been waiting for. Now I'm never going to let her go.' Well, that was more than twenty years ago. And now I have to let go."

Women all around the room began to blink. A few reached into their purses for tissues.

"I wanted to say something to you tonight that would let you know how much I love you. I found this poem, and it expresses exactly how I feel. It's called, 'What a Mother Thinks.'"

Tracy's mom cleared her throat and read from her card.

"I love you so much.
There is no way I can possibly put into
words how proud I am of you.
You're absolutely beautiful.

Sometimes when our eyes meet,
it's like gazing into a reflecting pool.
I see in you glimmers of my past.
Do you see in me hints of your future?
You are everything I ever prayed for.
There's nothing about you I'd change.
I love you more than you will ever know,
more than you will ever ask.
There's nothing I wouldn't give for you,
nothing I wouldn't do for you.
You are my daughter, and I will always love you
with a love so immense, so eternal,
I could never find a way to squeeze it into words."

Sierra swallowed hard and looked around the room. Everyone was crying.

"Would you please stand, honey? I'd like to bless you."

Tracy stood, and her mother stepped over beside her. They were about the same height. With her short hair, Tracy closely resembled her mom.

Her mother placed her still-quivering hand on Tracy's forehead, and paraphrasing Numbers 6, she said, "May the Lord bless you and keep you, Tracy Lynn. May the Lord make His face shine upon you, and be gracious to you. May the Lord lift up His countenance upon you and give you peace."

The two women looked into each other's eyes and exchanged unspoken words in the way only a mother and daughter can. Then her mom leaned over and, with a kiss on the cheek, whispered something in Tracy's ear that made her smile.

The phone rang, and Katie jumped up to answer it.

"I'd like to first get a picture of Tracy cutting the cake," her mom said. "Then please come help yourselves."

Tracy had positioned herself at the table with the silver cake slicer when Katie burst into the room and said, "Trace, you have to take this call."

"Just a minute," her mother said. "Picture first!"

Tracy smiled, her mom took the shot, and Katie called out, "Hurry up! You have to hear this."

Sierra watched as Tracy took the phone and covered her open ear with her hand. "Hello?...Yes...Yes...No...Where...Wait. Who is this?...Hello?"

She handed the phone back to Katie. All the younger women had gathered around her.

"What was that all about?" Heather asked.

Tracy closed her eyes and shook her head. "I knew this was going to happen."

"What?"

Tracy let out a deep breath and said, "Anyone want to go with me? The guys have kidnapped Doug. They said they won't let him go unless I come see him first."

"Where is he?" Tracy's mom asked, stepping into the circle.

"They chained him to the Balboa Island Ferry and paid the captain to let him ride all night," Tracy said.

"That doesn't sound so bad," Christy said. "I thought the guys were going to do something really wild."

"You haven't heard the worst," Tracy said. "They said I won't recognize him."

"Why?"

"I think they dressed him in some kind of costume."

"Jeremy wouldn't do anything like that to Doug," Tawni said.

"Guess again," Katie said. "I think that was Jeremy on the phone."

"What kind of costume could he be wearing?" Sierra asked.

Tracy looked around at her friends. "There's only one way to find out. Mom?"

"Go, honey. It's okay. Here! Take the camera. We'll save some cake for you."

# twelve

SIERRA SQUEEZED INTO THE BACKSEAT of Tracy's car along with Christy and Tawni. Katie and another girl were in the front seat and five more followed in Heather's car. Everyone in Tracy's car was talking at once, and the dignity of the earlier hour had vanished.

"I'm going to park on the Newport Beach side," Tracy said. "Let's all walk onto the ferry together. Watch out for these guys. I wouldn't be surprised if they had water balloons ready to launch at us."

"Do you think it's a trick?" Tawni asked.

"Could be," Katie agreed. "They could be setting us up. Maybe they didn't do anything to Doug, and they're just trying to get you to fall into their trap. Did you ever think of that, Trace?"

Tracy stopped the car at a red light and looked over at Katie. "No—think about it. These guys have far more reasons to pull a prank on Doug than they do me. I kind of wished we had changed clothes, though."

"There wasn't time," Katie said. "Your true love is in

desperate need of your assistance. How can you think of changing into the appropriate attire for a rescue?"

"I like this dress. I want to take it on our honeymoon, and I don't want those baboons to ruin it."

"Hey, that's my baboon you're talking about," Christy said.

"And mine," Tawni added.

"If anyone has anything to get back at Doug for, it's me," Katie said. "I should have been on the baboons' side tonight. Christy, remember when we went on the houseboat, and Doug gave me a black eye?"

"That was an accident," Christy said unsympathetically.

"It's always an accident with him, but he's gotten me good more than once."

The light turned green, and Tracy drove on.

"What kind of a costume would they put on him?" Tawni asked.

"Whatever they could find," Tracy said.

"Or whatever they could afford," Christy suggested.

"Gisele said she caught Larry calling around to costume shops last week. She didn't hear what kind of costume he was asking about, though."

"Oh, great!" Tracy said. "He might very well be a big baboon! Poor Doug, riding the ferry all night in a costume. I sure hope he keeps his sense of humor."

"You think it's a baboon costume, really?" Katie asked.

"Who knows," said Tracy. "It could be a grass skirt and coconuts, knowing these guys."

"I bet it's a Raggedy Andy costume," Tawni said.

Everyone started to laugh.

"Why in the world would you say that?" Sierra asked.

"Because Jeremy's old roommate had a perfect Raggedy Andy costume. I saw a picture of him in it from a party he went to with his girlfriend. I bet they put Doug in that Raggedy Andy costume."

"He would have thrown the red wig into the water," Tracy said.

"And what's wrong with red hair?" Katie asked indignantly.

"Nothing. It's the wig. Doug hates anything restrictive on his head. He hardly ever wears hats. A wig would drive him crazy."

Turning onto a side street, Tracy expertly parallel-parked the car. The girls were so eager that they piled out before Tracy had even turned off the engine. The car that was following them parked at the end of the block, and the other girls hurried to catch up.

"Does anyone have any money?" Tracy asked. "We need fare for the ferry."

Heather said she had twenty dollars with her, enough to cover everyone. The girls took off in a rush, all talking at the same time.

"Do you have the camera?" Sierra asked.

"Yes. It's right here. Everyone stick together and watch out for these guys. They're sneaky."

They rounded the corner and saw a large crowd waiting for the next ferry, which was approaching from Balboa Island, a short distance away.

"Do you see any of the guys?" Christy asked.

"No," Katie said. "Maybe they're on the ferry."

The girls stood together, looking around and talking at full speed. Sierra fixed her eyes on the ferry coming toward them. When she had visited at Easter, she and some of her friends had ridden on it over to Balboa Island. She remembered the ferry was pretty small, just large enough to hold four cars. The journey took about fifteen minutes.

It was dark across the water, yet plenty of light was supplied from the Ferris wheel and the Balboa Fun Zone amusement park to their right. As the ferry inched toward them, they saw a big yellow something in the front section.

"Tracy," Sierra said, tapping her shoulder, "what is that?"

Everyone looked to where Sierra pointed and squinted to see.

"Here he comes again," one of the men in the crowd ahead of them said. "Poor guy. I wonder if he's going to have to ride all night."

A man next to him said, "I heard someone say he's getting married this weekend. His girlfriend is supposed to come and make him promise not to chicken out."

The people around the girls all laughed.

"His fiancée is here," Katie said, loud enough for everyone to hear.

Now all eyes were on the girls, and the girls all looked at Tracy. She offered a weak smile to the curious crowd and gazed back out to sea.

"If I were you, I'd get while the going is good," one of the men said. "I heard someone say they were going to call the police."

"Oh no," Sierra heard Tracy mutter. "He's a big chicken."

"No, he's not," Christy said. "Doug is brave when it comes to difficult situations; you know that. The police will understand it's a prank."

"Christy," Sierra said, elbowing her and pointing to the big yellow blob in the front of the ferry. "Doug really is a chicken. He's a big yellow chicken. Look."

The ferry docked with a clunk, and poor Doug stood near the prow, dressed in a chicken costume, complete with a headdress, which Sierra imagined must be driving him crazy. He spotted them and called out, furiously waving his arms—or rather, his wings, "Trace! Over here! Hurry!"

All of them pushed through the crowd with quick apologies of "excuse me, pardon me" and dashed onto the ferry. Not one of the guys was anywhere to be seen. Doug's costume was a mass of bright yellow feathers, detailed and authentic enough for him to qualify as halftime entertainment at a pro football game.

"Are you okay?" Tracy asked, reaching for his hand and catching her breath. A bowling ball was attached to the end of a heavy chain locked around Doug's ankle.

"Get this head thing off me. It's attached in the back, and I can't undo it with these wings."

Tracy fumbled with the clasps. "Help me, you guys."

Tawni was the first to jump in, then Christy.

"Fare please," the attendant said as the ferry pulled away from shore, towing them over to the island. He was a local beach boy with long, sun-bleached hair hanging in his eyes. He seemed unaffected by the chicken on board.

"Here. I have it," Heather said, paying for all of them.

"Where are the guys?" Katie asked.

"Don't move, Doug," Tawni said, fiddling with the costume. "I've got it. Bend your neck, and we can get this off you."

He cooperated gladly, and the giant feathered head and long orange beak pointed toward the ground. Within two minutes, Tawni had the monstrous chicken head off him. A red-faced, heavily perspiring Doug looked at her with gratitude.

"The guys are on the island waiting for us," Doug said.

"Oh yeah?" Katie said. "I want to see their faces when we pull up and show them we've freed you."

"I'm not going anywhere with this bowling ball around my ankle," Doug said. Turning to Tracy, he touched her cheek with his feathered hand and said, "Thanks for coming. Sorry if this interrupted your party."

"Don't worry about it," Tracy said. "Are you all right?" Two tiny yellow feathers stuck to her cheek.

"Much better now, thanks. I've been developing a bad case of claustrophobia the past hour. It feels good to breathe clean air."

"You've been riding for an hour?" Tracy asked.

"I don't know. It feels like days."

"How are you going to take off the ball and chain?" Sierra asked. She knew she couldn't handle having something like that around her ankle. She would do better trapped inside the claustrophobic costume than be weighted down with a bowling ball around her foot—especially on a boat. The guys hadn't thought through how dangerous their prank could have turned if something had gone wrong on board.

"Larry has the combination to the lock," Doug said to Sierra. "Unless you feel like trying to figure out the combination, he'll have to get me off this big tub."

"I can do it," a man said. He was one of the many curious passengers on the ferry who had been observing the crazy scene. Without being invited, he knelt down by Doug's feet and put his ear to the lock. "Quiet, everyone!" he hollered. The stranger began to work the lock.

In less than two minutes, the man had the lock open. A spontaneous cheer rose from the girls and the observers. Katie, who was standing with Heather at the other end of the ferry, turned around to see what everyone was cheering about. Sierra considered joining them. She wanted to see the guys' reaction, too.

"This is what I do for a living," the man said, pushing up his glasses. "I'm a locksmith. Here's my card."

"May I pay you?" Doug said, slipping his foot out of the now open shackle.

"Nope. Consider it a wedding present. Just make sure you show up at the altar."

"No need to worry about that," Doug said.

Sierra noticed they were nearing the island. The guys had set up their own viewing area, complete with beach chairs, ice chest, and binoculars. She could see Larry standing in the middle of them with his hands cupped over his mouth.

He called out, "Why did the chicken cross the bay?"

"I thought they would have run out of those jokes by now," Doug muttered. He had unzipped the back of the chicken suit and was stepping out of it. His T-shirt and shorts were soaked with sweat. "Now it's time for me to play a little joke on them," he said, crouching behind one of the cars.

"Here, Tawni. Hide this." He handed her the big fluffy costume.

"Hide it? Where?"

"And Sierra, when I give the signal, you throw the ball and chain into the water. Ready?"

Sierra lifted the heavy ball. The ferry nosed its way into the dock, and Doug hid himself in a shadow at the edge of the deck. Grinning, he climbed onto the railing.

"Doug," Tracy yelled, rushing over to him, "what are you doing?"

"Playing the best trick of my life," he whispered.

# thirteen

THE FERRY DOCKED, and Doug yelled, "I can't take this anymore!" Then, with a quick nod to Sierra, he jumped feet first into the bay.

Sierra was startled for a moment. Then she remembered his instructions and threw the bowling ball into the water, far away from where Doug had jumped.

Tracy let out a loud shriek.

Larry bellowed, "What's he doing? There's a bowling ball on his leg!"

Katie immediately ran back to where Sierra and Tracy stood and frantically yelled, "Isn't anyone going to do something?"

Before they could stop her, Katie whipped off her jacket and scrambled over the side of the ferry into the water.

"You guys can't do that!" the ferry pilot called out to the swimmers. The pilot threw up his arms in frustration as Todd and Jeremy ran onto the ferry, with Larry and the other guys right behind them.

"It's okay!" Christy yelled at them.

"He didn't have the bowling ball on!" Sierra yelled.

"It was supposed to be a joke!" Tracy yelled.

Todd leaped over the side and swam over to Katie.

"I can't find him!" Katie screamed, surfacing in a panic.

"It's okay," Todd said, coming up beside her and shouting for her to calm down. "Doug is playing a joke on us."

"He is?" Katie treaded water and looked around.

From Sierra's vantage point, the water looked disgusting. It had a thin film of oil on the surface that caught the lights from the shore and made wobbly, distorted rings around Todd and Katie.

"Then where is he?" Katie cried out, scanning her surroundings.

Todd immediately dove down to look while Katie kept treading water.

"Is he on the other side?" Katie called out.

Tracy and Christy dashed to the other side of the ferry and searched the water, along with a dozen onlookers who hadn't exited yet.

Leaning out of his control booth, the captain said to Sierra, "Is there somebody still in the water? They can't do that."

"Three people are in the water. One of them hasn't surfaced yet, though," Sierra responded.

"That's it. I'm making the call," the captain said and ducked back inside.

"Doug!" Tracy screamed. "Doug!"

"Is he over there?" Tawni asked, her voice filled with panic.

Jeremy had his arm around her, and they were looking

back and forth across both sides of the water.

Tracy screamed out again, "Doug, this isn't funny!"

"I'm over here," a voice called from the side of the ferry where Sierra stood. She scanned the water but couldn't see anyone.

"Tracy, he's over here!" Sierra called out.

Immediately, two dozen people ran to that side of the ferry.

"What are you doing?!" Tracy yelled into the dark water. "Where are you? I can't see you!"

Todd surfaced, and Christy cried out, "Todd, he's okay. He's in the water somewhere."

"Where?" Katie asked, her head bobbing. Suddenly, a glaring searchlight shone from the side of the ferry, lighting up the water and revealing the heads of Todd, Katie, and far to the side, Doug.

"All right," the captain called through his bullhorn, "everyone out of the water. Now! I've called the authorities. This prank has gone on too long. Get out now."

Katie and Todd swam toward the shore, but Doug didn't move.

The light shone on him, and the captain called, "Get out of the water immediately."

"I'd like to," Doug said as the large audience on the ferry and on the shore watched him in the spotlight. "But you see, I, um…I seem to have lost my shorts somewhere here in the water and ah…"

The audience burst out laughing. Someone took a picture.

The locksmith stepped up next to Sierra and said, "Here. I have an extra pair."

He unzipped the small gym bag he had with him and threw a pair of swim trunks to Doug.

Everyone watched while Doug grabbed the trunks and then maneuvered underwater to get them on.

Katie and Todd were scrambling up the sharp rocks by the dock, trying to get out of the water. Suddenly, Katie let out a cry of pain. Sierra thought she heard Katie say, "My foot." But so much noise and confusion filled the air that it was hard to tell. The cars on the shore side were honking to get onto the ferry, a siren wailed as a police car tried to get through behind them, and everyone was heckling Doug as he dog-paddled toward the rocks.

"Come on," Tawni said. "Let's get off the boat."

She and Jeremy led the way, with Sierra, Tracy, and Christy right behind. The other guys from the group and three of the other girls were already off the ferry. They had gathered around the rocks, where Todd was trying to help Katie get up on level ground.

When Sierra arrived, she could see that Katie was in serious pain. She was lying on her side, soaking wet, shivering, and holding her ankle.

"Try not to move it," Todd said, leaning over her, dripping wet.

"What happened?" Christy yelled over the siren, which was now right behind them.

"She caught her foot between the rocks," Todd said. He flipped his hair back in his surfer fashion, sending droplets everywhere.

"I twisted it," Katie said between gasps for breath. "Ouch! It really hurts."

Sierra noticed that the vehicle with the siren was an ambulance, not a police car.

Larry motioned to the paramedic and called out, "Over here."

The crowd seemed to grow larger as the paramedic bent over Katie and began to ask her questions. Doug, who was safely out of the water and wearing the loaned swim trunks, which were too small for him, stood beside Todd. Christy and Tracy had joined them, but Sierra hung back with Tawni, Jeremy, and some of their friends.

"This turned out to be a mess," Tawni said. She held the bulky chicken costume in front of her.

"Maybe we should go back to Doug's house," Jeremy suggested. "Or were you planning to go back to Tracy's?"

"I think we should go to Tracy's, as long as Katie is okay."

One of the girls from their group ventured over to the thick of the action and returned to say the paramedics were taking Katie to the hospital. It was possible her foot was broken.

"That's awful," Sierra said. "Isn't she supposed to be in the wedding?"

"Not really," Tawni said. "Christy is the maid of honor, and Katie was going to do the guest book, I think."

"She might end up on crutches," Sierra speculated.

"I'm sure she'll find a way to blame it on Doug," Heather said.

"Well, if he hadn't jumped in..." Tawni said in Katie's defense. "She was acting out of concern. Obviously, she didn't know he had taken off the bowling ball."

"That shouldn't matter," Jeremy said. "Why would it be Doug's fault? Katie didn't have to go flying into the water like some superhero. Why did she feel responsible to save Doug?"

"That's the way she is," Sierra interjected, hoping to calm the brewing argument between Jeremy and Tawni. "Same with Todd. The two of them respond quickly in a crisis and then think about it later."

"If you ask me," Tawni said, "Doug was the one who wasn't thinking. It was a bad move for him to try to pull off this joke. He practically scared Tracy to death. I bet she's furious with him."

Tawni was right. Tracy *was* furious.

Katie was taken to the hospital, and Christy and Todd went along in the ambulance. The rest of the group gathered back at Tracy's house; anger was written all over Tracy's usually sweet face. Her mom invited them to come in and have some cake. Tracy was the only one who didn't eat any.

Doug didn't seem to take the incident too lightly either. He kept looking at Tracy as if hoping for a sign that she had calmed down.

"I think the locksmith was your guardian angel," Heather told Doug. "I mean, how many guys do you know who can open a lock like that and then just happen to have an extra pair of shorts with them?"

"What a ridiculous notion!" Marti spouted. "How absurd to think God would send help to save you from your own foolishness."

Doug immediately spoke up in agreement with her. "It was foolish. I can say before everyone here" —he looked at Tracy and attempted a sincere smile—"that I learned my lesson tonight. I'm finished with practical jokes. It's no fun when someone gets hurt. Or scared," he added.

"I should say not," Marti agreed. "I'm ready to go home. Who is going with me?"

Sierra looked around. She was the only one left of the group that had ridden over with Marti. Katie and Christy were still at the hospital, and Tawni and Jeremy had left earlier, since they had a long ride down the coast. "I guess I am," she said.

All the way home, Marti vented her concerns and frustrations about Christy's friends' foolishness. "It's time they grew up," Marti said. "You're new to this group, so you don't know them the way I do, Sierra. I've known these young people for years. It's absolutely ridiculous the way they carry on like immature teenagers. It's a good thing Robert wasn't there tonight. I'm sure my foolish husband would have been right in the middle of it all."

Marti pressed the garage door opener. "This only proves what I've thought all along. Christy must go away to school, or Todd will never mature. That young man hardly has an ounce of responsibility in his body."

Sierra thought of how Todd had turned down the invitation to go to Switzerland because he couldn't take any more time off from work. That sounded pretty responsible to her.

"There's no reason Christy shouldn't go to school in Europe. I can't understand why she would even consider passing up such and opportunity, to stay around here with friends like that."

"Don't you like Todd?" Sierra asked as Marti turned off the engine.

Marti looked shocked. "Of course! We love Todd like our own son. How can you ask such a thing?"

Sierra shrugged.

"My concern is for Christina. She is not the kind of woman who should marry young. This is her chance to see the world. Otherwise, she will regret it years later."

Sierra wasn't sure how Marti had come up with such logic. *I wonder how old Marti was when she and Bob married.* Sierra decided she had better not say anything, so she focused on keeping her lips sealed as they went inside.

On the kitchen counter was a note from Bob, saying he had received a call from Todd and had gone to the hospital.

"Who knows when they'll be back," Marti said. "I'm going to bed. Please make yourself at home."

"Thank you," Sierra said. "Good night."

"It's been a night, all right," Marti muttered. "If those two ever make it to the altar, I'll be amazed."

Sierra didn't know if Marti was referring to Doug and Tracy or to Todd and Christy.

# fourteen

THE NEXT DAY SPED BY in a wild and colorful blur. Katie and Christy had arrived home from the hospital late the night before when Sierra was already asleep. In the morning, Katie modeled the cast on her right foot and asked Sierra to sign it. Despite the trauma of the night before, Katie was in good spirits.

The phone rang all morning with calls from friends checking in on Katie. Of course, everyone had to go over his or her version of what had happened. Heather told them it was in the paper. Christy and Sierra ran downstairs to find the story, leaving Katie limping behind.

The write-up was on the second page of the local news section and consisted of nine lines describing a prank played by some college students on their friend who was getting married. The last line said, "Police Chief Sanders warned that such activities can be dangerous, as was evidenced by one of the teens' being taken to the hospital with a broken leg."

"Foot," Katie corrected Christy as she read the article

371

aloud in the kitchen. "I'm going to call them and tell them it was a broken foot, not a broken leg."

Before she had the opportunity to make good on her threat, the phone rang. Bob took it and went into the other room.

The three girls were still in their nightshirts when Sierra noticed the time. "It's almost noon, you guys. We should probably get dressed soon."

"It can't be that late!" Christy said. "I have to be at the church at four for the dress rehearsal, and then at six, there's a fancy dinner for the wedding party and relatives. I still don't know what I'm going to wear, and I need to call my parents."

Christy spent close to an hour on the phone with her parents, discussing Marti's plans for the Switzerland trip, which only seemed to stress Christy out more. She talked Sierra into ironing a blouse for her while she jumped into the shower.

Katie hopped around on her crutches but seemed to have lost some of her spring. The cast went up to her knee and had to be uncomfortable; also, she was probably still dealing with the trauma of having a broken bone.

Marti fluttered around the house, worrying about everything for everyone. Did Todd pick up his tux yet? Should they call Tracy's mom to see if she needed help on any last-minute details?

Marti followed Sierra up to the guest bedroom, where she put the freshly ironed blouse on a hanger in the closet.

Katie had stretched out on the bed and propped up her foot with some pillows.

"What about Doug?" Marti continued her worry-fest.

"Should Bob call him to make sure he has picked up the ring from the jeweler? And what about the marriage license? Todd and Christy will be required to sign it tomorrow as the witnesses. Do you think Doug will remember to bring it to the church?"

Marti finally left Christy, Katie, and Sierra alone in the bedroom when she realized she hadn't called her favorite department store to make sure the wedding gift had been delivered to Tracy's house.

"Remind me to elope," Christy said, towel-drying her long, nutmeg-colored hair.

"Oh?" Katie said. "Is this something we should start reminding you of very soon?"

"No," Christy stepped back into the adjoining bathroom and turned on the hair dryer.

Katie and Sierra exchanged glances.

"I give them six months," Katie said.

"What if she goes to Switzerland?" Sierra asked.

"She won't go. Would you?"

"Yes, I definitely would," Sierra said.

"So would I, but Christy won't. She hasn't been bitten by the same adventure bug that got you and me."

"I heard that," Christy said, turning off the blow-dryer. "And for your information, I think I'm going to go."

"You are?" Katie and Sierra said in unison.

Christy stepped back in the bedroom and said calmly, "I think I'm going to go with my aunt to check things out next week. I asked my mom to go with us, and she's going to talk to Dad about it. They'll be at the wedding tomorrow night, and she said she would tell me then. If Mom goes, then I'll go."

"Rats," Katie said. "I was hoping you would take me."

"O , I'm sure you would have a lot of fun hopping around urope on crutches."

"He , it's not as bad as that girl in the *Heidi* movie. What was her ame? The rich one from the city? She managed to get around the Alps in a wheelchair."

"Yes," said Christy with a laugh, "but she had Heidi and the gra dfather to push her around, and all you would have is Aun Marti and me."

Ju t then the door swung open, and Marti blew in, her face ink. Sierra wondered if she had radar that could detec when they were joking about her.

"I've canceled my account at that store," she said. "I ordered two settings of Doug and Tracy's china, and the store told me they delivered everything but the salad plates."

Sierra and Katie looked at each other. This did not seem like a tragedy.

"Only, just now they informed me that the salad plates are, in fact, in stock and available if I'd like to come down and get them myself. That means, if Doug and Tracy are going to receive the complete set, I have to pick them up. Who wants to go with me?"

Again Sierra and Katie exchanged glances. Then Sierra and Christy looked at each other.

"I need to finish getting ready for the rehearsal," Christy said. "I have to leave in less than an hour."

"My foot has been kind of sore," Katie said.

Sierra felt a tightening in her chest. She didn't want to go with Marti, someone she didn't particularly enjoy, on this stressful mission. Sierra knew if Doug and Tracy's wedding was anything like her brother Cody's, they couldn't even open the present until after they came back from their honeymoon. She was certain the salad plates would not be missed.

"Can't you ask the store to deliver them?" Sierra asked calmly. "I mean, didn't they deliver the rest of the china to Tracy's house? They should be able to deliver the salad plates, too. If not today, then certainly by tomorrow."

"That's right," Katie said, "And tell them to do a gift wrap."

Marti's worry-creased forehead began to smooth out. "I think you're right. Why should I have to pick up the salad plates? The store made the mistake, not me. I'm going to call them right back and tell them exactly that."

She breezed out of the room, leaving Katie, Christy, and Sierra to exchange glances.

"Yep," Katie said, stretching her hands behind her head. "Like I was saying, I hope you and your mother have a delightful time in the Alps with Aunt Marti. You couldn't pay Sierra or me to endure that nonstop for a week."

"Oh, I don't know," Sierra said. "Maybe if the price was right."

There was a tap on the door.

"Come in," Christy called out.

Uncle Bob poked his head around the open door. "Everybody decent?"

"Yes."

"Christy, Todd's here."

"Already? We're not supposed to leave for almost another hour."

"Well, it seems he hasn't purchased a wedding gift yet, and he thought maybe you could go shopping with him before the rehearsal."

Katie started to giggle. "Tell him to get on the phone with Marti right now, and he can chip in for some lovely salad plates. Or maybe the matching gravy boat hasn't been purchased yet."

"Katie, be nice," Christy said. "Uncle Bob, could you please tell Todd I'll be ready in about fifteen minutes, but we'll have to go shopping for a present tomorrow morning."

"Got it," Bob said, bowing like a gracious butler.

"Oh, wait!" Christy said. "What's Todd wearing?"

"Standard apparel for a beach bum."

"I was afraid of that. Could you also remind him this is a dressy occasion? He probably should go home to change."

"As you wish," Bob said with a smile, closing the door behind him.

"He's been to weddings before," Christy muttered, bending over and lowering her head so that her damp hair hung almost to the floor. She began to vigorously brush the underside. "I can't believe he thought he could show up in shorts and flip-flops."

"Are you sure it's formal?" Katie said. "My brother's wedding rehearsal was very casual." Before Sierra or Christy could comment, Katie answered herself. "But then my brother got married in a park in Reno, and the rehearsal dinner was at the Blackjack Buffet at the Starlight Motel."

Sierra started to laugh. "Are you serious?"

Katie nodded but didn't elaborate. Sierra decided it was best not to laugh.

Bob tapped again on the door and entered. "Mission accomplished," he said. "Todd will be back in forty-five minutes with bells on."

"Bells?" Christy questioned. "I'll be happy if he manages to find a pair of dress slacks and a clean shirt." Turning to Sierra and Katie, she said, "Is that too much to ask?"

Neither of them dared to answer.

Uncle Bob left, and Christy went to work on her makeup while Katie and Sierra discussed Christy's outfit options for the evening. They finally agreed on a simple short skirt and a different top than the one Sierra had ironed. It was a nice basic outfit that Katie convinced Christy would work well with either a casual or dressy escort.

Sierra admired Christy's calm response to everything that had been thrown at her all afternoon. She looked like the picture of repose and sweetness as she leaned toward the bathroom mirror to run the mascara brush over her eyelashes. Sierra wanted to be like that. Mild-mannered and happy in a deep, settled way.

"What are you two going to do all night?" Christy asked.

"Oh, we thought we would go Rollerblading," Katie joked. "Then maybe do a little jogging along the beach. Maybe join the neighborhood kids for some street hockey. You know, the usual."

Christy laughed. "Well, whatever you do, have fun." She swished out the door, leaving a faint scent of green-apple hair spray behind her.

"So what do you want to do?" Sierra asked Katie.

"I don't know. What do you want to do?"

Sierra laughed. "You know, we're pathetic."

"No we're not. Let's talk Bob into taking us some-where."

"Okay. Where?"

"I don't care. Any place that doesn't discriminate against one-legged redheads."

Sierra laughed. "Come on. Let's go coax him together. I have a feeling you have more experience at this than I do."

"You know it," Katie said, reaching for her crutches. "Come with me, Sierra, and I shall teach you the fine art of persuasion. Our target is the shy and unsuspecting Uncle Bob."

# fifteen

SIERRA TURNED OVER and pulled the covers up to her chin. She wiggled her feet and tried to get comfortable. The dark guest room was quiet except for the gentle ruffle of Katie's breathing.

It was after midnight, but Christy wasn't back yet. Sierra felt like a mother hen, worrying about her. Was she with Todd? Where they discussing her choice about school in Switzerland? Or was the wedding party playing some more practical jokes on Doug and Tracy?

Sierra and Katie had spent an uneventful evening going out to dinner with Bob and Marti and coming back to their house to watch TV. Apparently, Katie's art of persuasion was still in the training stages when it came to Uncle Bob. Of course, he was affected by Marti, who was still anxious about the wedding. She had spent most of dinner thinking of things they should worry about just in case no one else had thought of them yet. Marti had gone so far as to worry whether the air-conditioning would be turned on inside the reception hall so the cake wouldn't get mushy and tumble over.

Katie and Sierra had headed upstairs to bed at eleven o'clock, but since they had slept in so late that morning, Sierra couldn't sleep now. She thought about Amy and wondered what was happening with Nathan. Sierra hoped that Amy had listened to her message and would understand what she was trying to say.

What concerned Sierra most was that Amy's parents were having marriage difficulties, which seemed to make Amy eager for attention and love. Sierra hoped Amy wouldn't compromise her standards with a guy like Nathan in order to get the affection she craved.

Sierra heard soft footsteps coming up the stairs. The door opened slowly, and Christy tiptoed into the room.

"It's okay," Sierra whispered. "I'm still awake. Katie's asleep, but I don't think you could wake her if you tried. How did everything go?"

Christy followed the dim glow of the night-light and sat on the edge of Sierra's bed.

"It went well," she whispered. "I think everything will go smoothly tomorrow. It was so sweet when we were practicing and the pastor reached the part 'you may kiss the bride.' Doug took Tracy in his arms, and I thought he was going to kiss her! But he just looked into her eyes about an inch away from her face. I mean to tell you, Sierra, it was about the most romantic, totally make-you-melt scene in the world. Then I heard him whisper to her, 'Tomorrow, my love. Tomorrow.'"

Sierra smiled in the darkness. "This first-kiss pledge is really a huge thing for Doug, isn't it?"

"I think it's become a huge thing for all of us. Doug is sort of our group's symbol of purity. If he had kissed her tonight, I think I would have been mad at him. They would have come so close to their goal and then missed it by a few hours."

"Christy," Sierra said slowly, "is it strange for you to see Doug and Tracy getting married since you used to date Doug?"

"No." Christy paused before she continued. "In some ways, it doesn't seem like I ever dated Doug. I mean, he was more my friend, my buddy. We did a lot of things together, and I know he enjoyed being with me, but there wasn't any twinkle dust between us."

"Twinkle dust?"

Christy quietly giggled. "I don't know what else to call it. Sometimes when I look at Todd, it's as if God sprinkled a handful of golden glitter in the air that hangs between us. Nobody can see it but us. It connects us—strongly. I know there is twinkle dust between Doug and Tracy. They are going to be very happy together."

"Does that mean Tracy got over being mad at Doug about what happened last night?"

"I think so. She was pretty mad, though. I heard him say again tonight to his mom that his days of boyish pranks are over."

"Katie will be glad to hear that," Sierra said.

"I think you're right." A yawn escaped from Christy. "I'd better let you get some sleep," she said. "Sweet dreams."

She rose and headed into the bathroom, quietly closing the door. Sierra drew back the cover because now she was too warm.

*Twinkle dust,* she thought. *I like that.*

A contented smile rested on her lips as she drifted off to sleep. It seemed she couldn't stop smiling the next morning either. It didn't matter that Aunt Marti was in a high-strung tizzy over her worries. When Christy left to go shopping with Todd, it didn't bother Sierra to stay behind with Katie. Nor did it seem irritating that Katie, who was more uncomfortable today, kept asking Sierra to do little things for her. Sierra felt happy—happy deep down. She thought about Tracy all morning and wondered if she was feeling immensely joyful or if she was being driven crazy by everyone and everything.

Sierra thought nothing could rob her of all this happiness. After taking a long shower, she stepped into the room with a towel wrapped around her, ready to put on the one nice outfit she had brought along for the wedding.

Katie, who was standing by the bed where Sierra had laid out her outfit, immediately said, "I'm sorry, Sierra. It was an accident."

"What was an accident?"

"Your skirt. It got caught on the bottom of my crutch, and when I pulled it away, it ripped in three different directions. I'm so sorry. I don't think it can be fixed. Do you have anything else to wear?"

Sierra rushed over and examined the thin gauze skirt. She felt an angry frustration surging inside. First Amy had ripped her blue skirt and now this.

"No," she said sharply, "this is all I brought."

She had thrown in plenty of casual clothes when she had packed in her flurry, but she hadn't thought through her need for dressy outfits. Her thoughts had been fixed on her visit here at Easter when all she needed were shorts and sweatshirts.

"I feel awful," Katie said.

"Maybe I can sew it," Sierra suggested. Whenever she had thought about Doug and Tracy's wedding during the past few weeks, this was the outfit she had pictured herself wearing. It truly reflected her personality.

"I don't think there's time. Christy left with Todd while you were in the shower, and Marti said she wanted to leave early. I told her you weren't ready, so she went with Todd and Christy. Bob is downstairs waiting for us."

"What time is it?" Sierra asked.

"It's almost six o'clock."

"The wedding isn't until seven," Sierra said, examining the huge rip more closely. She knew gauze wasn't the sturdiest fabric, but still, why did all her clothes have to get ruined? She had only so many favorites.

"I know, but I'm supposed to be there early to stand by the guest book. Are you sure you don't have anything else you could wear?"

"I'm sure," Sierra said. It was depressing to realize how important her style had become to her and how devastated she felt when that foundation was rocked.

"This is all I brought," Katie said, looking down at her simple, forest-green dress. "Maybe Christy has something. Check her suitcase."

"I couldn't borrow her clothes," Sierra said.

"Don't worry. She'll understand."

*She may understand, but I won't be me if I'm dressed like Christy. You're the one who doesn't understand, Katie,* Sierra fumed silently.

Katie hobbled over to Christy's suitcase and bent down to open it. "Look, here's a dress right on top. Try this on. It might be a little big on you, but it's better than a pair of shorts, which is all I have to offer you."

Sierra took one look at the dress and tried not to grimace. It was fine for Christy, but definitely not something Sierra would ever choose to wear in public.

"I don't know," Sierra said, stalling.

"We don't have any other options," Katie said, rifling through Christy's clothes.

Sierra looked at her skirt again and wondered if she could turn the tear to the back or to the side. Then it wouldn't be so obvious.

*Why am I being so stubborn about this? I'm not usually obsessed with clothes. Am I?*

It occurred to Sierra that her trademark had been her distinctive outfits. In England, it had been her dad's old cowboy boots. Even Paul had commented on them. No one referred to her as "the young one" but as "the girl with the creative clothes." When she had met Amy the first day of school, they were drawn together by their similar outfits and their love of shopping at thrift stores and vintage shops. Sierra's clothes had become her identity.

A friendly tap sounded on the bedroom door, "How's it going in there, ladies?" Bob asked through the closed door. "We should be heading over there now."

Sierra looked at Katie and then at the dress.

"We're coming," she called to Bob.

She scooped up the dress and returned to the bathroom. Two minutes later, humbled and still a little frustrated, Sierra emerged wearing Christy's dress.

"You look adorable," Katie said with a congenial grin.

"My worst nightmare is that I would grow up to look adorable," Sierra said, shaking her wet locks. "Let me grab some jewelry and my shoes."

"What about your hair?" Katie asked.

"What about it?"

"You don't need to dry it or anything?"

"Nope. This is as good as it gets. I gave up on it long ago."

"I love your hair," Katie said. "It's like the symbol of a free-spirited woman."

Sierra had to laugh. Here she had thought her trademark was her clothes. "I'm a free-spirited woman who happens to be wearing a frilly little dress. Is there something wrong with this picture?"

Katie kept assuring Sierra she looked fine. All the way to the church, Katie talked about how if there was one thing she had learned in life, it was that your true friends love you no matter what. And the only people who qualify for true, true friends are those who pay attention to what a person is like on the inside.

"I think you're right, Katie," Bob agreed. He pulled out an index card from the black leather daily planner on the seat next to him. "Sounds a little like my quote for the week. Do you want to hear it? This is by Augustine: 'O soul, He only who created thee can satisfy thee. If thou ask for anything else, it is thy misfortune, for He alone who made thee in His image can satisfy thee.' That's rich, isn't it?"

"Read it again," Katie said.

Bob glanced from the road to the card and back to the road.

"Wait," Katie said. "Maybe you'd better read it, Sierra."

She was sitting next to Bob in the front seat. He handed her the card, and she read the quote.

"It's true, you know," Bob said when she finished. "It was my misfortune to spend nearly half a century looking for anything and everything that might satisfy me. I know now that only God can fill an empty soul."

For a quiet moment, Sierra and Katie absorbed his wisdom.

"Here we are," Bob said, breaking the serious moment as he pulled into the church parking lot. "This is the first wedding I've gone to as a believer."

They got out of the car, and, still smiling, Bob added, "I think I'm more excited about this wedding than anyone else is."

"Oh, don't count on it," Katie said, motioning to the steady stream of cars pouring into the parking lot. "This is going to be a wedding worth remembering."

*I'll remember it, all right,* Sierra thought ruefully. *I'll always remember this as the wedding I went to in a borrowed dress.*

# sixteen

AS SOON AS SIERRA, Bob, and Katie reached the front of the church, it became obvious Katie was late for her job as guest-book attendant. People were lined up to sign the book, and Marti was accommodating them by standing next to the podium and handing them the white-feathered pen.

"Katie, I'm so glad you're here," Marti's voice was like syrup: sweet and sticky. "Thank you," she said to a guest handing back the long plume.

Katie and Sierra slipped past the guests and went to Marti's side. "You sure you want me to take over? You look like you're having fun," Katie said.

"This is your job." Marti handed the pen to the next guest with a smile and a nod. "However, if you think you might have difficulty managing it…"

"Maybe I'll just stand here and greet everyone with you," Katie suggested. As soon as she spoke, though, she recognized someone in line and squealed, "Stephanie, I didn't know you were coming!"

Marti cringed visibly at Katie's loud voice, shaking her

head in disapproval as Katie left her post and made her way over to give the girl in line a hug.

Sierra wasn't sure if she should get in line to sign the guest book or find Bob, who had disappeared. She carried her gift over to the gift table, where one of Tracy's aunts who had been at the shower greeted Sierra warmly and took the gift from her. Sierra hoped Tracy and Doug would like the teapot. It seemed like a simple gift compared with Marti's china place settings and the silver tea service from Tracy's grandma that they had used at the shower.

*It's from my heart, and that's what matters most,* she reminded herself.

Sierra stood to the side and watched all the people enter the church's narthex. Bob was talking to Todd, and Sierra smiled when she saw Todd, the beach bum, dressed in a black tux. All the ushers were guys Sierra had met, and all of them were surfers, transformed in their formal wear—especially Larry, who was the largest guy Sierra had ever known. She wondered if it had been hard to find a tux big enough to fit him. He certainly looked good in it.

Tawni and Jeremy stood together at the guest book, and Marti gave Tawni a kiss that touched the air beside Tawni's cheek. Sierra walked over to join them.

"Hi," Tawni said, looking Sierra over with an expression of pleasant surprise. "You look nice. Is that a new dress?"

Sierra swallowed a scream. "Not exactly." Wearing something that her sister approved of was not something Sierra normally did. Actually, it was a dreaded thought. Tawni's approval meant that Sierra had sold out her unique style and become like everyone else. She couldn't do that. She had to remain unique and be noticed for it.

When Sierra didn't offer any more explanation about the dress, Jeremy asked, "Should we sit on the bride's side or the groom's side?"

"I don't think it matters when you're friends with both of them," Tawni said.

"Maybe not," Jeremy said, "but let's ask one of these guys in the monkey suits."

He led Tawni by the hand over to Todd and said to him, "What are you doing out here? Isn't the best man supposed to be back there making sure the groom doesn't pass out or something?"

Todd laughed. "They didn't need me, that's for sure. Doug had enough photographers and fathers and grandfathers and uncles with him to keep him busy until the organ cranks up." He smiled at Tawni and Sierra, giving them both a chin-up nod.

"That's a nice dress," he said to Sierra.

She clenched her teeth and forced herself to smile. "It's vaguely familiar, don't you think?"

Todd didn't catch her comment because a tall, good-looking guy with dark, wavy hair and chocolate-brown eyes strode up to their little group and gave Todd a punch in the arm.

"Hey, Moon Doggie," he said sarcastically. "What's up, dude?"

Todd gave him a punch back and said, "Hey, dude! How you been? I heard you were getting married."

"No, not me," the guy said, turning to check out Sierra and Tawni. It felt like a visual X ray.

"You know Jeremy," Todd said. "This is Sierra and Tawni Jensen."

The guy gave Sierra a polite nod. Then he offered his hand to Tawni and held it just a little too long, Sierra thought.

"This is Rick Doyle," Todd said. "We go way back."

"Christy's here, isn't she?" Rick asked.

Todd nodded. "She's the maid of honor. You won't be able to miss her."

"And you two are still...?" Rick tilted his head and looked at Todd.

Todd didn't reply. He stood his ground with his arms folded across his chest, waiting for Rick to complete his question. Sierra thought she saw a hint of laughter in Todd's silver-blue eyes.

"Never mind," Rick said, throwing up his hands. "Why do I bother to ask?"

"Beats me," Todd said.

"Beats you," Rick repeated under his breath, letting out a huff. "Like I ever could."

"I think we should probably go inside," Tawni suggested.

"Good idea," Rick said. He held out his arm to Tawni, inviting her to take it and let him usher her down the aisle.

Tawni refused his offer by turning from him and taking Jeremy's arm. Rick recovered flawlessly from Tawni's snub, and for a moment, Sierra thought he was about to make the same offer to her.

Before Rick had a chance, though, Todd stepped in, and in a calm, steady voice, he said, "May I escort you to your seat, Sierra?"

She slipped her hand into the crook of his tuxedoed arm and let Todd usher her down the aisle on the bride's side. He stopped about six rows back, and Sierra took little steps in until she was next to Jeremy. Tawni was on the aisle.

A thick white satin ribbon roped off the end of the pew from the center aisle. Bright nosegays of summer flowers were gathered in the middle of white bows on the end of each pew. A long white runner went down the middle of the church and came to an abrupt halt at the altar.

As tender piano music filled the air, Sierra could feel her heart beating a little faster in this beautiful, holy place. She drew in the heady fragrance of the flowers. Two tall wicker baskets at the front of the church spilled over with a colorful assortment of roses, carnations, statice, and ivy. A brass archway laced with ivy and roses stood between the two flower arrangements. Sprinkles of baby's breath dotted the ivy and flowers, giving it a touch-of-heaven look. In front of the archway stood a kneeling bench covered in white satin.

"Have you seen the dresses yet?" Tawni asked, leaning over Jeremy and whispering to Sierra.

She shook her head.

"Me neither. I wonder what they'll look like, because I know she wanted a garden theme. It's beautiful, isn't it?" Tawni asked.

Sierra nodded.

More guests entered in a steady stream. All the aisle seats and the first five rows were packed. Now the ushers were filling in the row where Sierra sat. She turned to see that the guest who lowered himself into the place next to her was Rick. Giving him only the slightest nod and smile, Sierra looked back toward the front of the sanctuary. She shifted in her seat and found she had involuntarily moved a pinch closer to Jeremy and farther away from Rick. Sierra didn't know why, but he gave her a creepy feeling. She usually was a good judge of character, and this was one guy she didn't like.

The church continued to fill with guests.

Rick leaned over, his musk-scented aftershave coming too close to Sierra's nose for her liking. "Looks like this is the event of the century," he murmured.

Sierra didn't feel compelled to respond.

"You would think they were the only two people who ever decided to get married," Rick mumbled in Sierra's ear. "There must be 300 people here. And there's more coming. What a mob! You think they're all here to see Doug's lips finally lose their virginity?"

Without turning her head, Sierra stated flatly, "Well, it must be a sight worth seeing. You're here, aren't you?"

She heard no sound from Rick in response. About a minute later, he stood and, excusing himself, stepped over people all the way to the side aisle. Then he disappeared into the narthex.

"What did you say to him?" Jeremy whispered.

Sierra shrugged and used her eyes to convey her innocence to Jeremy.

He smiled at her and said, "Don't give me that." He tilted his head and looked at Sierra with the same kind of tender big-brother look Wesley gave her. "I probably shouldn't tell you this..."

He paused and glanced at Tawni. She was watching the people being seated across the aisle. Sierra noticed that Rick was one of them. He had found some other, more attentive young woman to sit beside.

Jeremy looked at Sierra again and said, "Tawni told me I should tell you, but I wasn't sure."

"What?" Sierra said. Her curiosity was stirred by the look on Jeremy's face. He seemed tender and concerned. She couldn't imagine what it was he wanted to tell her.

Just then the piano music stopped. All eyes went to the front as the minister stepped out from a side door. Facing the wedding guests, he positioned himself between the altar and the kneeling bench under the garden arch. Sierra knew Jeremy couldn't finish his sentence now, but it didn't matter. Right behind the pastor, in a straight line, came Doug followed by Todd and two other groomsmen. They all wore black tuxes. Doug had a single white rose adorning his lapel. He stood to the right of the garden arch and turned to face the guests with his hands folded in front of him.

Sierra had never seen a face brimming with so much dignity and honor. Clearly, Doug took this ceremony seriously. She knew no goofy smiles or gestures would be exchanged with the groomsmen as she had seen in other weddings. Doug's expression made it clear this was a holy moment between himself, his bride, and the Lord.

A reverent hush fell over the sanctuary.

# seventeen

SUDDENLY, THE SILENCE was broken as the pianist began to play a lilting classical piece that Sierra vaguely recognized. As the song filled the air, Doug's parents were ushered in, with Tracy's mom and grandparents following.

An angelic little girl wearing a wreath of flowers in her blond hair started down the center aisle, one foot placed carefully in front of the other. She held a tiny garden basket in her hand. Halfway down the aisle, she remembered to take out some of the pink rose petals and sprinkle them on the white runner. Her task seemed to become more difficult as she dropped the flowers. Step, stop, take out one petal, drop it. Step, stop, repeat the one-petal drop.

People were smiling, whispering, and craning their necks to see the flower girl dutifully complete her journey to the front of the church. She received a subtle wink from Doug when she reached her goal. Then, with continued careful little steps, she made her way to her post.

The first bridesmaid, a relative of Tracy's, began her

slow walk down the aisle with the music lifting into the air. She wore a long, flowing gossamer dress in pale lavender and a wreath of flowers and ivy around her head. Instead of a bouquet of flowers, she held what Granna Mae called a gathering basket. It had a long, flat bottom made for collecting cut flowers from the garden. From this bridesmaid's gathering basket tumbled a cascade of summer garden flowers. Sierra thought it was clever and exactly like Tracy to think of something so creative.

The second bridesmaid made her way down the aisle in the same outfit, only her dress was a pale pink. Then came Christy in pale blue. Her long hair hung over her shoulders, curled perfectly at the ends. The wreath of flowers about her head was thicker than the other girls'. Her gathering basket bubbled over with flowers so that it looked as if she had just stepped out of a garden in full bloom.

Christy's round cheeks glowed. Her clear eyes danced, taking in the rose petals on the runner, the guests smiling along the aisles, and the bows and flowers strung along the way. Sierra watched as Christy looked up to the front of the church. Her eyes stopped their merry waltz when she saw the best man. Her gaze fixed on Todd, and she didn't seem to blink the rest of the way down the aisle.

Sierra smiled when she saw the expression on Todd's face. He seemed mesmerized by Christy's appearance. His mouth hung open slightly, and his eyes had grown wide and stayed fixed like that as he, too, didn't seem to blink.

In the pew two rows in front of Sierra sat Christy's parents and her younger brother. Bob sat next to him, and Marti was on the other side of Bob. She noticed both

Christy's mom and dad dabbing at the corners of their eyes after their daughter floated past them.

Out of curiosity, Sierra glanced across the aisle at Rick. He sat a head taller than the young women who were perched on either side of him. His back was straight, his chin stuck out, and his lips were pursed together. One eyebrow was raised slightly. He wasn't taking his eyes off Christy either. Sierra decided she would have to ask Katie about this guy. If anyone could fill Sierra in, it would be Katie.

The piano music came to a sweeping finish as Christy took her place at the front. The organist picked up right where the piano ended. Grand and glorious, the music of the traditional wedding march boldly flew from the shiny organ pipes and filled the church. Tracy's mom stood and turned toward the entrance. The rest of the guests took her cue and stood as well. Sierra peeked at Doug. He straightened his shoulders and seemed to draw in a deep breath. Then his face lit up. Sierra knew Tracy had appeared in the doorway and had started down the aisle. Not because she saw Tracy, but because it was written all over Doug's face.

*Now, that is the look of a man in love!* Sierra thought, sighing. *He's about to burst. I think I even see tears in his eyes.*

Without warning, a fresh batch of tears sprang to Sierra's eyes, blurring her vision. How could anyone keep from crying after seeing the expression on Doug's face? Sierra quickly wiped away her tears and turned to look at the bride.

Petite Tracy securely held her father's arm. Her dainty steps barely ruffled the rose petals strewn along her path She was clothed in white from head to toe. Her dress had a delicate lace inset on the bodice, and the long sleeves were made of the same sheer lace. The full skirt was sprinkled with pearls and behind her flowed a long satin train.

As magnificent as the dress was, it wasn't the gown that was most noticeable. What stood out more than anything was the radiance of Tracy's heart-shaped face beneath the thin veil of lace. The veil hung around her like a wisp of a cloud and seemed to tumble like a waterfall from the crownlike wreath of all-white flowers that she wore so elegantly on the top of her head. In her hand she held one long-stemmed white rose. Tracy was the picture of virtue and purity. To Sierra, she seemed to be a walking work of art. And the sight of her seemed to make everyone want to cry.

A rustling filled the church as the guests sat down.

The pastor spoke up. "Who gives this woman to be wedded to this man in holy matrimony?"

"Her mother and I," said Tracy's dad with a tremble in his voice.

He squeezed Tracy's hand. Doug stepped forward. Tracy's dad symbolically took Tracy's hand out of his and placed it into Doug's. Then he let go of her and went to the empty seat next to his wife.

Doug not only grasped Tracy's hand when it was given to him, but he also tucked her arm through his and pulled her close. Together they climbed the three small steps that led to the kneeling bench under the archway. The scene created a beautiful picture, the two of them standing there before God and the many witnesses. Sierra hoped with all her heart that one day her wedding would be this sacred and beautiful.

The pastor began by stating in a rich, rolling voice that marriage was a holy institution and not to be entered into lightly. He read Scripture and talked about the mystery of God's design in directing two people to be knit together in love.

"God's Word makes it clear that a man is to leave his mother and father and cleave to his wife. The two are to become one flesh. These are your instructions then," the pastor said. "You are to leave your parents, cleave to one another, and allow God to weave your lives together." He solemnly told Doug and Tracy that it would take everything in them and a strong relationship with Christ to make their marriage a lasting one.

"I now have instructions for you, the guests," the pastor said, looking beyond Doug and Tracy to their family and friends. "You are to pray for this young couple. Encourage them. Love them. Always expect the best from them and be ready in times of adversity to offer your support to them. I charge you to nurture this union."

He motioned for Tracy and Doug to kneel. Doug helped Tracy lower herself onto the soft kneeling bench. The minister stretched out his hand over the couple and prayed for them, for their marriage, and even for the children that might come from their union. Sierra silently agreed with the minister as he prayed for God's richest blessings on Doug and Tracy.

When they stood again, the minister instructed them to hold hands, face each other, and repeat their vows.

"I, Doug, take you, Tracy, as my lawfully wedded wife. I promise before God, our family, and our friends to love, honor, and cherish you until God takes me home to be with Him."

"I, Tracy, take you, Doug, as my lawfully wedded husband. I promise before God, our family, and our friends to love, honor, and cherish you until God takes me home to be with Him."

The pastor motioned for them to exchange the rings. Todd reached out his hand and placed the ring in Doug's open palm.

Looking into his bride's eyes, Doug lifted her left hand and slowly inched the ring onto her finger. "As a constant reminder of my never-ending love for you, I seal my vow with this ring."

Tracy turned to Christy. It appeared to Sierra that Christy was wearing Doug's large wedding band on her thumb, and now she easily slipped it off and handed it to Tracy.

Lifting Doug's hand, Tracy pushed the ring on and repeated the words. "As a constant reminder of my never-ending love for you, I seal my vow with this ring."

The couple then turned to face the minister, and the piano played a gentle tune. A young man stood by the piano and sang into a handheld microphone a popular Christian love song that Sierra had heard once before at a wedding. As she listened, she looked down at her gold ring.

*Father God, this ring is already becoming a constant reminder of Your never-ending love for me,* she prayed silently. *I vow to stay pure and save myself for the man You want me to marry, and I seal my vow to You with this ring.*

She clasped her hands together in her lap and for the

first time was glad her ring was gold and not silver. It symbolized something strong and powerful. Sierra liked that it didn't resemble all her other fun jewelry. This ring was special, just as Wes had said. It was set apart from all the rest. And in a way, at this moment, that's how she felt.

# eighteen

THE FINAL NOTE escaped from the singer's throat. He returned to his seat, and all eyes returned to Doug and Tracy, who had stepped away from the arch, each on the appropriate side, and walked around until they met at the altar.

"In thanksgiving for their purity before God and between each other," the pastor said, "Doug and Tracy are offering a sacrifice of praise to the Lord. Each of them now presents a gift on the altar."

Tracy laid her long-stemmed white rose on top of the altar. Doug unpinned the white rose boutonniere from his lapel and laid it down. The pastor swung the kneeling bench out from under the arch so that it resembled a garden gate. Doug and Tracy joined hands and walked through the gate together. They stood just on the other side of the arch and looked intently into each other's eyes.

"By the power vested in me by the State of California and as a minister of the gospel of Christ the Risen Savior, I now pronounce you husband and wife."

There was a pause.

The minister smiled and said, "You may kiss your bride."

Sierra held her breath. It seemed as if the hundreds of well-wishers around her were doing the same thing. Out of the corner of her eye, Sierra saw Jeremy reach over and take Tawni's hand in his. They all sat perfectly still, waiting.

Doug carefully took the ends of Tracy's veil and lifted the sheer fabric over her head so that it tumbled down her back like fine mist from a waterfall. Tracy, with unveiled face, tilted her lips toward Doug and looked into his eyes.

He looked back at her. They acted as if they were oblivious to the hundreds of guests clinging to the edge of the pews and inwardly cheering, "Come on, kiss her!"

Doug took Tracy's sweet face in his large hands and whispered something to her. He tilted his head just right and slowly drew closer to her upturned face.

Then their lips met.

Sierra bit her lower lip and blinked fast to stop the tears from coming.

It was a long kiss. A slow kiss. A tender, unhurried, and wonderfully romantic kiss. Doug slowly drew away from Tracy and opened his eyes as if everything were in slow motion. A huge smile broke across his face, and Tracy let out a little giggle.

Someone broke loose with a "Bravo!" and spontaneously, all around the sanctuary, friends and family were rising to their feet, clapping and cheering.

Doug turned to greet the outburst with a look of surprise. Tracy looked startled, too. And a little embarrassed. Then she started to laugh and motioned for Doug to look up in the balcony. Everyone turned to look. There stood the ushers in a straight row, holding up large numbered cards that read: 10.0, 9.8, 9.9, 10.0, 10.0.

The church filled with bursts of laughter. The organ cranked up extra loud, and in the church steeple, bells began to ring. Tracy took Doug's arm, and with joyful tears rolling down their cheeks, they began their march down the center aisle. Everyone was standing, still clapping, still cheering, as the newlyweds hurried out the door at the back of the sanctuary.

Todd and Christy followed them, smiling broadly and whispering to each other as they walked arm in arm across the crushed rose petals. It seemed to Sierra that they, too, were oblivious to the rest of the world and that they gave the appearance of floating rather than walking.

The rest of the party exited. The ushers came down from their judges' booth and began to dismiss the guests by undoing the ribbons and directing everyone down the center aisle, one row at a time.

The mood was the most festive Sierra had ever experienced at a church service or wedding. People were talking, laughing, and greeting each other with big hugs. Sierra followed Tawni and Jeremy out of the church. They were still holding hands and talking in a close way that indicated they wanted to be alone. As soon as Sierra was out of the church narthex, she took off ahead of Tawni and Jeremy as the guests all headed for the building where the reception was to be held.

As she entered the large gymnasium, Sierra thought the decorating committee had done a pretty good job of dressing up the place. Dozens of small round tables were decorated with tablecloths of soft pink, lavender, and blue, just like the bridesmaids' dresses. Huge ferns hung from the basketball hoops. The three-tiered cake graced the center of the long serving table. Sierra noticed that it was holding its shape quite nicely. Marti would be relieved that it hadn't crumbled in the August heat.

In the far corner was a white-carpeted area with a decorated archway woven with ivy and bright summer flowers. Sierra guessed that that was to be the receiving line. She couldn't wait to give Doug and Tracy her best wishes. But it would probably be a while before they formed the line, since more pictures were being taken.

Finding an empty table, Sierra sat down and tried one of the pastel mints in a dish next to a vase of fresh flowers. Katie made her way over to the table and leaned on her crutches.

"Was that a wedding to remember or what?" Katie slid the crutches under the table, and Sierra pulled out a chair for her. "Did you see their kiss? Of course you did. Everyone did. I didn't know the guys were going to do the numbers up in the balcony. What a scream!"

Katie's flushed face matched her red hair. She sat down and said, "Man, I'm pooped from trying to get around on this stupid foot. I can't believe I have to wear this cast for a month. This is so pathetic."

Sierra noticed Rick pulling out a chair for a slender brunette a few tables over.

"Katie, who is that guy?"

Katie looked over her shoulder and, with wide eyes, leaned toward Sierra and said, "Don't go there, Sierra.

Trust me on this one. Stay far away from him."

"I don't think you have to worry about that. He's the one who wants to stay far away from me." Sierra told Katie about her exchange with Rick and how he had gotten up and moved right before the ceremony started.

Katie started to laugh and said, "I wish I'd been more like you a few years ago." She shook her head.

"You didn't date that guy, did you?" Sierra said.

"If you could call it that. He was my first kiss. Can you believe that? What was I thinking?"

Sierra was amazed.

"Actually, that's a dumb question. I know what I was thinking. I was thinking, if he's good enough for Christy to kiss, then why can't I kiss him, too?"

"You aren't serious," Sierra said, her eyebrows coming closer together as she scrutinized Katie's expression. "Not our Christy! Christy Miller? She didn't go out with that guy...did she?"

Katie nodded.

"And she kissed him?"

Katie leaned forward across the table, nearly toppling the bowl of mints. "Let me just say, Sierra, that you need to understand that with Rick, he is the kisser and you are the kissee. I don't know that I could say that Christy ever initiated a kiss with him, but yes, he did kiss her quite a few times. He was crazy about her. She was like this unattainable prize to him. I'll admit it: I was jealous of her. So when Christy broke up with Rick and he showed a little interest in me, of course I gobbled it up."

Sierra still had a hard time imagining that both of these

friends, whom she deeply admired, had ever given any part of themselves to a guy like Rick. He seemed like an incurable flirt to Sierra.

"Oh, the things we do when we're young and stupid," Katie said, leaning back and shaking her silky red hair. "If it weren't for the grace of God, we would all be a sad bunch of losers, wouldn't we?"

Sierra slowly nodded. She was thinking of Amy. "So how did you figure out that you shouldn't be investing your kisses in Rick?"

"Investing my kisses," Katie repeated. "I like that. I don't know. It just all fell apart. There wasn't anything to hold it together. Then I fell in love with Michael. You remember my telling you about him in England."

"He was the exchange student you stopped going out with because he wasn't a Christian, right?"

Katie nodded. "That one was really hard. We were together for a long time. It still hurts when I think about him. Christy was such a great friend to me during that time, though. Right away she told me exactly what she thought of us getting together, and then she let me live my own life, even though she thought I was making a huge mistake."

"Do you think it was a mistake to go out with Michael?"

Katie paused. Then, curling up her lower lip, she said, "Yeah, I guess, looking back, it wasn't the wisest choice. I emotionally poured myself out. You know, I kept praying for him and talking to him about the Lord. I was so sure he would 'see the light,' as they say. It cost me a lot inside—in my heart, where it really counts."

"But you said Christy didn't try to persuade you not to get involved with him. Weren't you close friends?"

"Oh, the best! I think Christy did the right thing. She told me what she thought, and I know she prayed long and hard for me, but then she let me go my own way and just continued to be a consistent friend through it all. Then, when I crashed and burned, she was right there to salvage the wreckage."

Katie's glance moved past Sierra to someone standing behind her. Katie's green eyes flashed a look of delight as she practically shouted, "You came!"

Sierra turned to see Antonio, a guy from Italy whom she had met on the beach last Easter. Sparks had flown between Katie and Antonio then, and obviously that interest was still alive inside of Katie.

"I heard you are a movie star." Antonio's rich accent washed over both of them. "Something about a cast of thousands." He stepped over to where Katie had planted herself and leaned down to kiss her lightly on each side of her face.

"Only one cast, Tonio," Katie said, her eyes still gleaming. "And it's on my foot."

"Tsk, tsk, tsk," Antonio said, shaking his head and clucking his tongue in a way that was decidedly European. "This is such a pity. I was hoping you would go waterskiing with me tomorrow."

"I can still sit in the boat and hold up the flag," Katie said.

Antonio laughed. Then he turned to see who was sitting with Katie. "Sierra! I did not know it was you."

He bent over, and before she knew what he was doing, he brushed his lips faintly against the side of each of her cheeks. She immediately felt herself blushing.

Behind them a surge of voices rose, along with cheers and applause.

"It looks as if the bride and groom have finally arrived," Antonio said. "Come with me, Katie, Sierra. Let's get in their giving line." He held out an arm for each of them.

"Tonio," Katie corrected him, rising with the help of his strong arm, "it's a receiving line, not a giving line."

"For you, perhaps. For me, it is a giving line. I'm giving the bride a kiss."

# nineteen

STANDING IN THE LONG LINE behind Katie and Antonio gave Sierra a chance to think. So many things had impressed her during the past few hours. The emotionally powerful ceremony had awakened a new sense of longing within her. It wasn't just a desire to be loved deeply someday by a man like Doug; it was a sense of responsibility to prepare now for that man.

She remembered what the pastor had said about God's mysterious design in directing two people to be knit together in love. It was all a mystery to her. She was sure the only way to navigate a marriage relationship was the same way she should be handling her dating years now—by praying hard and trusting God each step of the way.

What Katie had said a few minutes ago at the table had helped her decide what to do about Amy. Sierra now knew that it wasn't her responsibility to change her friend's heart and mind. Only God could do that. She could certainly state her opinions loudly and clearly, and she had never had a problem doing that. But Sierra needed to learn from

Christy's example by standing back and simply praying for her best friend.

Antonio stepped out of the line.

Katie smiled at Sierra, "He's going to get me some punch. Is that guy the ultimate gentleman, or what?"

"I like him, too," Sierra said.

"You do?" Katie's countenance fell.

"Not like that," Sierra said, laughing at Katie's expression. "I mean, I think he's a great guy. I know he has a deep love for the Lord and that makes him..."

"Irresistible." Katie finished the sentence for her.

They both laughed. The line inched forward. Sierra brushed the curls off the side of her neck.

"Is that a purity ring?" Katie asked, eyeing the gold band.

"Yes. My dad gave it to me last week. After watching Doug and Tracy place their roses on the altar, I have to admit, I was ready to start a nationwide purity campaign."

"It's already been done," Katie said.

"I know. But you know what I mean. If more of my friends had examples like Doug and Tracy, I think they would be more deliberate about who they date and about saving themselves for marriage."

"You're right," Katie agreed. "I bought myself a ring." She held up her right hand and showed Sierra the simple, silver-twisted band. "My parents aren't Christians, so I wasn't expecting my dad to surprise me with a father-daughter bonding moment or hand me a little velvet box and everything."

A lump caught in Sierra's throat. She did have a Christian dad who had gone to the effort of making their

dinner a special occasion. He had handed her the little velvet box. And all she could think of that night was how
embarrassed she was.

*I wish I had worn the corsage. I wish I had been more appreciative,* she
thought.

"Some of my friends went to those nationwide cam-
paigns while they were in high school," Katie said. "They
signed cards or something, and their whole youth group got
rings to wear. Our youth group somehow missed out on all
that. Or maybe they went and I didn't go for some reason.
Anyway, I decided to make my own purity vow. So I bought
this ring and took myself to the beach one morning really
early. I sat on this big rock and read my Bible and sang and
then put on the ring."

Just then Antonio returned with the punch.

"Here you are," Antonio said, handing a glass to Katie
and one to Sierra. "I see we're almost to the front of the
line. Good work, ladies."

Within three short minutes, they had reached the
reception line and were shaking hands with a string of
Doug's and Tracy's relatives and the wedding party and con-
gratulating them all. Sierra received a hug from Todd and
then a crushing hug from Doug. He was still looking hap-
pier than any man alive should be allowed to look.

Sierra kissed Tracy on the cheek. She had to. Tracy
looked so beautiful that a hug wasn't enough. And it wasn't
enough for Antonio either. He soundly kissed Tracy on
both cheeks and pronounced an Italian blessing on the
couple.

Sierra then gave Christy a hug and told her how beautiful she looked.

"Not only beautiful," Antonio said, overhearing Sierra's comment. "Christina, you are radiant. I predict you will catch the croquet."

"Not the croquet," Katie said, playfully swatting at Antonio's arm. "The bouquet."

"Oh. It is not long-handled wooden mallets you Americans throw at your guests?"

Katie seemed to come alive around Antonio and gobbled up his teasing. "No, it is not long-handled wooden mallets," Katie repeated in her best imitative Italian accent. "It's long-stemmed, fragrant flowers."

"No!" Antonio said in mock surprise. "Once again you have shown me that I would be lost without your instruction in this strange land in which I sojourn." He slipped his arm around Katie's shoulder.

"The only strange land in which you sojourn, Tonio, is your own mind," Katie teased.

He shot right back. "And you would know this, because you have been there?"

"Been where?"

"In my mind."

"Actually, instead of 'in,' we say 'on my mind,'" Katie began.

Then it seemed to dawn on her that he had given her a sweet compliment. Sierra suspected she was watching another budding romance among her friends. Now she truly was the odd one. The young one. The unattached one. The one in the "adorable" dress.

Sierra sat quietly with all her friends—the couples—and did some thinking.

Nearly an hour later, Tracy threw the bouquet. All the

eligible young women gathered outside the church for the big moment.

"It's a fake, you know," Katie said. "Tracy carried a single white rose, remember? This bouquet is for tradition's sake."

"I still think it's a wonderful tradition," Tawni said, taking her place next to Sierra. It almost appeared she was placing herself at the best probable angle to catch the bouquet.

The photographer snapped a couple of shots while all the guys stood to the side, cheering for their favorite. Christy was, of course, the most adored candidate. On the count of three, Tracy tossed the bouquet over her shoulder and high into the air.

Sierra looked up into the summer evening sky and realized it was coming right toward her. With a leap, she could snatch it. But something deep inside her spoke. Not a voice, really, but more than a thought. Clearer than a feeling.

*Wait.*

Sierra didn't leap. Tawni stretched her long, limber arms and snatched the bouquet. The joy of her victory was immediately evident. She waved the bouquet in the direction of all the guys, and they began to rough up Jeremy, telling him that now the pressure was on to catch the garter.

Tracy lifted her gown only slightly, revealing the fancy lace garter around her middle calf. Teasing comments about her modesty pelted Doug as he removed the garter. The eligible and not-so-eligible guys lined up, pushing and joking.

Without much warning, Doug turned his back to the rowdy bunch and said, "Here it comes!"

The elastic garter shot straight into the air, and like a bunch of pro basketball players, the guys all leaped to catch it. Not until the huddle of men peeled themselves off each other were they able to see who had caught the garter.

"Rick Doyle?" Christy spouted. Her face seemed to turn a little gray. "I didn't know he was here," she whispered to Katie.

Sierra wanted to say, "Well, Rick sure knew you were," but she decided to leave that one alone. Apparently, Christy's memories of this guy were not exactly heartwarming.

Tawni and Rick posed for the photographer. Sierra noticed how perfectly Tawni stood and smiled, her head at just the right angle. She was a natural in front of the camera.

"Here, take a handful," a woman said, thrusting a bag of birdseed in front of Sierra. "Instead of rice," she explained. "It's organic."

As Sierra grabbed from the bag, a white Rolls-Royce pulled up in front of the church, complete with a chauffeur wearing a black cap. He got out and opened the car's back door. Tracy kissed her mom and dad good-bye and then linked her arm in Doug's as they merrily dashed for the get-away car.

"Now!" the lady with the birdseed called out.

Doug and Tracy were showered with thousands of tiny bits of birdseed that their cheering friends tossed in the air. Tracy lifted her long skirt slightly as she slid into the Rolls's backseat. Doug held the long train for her and then ducked his way in beside her. The chauffeur shut the door and walked calmly around to the driver's side as if he did this every day.

"'Bye. Have fun! See you," everyone called out.

"Where are they going on their honeymoon?" Sierra asked.

"Maui," said Tawni. "Didn't you know? They're going to Bob and Marti's condo."

"Sierra," Jeremy said. "I started to tell you something right before the ceremony."

"Oh, yes." She had forgotten.

Jeremy gave Tawni a smile, and taking Sierra's elbow, he led her away from the crowd to an open spot on the church lawn.

"It's about my brother," Jeremy said. "I think you should write to him."

"Why?"

"Well, it's just that he's..."

"Is he okay? I mean, he isn't in trouble or dying or anything, is he?"

"No, Paul is doing great. Really great, actually. Better than ever. I honestly think you've had a lot to do with that."

"Me? How?"

"I know you've been praying for him. But it's more than that. Here. I don't know how to tell you any other way."

Jeremy pulled a piece of paper from his pocket and unfolded it. Sierra immediately recognized the bold, dark letters of Paul's distinctive handwriting.

"Right here," Jeremy said, pointing to the last paragraph. "He's talking about going on these walks in the highlands of Scotland where my grandmother lives, and then he says...well, you read it."

Sierra took the letter and read aloud: "You'll probably laugh, but the face I keep seeing in the clouds above this 'bonnie' land is Sierra's. Last June, in Portland, I thought I could pat her on the head and send her out of my mind. But look. She's followed me here. She told me God has put His mark on my life. Do you think that's true? What does it mean? What does God want me to do with my life?"

Stunned, Sierra looked at Jeremy and said the first thing that came to her mind. "These are Paul's private thoughts. I don't think he meant for you to show them to me."

"Maybe not, but don't you see? He needs some encouragement right now, and I think it should come from you."

Something deep within Sierra spoke to her again. Not a voice or a thought. Clearer than a feeling.

*Wait.*

In that moment, it didn't matter to Sierra that she was the youngest or the only one without a boyfriend. It didn't even matter that she was wearing Christy's dress. She was finally beginning to recognize her true identity. Bob's quote from Augustine came back to her: "For He alone who made thee in His image can satisfy thee."

Reverently, Sierra folded the piece of paper. The gold band on right hand caught the light as she handed Paul's letter back to Jeremy.

"This may sound overly simple," Sierra said, "but I believe God will meet Paul right where he is. And God's the only One who can answer questions like these."

Jeremy looked at her for a moment, his handsome face expressionless. Then he said, "I think Paul would like to get a letter from you."

"Maybe he would," Sierra said. Then, with a smile and a

pat on Jeremy's broad shoulder, she added, "Tell him to write me first."

With a swish, she turned and headed back to join the others. Sierra felt full of hope and confidence in God. She knew who she was. And she knew Whose she was.

Whatever mysterious plan God had for her life, it would be an interesting one. As Christy had said earlier, God writes a different story for each person. Sierra decided hers might not be a bestseller or even a thriller. It certainly wasn't a romance. But it was turning into a fine mystery. And she could live with that.

# Happenstance...
# or God's Great Plan?

*She's the bold, free-spirited type. She's cute, she's fun, and she's following God. She's Sierra Jensen, Christy Miller's good friend, ready for her junior year of high school! All twelve books in the popular Sierra Jensen series come together in four volumes to reveal the ups and downs of Sierra's incredible God-led journey!*

**Volume One:** In *Only You, Sierra*, she's nervous to be the "new girl" after her family moves to Portland and wonders if meeting Paul in London was only by chance. Just when everything important seems to elude her, all it takes is one weekend *In Your Dreams* to prove otherwise. But even a vacation doesn't keep her troubles away in *Don't You Wish*.
*Available Now!*

**Volume Two:** Paul's voice lives in her memory, but now it's loud, clear, and right behind her in *Close Your Eyes*. With summer fast approaching, it is *Without a Doubt* bound to be Sierra's best yet. In *With This Ring*, she can't help but ponder the meaning of first kisses and lifetime commitments.
*Available Now!*

**Volume Three:** An exciting trip to Europe challenges Sierra to *Open Your Heart* to loving others without expectations. At the start of her senior year, only *Time Will Tell* the truth about Sierra's friendships. And in *Now Picture This*, she wonders if her relationship with Paul is as picture perfect as she thinks!
*Available July 2006!*

**Volume Four:** In this final volume, Sierra Jensen's only just beginning the roller coaster of adventures leading up to college. Join her in this exciting, challenging time of faith and fun!
*Available August 2006!*

**www.ChristyMillerAndFriends.com**

# Don't Miss the Next Chapter in Christy Miller's Unforgettable Life!

Follow Christy and Todd through the struggles, lessons, and changes that life in college will bring. Concentrating on her studies, Christy spends a year abroad in Europe then returns to the campus at Rancho Corona University. Will Todd be waiting for her? CHRISTY AND TODD: THE COLLEGE YEARS follows Christy into her next chapter as she makes decisions about life and love.

CHRISTY AND TODD: THE COLLEGE YEARS by Robin Jones Gunn

Until Tomorrow • As You Wish • I Promise

# SISTERCHICK® Adventures by
# ROBIN JONES GUNN

### SISTERCHICKS ON THE LOOSE!

Zany antics abound when best friends Sharon and Penny take off on a midlife adventure to Finland, returning home with a new view of God and a new zest for life.

### SISTERCHICKS DO THE HULA!

It'll take more than an unexpected stowaway to keep two middle-aged sisterchicks from reliving their college years with a little Waikiki wackiness—and learning to hula for the first time.

### SISTERCHICKS IN SOMBREROS!

Two Canadian sisters embark on a journey to claim their inheritance—beachfront property in Mexico—not expecting so many bizarre, wacky problems! But there's nothing a little coconut cake can't cure...

**AVAILABLE NOW!**

www.sisterchicks.com

# More SISTERCHICK® Adventures
## by
# ROBIN JONES GUNN

### SISTERCHICKS DOWN UNDER!

Kathleen meets Jill at the Chocolate Fish café in New Zealand, and they instantly forge a friendship. Together they fall head over heels into a deeper sense of God's love.

### SISTERCHICKS SAY OOH LA LA!

Painting toenails and making promises under the canopy of a princess bed seals a friendship for life! Fifty years of ups and downs find Lisa and Amy still Best Friends Forever…and off on an unforgettable Paris rendezvous!

### SISTERCHICKS IN GONDOLAS

At a fifteenth-century palace in Venice, best friends/sisters-in-law Jenna and Sue welcome the gondola-paced Italian lifestyle! And over boiling pots of pasta, they dare each other to dream again.

**AVAILABLE NOW!**

www.sisterchicks.com

# About the Author

Robin Jones Gunn grew up in Orange County, California, where both her parents were teachers. She has one older sister and one younger brother. The three Jones kids graduated from Santa Ana High School and spent their summers on the beach with a bunch of "God-Lover" friends. Robin didn't meet her "Todd" until after she had gone to Biola University for two years and spent a summer traveling around Europe.

As her passion for ministering to teenagers grew, Robin assisted more with the youth group at her church. It was on a bike ride for middle schoolers that Robin met Ross. After they married, they spent the next two decades working together in youth ministry. God blessed them with a son and then a daughter.

When her children were young, Robin would rise at 3 a.m. when the house was quiet, make a pot of tea, and write pages and pages about Christy and Todd. She then read those pages to the girls in the youth group, and they gave her advice on what needed to be changed. The writing process took two years and ten rejections before her first novel, *Summer Promise*, was accepted for publication. Since its release in 1988, *Summer Promise* along with the rest of the Christy Miller and Sierra Jensen series have sold over 2.5 million copies and can be found in a dozen translations all over the world.

For the past twelve years, Robin has lived near Portland, Oregon, which has given her lots of insight into what Sierra's life might be like in the Great Northwest. Now that her children are grown and Robin's husband has a new career as a counselor, she continues to travel and tell stories about best friends and God-Lovers. Her popular Glenbrooke series tracks the love stories of some of Christy Miller's friends.

Robin's bestselling Sisterchick novels hatched a whole trend of lighthearted books about friendship and midlife adventures. Who knows what stories she'll write next?

You are warmly invited to visit Robin's websites at: www.robingunn.com, www.christymillerandfriends.com, and www.sisterchicks.com. ozen translations all over the world.

Now that her children are grown and Robin's husband has a new career as a counselor, Robin continues to travel and tell stories about best friends and God-Lovers. Her popular Glenbrooke series tracks the love stories of some of Christy Miller's friends. Her books *Gentle Passages* and *The Fine China Plate* are dearly appreciated by mothers everywhere. Robin's bestselling Sisterchicks novels hatched a whole trend of lighthearted books about friendship and midlife adventures. Who knows what stories she'll write next?

You are warmly invited to visit Robin's websites at: www.robingunn.com and www.sisterchicks.com. And to all the Peculiar Treasures everywhere, Robin sends you an invisible Philippians 1:7 coconut and says, "I hold you in my heart."

# Excerpt from *Secrets,*

## Book One in Robin Jones Gunn's
## Glenbrooke Series

JESSICA MORGAN GRIPPED her car's steering wheel and read the road sign aloud as she cruised past it. "Glenbrooke, three miles."

The summer breeze whipped through her open window and danced with the ends of her shoulder-length, honey-blond hair.

"This is it," Jessica murmured as the Oregon road brought her to the brink of her new life. For months she had planned this step into independence. Then yesterday, on the eve of her twenty-fifth birthday, she had hit the road with the back seat of her used station wagon full of boxes and her heart full of dreams.

She had driven ten hours yesterday before stopping at a hotel in Redding, California. After buying Chinese food, she ate it while sitting cross-legged on the bed watching the end of an old black-and-white movie. Jessica fell asleep dreaming of new beginnings and rose at 6:30, ready to drive another nine hours on her birthday.

*I'm almost there,* she thought. *I'm really doing this! Look at all these trees. This is beautiful. I'm going to love it here!*

The country road meandered through a grove of quivering willows. As she passed them, the trees appeared to wave at her, welcoming her to their corner of the world. The late afternoon sun shot between the trees like a strobe light, striking the side of her car at rapid intervals and creating stripes. Light appeared, then shadow, light, then shadow.

As Jessica drove out of the grouping of trees, the road twisted to the right. She veered the car to round the curve. Suddenly the bright sunlight struck her eyes, momentarily blinding her. Swerving to the right to avoid a truck, she felt her front tire catch the gravel on the side of the road. Before she realized what was happening, she had lost control of the car. In one terrifying instant, Jessica felt the car skid through the gravel and tilt over on its side. Her seat belt held her fast as Jessica screamed and clutched the steering wheel. The car tumbled over an embankment, then came to a jolting halt in a ditch about twenty feet below the road. The world seemed to stop.

Jessica tried to cry out, but no sound came from her lips. Stunned, she lay motionless on her side. She quickly blinked as if to dismiss a bizarre daydream that she could snap out of. Her hair covered half her face. She felt a hot, moist trickle coursing down her chin and an acidic taste filling her mouth. *I'm bleeding!*

Peering through her disheveled hair, Jessica tried to focus her eyes. When her vision began to clear, she could make out the image of the windshield, now shattered, and the mangled steering wheel bent down and pinning her left leg in place.

Suddenly her breath came back, and with her breath came the pain. Every part of her body ached, and a ring of white dots began to spin wildly before her eyes, whether she opened or closed them. Jessica was afraid to move, afraid to try any part of her body and find it unwilling to cooperate.

*This didn't happen! It couldn't have. It was too fast. Wake up, Jess!*

Through all the cotton that seemed to fill her head, Jessica heard a remote crackle of a walkie talkie and a male voice in the distance saying, "I've located the car. I'm checking now for survivors. Over."

*I'm here! Down here! Help!* Jessica called out in her head. The only sound that escaped her lips was a raspy, "Ahhgg!" That's when she realized her tongue was bleeding and her upper lip was beginning to swell.

"Hello in there," a male voice said calmly. The man leaned in through the open driver's window, which was now above Jessica on her left side. "Can you hear me?"

"Yeath," Jessica managed to say, her tongue swelling and her jaw beginning to quiver. She felt cold and shivered uncontrollably.

"Don't try to move," the deep voice said. "I've called for help. We'll get you out of there. It's going to take a few minutes, now, so don't move, okay?"

Jessica couldn't see the man's face, but his voice soothed her. She heard scraping metal above her, and then a large, steady hand touched her neck and felt for her pulse.

"You had your seat belt on. Good girl," he said. The walkie talkie crackled again, this time right above her.

"Yeah, Mary," the man said. "We have one female, mid-twenties, I'd say. Condition is stable. I'll wait for the ambulance before I move her. Over."

Jessica felt his hand once more, this time across her cheek as he brushed back her hair. "How ya' doin'? I'm Kyle. What's your name?"

"Jethica," she said, her tongue now throbbing. From

the corner of her eye she caught a glimpse of dark hair and a tanned face.

"I saw your car just as it began to roll. Must have been pretty scary for you."

Jessica responded with a nod and realized she could move her neck painlessly. She slowly turned her head and looked up into her rescuer's face. Jessica smiled with surprise and pleasure when she saw his green eyes, straight nose, windblown dark hair, and the hint of a five o'clock shadow across his no-nonsense jaw. With her smile came a stabbing throb in her top lip and the sensation of blood trickling down her chin.

"So, you can move a little, huh?" Kyle said. "Let's try your left arm. Good! That's great. How do your legs feel?"

Jessica tried to answer that the right one felt okay, but the left one was immobile. Her words came out slurred. She wasn't sure exactly what she said. Her jaw was really quivering now, and she felt helpless.

"Just relax," Kyle said. "As soon as the guys arrive with the ambulance, we'll get you all patched up. I'm going to put some pressure on your lip now. Try breathing slowly and evenly like this." Kyle leaned toward her. His face was about six inches from hers. He began to breathe in slowly through his nose and exhale slowly through his mouth. The distinct smell of cinnamon chewing gum was on his breath, which she found strangely comforting.

Jessica heard the distant wail of an approaching siren. Within minutes she was in the middle of a flurry of activity. Some of the men began to stabilize the car while several others cut off the door to have more room to reach her. Soon a team of steady hands undid Jessica's seat belt, removed the steering wheel, and eased her body onto a long board. They taped her forehead to the board so she couldn't move her head, and one of the men wrapped her in a blanket. They lifted the stretcher and with sure-footed steps walked up the embankment and carried her to the ambulance.

Jessica felt as if her eyelids weighed a hundred pounds. They clamped shut as her throbbing head filled with questions.

*Why? Why me? Why now, right on the edge of my new beginning?*

With a jolt, the men released the wheeled legs on the stretcher and slid Jessica into the back of the ambulance. One of them reached for her arm from underneath the blanket, and running a rough thumb over the back of her left hand, he asked her to make a fist.

Another paramedic spoke calmly, a few inches from her head, "Can you open your eyes for me? That's good. Now can you tell me where it hurts the most?"

"My leg," Jessica said.

"It's her left one." Jessica recognized Kyle's strong voice. His hand reached over and pressed against her upper lip once more.

The siren started up, and the ambulance lurched out onto the road and sped toward the Glenbrooke hospital.

As the stretcher jostled in the ambulance, the paramedic holding Jessica's left hand said, "Keep your fist. This is going to pinch a little bit." And with that an IV needle poked through the bulging vein on the top of her hand.

"Ouch," she said weakly.

She felt a soft cloth on her chin and lips and opened her eyes all the way. Kyle smiled at her. With one hand he pressed against her lip, and with the other he wiped the drying blood from her cheek and chin.

"Can you open your mouth a little? I need to put this against your tongue," he said, placing a swab of cotton between her tongue and cheek. "The bleeding looks like it's about to stop in there. Now if we can only get your lip to cooperate, you'll be in good shape. We'll be at the hospital in a few minutes. You doing okay?"

Jessica tried to nod her head, but the tape across her forehead held her firmly in place. She forced a crooked, puffy-cheeked smile beneath the pressure of his hand on her lip.

Jessica felt ridiculous, trying to flirt in her condition. Here was the most handsome, gentle man she had ever laid eyes on, and she was a helpless mess.

*He's probably married and has six kids. These guys are trained to be nice to accident victims.*

The full impact of her situation hit Jessica. She *was* a victim. None of this was supposed to happen. She was supposed to enter Glenbrooke quietly and begin her new life uneventfully. Yes, even secretly. Now how would she answer the prying questions she was sure to receive at the hospital?

As tears began to form in her eyes, she remembered that today was her birthday. Never in her life had she felt so completely and painfully alone.